GURKHAS AND A GRAND PIANO

By

Peter Slaney

CHAPTER 1

NOW HERE AND THERE

The knitting needle my mother said she pushed into her womb, when she was pregnant, failed to stop my birth, although that had been the plan. My mother blames her sister for the impulsive act. Dorothy, my mother's sister (with whom she and my father lived then) had declared: 'I'll not have a baby in *my* house' and my mother, pregnant, didn't want to be homeless. But the needle failed and I suppose the sisters came to terms and so on the morning of January 4th 1932, I was born. It was early morning, just as the factory hooters were summoning their employees, father among them, to look sharp and clock in.

Hooters played another significant part in my life, but this time nothing to do with factories but The Blitz when their stomach-churning wailing announced the approach of German bombers, both by day and by night. The urgent grabbing of gas masks followed by the dash to the claustrophobic, sweaty Anderson shelter built into a pit in the garden where we would bravely peep out from the tiny doorway like
meercats before sundown watching for tell-tale enemy vapour trails. The eight years between those two wind-driven messages however was a period when I did manage latterly to learn quite a lot.

At the time of my conception, my father, Sidney, Joshua, Henry and my mother, Maud, Lilian, could well have already been living with mother's sister Dorothy (a name she adopted by Deed in place of her given names Alice, Ivy) and her husband Arthur Parsons at 3, Tudor Villas, Chase Road, Southgate, a swanky, leafy suburb of north London. Arthur worked in the finance department of the local Electricity Company. Dorothy divorced him because of a bigamy charge emanating from South Africa. I'll leave you to work that one out. Dorothy, so my mother later told me, disliked children to the extent of saying that they should be born and hatched like eggs rather than the messy way that Nature has devised for humans (mother and Dee had a love-hate relationship for many years and

2

sniping at one another was a skilled pastime). Thanks to that frame of mind, mother was scared to tell her that she was expecting a baby in case Dorothy (pushing the blame on Arthur, her unsuspecting husband) threw her out. Hence the episode with the knitting needle, which patently didn't work. Whether she also tried hot gin, another shady Victorian abortion technique, or not remains an open question. As much as she is supposed to have disliked children, Dorothy also stood accused of liking to swank about being a 'Government Officer' – which meant clerk, I suppose. To this extent, mother would disparagingly tell that while the house looked smart, due to Arthur's lowly income as a clerk, he and Dorothy could not live in the style to which she would like to become accustomed and had to make do with deckchairs in the lounge. In mother's words, it was all 'fur coats and kippers'. This prickly sisterly relationship lasted most of their lifetime yet on the surface all was hail fellow, well met. Looking back on the Southgate I knew during my teen-age years, I cannot recall seeing one single factory. It was a quiet, residential, sort of up-market part of Middlesex, peopled by professionals living in mock Tudor houses set in tree-lined roads; in fact, all very desirable and very 'suburban-county'. It was plainly where the country met the northern fringes of Greater London. So I must conclude that my mother had a supernatural hearing ability or was being a bit fanciful when telling me about my arrival coinciding with the factory hooters, the nearest of which would have been in Edmonton, three or four miles to the south. Sometime between the 4th January and the 21st February 1932, my mother and father must have remembered my mislaid second Christian name. My Birth Certificate shows me as just plain Peter, whereas my Baptism Certificate shows Peter Armitage, a much loftier-sounding name and one I like. I adopted its use after 14 September 1977, when following enquiries, I received a copy of my Baptism Certificate from the Vicar of St. Mary's Church, Lansdowne Road, Tottenham, where the event obviously took place.

During the 1930's, if you were more than a few miles out from the centre of London, you couldn't help noticing that everywhere was becoming more rural. Islington, Stoke Newington and Tottenham had been pretty well built up during Victorian times and were the last bastion of the old order going north. Edmonton had been a rural village on The Great North Road in the mid 1800's and was now being newly built up in the nineteen twenties and thirties with the snobbier neighbourhoods of Southgate and Palmers Green lying slightly to the west of The Great North Road. In the 1920's, following the Great War, and into the 1930's following 'The Depression', building development had gone ahead at a great pace creating new towns each with their newly designed styles of houses where only open fields once stood. Gone were the seemingly endless rows of cloned terraced houses further south, as in Tottenham where my relatives all lived. Now, in Edmonton a terrace would contain perhaps no more than ten houses at most, or even as few as six. Farther north still, out to Chingford and Epping Forest and Enfield, the countryside became even more obvious. As a young boy, I can clearly remember our streets being lit by gaslight, which cast a diminishing yellow veil of light for about ten to twenty metres around each lamp. During autumn and winter, when London suffered the throat tickling, sulphurous fogs we knew as 'smogs' caused by all the coal smoke mixing with the already foggy, damp atmosphere, the yellow lamplight took on a gloomy, almost threatening appearance. The lamps were tended by gas fitters who came around, propping their ladders against the special support bar just below the lamp to clean the panes of glass, change the incandescent gas mantles which often burnt out, or attend to the on/off switch for the gas supply. Each lamp had a pilot light which remained permanently alight and had to be properly maintained to keep it burning at just the correct setting. Coal for cooking stoves and fires was delivered to homes by the coalman with his horse and cart and the horses were usually quite large, docile, shaggy creatures, content to feed from their nosebags from time to time. Most coalmen's skin seemed to be universally black and begrimed and they wore, by unspoken rules, a uniform of tough dark blue or black trousers held up by braces and a belt over a collarless shirt with sleeves rolled up to the elbow, a spotted cotton scarf knotted at the throat and a one-piece leather cap and back protector. They didn't suffer from the same cautionary awareness as the hoodies of the noughties, almost one hundred years later. Their trousers always seemed to be tied just below their knees with a leather thong and hung down loosely to their strong, black boots. If you ever see the Rex Harrison, Audrey Hepburn film version of 'My Fair Lady' based on the George Bernard Shaw book 'Pygmalion', the character

Henry Higgins is a typically iconic portrayal of a coalman. They were all of seeming superhuman strength, each appearing to lift their sacks of coal and carry them on their backs with some ease. These sacks could weigh up to one hundredweight (112 lbs, or in more modern terms 50 kilos) so it was a very strenuous job, especially when you consider that they had to look after their own horses while out on the delivery run. All towns those days had horse-troughs along the roads for the animals to drink at and the delivery man to fill up the horse's drinking bucket from and which he hung from a hook beneath the cart. Oddly enough, I don't recall coalmen wearing a top coat in winter time – perhaps they might sport an old waistcoat, but not much more.

The valley of the river Lea in which I lived, ran directly north to south stretching from Ware in Hertfordshire down to the very heart of London, where it joined the Thames at Blackwall, midway between the Isle of Dogs and "The Docks". The Docks was a great commercial area of the river comprising the Royal Victoria, Royal Albert and King George V docks where, thanks to the busy variety of shipping, most of the imports and exports to and from London, the Home Counties and beyond were handled. There were barges everywhere with dockside cranes dangling great loads of goods up from the holds of the ships and lowering them into the waiting barges. This area became a prime target for the German bombers during the Blitz on London in 1940-41. Upstream a few miles, as the Lea passed through Walthamstow and Tottenham, factories and timber yards had grown up along its banks. Harry Lebus, famous as the 'G Plan' furniture manufacturer and John Dickinson, the makers of "Basildon Bond" paper products and where my father and cousin John worked had their yards and factories established between Lea Bridge Road and Ferry Lane. Raw timber and huge rolls of paper the size of round straw bales but weighing infinitely heavier, were transported by horse-drawn barge from the London Docks to be unloaded right on their doorsteps, whilst other barges continued upstream carrying raw materials to the linoleum factory beyond Edmonton, lead to Eley's Shot Tower and steel to the British Enfield Small Arms works even farther on. Each bank of the canal had a towpath (a self-evident name) along which the great heavy Shire horses would patiently plod along. Around their necks were large, padded halters which rested on their front shoulders and attached to these was a strong tow rope fastened just off-centre of the bow of each twenty metre long barge. The bargee steered his vessel with a large rudder at the stern end and the whole thing was open to the elements, so if it rained, he – and his horse – got very wet while the precious cargo was safely covered under a huge tarpaulin. (No Health and Safety in those days)! By the time the barges reached Waltham Abbey, nowadays just on the northern fringe of the M25, it was countryside without a doubt. The ancient Abbey standing in the water meadows just the other side of the pretty little hump-backed bridge and lock-keeper's cottage (and where we often fished for roach, perch and dace) could easily have been the backdrop for Constable's "The Hay Wain".

The London and North Eastern Railway ran from Liverpool Street mainline station in London out through the suburbs and then followed the Lea Valley on to Peterborough, Grantham and eventually Edinburgh. Black painted steam goods trains hauled their great crocodiles of open wagons loaded with coal alongside the river and the New River Canal running parallel, to Brimsdown Power Station at Ponders End. Green liveried express trains thundered beneath plumes of smoke and steam on their way to or from the north and each train left behind its own aura and sooty smell which tickled the throats of us watching, 'train-spotting' boys, imprinting our juvenile minds with the magic of the steam train. This is the area that will be the venue for the 2012 Olympics, which at the time of writing is still three years hence. I only hope that all the vast amount of money being spent will be eventually beneficial and worth it compared to the other National extravagance, the Millennium Dome which patently was not.

Mother's and Father's roots were all very firmly embedded in Tottenham, post-coded in those days as London N17 and apart from one or two exceptions, that is where most members of each family stayed until they died. Father was born on the 31st. of January 1901 and was I believe the second of three sons. His mother died of cancer before I was born and I never met his father, who I was told by dad had remarried and gone to live in Thundersley, Essex. From the little I did hear of him, it seems he was a bully, perhaps through an overdeveloped sense of Victorian strictness.

I knew my father, comparatively speaking, for only a few years. By the time I was seventeen, I was living away from home in the Linden Hall Hydro Hotel opposite Boscombe Gardens, Bournemouth and after that I went straight into the Army. After the age of twenty eight, I never saw him again. During that ten or eleven years, we met only when I went home on leave, when we might spend the occasional Saturday night or Sunday morning down at the Chine Hotel in Boscombe Gardens where buxom Millie kept the bar with a pair of marmosets in a glass fronted cage at the foot of the stairs to keep her company. On those occasions the possibility of him dying before I was thirty did not occur to me, nor, I suppose, to him. So we never did really talk earnestly about those things which matter and which I would dearly love to know about now. I miss not having had these later years of his fatherly companionship. And having no brothers or sisters has meant that I have not had a meaningful sibling family life either. Now aged 76, I would love to be able to spend time with a brother or sister, their families, have nephews and nieces and to see their youngsters grow up. I would also love to be physically closer to our son, Mark, who now has a family of his own, nearly a thousand miles away in the far north of Scotland, probably nearer the Arctic Circle than Norma and me in south Devon.

Dad was a truly "gentle man", five feet nine inches tall, dapper, helpful to everyone and slow to anger. Maybe this latter characteristic was a pendulum swing away from his father's temperament. He could be humorous despite being dogged by ill health for most of his life. He died on the 22nd of January during the bitter winter of 1962 from a heart attack, in bed, after making love to my mother. She also once told me that his last words to her were, 'That's the best yet.' Moments later he gasped and died, lying beside her, no doubt expecting a goodnight cuddle. At the time, I was at the other side of the world with Norma in South Malaya. The trans-world telephone link between Bournemouth and Malaya was a tenuous one to say the least and it was little wonder that when mother and I spoke to each other it was traumatic for both of us. "Shout" at each other might be a better description as every few moments everything was blotted out by an all-consuming crackling through the earpiece which threatened to deafen us. In between times, mother was barely audible and it took me some time to grasp what she was trying to tell me - that dad had died the night before. I tried to comfort her by getting her to understand that I would see about getting home on compassionate leave. I saw my commanding brigadier without delay, but my request was turned down on the strict military reasoning that as dad was now dead, my presence in England would do nothing to change his condition. Mother had sisters who would have to rally round and in any case, Norma's parents were only just "round the corner".

'No, Peter, I'm terribly sorry, but the Army can't spend all that money on your fare home when you probably wouldn't even get back in time for the funeral.'

That night, in the Kluang Garrison Church with Norma, I extemporised on the organ for an hour or so, playing whatever melodies and harmonies came beneath my fingers. I hope it wasn't just melodramatic nonsense, but felt better for it and to her everlasting credit Norma was complimentary, saying that she found it very moving. I used to play that organ most Sundays at morning service. It was a foot pumped instrument with two manuals and about a dozen stops for creating the different "voice" effects. The more stops chosen the more air was needed, with the performer pedalling furiously to keep up the pressure if the music was not going to wheeze to a gasping halt – little wonder that the diminutive Christian Indian lady who took it in turns with me to play on Sundays never used more than three stops. In the heat of tropical Malaya, the price of full-blooded volume was sweat, lots of it. Modern-day gymnasia have a similar piece of equipment but without the keyboard(s) and charge a lot of money for using it. Pity the church committee hadn't thought of renting out the organ and calling the building the Kluangym Church. They might have made a bit of money out of it.

As a young man, dad had been good looking but unfortunately a lifetime of almost permanent illness had taken its toll of his features which became drawn, giving him a haunted look of apprehension, as though he was waiting for the next unannounced spasm of pain to strike. According to him, he had suffered in his younger days from chalky teeth causing the enamel to crack and break up, which must have caused him a lot of toothache. Nowadays, we might assume he had a calcium deficiency in childhood. He saw his dentist who told him that his condition was incurable and that the only remedy was for him to have all his teeth extracted, which he eventually did. (Sounds like a bit of post-Victorian 'kill or cure' to me). Dad swore that the dentist had used a cracked hypodermic needle to inject the cocaine and instead of it going into his gums, it went down his throat into his stomach and this, he claimed, was the cause of his severe gastric and duodenal ulcers. He suffered agonies from these for many years, nearly dying on occasions from loss of blood by haemorrhaging, sometimes in the street on the way to or from his work.

***

NO PASSAGE HOME

For years he had suffered. Now shoppers just
stood –
he'd collapsed on the pavement, vomiting
blood.
From hospital later he'd been full of hope,
his insides much smaller, just able to cope.

Enduring wartime, taking our chances
with bait and picnic, rods like knights' lances
we'd bike to the country, escape our bombsite
never quite knowing if we'd last the night.

Too ill and too young to join up and fight,
drones moan through darkness – white rods of
arc light
weld bombers to belching blast-furnace sky.
Grim heavenly gamblers – whose turn to die?

Bombs did not get him, he went soon enough.
Not there for his ending, that man I loved;
Career Army posting sending me East
while that Arctic winter his heart stopped.
Deceased.

***

He also suffered from a condition of the blood known as Giant Urticarea making him susceptible to certain foods. Without warning, he would develop huge lumps and bumps all over his body and there were occasions when his face and scalp were so badly

9

affected that he was barely recognisable. He blamed baked beans for his skin troubles! His pride must have taken a bad dent at times like these as he was unable to get his hat on! It was as though he had been stung by a thousand bees and in those years and unlike today's medication, antihistamines, there was no known cure. This combination of terrible afflictions meant that he was permanently locked into a lifetime of dieting and in this, mother performed culinary miracles for him. From knowing absolutely nothing about cooking when they first got married, she became, by necessity, a very competent cook. On her own admission, her first breakfast offering to her new husband had been bacon and mushrooms - only the mushrooms looked more like dried black buttons and the bacon reduced to a strip of pinkie-brown leather.

So with his full set of dentures and the consequent loss of gum and facial structure, dad developed quite deep lines beneath his cheeks and around his mouth which tended to make him look older and more serious than he really was. Nevertheless, he did maintain a keen, somewhat dry, sometimes boyish sense of humour, when his eyes would twinkle while he waited for the penny to drop among his audience. On one occasion, the three of us went to visit my cousin Rosie and her husband George (Adams) at their garage business at the top end of Seven Sisters Road in Tottenham. They also lived there above the premises which opened onto the pavement. The petrol pumps swung out over the pavement to serve the cars at the curbside and George had just finished serving a customer and was putting the pump back when dad approached him from behind. Proffering his Ronson petrol lighter he said flippantly,
'Fill 'er up, mate.'
Without turning to see who it was, George said over his shoulder 'Piss orff.' Then seeing the three of us, he grinned, 'Bloody 'ell mate, you got me goin' then.'
Locking the pump away against the wall, he said cheerily, 'Come on in. Rosie'll be pleased to see you all.'
While Mum and Dad were in the sitting room chatting, George took me to a back bedroom, produced a Webley .22 air pistol and bet me I couldn't shoot out the top windows of an empty warehouse at the bottom of his garden. He lost his bet, as I suspect

he knew he would and rewarded me with a half crown.

As a young man, not long out of school, dad lived at home with his parents and his father had put him to work at a local printers. This was before all the safety equipment we take for granted now became necessary. Machinery then was still no doubt stuck in the early Victorian age when small boys scrambled beneath working machines to sweep up the dross – and indeed climbed inside chimneys to brush down the soot. At about the age of seventeen, by which time dad had received his share of anonymous white feathers for not volunteering to fight the Germans in the first Great War of 1914-1918, he had an accident at work, getting his right hand trapped in a machine. This took off the top joint of his fourth finger, severely broke the tip of his little finger and burst his middle finger vertically. Following, to me, not very adroit surgery, he regained the use of his hand, but it was always deformed, the little finger ending in an almost right angled hook. His post-operative treatment included soaking his hand each day in a mixture of his own urine and Condy's crystals, (Potassium Permanganate) which turned everything they came into contact with a deep bluey purple colour. Presumably they had some remedial effect and no doubt had some antiseptic properties. When I was about the age of thirteen, I discovered during a home experiment on the dining table that when Condy's crystals were heated in a crucible with sugar, they exploded! That made a bit of a mess in the living room.

Dad said he told his father that he wanted financial compensation for his injuries so that he could buy the little grocery store which was for sale just down the road from where they lived. But his father rejected the idea of having an entrepreneur in the house, insisting that dad accept the firm's offer of a free seven year apprenticeship with the assertion that this was by far a safer thing to do, and so dad became a lifelong printer. As a young man now in his mid-twenties and fully qualified in his trade, he was indeed earning quite good money; enough, in fact, to be the proud owner of the latest Rudge Special motorbike, various sets of fishing tackle and some sporting guns. According to him, one of these was a beautifully crafted folding "four-ten" gauge, slightly smaller than a standard twelve bore, but equally effective over shorter ranges. It had been owned by Georges Carpentier, the French Light Heavyweight World Champion who fought Jack Dempsey in 1921 for the world title, the fight being stopped in the 4th round after Carpentier broke his thumb. Inlaid in the butt was a gold plaque with the champion's name and date of his world title fight and for good measure, the barrels were inlaid with filligree silver, obviously the work of a master gunsmith. When dad was working nightshifts, he would get back home early in the mornings and often while it was still dark, set off on his motorbike to the Tottenham or Hackney Marshes for some shooting, or the river Lea or any of the local reservoirs to fish.

Then, when he was about twenty eight, he met mother. She was twenty months younger than him and a very attractive, vivacious "flapper" who at the time was engaged to Billy Martin. Billy had gone to Australia to seek fame and fortune and was to send for mother when he had done so - or at least done well enough for them to become married. He had sent mother a local Australian opal (in her subsequent conversation it becomes a blue-white diamond – but they come from South Africa, not Australia) telling her she could have it made up into any style of engagement ring she wanted. But Cupid's arrow had found its mark elsewhere and dad fell in love with mother, who, being quite flighty must have responded, despite her attachment to Billy. Speaking of those days to me at one time she gaily said without a trace of remorse,

'Oh, I wrote to him telling him it was off.'

'What happened to the opal? I asked.

'Dee's Arthur said he knew a gem dealer in Hatton Garden who would have it made up for me cheaply. But I never heard another word from him, not then, or after he and Dee divorced. The bugger must have stolen it for himself.'

She went on to say how thrilling it was to be collected from her work in Regent Street, London by this handsome young man dressed in his leather overcoat, flying helmet, goggles and gauntlet gloves on the latest in motor cycles. I should have found out whether he wore the fashionable breeches and boots as well – all veryt Biggles looking. At that time, she was in charge of the packaging department of Morny Frères, the famous perfumiers, having been promoted into the job by the manager, a Mr. Pettitt who, although married, also looked upon her with great interest... I got the feeling that my mum was one for the boys, especially as she said that before she knew Sid, she and her elder sister Dolly (Dorothy) would dress up and go to Finsbury Park to join the weekly evening promenade to see and meet the boys before going to a dance. While she worked in London, mother would spend her lunchtimes walking round the West End studying the latest creations displayed in the windows of the great couturiers. She would draw the outfits she saw, buy some appropriate materials and have them made up by a friend of hers who she said was a "Court Dressmaker". She and Dorothy were always dressed at the height of fashion.

Eventually on the 8th February 1930, mother and father (I still find it difficult to call them Mum and Dad) were married in St. Mary's Church, Lansdowne Road, Tottenham. Dad was sufficiently bowled over by his newly acquired bride to suffer a severe attack of amnesia, leaving home with only a couple of suitcases of clothes. His motorcycle, guns and fishing tackle were left in Thackeray Avenue where no doubt his father duly disposed of them to the benefit of his own pocket. Dad was now not just a printer, but a proud husband to boot, totally infatuated with Maud Lilian who was, from then on the centre of his world.

According to dad, the little grocery shop he had hankered after following his accident flourished under its new management, eventually becoming the first in the chain of Lipton's stores, later to become one of the country's leading grocers with "Tommy" Lipton becoming a famous international millionaire with a string of racehorses and racing cars. Whether "Sid" Slaney would have achieved a similar status, we shall never know. I've got more than a sneaking suspicion that The Liptons were already a wealthy family irrespective of this little fact or fantasy corner shop enterprise. I'm uncertain of the veracity of this story as I am unable to find any factual evidence for it. It would be nicely sad to think it was as Dad described. From the time of his accident, Dad tended to play everything "on the safe side", a tendency which must have been reinforced by his experiences of the depression and General Strike of 1926. During the strike, dad had to go each day to his Union headquarters at Blackfriars, near London Bridge to "sign on" the dole and where, if they were lucky, he and his brother printers would be offered a day's work. If none existed, or if they were not chosen by the Father of the Chapel, they would have to return home empty-handed apart from his tiny dole allowance. Eventually, after the strike was all over, he managed to find a job in London working five nights a week for what was then quite a good wage of £9 per week. It was what he had managed to save from this job which gave him enough money to get married.

At the time of their marriage, Dad's family home was 114 Thackeray Avenue, Tottenham, only a street or two away from mum's home at 27 Seymour Avenue. As far as I can determine at the moment, Dad's family consisted of three brothers, himself, Walter the eldest and Jim, the youngest and two sisters, Alice and Jessie. As Victorian families go, this was not overly large. According to dad, unlike his strict father, his grandfather was out of a different mould. Here's another fact or fantasy story. His Grandfather had been the Landlord of "The Three Tuns" public house in Aldgate in the heart of London. This was supposed to have been a very famous eighteenth and nineteenth century coaching inn. Grandfather had also been a great swimmer, owning his own "Academy of Swimming" at the turn of the century when swimming was fast becoming a respectable sport, and again according to dad, Grandfather had accompanied Captain Webb in his attempt to swim the English Channel. So the story goes, when he, grandfather, got to within a mile of the French coast he was forced to give up due to cramp. Although I have scanned one or two books on Captain Webb and his exploits, I was unable to find any reference to Great Grandpa Slaney having been with him, either as a companion swimmer, or in the safety boat, although reference is made to a crew member being a certain Mr. Stanley – spelling mistake? I have yet to find whether the dates tie up, so this remains something of a grey area in our family history. However, the story continues with Grandpa making it known that he would leave The Three Tuns to the first of his descendants who could swim to his satisfaction. None did, so he married his head barmaid and left everything to her. A nice story, but so far uncorroborated. Dad always said that he could have swum well enough to satisfy his Grandpa but had been prevented from doing so by dislocating both his shoulders while at school. His somewhat unusual way of achieving this was to let go while hanging upside down on the parallel bars in the gymnasium - a particularly painful way to decline the future ownership of an historic pub! It meant that for evermore, the best method of swimming he could find was known as "The Trudgeon", a kind of lop-sided sidestroke. As my time with dad had been so very short, I was never able to pursue

14

any of these stories in any greater detail and find out which grandfather it had been, paternal or maternal and what subsequently happened to him. Perhaps now in retirement, I or some future generation may have the time and inclination to find out more. A simple check through the internet reveals that there is no Three Tuns in Aldgate, at least not now, but there is one in Marylebone, just off Oxford Street.

I met dad's brother Walter after the war, following his repatriation from prison camp and when he had been reinstated as a bus driver by the LPTB (London Passenger Transport Board) driving a number 76 from Tottenham Hale to Victoria mainline station in London. He would make perhaps two or three round trips a day driving his double-decker Guy bus and in those days, unlike today, each bus had a conductor as well as driver. The conductor was responsible for selling the tickets from a hand-held clipboard which had different coloured tickets representing the various stages at which passengers boarded. A hole was punched in the margin of the ticket by a little machine worn by the conductor on a shoulder cross-belt and which rang a bell each time. From the other shoulder hung a leather money pouch with various separate pockets in it for coppers and silver. Childrens' "Conductor's Outfits" were almost as popular as "Cowboy and Indian" outfits in the 1930's. The conductor also signalled to the driver by either a press-button bell at the exit platform, or by a long pull-wire which ran the length of the bus above the seats. Passengers were expected to ring the bell once to request the driver to stop at the next stop. Conductors were usually cheery souls, particularly during wartime when women were recruited as "Clippies". Everyone on board was a "Ducks" or "Darlin'" at a time when it was normal for younger people to give up their seats without a second thought to the older passengers, especially to pregnant women. Clippies' "His" or "Her" passengers were helped on and off the bus and given help to stow any bulky luggage beneath the stairs. Smoking was allowed upstairs, but not on the lower deck.

During the war, Walter had been in The Royal Engineers and taken prisoner in Crete when the Germans landed the first ever airborne invasion force on the 20th. of May 1941. He had been in captivity for the remainder of the war in either Stalag VIIIB or Stalag 344 and forced to march hundreds of miles westward as the

15

Russians advanced on the Eastern Front. During this his feet became so badly damaged that he lost the skin off both and had replacement skin grafted onto them by a German doctor. Whether this was experimental surgery or not, we don't know, but it is in stark contrast to some of those less fortunate in other camps. Walter also managed to keep a .303 rifle bullet hidden and which he said he had kept for himself if ever the going got too tough. Quite how he proposed using it, I shall never know as I doubt the Germans would have provided him with the appropriate Lee Enfield rifle to do it with. No, I'm sure he meant to keep it just as a memento. I do remember as a small boy of thirteen holding that bullet, smooth and shiny brass with its bright, pointed silver end. Walter and Winnie had one son, Bryan and one daughter, Iris.

Dad's brother Jim I never met. Apparently, he had volunteered for the Royal Navy and had died of a fever somewhere in western Africa such as The Gold Coast while sister Jessie married John (?) and went to live in Rhodesia. They had one daughter, Sandra. Alice, the other sister married Ernest Gooderham and went to live in Enfield where Ernest was a signalman on the L.N.E.R. They had two daughters, Norma and June. So from dad's side of the family, I obtained five cousins, none of whom I have really managed to keep in touch with. My last contact with Norma's family was when I went fishing one day with Jim (Stansfield) her husband, but that was in 1947 when we were still living in Palmers Green.

On the other hand, I grew up with Mother's sisters and their offspring. Oddly enough, I never met any of her brothers, only the sisters and I knew them all intimately. As a family, they had lived at number 27 Seymour Avenue, Tottenham. The matriarch, my grandma, was Alice (Cates), an erstwhile school teacher whose parents had been in the confectionery business. Grandpa was Henry Armitage, nicknamed "Tim" by grandma. He was a painter and decorator employed by Mr. Couchman, the landlord of the many houses in the Seymour Road/Thackeray Avenue area. Grandpa Tim was a Journeyman Decorator whose job it was to repaper and paint all the various houses as they became empty or in need of refurbishing. Often he would be laid off for lack of work as in those days, houses were let to families for lifetime renting which meant that it could be many years before a property came up for re-letting. His terms of employment laid down that he could not work for anybody else, which meant no wages at all, so he was dependent upon a reasonable turnover in tenants to keep his family provided with all the necessaries. Thank heavens for "Flitting" as it was known, when destitute families, unable to pay the rent would take off in the middle of the night to find rooms elsewhere. At least having sons meant that grandpa and grandma would be able to rely on contributions to the family income from sons while they lived at home - and the daughters too if they could find work.

Regrettably, for nearly all the years I knew him, grandpa laid on a day couch in the front parlour, unable to move, let alone work, due to chronic angina. The slightest exertion and he would collapse back onto the couch gasping for breath and wincing with the pains in his chest. In those days there were no little pills to pop under your tongue to relieve the condition. So he was condemned to a life of almost total inactivity with no further likelihood of any income (there was no State benefit then). Even after they married and left home, the children still contributed towards keeping grandpa and grandma in the house. Daughter Violet even moved to the house next door to number 29 sometime after she married, especially to keep an eye on them and help out whenever possible. She lived there with husband Arthur and her two sons, Arthur and Geoffrey for many years, including through the '39-45 War.

What I really can remember of him was as a lovely old man whose skin was beginning to take on that thin, papery, alabaster appearance of age and infirmity (which often came early in those days), with receding hair and a walrus moustache. He was so grateful for everything that was done for him, although this really didn't amount to very much. The one photograph I have of him as a young man shows him striding out in his dandy suit and curly brimmed Derby bowler hat with a very humorous air about him. He must have been quite a lad in his younger days - every bit the Victorian bobby-dazzler! In his later days he had heard Arthur Tracey, "The Street Singer", who was famous as an entertainer on the various Variety halls. His signature tune was "I'm only a Strolling Vagabond" and Tim loved this song more than any other. He and Grandma had neither a radio, nor piano, so their only contact with music in the outside world was when the organ grinder wheeled his barrel organ round the streets, churning out his small library of tunes from perforated paper reels. Why or how the habit came about, but organ grinders in those days often sported a small monkey on a chain which would sit on their shoulders while they were turning the crank handle. Some of the monkeys were also taught to hold out the collection cup for pennies from the audience. When Tim lay obviously dying, mother said how much she would love her dad to hear that tune again and she decided it was up to us to make it possible. She saw a piano accordion in a pawnbrokers shop and bought it for me to practice on and although I had never seen the music, made my own arrangement of it to play to Grandpa.

'Thankyou, son, that was wonderful. Just like the old days,' he whispered, tears streaming down his pale, parchment cheeks and as he grasped my hand, thanking me with all his heart for that moment of happiness.

The next time I went to see him was to kiss his cold forehead as he lay in his coffin, still in the front parlour waiting for the undertakers to take him away. My final tribute to him was in 1951, shortly after I had been commissioned when mum took me on a tour of all her sisters to show me off in my Number One blue uniform complete with a single pip on each shoulder as a second lieutenant, the first – and only- officer ever to come from the combined Armitage/Slaney families. In those days, it was a requirement of military tradition that all ranks should stop and salute funerals if they passed in the street and when we went to White Hart Lane Cemetery to see Grandpa's grave, it seemed quite natural to me to give him the benefit of that tradition by saluting his headstone.

All the houses in Seymour and Thackeray Avenues were identical, all built during the late Victorian period towards the end of the 1800's. The terraces of about twenty or thirty houses were laid out so that each neighbouring house was a mirror image of the one next door. Each had a tiny front garden, no more than perhaps six feet deep and with a low front wall and railing onto the pavement. Every front room, or parlour, had a small bay window and each neighbouring entrance hallways ran parallel to one another from the front doors, separated only by one common wall. Usually, there were three bedrooms upstairs, lit by gas and no bathroom or toilet in the house at all. Toilets, known as privies, were in a shed in the back garden. With large Victorian families, there was a considerable degree of overcrowding, particularly when it came to bedtime and in mother's house, her mother and father had the front bedroom and the remaining two rooms had to be shared by three sons and five daughters, which meant sleeping in shifts. Try as they may, domestic hygiene was poor and mother has said that even when the older brothers and sisters had married and moved out, bugs would still come out of the cracks in the walls and plasterwork to finish up in bed with her. There was no carpeting in the house to speak of, the floors being covered in a dull brown, patterned linoleum, often badly cracked due to all the scrubbing and washing it had to have each day.

Downstairs, the hallway provided access to the front parlour and back room which served as kitchen, dining room and sitting room on weekdays. Further back came the scullery and the back door into the garden. Under the stairs was usually a storage cupboard which also housed the gas meter. Everybody washed in the scullery and had their weekly bath in a tin bath in front of the kitchen range. The front parlour had a marble fireplace with a large black marble clock on the mantelshelf. The clock was in the classical style, flanked by Corinthian columns and rearing stallions being held in check by naked Greek warriors holding the reins in one hand and a shield to cover their manhood in the other. The general purpose back room had one window looking out over the garden and set into an alcove was the cooking range which dominated the entire room and which demanded the weekly chore of being black-leaded to keep it shiny. The temperature of the oven was adjusted by altering the flue in the chimney and the whole arrangement was heated by a firebox set to one side of the oven and fed with coal through removable rings on the hotplate, similar to today's solid fuel Agas. Every drop of hot water used was heated in kettles or pans on top of the stove and there was usually a kettle sitting on one side of the hob keeping almost on the boil for tea making when needed. In the middle of the room was a large wooden table covered with first a washable oilcloth and this took the place of a tablecloth for meals as it needed no laundering. Between mealtimes, a velveteen cloth with a tasselled border was spread over the table to make the room look less functional. As there were so many people to seat when everyone was at home, trestles were more favoured than chairs. In fact the only two soft chairs in the room were the two armchairs that specifically belonged to grandma and grandpa, set on either side of the range.

In the scullery was a copper for doing the washing and which was like a large iron cauldron set into a brick surround with a fire box beneath, a tap on the front and a circular wooden lid on top. Alongside this was a dull mustard coloured glazed earthenware sink with a single brass cold water tap and a wooden draining board, leaving just enough room for the mangle with its two wooden rollers and cranked at one end by a handle on an iron wheel with "S" shaped spokes. Dependent upon the pressure applied by the tensioned spring onto the rollers, every last drip of water could be squeezed out of the washing before it was hung outside in the garden to dry.

The washing line in the back garden was supported by a long notched wooden prop to keep the sheets from dragging on the ground as they flapped in the breeze. Without the benefit of modern fabric conditioners, much of the washing finished up like clean, fresh smelling cardboard. All the water squeezed out of the washing was re-cycled, either as washing water, or if really surplus would be used on the garden.

The lavatory was a single-holer, situated in a small wooden garden shed with an iron water cistern supported on brackets above the lavatory itself. The chain for flushing ending in either a piece of wood or more usually a small iron ring dangled down beside the seat. Toilet paper was a luxury and it was far more usual for families like ours to save various pieces of paper including newspaper, torn into sheets nailed behind the lavatory door or sometimes threaded onto a loop of string. The art of making a visit more comfortable was to spend a little time crumpling and rubbing the sheets of paper together to render them softer for the job in hand... I never did find out how much printing ink became transferred to waiting posteriors. As a child, the one thing that I always used to wonder at was why my grandparents had to live in such a house. Surely they must have been well off enough to have a bigger, more modern house than this. Especially if they had a factory which printed their very own name inside the glazed bowl of the lavatory and moulded into the cast iron of the cistern. It said on both very clearly "Armitage ware", but in those days I didn't know any better. The garden was about forty or so feet long by about twenty feet wide with a central cinder path running the length of it to the little shed at the bottom. On either side were flower beds and vegetable plots. The soil was rich and dark, no doubt from the night soil which would have been spread on it before the flushing toilet was provided. The resulting vegetables were superb – (no, you'd better believe it) - so full of flavour despite being over-boiled, which was the way they were treated then. Many people rented allotments from the local Council which demanded that no more than a certain proportion of the land could be used to grow flowers. The major part had to be given over to growing vegetables and this was strictly enforced during wartime. The one thing which was very noticeable about life then was that neighbours stuck together. There was a sense of community which meant that nobody thought twice about knocking on next door to ask for a cup of sugar until next pay day. Those neighbours who made a habit of asking too often, though, were soon branded as scroungers. This neighbourly brotherhood came into its own during the War, when everyone looked out for each other, coming to the rescue – literally - in time of need, particularly after a bombing raid.

This then, is the life and times background to my family.

CHAPTER 2

MOTHER AND HER FAMILY

I knew all of mother's sisters and their families well. Her brothers, I never met. Henry was a baker and confectioner and worked at a local bakery (Eumig's?) and mother was his favourite. She was the baby of the family and was born on the 21st.of October 1903 as a weakly child in much need of fussing and caring. Her early diet included a mixture of tonic wine beaten up with egg yolks and malt and if Henry was doing any baking at home and making up royal icing, he would always give mother the left over raw egg yolks in fresh milk as a drink. When at home at weekends, he would always make sure that mother got the biggest chunk of bread dipped in the roast gravy. Whether all this had any bearing upon her health, I don't know, but she finished up the healthiest and longest living of all of them, eventually dying of cancer shortly before her ninetieth birthday at Easter in 1993. She was cremated at Efford Crematorium in Plymouth on Friday the 24th. of April with just Norma, my second cousin Alyson Armitage and me as witnesses. It was a most awful day; cold, raining in torrents and a high wind, making it not only a sad occasion, but more like a setting for some Victorian melodrama, quite Gothic and oddly detached from reality. The chaplain didn't know mother from Adam and when he asked me if there were any words I wanted him to say at the moment of committal, I said 'No' as I certainly didn't feel it appropriate for a total stranger to say anything at all, especially in the oleaginous, "religious" voice certain vicars adopt for these occasions. We left the Chapel after the service, which took every bit of fifteen minutes, stood outside in the bleak, cold, wind and wet while the Undertakers talked in hushed voices about what to do with the ashes. I asked them to scatter them in the cemetery. Later, the crematorium wrote asking whether I would like, at a charge of £25.00 or whatever, for Mother's name to be entered in the Book of Remembrance, an offer I declined. Plymouth, after all, meant nothing to her. In later years, I couldn't guarantee ever needing to go back to Efford Crematorium, unless by some quirk of fate it was my turn to be cremated there.

Mother spent little time at school, partly because of her state of health as a child and partly because she seemed to be a past-mistress at the art of playing hookey, telling the teachers that she was wanted at home to look after her baby sister, or her mother was ill, or some such similar concoction of lies. She really wanted to be a boy and seemed to fight against femininity as a child. She told us on one occasion that to show her resentment against being taken shopping *as a little girl,* she was in a hardware shop one day which had bundles of firewood in one corner and she suddenly took it into her head to pull down her knickers and urinate on the wood - presumably because she thought boys might have done it. She sounded quite proud of herself when telling the story, giggling at the terribleness of what she had done. She and her family certainly had a few weird ways of doing things! Certainly I remember tales of her father calling her to go out into the street with a bucket and spade to see if the coalman's or milkman's horse had dropped any "brown apples" which were used to fertilize the rhubarb and roses. Just the job for a boy!

Her periods started at a very early age and she thought nothing of them, although the bleeding would be so profuse as to run down her legs, a situation not helped by the fact that there were no tampons then. The only help came from pieces of rag held in place by knickers and quite often, rag wasn't handy in times of need. The situation at school became difficult when the headmistress told grandma that she could no longer have mother as a pupil, as her periods had started and it was against the rules for her to stay on there, so at the age of about fourteen, mother left. She must have been a pretty, precocious girl who loved flirting with danger. On her own admission, she often paid no attention to circumstances which would have left other adults, let alone girls of her age, full of inquisitiveness. She attracted the attention of a family by the name of Levacque who lived locally. Herbert Levacque was a famous racing motor cyclist who was eventually killed at Le Mans. As the Great War ended, the Lavacques who by now had two or three children of their own asked mother whether they might approach her mother to see whether they could take her to live with them as a companion to their own children. Mother said they wanted to adopt her, but that might have been a slight exaggeration. Had they done so, or taken

23

her to live with them, mother would no doubt have experienced a very different lifestyle. For a short time anyway, as it turned out, as Herbert was killed in a racing accident.

As it was, mother used to go almost every day to their house where Mrs. Levacque would give mother lessons in "culture" by showing her how to lay tables properly, using the very finest Irish linen cloths and napkins and this all no doubt played its part in mother's eventual attitude to life. While we owned Opus One Restaurant, I took mother along one day to the Montague Motor Museum at Beaulieu where to her excitement, she saw a photograph in the Hall Of Fame depicting Herbert Levacque on his bike. Mother immediately wrote to his Grace, Lord Montague telling him of her connection with "Bert" and received a nice personal reply, which unfortunately has been destroyed or lost together with many other mementos.

Eventually, mother got herself a job at Morny Frères, the perfumiers and rapidly worked her way up the ladder to take charge of the packaging department, personally wrapping, boxing and tying with silk ribbons all the perfumes and soaps which went to The Royal Family and for special orders elsewhere all over the world. While there, she caught the eye of the Manager who seemed to take an inordinate interest in her and in mother's coquettish way she would say that "he seemed to be quite fond of me." To what extent, we shall never know, but the impression is that had he not been already married, I suspect there might well have been a romance there.

Mother was christened Maud, Lilian, but was always known in the family as "Maudie", "Mick" or "Mickie". When she went out to work again while I was a child, she wanted, for some odd reason, to be known as "Mollie" and this stuck for the rest of her life among those who knew her. Personally, I quite like the name Maud. All her sisters also had floral names, Alice Ivy, Lilian, Violet, Daisy.

Daisy was the eldest sister who married Alfred Carter and lived at no. 10, Springfield Road, Tottenham not far from the Lebus furniture factory I mentioned earlier. They had four daughters, Rose, Doris, Billie and Shirley. Uncle Alf was a stevedore at the London Docks and so long as he had his pint or two (or three) down at the local and his permanent packet of Goldflake cigarettes, he was contented. He seemed to treat Daisy and the children well enough, although after his drinks, he could be a bit difficult at Saturday or Sunday lunchtimes. One day mother was walking along with me and must have been carrying me with me facing over her shoulder. Alf walked up alongside her

"'Ello Maudie, I see 'e's started early, then." Mum was nonplussed until she looked at me and saw that Alf had put his cigarette in my mouth.

Violet was the next eldest. She and mother got on well together and one day she whispered, "Come upstairs Maudie, I want to show you a secret." When they had shut the door, Vi pulled open a drawer in the dressing table and showed mother all the tiny knitted clothes she had made. Mother was mystified and asked where Vi had got them from.

"I knitted them myself", she said.

"What for?"

"Well, that's the secret. I'm going to have a baby, but don't tell Mum or Dad, they'll murder me."

But it wasn't too long before her Mum did find out and came downstairs one day shouting,

"That bitch is going to have a baby!"

Mother's inability to comprehend Vi's situation helps demonstrate her total lack of knowledge of sex as a child and even into later early married life. She admitted to us that on one occasion when she was quite grown up, she had come back home after being out and had gone into her parents' bedroom to say her customary "goodnight" and found them having intercourse and had been not only mystified, but disgusted to the point of anger by what they were doing.

Three days later, after the secret draw event, Vi got married to Arthur Paulson, but baby Dennis was stillborn. They went on to have two more sons, Arthur and Geoffrey. Arthur became a very talented conjurer, or illusionist as he preferred to be called and joined the Magic Circle in which he later became a member of the Inner Magic Circle, a step up in the hierarchy. He was never at a loss to entertain people, having a good line in patter and always able to magick something out of thin air. He was a large, shall we say "chubby" man, always good humoured and ready to help anyone. Right to the end of his life he was always giving shows, and always free of charge, particularly for such organisations as "Help the

Aged" and other charities. He knew and had worked with many of the famous magicians of the 1950's to 1980's such as David Nixon and Tommy Cooper.

For years, Arthur had suffered from emphysema, a crippling lung condition, where the slightest exertion would leave him gasping for breath, much the same as Grandpa Tim with his angina. After his mother Vi had died when they were living together in Ashburton, he moved to Tavistock, but his lung problems got worse. He couldn't work and finally depended upon a charity to provide him with a small flat in a block of almshouses which gave him sheltered accommodation. It was here that I eventually found him in 1994, when I discovered his whereabouts. While Arthur and Vi were in Ashburton, Geoffrey had also lived at home, ostensibly helping run their tiny guest house, but the two brothers split up when Vi died. Arthur had found out that Geoffrey was spending more of their joint income from the guest house than it was producing and to make matters worse, it had also suddenly dawned on him that his brother was homosexual. The day that Norma and I first went to see Arthur in Tavistock, he had just received a letter from Ashburton Social Services to say that Geoffrey had died and as they had been unable to find any relatives who could take care of his final arrangements, they had given him a pauper's funeral and buried him in one of the local churchyards at the State's expense. Such personal effects as there were would be sold off to recover some of the costs. Although Arthur was obviously upset by his brother's death, he just couldn't reconcile himself to Geoffrey's sexual proclivities. He himself got married, but it didn't last very long, returning him to a state of lonely bachelorhood.

About a year later, I received a telephone call from Derriford Hospital to say that my cousin, Arthur Paulson was in Hound Ward, seriously ill. Norma and I went to see him and when we arrived, he was struggling to get out of bed, shouting for an orderly to help him go to the lavatory. He was in a seriously distressed state of mind and we were asked to wait while they helped him. When we were allowed to go and see him, he was lying propped up in bed, utterly exhausted, but as soon as he saw us, he started to relax and resume his old cheerful, anecdotal ways. He reminisced about all manner of things that had happened to him, reminding me of the wartime days we had spent together as families. We both knew he was desperately ill and it was no great surprise when a few days later, I received another call from the hospital to say that he had taken a turn for the worse and could I please come as soon as possible. I dropped everything and drove the eighteen or so miles as quickly as I could, but the traffic was very heavy and it took me about forty minutes to get there, only to be told that I had missed him by five minutes. The nurses were tidying him up and when I arrived at the bedside, he was still normally warm and looked just as though he had dropped off into a wonderful peaceful sleep and looked much younger and as though all the cares of his illness had fallen away. I felt sad that I was not there to be with him at the end – I think he would have appreciated some family company.

I telephoned around to start dealing with his affairs and managed to get permission from the Housing Trust to go into his flat and in going through his papers, I came across a "do-it-yourself" Will made before he knew that Norma and I lived so close to him now. His Will had appointed a local "Help the Aged" bus driver as Executor, so he and his wife had the legal right to go through everything and not me, although I was his nearest surviving relative. He had left his pitifully few remaining possessions to "Help the Aged" including a handful of shares he had in some obscure company which had gone into liquidation some years earlier and so were worthless. Between his Executors and me, we arranged for him to be cremated at Efford, as my mother had been. By at least having his personal papers, I tracked down some of his old wartime buddies who had been in the R.A.F. with him and as a result, they were able to arrange for him to have his funeral with full R.A.F. honours. About three of his air force colleagues managed to get to the funeral and his best friend and wife, Norma and I all went to lunch together at "The China House" pub on the quayside in Plymouth. There, his friend told me about the time when volunteers had been called for to drive radar trucks to a new RAF station being set up in France at the time of the Normandy landings. He and Arthur had volunteered and having arrived safely, had just finished unloading their trucks when they were instructed to get back to one of the nearby ports to help. It was necessary for them to get their trucks down to the beach to help clear things away. When they got there, what they had to help "clear away" were all the dead bodies washed up on the beach of their comrades whose landing craft had taken a direct hit. This trauma must have shocked Arthur into silence, as he never ever mentioned it or anything connected with his wartime service it to anyone. He carried this horror around with him for over fifty years.

Following his cremation, I eventually arranged for Arthur's ashes to be scattered in the churchyard at Tavistock among the graves of his recently departed "Help the Aged" friends. I felt that the charity could then pay their respects to him as and how they saw fit rather than have his ashes dispersed somewhere in Plymouth where nobody knew him and where we would one day most likely leave.

Geoffrey, his brother, was a "strange" boy as far as most of the family were concerned, preferring even at the age of ten to dress in his mother's clothes (those that could be made to fit him). He spent all his spare time playing with cardboard theatres and making himself up, complete with a beauty spot on his cheek. Later, he managed to get himself a job connected with the theatre, working in the box office, but later going into the wardrobe department. Come to think of it, Vi had some funny ideas about him too. I remember one day her saying to my mother 'Can't understand it, Micky, he even buys shirts with funny little tails', and with that she hauled mum off to the garden to see these 'tailed shirts' blowing on the washing line. Most men's shirts at that time were tail-less, being more like thigh length smocks without collars, which were added later with the help of collar studs if the men wanted to dress up a bit. At one time, Geoffrey was also doing some work with BBC TV as a dresser and was at that time living with Alec Bregonzi, an actor whom we met once or twice, but only once actually saw on TV in a period play.

Uncle Arthur, the father, was a diminutive, quiet, inoffensive man who was just a breadwinner and kept in his place. I recall that he worked in the despatch department of a large factory or paper mill trundling pallets of goods around, quite possibly involving him in a lot of manual work, as his hands were as rough and tough as the bark of a tree. I don't think I ever saw him in anything other than his shiny blue working suit and when he was at home, he would change the jacket for a cardigan of some sort. I think he had one other suit "for best", but that was worn only at funerals and weddings or very special outings. Vi herself was always generous to a fault, but lived in some kind of dreamworld, as did her two sons. Reality was always

28

somewhere else and if by exaggeration they could be made to appear to be doing something "really important", but which was in fact quite mundane, so much the better. In the 1930's they must have had some money coming in from somewhere though, as they lived in quite a nice large house out towards Enfield and were among the first people to have television in about 1938. I can remember going to see them one weekend and all seven of us crowded round a large walnut console in the corner of the room and when the front doors were slid open, the TV screen was tiny - no more than about eight inches by six and the black and white scene hinted more at two shades of blue with the presenters speaking in clipped Oxford accents. In those days, and indeed in the immediate post-war years, all the presenters on TV and even the newsreaders on the radio wore evening dresses and dinner jackets. Everything was so "proper". Only casts of stage plays and comedians on stage could get away with wearing ordinary clothes. Even in films the actors tended to wear slightly more formal clothes, unless they were in costume dramas.

Aunt Lilian married Johannes (Jack) Pichowski and they had one son, John and one daughter, Peggy. Jack worked for the Tottenham Council and his father was born in Warsaw and his mother was born in Rotterdam, both around 1860/70. He himself was born in Dalston, London, so was half Polish and half Dutch, but English by birth. He and Lily were both very sweet, gentle people and they lived at 127 Roseberry Avenue in Tottenham, not far from the Pickle factory and when the wind was in the wrong direction, there was an all pervading smell of vinegar and sweet boiling vegetables. It was from there on Christmas Day 1947 that my dad, John and I we walked the two or so miles to White Hart Lane to watch Tottenham Hotspur play Arsenal and that was the last football match I ever attended. In those days, the games were very clean, with very few fouls and everyone expected good behaviour from the spectators. The players each got about ten pounds a week, which was considered good money then.

John, my cousin had been in the R.A.F. during the war based at Trincomalee in north eastern Ceylon (now Sri Lanka) and in 1947 was now either demobbed or about to be. He went to work at John Dickinson's, as did my father but John stayed with them until he retired, complete with company pension, unlike my father who got nothing for all the years of service he put in with them. Company pensions were a rarity in the 1940's, with employees being mostly expected to retire with a gold watch for good service and to live on a small Old Age Pension of a few pounds a week. John married Doreen and they have one son, Paul and one daughter whose name I can't recall. Carrying on the family tradition, Paul became a printer too, but tragically lost one eye when molten print lead splashed into his eye. He moved with Nola, his wife to Dartmouth where he became manager of the Dartmouth Royal Naval College printing department. Unfortunately, when due to MOD financial cuts back his department was closed down he was made redundant in about 1994 and did not find alternative employment until 1996.

Then came Alice Ivy, otherwise known as Dorothy or Dee who was briefly married to Arthur Parsons and divorced before any children appeared on the scene. Arthur was apparently quite a good pianist, but was also a good "fiddler", having been sent to prison for embezzlement (now changed to bigamy). As I have mentioned before, he also managed to "lose" mother's opal (now, in mum's chat with us a blue-white diamond) which Billy Martin sent to her from Australia, saying he could get it mounted by a friend of his in Hatton Garden in London, which is, or was the centre of the international gem trade. After their divorce, Arthur was never seen again by any of the family and Dee became a confirmed divorcee working in local government at Middlesex County Hall, on the Thames Embankment where she was a clerical officer. To give you some idea of the inherited power this gave her is best demonstrated when in 1947 she telephoned the North Middlesex Hospital one day to find out how dad was after his partial gastrectomy operation. His ulcers has become so critical that it was touch and go as to whether he would survive his last haemorrhage - he had lost so much blood. He had been admitted to the hospital to undergo this experimental operation which entailed surgically removing about half of his stomach where the ulcers were and rejoining the two cut ends like joining two lengths of hose together. In fact, it was one of the very first such operations to be performed in this country. While he was recovering, it was still quite difficult for mother and me to get in to see him as there were very strict visiting hours and Matrons those days ruled the wards with rods of iron. It was during this period that Dee telephoned to ask whether she might come to see her brother-in-law - and the hospital virtually laid out the red carpet for her as she was deemed to be an official visitor from County Hall. She was escorted to dad's bedside and given quite the V.I.P. treatment. I don't know that dad was though, as he had to endure having a rubber tube passed up through his nostrils into what remained of his stomach and through this he was fed with milk and morphine to both nourish him and sedate him at the same time. When he was eventually discharged, it was with the warning that he should not expect to be able to return to normal living and eating. Because he now had only half a stomach, he would have to eat small snacks and meals frequently each day to make up for not being able to eat three normal size meals. But at least he didn't suffer again to my knowledge from his ulcers. I can't help comparing what he had to go through for his cure compared with me. Suffering from a similar condition, I was lucky and benefited from the latest research carried out by Mr. Barry Marshall, an Australian doctor, who had discovered that most ulcers are caused by a bacteria called helicobacter pylori and that these can be eradicated from the stomach by a special cocktail of simple antibiotics. I'm glad to say that although he didn't receive much recognition at that time, I understand that he later received a Nobel Prize for the Advancement of Medical Science

Apart from the early days at Seymour Avenue, when Dee, even then, was considered to be the "arch bitch" by one or two of her sisters, all the family got on pretty well together and so did all we cousins. In all, I had eight that I knew of from the sisters and I suppose I must have had some from either of the two brothers when they got married, but I never met them. Daisy, Vi and Lily and their families all lived fairly close to one another in Tottenham, but Dee had moved to the much more classy area of Palmers Green where she lived in a very nice two bedroomed flat in a modern block called Connaught Grange on the North Circular Road, halfway between Green Lanes and the Cambridge roundabout, which was dominated by the pub of the same name.

During her years there, she had a "man friend" called Harry Evans who was Managing Director of Burtishes, the makers of Consulate shirts, pyjamas, ties and men's wear. They are still famous for their "Tern" range of shirts. Harry was also a director of Tottenham Hotspur football club and was a friend of the local Chief Constable, which is maybe why he was never pinched by the police for being drunk in charge of his car! Harry was a Cockney through and through. A big man who carried himself very loosely, giving the appearance of a great shambling giant, but always impeccably dressed in his blue suit and spotted tie. He looked so relaxed all the time - and probably this had something to do with his daily intake of scotch. His conversation was peppered with Cockney rhyming slang, so when we met, I was always invited to share a "pimple" (and blotch - scotch). Trousers were "strides", suits were "whistles", hats were "titfers" and so on. After a heavy bout of drinking, you were likely to suffer from "red minces" (mince pies - eyes). He drove an immaculate Vauxhall Fourteen black saloon, but weaved from side to side in the road, threatening to run over unwary pedestrians at any moment. It was amazing that he never appeared to have any accidents. I suppose everyone had plenty of time and managed to get out of his way, no doubt because he never drove at more than fifteen to twenty miles an hour - anywhere! Harry was married and lived in the poshest part of Palmers Green, but I never got to meet his wife.

CHAPTER 3

I ARRIVE

It wasn't until I was well over fifty that mother told me about my arrival into this world and I suppose I am quite lucky to be here at all. She said how much she wanted a child and kept begging dad to have one. He had said "No" in the early days of their marriage because he wanted to wait until he had the security of a regular job and steady income. Following their wedding in the February of 1930, they went to live with Dee and her husband Arthur, whom she called "Bo" in their new house in Chase Side. By then, dad had managed to save enough money from his night-work job to be able to afford some hand-made furniture from Maples of Tottenham Court Road in London. He and mother had chosen a bedroom suite consisting of a double bed with headboard and curved footboard, tallboy, dressing table and stool and double wardrobe, all in figured walnut. The bed had an iron frame latticed with springs and covered with a woven wire mesh anchored to the frame on which was the flock stuffed mattress, not at all like today's modern interior or pocket sprung mattresses. As a result, the bed was more like a trampoline so that when two people lay side by side, they would inevitably roll together into a valley down the centre of the mattress.

When I was eventually "on the way", mother told Dee she was expecting a baby. Dee was apparently horrified to think that her new house was going to be polluted by squalling babies, nappies and prams. It was her view that the whole business of women carrying babies around as foetuses in their swollen bellies, to have them painfully emerge all bloody and horrible from some unmentionable place was an anathema. She had told mother that "babies should be laid like eggs." But who was expected to sit on them until they were hatched was never suggested. It would seem that she made herself quite plain regarding my forthcoming arrival not fitting in with her own domestic plans " . . . and in any case, Bo would not approve." So mother told me that she tried the "knitting needles" abortion technique, but it obviously didn't work in my case. It is possible, of course, that all this prodding contributed to the fact that I was eventually born ruptured, with a hydrocele and a "capit" on my head the size of an ostrich egg! So, although according to mother it was Dee who did not want a baby in the house, it was strange how doting she was when Mark came along when she would come and baby-sit for hours, playing on the floor with him while Norma and I went out. In that respect, she was a good as any grandma could be - unlike the real grandmother.

When Norma was first pregnant, she didn't want to publicise the fact to all and sundry too far in advance. She and I had come back from Malaya to live in Knyveton, mother's house. But the arrangements did not work out and after a short while, Norma said she wanted to go to live back at Netheravon with her own parents. My mother was furious and so began a period of hostility between her and Norma. From Netheravon, we went to live in Guildford Court, a block of flats in Bournemouth, overlooking the Upper Pleasure Gardens and it was here that Mark was conceived. It would seem that one day, mother was met by someone in the street in Boscombe who had asked her what she thought of the good news. "What good news?" "Norma's going to have a baby." That did it! Mother accused us of deliberately excluding her from news of the happy event and the atmosphere became even icier than before. So it was not until Mark was several years old that we had buried the hatchet sufficiently for mother to share the baby-sitting with Dee.

So it would seem that because of my arrival, mother and father were invited to leave Tudor Villas. The hunt for somewhere permanent to live began and there was quite a lot of new building going on in Edmonton at the time in a huge estate development out towards the Lea valley. One weekend, mother, father and I as a babe of eighteen months went to look at some new houses in the Middleham Road area. These were all identical two bedroomed houses laid out in terraces of sixes and consisting of a front lounge, back dining room and kitchen and upstairs were two bedrooms and a bathroom. The overall development was for about two hundred houses, but at the end of the site nearest the main road was a little cul de sac with a small development of only about sixteen houses in four terraces. The far end of the cul de sac ended at the rear wall of the St. John Ambulance Brigade Hall whose frontage was in Claremont Street, an older Victorian road of somewhat run down houses when compared to these of the new 1930's design. This cul de sac was

Middleham Gardens and being cut off from the remainder of the estate was much quieter and ideally suited to anyone who was going to raise a family. There was no traffic to speak of except the weekly coalman, dustcart, milkman, Walls ice cream salesman on his tricycle and a mobile hardware shop. This last was a brown painted Morris Commercial van which would arrive festooned on the outside with brushes and coir doormats of all shapes and sizes, while the inside was stacked out with drums of floor polishes and paraffin, methylated spirits and paint, dusters and mops, pots and pans, screws and nails, hammers and chisels - in fact almost everything a budding D.I.Y. person could wish for. With all that collection of cleaning materials on board, the van had its own particular smell, one I'm instantly reminded of when I delve under the kitchen sink for polish or soap. Cullens was another example of enduring memories of childhood smells. As with all good grocers of the day their shops were fitted out with mahogany counters and shelves, with food storage drawers and bins containing all manner of sugars and spices, loose teas and coffees. Together with the smells of cheeses, slabs of butter and sides of fresh, real smoked bacon (unlike the watery, chemical flavoured stuff we get palmed off with today), they have indelibly imprinted my olfactory senses with that certain entrancing smell. I remember distinctly the way the shopkeeper would serve your butter, cutting off a chunk with one of his pair of wooden, ridged bats, then expertly turning it this way and that on a damp marble slab, patting it into a square, forcing out tiny drops of salty water and finally holding it between his bats putting it onto a square of greaseproof paper, and folding it neatly for you to put in your string or bag or woven basket. Anyway – back to the houses . . . The terrace houses were being sold at £495 and the semi's at the ends were £10 extra because of the extra strip of land they had at the sides of the houses. All the gardens were just raw fields, staked out with chain link fences and because it was all so newly developed, the local farmers were still grazing their sheep in the gardens. Mother took a fancy to number One, the first semi in the tiny Middleham Gardens development so went off to find the Estate Office to see if they could have it. They were told they could if they put down a deposit on it there and then, so they rummaged around in their pockets and found just ONE POUND and that became their deposit on their first house. They managed to get a mortgage from The

Halifax Building Society and so "Silverlea" became the first real home of their own. Dad painted it maroon and white. Down the left-hand length of the garden ran a long "right of way" onto which backed all the other gardens of the houses in that neighbouring part of Middleham Road. By using the right of way, short cuts could be taken through various parts of the estate, bringing you out in Ingleton Road, right near Fore Street, the main road through Edmonton. About halfway down the right of way, the Snell family had built a tiny garage for their brand new black Ford Eight which was their obvious pride and joy. Every weekend it would be backed out of the garage and washed and polished, irrespective of the fact that it had not been used during the preceding week. Then it would be put back once more into the garage, ready for the following weekend's wash and brush up or that special journey which never came. During the war, with petrol rationing and only a couple of hundred miles on the clock, they offered it to dad for £45, but he said he couldn't afford to buy it and in any case didn't have a car driver's license.

Dad built a conservatory onto the back of the house; in those humble days it was called a "lean-to", so we could go out of the French door through the lean-to and into the garden. Nearest the house, he and mother built a rockery, followed by a lawn, beyond which was the fishpond. A wooden archway to one side of the pond led down into the vegetable garden and the garden shed. They worked like slaves on that garden and it won quite a few local prizes for the best kept garden and lots of people used to come down the right of way just to look at it. At the waterfall side of the pond, was a red hatted garden gnome who permanently fished, but I assassinated him with my air rifle after a few years, when I was about twelve. I succeeded in blowing his head off with some well-aimed shots from my bedroom window! Wow – vandalism! Actually, I had only wanted to see the chip mark on his head from the impact of the lead slug, but it obviously carried more clout than I had allowed for.

Once mum and dad had got everything established, Silverlea became a favourite Sunday afternoon venue for family visitors. Mother had become a very good cook - a far cry from when they had first married. Now, thanks to the Bel cream maker they had bought at the Ideal Home Exhibition at Alexandra Palace in 1937 and the garden produce, tea times became a feast of salads, hot scones and

36

soft fruits and cream. Some of the food remains in my memory very clearly. Dad grew the most wonderful Cos and round lettuces, celery, Webb's Wonder red radishes which set your mouth on fire and White Icicle ones that didn't, plus tomatoes which smelled deliciously of cat's pee (now we might say sauvignon blanc). His garden peas, runner beans and new potatoes were magic. I say dad's, but mother also had an equal hand in things. So with all those things, plus tinned salmon and Heinz salad cream, it was little wonder that almost every Sunday we could be guaranteed another batch of family visitors.

My early days seemed to be spent in a sun hat and toddler's knitted bathing costume, stumbling around the garden "helping". My hair was so blond it was almost white and as a laugh for visitors, I would be treated (no permission granted) to a showering from the garden hose. But inevitably the day came when it was time for me to go to school, when I was about four or four and a half I went to the local Church School in Edmonton in a little road behind The Law Courts and what I did there is now a mystery to me, except that according to mother I came home one day saying "Look mummy, we learned this today" and picked out the notes of a tune on our piano. Mother always said that she bought the piano as a result of that little incident. I can't quite get the timing right though because if we got the piano as a result of me learning those notes, I don't quite see how I could have played them on a non-existent piano. I certainly don't recall us having any piano before the one we bought from Nathaniel Berry's in Fore Street, near the Angel roundabout in Edmonton. But I remember that piano well. It was an overstrung upright in a modern rosewood case and with a "practice stop" lever at one end of the keyboard which, if used, lowered a felt damper down in front of the hammers to deaden the sound of the strings struck. How very neighbourly! To make sure that we got the actual piano we had seen in the shop, mother put a small lipstick cross on one of the labels inside the case, just under the lid while the salesman wasn't looking. It was a very good piano and one I would be quite happy to have today in place of my now missing Yamaha grand.

I was given a red pedal car in which I raced up and down the garden endlessly. One day, when I was about four, I must have managed to get out of the garden gate and started pedalling along the road to some unknown destination. The first mother knew of my escapade was when a policeman called to tell her I was in custody at North Edmonton Police Station and could she please come and collect me. It seems that I had managed to pedal round the estate and into Fore Street, past Heraud's Stores, the main departmental store in Edmonton. Turning right I passed The Phoenix public house, which usually had black, sad looking prams and sadder looking children inside them parked outside while the mums were inside having their stout. I crossed the North Circular Road at The Angel roundabout and headed north together with all the trolleybuses and other cars and lorries past the Alcazar wrestling stadium and out towards Enfield. The police must have managed to find out from me where I lived and a constable had been sent cycling all the way back to tell mother, who by now distraught, had to catch a trolleybus to where I was.

"Right you little bugger, you pedalled your way here, now you can bloodywell pedal all the way back!" After that, mum got a telephone put in (Tottenham 6840, I remember).

Dad had now got himself a permanent job at Dickinsons, the printers and papermakers in Tottenham (The Basildon Bond people). I was at school and mother may well have got herself a small part-time job too. Dad used to cycle to work every day on his "Hercules" pushbike, taking his lunch sandwiches in a box together with his flask of tea, rather than spend money in the canteen. When he came home at night, he would be scrupulously clean, but reek of printers' ink and the solvent he used to clean up his machine - and himself at the end of each day. He would go to work ready dressed in his overalls and managed to keep them pretty clean, despite handling ink and printed paper all day long. By then though, thanks to his apprenticeship training, he was a machine "minder", rather than the one who actually did all the humping and heaving. Dad had to set the print in the bed of a machine half the size of a bus and make sure that it all "registered" properly, so that when doing colour runs, the various colours printed during each run matched edges accurately. This was where his skills came in. he used to pride himself on never having a picture "out of register", no matter how small and detailed it was.

Although we seemed to manage reasonably well on the money which he and mother brought home, it was never enough for us to have such luxuries as a car or regular holidays, so the house and garden were the beneficiaries. In any case, a large part of my childhood was taken up by the War, when holidays were a dream rather than a reality. Every spare moment went into making "Silverlea" the envy of many neighbours and visitors to the area. I recall helping dad fix up the fountain in the fishpond. It was just before the war, so I suppose I must have been about six at the time. Dad had been to London and bought a new Pratt and Whitney electric water pump. He had put in the necessary piping and cabling, so now just had to connect the electrics.

'Just hang onto that,' he said, handing me one end of the electric cable, 'I'm just going indoors to make up a connection.'

He left me holding one end and disappeared into the house to fit the plug to the end of the wire and plug it into the electricity socket. Shortly after he went into the house I was catapulted through the air with an intense buzzing feeling ripping through my body. Fortunately, because the live end I had hold of was secured to something, my somersault pulled the cable from my hand as I fell, otherwise I would have been electrocuted for sure - and so would anyone who came to my help if they touched me without themselves being insulated. It was my first encounter with electricity and has made me very wary ever since. It's an energy force you can't see or smell, only touch at your peril.

We did, however, at last manage a holiday for a week, probably that same year, with cousin Rosie and her husband George (who had the garage), going to stay at a boarding house somewhere in Eastbourne. I have an old photograph of dad and me on the promenade with a very distinctive hotel in the background. It must have been very new then, as it is typically 1930's architecture. It's still there now.

As a result of my apparent aptitude for music, mother took me a few doors down the road to Mrs. Boston who taught piano for about sixpence or a shilling (2 1/2p or 5p) per lesson. She had thick pebble glasses which made her eyes seem to pop out of her head, rather like frogs' eyes and she had the most dreadfully ill-fitting set of dentures possible. Every time she opened her mouth to speak, her upper row of teeth would part company with her gums and drop with a little clunk onto her bottom set like a miniature portcullis falling into place. With a moist sucking noise, she would induce them back into place long enough to say a few more words, when the whole process would be repeated. Under her tuition, I made some progress and showed that I could memorize my pieces very quickly. She used to show me off to mother when she came to collect me, by getting me to play something and taking the music away from in front of me so that I could carry on from memory. This little trick earned me a penny reward which I was quite happy to have. The trouble was that she was rather lax when it came to me playing wrong notes, letting me get away without correction - other than for the very obvious mistakes. As a consequence, I still play some of my childhood pieces with those same wrong notes when I play them from memory. Somehow, my brain simply refuses to go into "edit" mode and get rid of them.

From church School I went on to Rainham Road School, a junior school about fifteen minutes walk from home. It was a typically suburban Gothic style Victorian building on three floors with a playground at either end and on the outskirts of one playground was a detached building which was the metal and woodworking workshop. This had been erected as a very much later necessity as those two skills were much in demand in those pre-war days. The whole school was surrounded by iron railings - perhaps intended to keep the inmates in rather than the other way round. Inside, years of polishing the woodblock floors had given the entire building a certain waxy, clinical aroma. Institutional wax polish was designed more for efficacy than perfume. The floors were linked by stone staircases which echoed like caverns and outside, the playgrounds were covered in a coarse tarmac resembling a black lemon grater which took the skin off your knees in no time if you fell over.

The local corner shop was Hucklesby's, a Victorian building, having two stone steps up to the front door. Inside, were bare floorboards, waxed with what must have been the same institutional stuff as the school used. Who knows, perhaps there was only one brand of wax polish for the whole of Great Britain. The shop sold newspapers and comics, tinned food, cheap toys, cap-guns, sweets, Wall's ice cream, matches, paraffin and brushes. Among the sweets were liquorice sticks; long, solid, pliable, black sticks and also hollow ones like sweet, black, sticky straws. The hollow ones were sold to go with packets of sherbet and by tearing off one corner of the packet, the hollow tube could be inserted into the sweet white powder which when sucked up would explode as a mouthful of lemony tart foam as it dissolved. They also sold a strange kind of shrivelled yellow stick you could suck and chew and as the end became like eggyolk coloured string, it gave off a strong flavour not unlike turmeric – which it actually might have been. I never did find out. It lasted for ages and needed lots of teeth cleaning afterwards if we weren't to look like junior vampires. One dangerous small toy was the metal bomb. This was like a tiny hand grenade which came apart. Inside you could pack in a few caps and putting the two halves back together, held in place by a small but strong elastic band, the bomb was hurled into the air by its string tail and it would explode on impact - hopefully with the ground and not someone's head!

Only two of my Rainham teachers remain in my memory. Mr. (Hoppy) Barnett had one wooden leg and the other was crippled in some way, so he used crutches all the time; perhaps he was a World War One veteran who had seen active service and had become a casualty. He could get around pretty well though, particularly when it came to going downstairs, having perfected the method of holding his wooden leg out in front and slipping from the edge of each stair on his better foot. It was amazing to watch how quickly he slipped and slithered down as though skating on a tiny tea tray. Apart from his teaching general studies, he also indulged in making home-made wine at school. Our ink used to come in one gallon stone jars each stoppered by a tough rubber bung. These became his fermenting jars when finished with. One day in a geography class, there came a loud bang from the map cupboard and when he opened the door, a red, effervescing cherry red liquid flowed out onto the floor, leaving the map cupboard smelling like the Last Chance Saloon for weeks after. The other teacher was a Mr.Rubinstein who was instrumental in getting me into the Tottenham Grammar School. He was, apart from other things, in charge of the school garden and it was there that I got my first taste of kol rhabi. Each day we also received a quarter pint bottle of milk at morning break. These were stumpy little bottles with wide mouths sealed with round cardboard caps in the middle of which was a lightly scored inner disc you would push open with a fingertip. I always licked the cream off the inside of the cap first - that was the best bit! My first experience of bullying came at Rainham school from a boy called Smith. A tough James Cagney-like figure who enjoyed going round making boys less aggressive than himself do various things against their will - or suffer the consequences. Sooner or later, it was my turn to receive his attention and we finished up having a fight during which I managed to land a lucky punch in his eye which made him break off the fight, swearing to "get even one day". For some weeks, I kept a low profile with butterflies in my tummy in case he should pick on me again, but he never did. The catchment area for the school took in all sorts of boys from diverse families, mostly of the working/artisan class, so we had the roughs and toughs and the "nicer" boys and girls from the Middleham area. Among the roughs and toughs was a boy we called Arnold - "Bonker" to us - (can't think why). His home life must have been pretty awful I felt, as for some arcane reason he had had all his hair shaved off except for a small fringe at the front. He had head lice and I supposed it was the only way they could be deprived of their nest. He smelled dreadful and wiped his snotty nose on the cuff of his frayed jacket or shirtsleeve. He may well have been quite a nice person if we had got to know him, but we all steered clear of him, so he remained an outsider to most of the school. I wonder what he went on to do with his life?

In the main school hall were two long display cases like they have in museums, each about twelve feet long with an apex shaped top making them look like very low greenhouses. The few artifacts which were on display could be got at only by unlocking the window panels. One day, one of the boys managed to smash his arm through one of the panes of glass and had to be rushed off to hospital to have it all stitched up. The ambulance was a Morris Commercial, painted white with a large red cross on the sides and back doors. On the left of the driving cab on the outside was a big brass bell which could be rung by the co-driver reaching out of his window and vigorously shaking the rope which had a big round weight on it. An obvious job for Quasimodo. No sirens or electric bells yet then . . . The stretchers were just a piece of thick canvas stretched between two poles and which slid into runners in the back of the ambulance. These were to see really heavy duty in the years that followed when we suffered "the Blitz". Fortunately, I was never a customer and can't remember ever having to ride inside an ambulance.

Childhood Christmases remain, somewhat hazily, in my

memory. It was usually a time for family get togethers, when after a traditional Christmas Dinner with loads of puddings and custard the King's Christmas Day Speech was always reverently listened to on the radio, when everyone would get sat comfortably, cups of tea in hand, to hear what he had to say to his Empire. Later, after an afternoon rest, washing up done and supper sandwiches made, the partying really began. Cousin Geoffrey and I would manage to empty the dregs from the various bottles and quite enjoy ourselves, before being conscripted into playing the piano for popular songs and carols. Real fir trees were decorated with tinsel and real candles in little tin cups which attached to the ends of the branches with spring clips (imagine the fire risk)! Lots of little presents, especially for us kids; battery powered tin cars and trains – no plastic in those days, magic lanterns with slides of what the makers thought were interesting places, Meccano sets for budding builders and engineers, roller skates – if you were old and lucky enough, bus conductors' and cowboys' outfits complete with six-shooter cap guns, kaleidoscopes and metal model aircraft. I remember one particular metal toy of mine was a Mercedes racing car built by the German firm of Schuko, battery powered and with a wire remote control steering wheel which could be driven all over the room avoiding grown-ups' feet (with practice). One such model recently came up for auction making well over one hundred pounds. Whether the toys of today will ever become collectors' items as were those of the earlier days, is anyone's guess.

CHAPTER FOUR

THE WAR YEARS

It was while I was at Rainham Road School that the Second World
War started. War was declared on Germany on the 3rd.of September
after what was considered by many to be a weak attempt to dissuade
Hitler from his expansionism into Europe. Mr. Neville Chamberlain,
our Prime Minister had issued ultimatums to Mussolini, Italy's
dictator and to Hitler warning them that if they did not stop invading
their neighbours, Great Britain would invoke her various treaties and
rally to their aid. In the previous August, Chamberlain had told The
Axis Powers that we would fulfill our guarantee to Poland and
defend them if necessary. Only a year earlier, Chamberlain had
returned from a meeting with Hitler in Munich announcing that he
had secured "Peace in our time", but almost before the ink was dry
on the agreement, Hitler had again moved westwards, threatening
Belgium, Holland and France. After more cabinet meetings and
delays, it was eventually decided after much deliberation and stalling
to declare war on Germany. But Parliament was not happy with
Chamberlain's leadership and it was decided to reconstruct a
coalition government led by Winston Churchill.

There then followed a period known as "The Phoney War",
when nobody seemed to know what was going to happen next.
Germany was consolidating its gains in Europe and although
everyone expected them to march westwards yet again, no-one knew
when, or by what route and in what strength. So we sent what was
known as The British Expeditionary Force (BEF) of 150,000 men to
France and Belgium to help them defend themselves when the big
push did come. But because those two countries collapsed quickly,
France became a divided country with the surrendered southern part
of France governed by their own Marshal Petain, who seemed
content to work under German occupation. The beleaguered BEF
situated in the northern part had to defend themselves almost alone
against the advancing German army. This led to the greatest
evacuation ever mounted across the sea from Dunkirk to the south
coast of England. Hundreds of tiny boats, fishing boats, family
motor boats, yachts, anything that could float and crewed by

volunteers were being mustered from every harbour between The
Medway and Weymouth and beyond and anything capable of
crossing The Channel was pressed into use including the old seaside
paddle steamers. These were escorted backwards and forwards by
the Royal Navy, lifting our beleaguered soldiers off the beaches.
Many ships and boats of all sizes were lost by enemy action, but in
true British Bulldog fashion, we turned this disaster into a national
victory. In the final analysis, just over a third of a million men were
evacuated back to England, including almost 140,000 Frenchmen. It
was the greatest feat of Naval organisation.

Up to that point in the war, we in Britain had only known that
the BEF was in trouble in France and having to withdraw. We had
not seen a single German aircraft in our skies, so at home, everything
was peace and quiet. Hence the misnomer "Phoney War". In 1938,
the Government had drawn up plans for the evacuation of about 1.5
million children from designated danger areas to safer places "in the
country", so that should war be declared, everything was ready to
swing into action. In the September of 1939, as soon as we declared
a state of war to exist between us and Germany, the evacuation plans
were put into operation. Almost all children up to age of about
twelve or so living in built up areas such as London, Southampton,
Plymouth, Birmingham, Liverpool were moved out by train and bus
to be billeted with strangers in equally unknown villages and towns
in the country. Some were sent abroad to America and Canada.
Right up to the moment of departure, parents had little or no idea
where their children were going "until further notice". We kids were
all equipped with smelly rubber gasmasks in little rectangular
cardboard boxes tied round our necks with string. We were all
expected to carry a couple of spare changes of underwear, shirts and
socks and coats, plus a small supply of food ration to see us through
the first day or two in our new homes. This entire luggage was to be
in one small case which the child could carry, or where people were
not sufficiently well off to have such a thing as a case, wrapped in
brown paper bundles and tied with string. Each of us had a label tied
to a lapel to show who we were. We did some gas mask practice -
just in case. They were made of black rubber with an oval mica
eyepiece and had a droopy nose-piece at the end of which was taped
one or two perforated cans of crystals which were intended to filter
out any gas. The whole contraption was held in place by rubber

45

bands over our heads, making us all look like mutant baby elephants.
We were shepherded onto trains and amid tearful parents wailings and shouts, steaming off to our unknown destination in a benignly intended odyssey whose purpose was the very opposite of that now befalling millions of Jews at that time in central Europe. In some lucky cases, as with me, certain mothers were chosen to help conduct the battalions of children to their new homes, assisting the Billeting Officer sort them out for dispersal. I left Edmonton railway station with mother in charge of a carriage-full of bewildered children, not knowing whether they were going on a picnic or simple day's outing. Many a childhood trauma must have been born that day. As I now know, the L.N.E.R. steam train took us out through north east Middlesex into Hertforshire and on to Braintree in Essex, then a sleepy little market town near Colchester. It was all very rural, nestling between Chelmsford and Bishops Stortford. Nowadays, it is barely in the country as the northern fringe of the M11 runs just south of the town with busy Gatwick Airport only a stone's throw away. As with so many other once beautiful towns, modern developers have ripped the heart out of it, replacing local village stores with ubiquitous Boots, Marks and Spencer's, Tesco et al.

After a few false starts, I was eventually billeted to mother's satisfaction with Mr. and Mrs.Pockock, a bank manager and his wife who had a golden cocker spaniel they called "Future". They had a very nice modern house, but on the opposite side of the road was the local Calor gas depot, so the frequent clanking sound of gas cylinders being stacked and rancid mustardy smell of gas often wafted over the road when the wind was in the wrong direction. Mother stayed for a few weeks, leaving dad to cope on his own. But after a while, she had to make other arrangements for me to go to another family before leaving me on my own with them. It was felt that it would be in my best interests if a billet could be found for me where there were other children of my own age and eventually she found the Cornell family who lived, I believe, at no. 166 Cressing Road. Gwen, the daughter, was about nineteen and had a boy friend, Larry, so she wasn't really compatible with me at eight years of age. But the son, Noel, was about ten, and consequently he and I were expected to get on well together, irrespective of our individual personalities. It must have worked out reasonably well and mother went home to Silverlea.

The Cornell's house was at the end of a small group of houses well down Cressing Road, almost on the outskirts of the town. Not much farther on down the road we could stand with our legs apart, claiming that half of us was in Braintree and the other in the village of Cressing. I went to the same school as Noel and seemed to settle in well there, getting an honourable mention from my teacher one day for having written an essay describing the table as "laden" with food. 'Oo, that's a very good word to use, Peter.' Apart from the daily walks to and from school, I remember little else about what I did there. Noel's sister, Gwen, was a Licentiate of the Royal Academy of Music, but I don't ever remember her playing the piano. Come to think of it, I don't even recall whether the Cornell's had one – it's all a bit foggy. Over that winter of 1939/40, the snow fell so thickly that we wore Wellington boots to go to school and it often came over the tops of our boots, making our socks wet and freezing our feet. The hedgerows along the road and round Berry's Field belonging to a local builder were thick with dark red hips and haws, some of which I used to nibble, each one an astringent tobaccoey flavour, temptingly pleasing to the taste buds, but carrying an inbuilt warning that too much indulgence *might* just be bad for my tummy. We had nothing quite like it in London, where later, I had to ride my bike quite a long way before finding equivalent hedgerows. But here, not fifty yards from where I was living, I could indulge in the peace and quiet of nature any time I wanted - not that I really appreciated it then, I suppose. The undisturbed snow on the fields and hedges twinkled in the sunlight, bringing into stark relief the various birds which flew backwards and forwards collecting what food they could find. It's a pity that those self-same birds suffered from us children when in springtime we robbed their nests of their long awaited eggs. Pricking holes at each end of the shells and blowing out the contents and laying the fragile shells in our own little cotton wool nests. We had them in the palest of blues, some speckled with tiny black spots, others just plain cream or faintly green coloured - all potential chicks whose futures had been obliterated by the avarice of us junior collectors.

The evacuation plans had not taken account of the adverse effect that might happen to the children themselves as being separated from their parents at such a crucial time in their lives led to all kinds of psychological problems. Bed-wetting was common

47

among them, leading to many "foster parents" becoming physically unkind to their charges. Some children were considered to be nothing more than unpaid skivvies, to wash and clean, run errands and work as dictated. Some even had to sleep out of doors in sheds. Is it any wonder some children grew up full of resentment and hatred for grown-ups?

Eventually, by the spring of 1940, the Government reconsidered the situation and came to the conclusion that as England had not been obliterated under a blanket of bombs and that there was no sign of Germany mounting an invasion, they could relax the evacuation order and allowed those parents who so wished to have their children back home with them. Mum took the opportunity to collect me around the beginning of May and took me home to Silverlea as to all intents and purposes, the Phoney War had not developed into anything to worry about too much. People were becoming complacent. On the 10th. of July, however, the situation suddenly changed. Goering ordered his bombers to attack our airfields in the south east. Thankfully, we had developed a new system called "Radar", an electronic early warning device which enabled observers to plot enemy planes on their screens and so able to give Fighter Command information about their distance, height and speed of approach. With this device and the Observer Corps, most incoming bombers were known about before they arrived over their targets, allowing our Hurricanes and Spitfires to scramble and get up to fighting height in time to intercept them. This did not entirely stop the bombers from getting through - merely thinned them out a bit! The Battle of Britain had started with the main targets being not only our airfields, but the radar installations situated along the south east coast. From time to time, the attacks came further north westward from Kent and Sussex, resulting in enemy planes actually beginning to appear over the outskirts of London. At first, the sight of all the planes getting mixed up among a cat's-cradle of vapour trails as they fought it out with one another was new to us on the ground. We cheered as "Our Boys" shot down an enemy, watching it spiralling down leaving a trail of grey-black smoke behind, to disappear somewhere beyond our immediate skyline. It wasn't so good when it one of ours that did the plummeting to earth.

At about that time, a month or two after I had left the Cornell's, a lone German bomber may have found himself off course

48

in East Anglia and before turning for home decided to drop his landmine rather than take it fully armed all the way back to Germany. It had landed a couple of doors away from the Cornell's, totally demolishing that end of the terrace, including their house too. In 1994, Norma and I were visiting that part of the country and out of curiosity, we drove along Cressing Road to see where I had lived, hoping to see no. 166 among all the other pebble-dash houses, but it was not there. Right in the middle of that part of the road was a small group of much more modern houses which had been built to replace those destroyed in 1940. I had not recognised number 166's replacement.

For almost two months, the Luftwaffe concentrated their efforts on bombing our airfields and radar stations. We now knew that the Phoney War was well and truly over and that the real shooting had started. During the first few months of the war, those people who had large enough gardens were issued with the necessary shaped sheets of corrugated iron, nuts and bolts and instruction leaflets explaining how to assemble what were to become their "Anderson" shelters. Deep holes had to be dug into which these iron huts were placed and covered over with a foot or two of earth as extra protection. London is built on the clay beds of the Thames valley and to dig down six feet inevitably meant reaching the water table, so the majority of the shelters began to fill with water. To counteract this meant lining them with concrete back up to ground level and just for good measure all the bunk beds were built up on stilts - just in case. But even so, the shelters were nearly always damp and none too healthy for long periods of occupation. Even so, it was our somewhat more comfortable taste of what our senior generation had had to endure in the trenches only a mere twenty five years earlier. For those families whose garden was not large enough, they received a "Morrison" shelter made of four thick angle iron legs bolted to a steel top. As this was about six feet square, it served many a family as a dining table.

On the evening of the 7th. of September 1940, the air raid sirens started wailing with what was to become the familiar but feared rising and falling moan signalling the approach of the enemy. We dutifully trooped down the garden to the shelter and in the early evening sky saw the barrage balloons floating in the skies of London looking like huge droopy silver sausages with tail wings. Each one was tethered to a winch on the ground by a steel cable which was meant to deter planes from flying low to get a more accurate drop for their bombs, the theory being that if they could be kept higher, the anti-aircraft guns had a better chance of hitting them. As darkness began to close in, the searchlights picked out the bombers in their pencils of brilliant white light, but this still didn't necessarily mean that the guns could hit them any the easier. It was all a bit hit and miss really as the gunners had to estimate the height that they wanted their altitude sensitive fuses to detonate, then predict how much it was necessary to "aim off" in front of their chosen target in the hope that if they got both nearly right, the explosion and shrapnel of their shell would hit the plane. Sometimes, the shells didn't explode, coming back to earth either to explode there or to rest in the ground waiting for something to trigger the detonator. Either way it added to the deaths and injuries inflicted by the Germans. As the evening wore on and wave after wave of bombers inexorably flowed over London, the noise of gunfire, bombs exploding, engines of planes either droning towards or away from us, plus the screaming of engines belonging to the planes diving to crash on the ground who knows where, mounted to a crescendo. This attack had been aimed at the heart of London with the docks as the prime target. High explosive and incendiary bombs rained down in their tons, saturating the centre of London in a raging inferno that was to spread farther and farther as each successive wave of bombers used the flames as their aiming mark. This was all happening no more than about five or ten miles away from Middleham Gardens and by the light of the fire-enflamed red sky, mother was able to read the time quite clearly on her tiny ladies wrist watch. As the raid progressed, bonded warehouses lining the docks and filled with spirits such as rum for the Royal Navy, paint stores and timber warehouses all fuelled the inferno. Before long, the heat was so intense that the tarmac road surfaces began to boil and ignite, making rivers of fire through the already burning buildings, preventing the ambulances and fire engines from getting through, or almost worse, themselves becoming trapped in those rivers of fire. Fire boats stationed in the Thames worked through the night pumping their plumes of water onto the warehouses along the embankment in an attempt to keep those which had not already burst into flames from doing so. The others were too far gone to save and were left to burn themselves out. That night, almost two thousand Londoners were either killed or injured and we learned later the next day on the radio that the same pattern of devastation had been taking place in other major cities and dock areas such as Coventry, Southampton, Plymouth and Bristol. I had been taken back to London in time to become involved in what became all-out war against the civilian population, the like of which had never been seen before. The bombing continued by night and day with the hope that the will of the people would crack and that by undermining our morale, it would bring down the Government of the day. The Germans were wrong. It merely stimulated people to redouble their war efforts to make more and more munitions, more planes and ships and by "Digging for Victory" every square inch of land was used to grow food. Flower beds were dug up in favour of vegetables, every back garden which could spare a yard or two of space rigged up chicken coops or rabbit hutches. We had white Aylesbury ducks on our pond.

Everybody tightened their belts and rationing was introduced so that food and clothing, furniture and other necessities were strictly controlled. Luxuries were a thing of the past, unless bought on the "Black Market" which flourished in the hands of the spivs and fly boys. Private car owners were lucky to receive one gallon a petrol a week as their ration and then they were to be used mainly for essential journeys only. Had the Germans concentrated on wiping out the RAF on the ground, they could have won an enormous victory, but as it was, by switching to bombing the towns, our heavy industries managed to produce more fighters and bombers which enabled the RAF to regroup and re-equip. If anything, the RAF now experienced a shortage of pilots rather than the planes for them to fly, despite recruiting pilots from Commonwealth and foreign countries which had been overrun, such a Poland, Czechoslovakia and from Free France. Lads as young as eighteen or nineteen were qualified as pilots and thrown into the air battles with only a handful of hours flying experience. Only the lucky few, who learned quickly, survived.

As the raids continued, the German planes often overflew London, coming north to bomb power stations such as the one at Brimsdown which supplied electricity to the British Enfield Small Arms company nearby, which was also an obvious target. The railway line which ran alongside the river Lea was also a target, as was our gasworks. They all got their fair share of attention and what was left over, we got, quite indiscriminately dropped on our houses. Although Silverlea was never hit, there were several near misses. It was the job of the Air Raid Wardens to patrol the neighbourhood making sure that when the sirens sounded, residents blacked out their windows or switched off their lights and took cover in their shelters. They were also expected to help the fire brigade and ambulance crews wherever necessary. Their equipment was a proper military gas mask and a white steel helmet with a large black "W" painted on it and an armband identifying them as "Warden". One night, the siren sounded, by now "as usual", and Iris, the daughter of the Doubledays, whose house backed onto the right of way about level with our shelter, had been in the bathroom. She ran out to their shelter leaving the light on and without the curtains drawn. The Warden spotted the light. "Turn that light out". No response, naturally, as the house was now empty. "Turn that light out". Nothing happened. "Will you turn that bloody light out!" at which point we all heard the familiar sound of a German bomber coming close and all dived for cover. The solitary light had perhaps given the bomber a target to aim at and it had released its bomb which fell a short distance away hitting Maison Owide's hairdressing salon. One of the steel joists from the shopfront was hurled like a monstrous javelin straight through the side of a house only ten yards (9 metres) away from us, transfixing the staircase just as the son, Ronny Heinz was running downstairs to get into their shelter. It narrowly missed him, but he was hit by some of the flying masonry and in later years, I couldn't help thinking it was ironic that with a name like theirs, Germanic fate could have at least given their house of all a miss. Daylight raids gave us the spectacle of watching the aerial dogfights as our nimble fighters dodged and wove round and through the solid formations of Dorniers and Heinkels, Junkers and Messerschmitts. A Heinkel came over low one afternoon with smoke streaming from an engine, chased by a Hurricane pouring bursts of machine guns bullets into it. We could clearly see the crews of both planes as they passed overhead and we all cheered and waved, totally oblivious to the anguish of those four or five Germans as at worst they plunged to their probable deaths somewhere none too far away. At best, if they survived, they would end up being given a cup of tea and a cigarette by fair-minded people before being marched away by the local Bobby or Home Guard. Funny people, we English...

Each day during the Blitz, dad cycled to work and as a result of all the broken glass in the road went through puncture repair outfits as though they were going out of fashion. During one Sunday raid he lost his temper, shouting "Listen to all those silly buggers sweeping that glass into the road again. I bet I get another bloody puncture tomorrow." What he was in fact hearing turned out to be a shower of pieces of aluminium from a bomber which had blown up almost immediately overhead. We kids added lots of bits and pieces to our collection that day. We used to scour the streets for souvenirs, picking up all sorts of pieces of twisted metal, nose cones of shells with the altitude fuse rings still intact, shards of shrapnel, spent bullets and bullet cases, all bright and shiny. The danger came from any chance encounter with a "Butterfly bomb". These were quite small, about the size of a tin of baked beans, with little wings which sprouted out of the end on a stalk and the idea was they would lodge in rooftops and gutters of buildings to explode some time later, especially if they were disturbed accidentally. Sometimes they were incendiary and sometimes they were explosive anti-personnel bombs and were to be reported to a Warden if we saw them. He was expected to guard them until a bomb disposal team could come, or if they burst into flame, deal with them with any stirrup pump which came to hand. Most households had been issued with one of these foot and hand operated pumps like large bicycle pumps with hoses attached and which stood in buckets of water, although most people used them for watering the garden when not wanted for more serious purposes.

In response to the Blitz, the War Cabinet decided to retaliate and bomb Germany, with Berlin being the prime target to begin with. The Germans responded by now naming us as "The Aggressors", feeding the German population propaganda by radio and in all their newspapers and not necessarily saying what they had done to us, of course. The effect of our counter attack was that Hitler called off his air raids on us to better defend the Fatherland, which meant that The Battle of Britain drew to a merciful close. We still had air raids, but not of such intensity as during that dreadful three or four months which began in the early September of 1940. People began going out again to the cinema and dance halls. As a family, we would often walk the few miles to see relatives in Tottenham and as every day passed without further injury, we became very party-minded, often spending until late at night singing and telling jokes or inviting neighbours in for a drink, especially if their son or daughter was home on leave from the forces. If there was a night raid, we would all sleep under the stairs or kitchen table, or even in the shelter and walk home the next morning. Impromptu parties would break out at the most unexpected times. Cousin Arthur (Paulson) was home on leave one weekend when we went round to see Aunt Vi. A raid started and as one or two bombs dropped a bit too close for our liking, we all dived under the Morrison shelter. Being nimble, I was among the first, only to be landed on by Arthur who weighed in at about fourteen stones. We always said that he flung himself on top of me to protect me, but in the process he nearly broke my ribs. When the raid ended, we climbed out unscathed and went back to our partying to carry on where we had left off.

Arthur was a very good magician and his younger brother, my cousin Geoffrey a good pianist. My mother had quite a good singing voice and always said that she had had her voice "trained" when she was young, but by whom or to what extent, I never knew. But to give her her due, she could sing very well, choosing songs from Ivor Novello shows, and the then very popular "Trees" and "Because" (this last song was made popular by Deanna Durbin, a wonderful singer actress from Hollywood). Aunt Vi could always be relied upon to make mountains of sandwiches, even during the rationing, thanks to her clandestine relationship with Fred Miller who owned the local cafe at the corner of Bruce Grove. She also helped her son Arthur with his illusions. Other cousins and friends who could dance or sing were roped in so that between us we could put on a show of about ten acts. Thanks to Arthur's seemingly never ending supply of Max Factor stage make-up and some devoted dressmaking from bits and pieces of material cut from unwanted curtains, we put together a creditable Concert Party. Arthur adopted the stage name of "Sonny Paul", assisted by his mother, known as "Irene". My Mother became "Molly in Song". Geoffrey and I remained Geoffrey and Peter "at the piano", although as I have said earlier, Geoffrey preferred to dress as a girl, which made it a bit difficult to go on calling him "Geoffrey at the piano"!

As the bomber raids tailed off, Hitler introduced us to new

threats known as the V1 and V2 missiles. The V1 was a ramjet engined flying bomb packed with one ton of high explosive and launched from special ramps in Belgium or France. Under gyro compass control it would fly on a predetermined course until its fuel ran out, when without warning, the bomb would glide to the ground, exploding on impact. They were propelled by a highly efficient engine which made a very distinctive raspberry-farting noise and as they flew very fast but low, they were easy to spot. The trouble was that once they arrived over built up areas, they would do untold damage wherever they came down, unless they could be made to explode in the air. They weren't easy targets for the ack ack (Anti-Aircraft) guns and if the radar could pick them up in time while they were over the Channel, our fighters could get up to intercept them, but they didn't have much time to do it. A dangerous, but effective way was devised by some of our more "adventurous" pilots, which was to dive to gain speed and then fly alongside the Buzzbomb, or Doodlebug as we called it, and tip one of its wings to upset the gyro, putting it into a lop-sided attitude which caused it to go out of control and crash before getting over a built up area. V2's were the first proper ballistic missile and had been developed by Werner von Braun, a rocket scientist in Germany during Hitler's reign of terror. Although von Braun had been much more interested in the purely scientific development of rockets, Hitler seized the opportunity to pressgang his knowledge into use for the Third Reich and with slave labour organised by Albert Speer built the necessary launch sites for them. These weapons incidentally gave us the name for our concert party and "The Rocketeers" was launched for the benefit of those people displaced from their homes by enemy action. We travelled the countryside giving free concerts in Town Halls, Corn Exchanges and Red Cross or St. John Ambulance Centres in all weathers in an attempt to cheer up those who had just been made homeless.

The rockets arrived totally unannounced and literally out of the blue. Soon after being launched in Western France or Belgium, they became supersonic for their short flight across the Channel to land almost anywhere and although most were targetted onto London, they could sometimes go astray and overfly or fall short of their hoped-for destination. By the time they were used, it was early 1945 and I was by then a pupil at Tottenham Grammar School in White Hart Lane, not far from the Tottenham Hotspur football stadium. We had all finished our lunch one day in the school hall and had gone outside to wait for the afternoon lessons to begin at 2pm. Usually I played football with my chums, but on this day I decided to sit in a quiet sunny corner overlooking the school garden where two of our teachers, Fred Sales and Fanny Adams sometimes sat talking to one another. Beside the garden at the edge of the playing field was parked an old Tiger Moth plane which the Air Cadets used to do some training. Without any warning, there was an enormous explosion which must have deafened me for a while as well as flinging me around a bit. Fortunately the corner of the school building had protected me from the direct effect of the blast and I can remember quite clearly regaining consciousness and coming to my senses in time to see the effect of the explosion on the houses at the far end of the playing field. Almost as though in slow motion, all their front windows clouded over as though splashed with milk and as the panes of glass shattered, the curtains were all sucked out through the gaping windows to flap like washing in the breeze. As the dust settled and I struggled to my feet, I slowly became aware of what had happened. The Tiger Moth was a jumbled heap of metal and fabric and as I stumbled round the corner, I saw that a group of houses which had recently stood just opposite the school gates had disappeared. The playground in which I would normally have been playing football had taken the full force of the blast and resembled a battlefield with building debris and broken glass everywhere. Boys were lying groaning and some bleeding from their injuries. Some were obviously dead, one with a small hole between his eyes where he had been hit by a solitary piece of shrapnel, another from his lungs having collapsed as he was caught in the vacuum behind a surface shelter. Others trapped under fallen masonry, were being hauled out to safety by teachers and the older, uninjured boys. One boy Burns, whom I never knew really well, was lying with just the stump of his arm left with Mr. Mitchell, my favourite English Master applying a tourniquet made from his handkerchief, twisting it with his fountain pen in an attempt to staunch the loss of blood. Some week or two later, I went to see Burns in hospital and gave him our whole month's ration of chocolate.

* * *

NO COUNSELLING THEN.

'Football?' my pals asked. 'No, not me
today'.
I had revision to get through. No way
could I chance failing tomorrow's big test –
proud parents expecting I'd do my best.
Reading deeply lost in thought my world
crashed
about me – confusion, brick walls all
smashed,
red rubbled crater, glass shards, boys cry
for 'Mum' and 'Help, please come'!
Soon some will die.

Amid evil's destruction and mind-numbing
noise,
on pumping stumps of victimized boys
black-gowned masters flock like crows
twisting school ties with pens, knotted like
bows.

Dear God, why now? Who's really to blame
for this V2 weapon joining life's game?

* * *

There used to be a pawnbrokers in Fore Street, Edmonton
where you could buy all manner of unredeemed articles from cups
and saucers to sewing machines, bicycles to "Box Brownie" cameras
and one day I saw a B.S.A. air rifle which I got dad to buy for me.
The shopkeeper said it needed mending and I think dad paid about
seven shillings and sixpence or so (35 pence) for it and when we got
it home and taken apart, dad found that the main spring had broken
and the leather washer in the air compression chamber had dried out.
He found a suitable replacement spring and soaked the washer in
some soapy water to soften it, then some grease and put the rifle
together again. The spring was so strong that I could only just work
the pump lever to compress the air. The next problem was that we

couldn't get the right size 0.22 pellets for it; all we could get were 0.177s. So dad overcame that little problem by making a special mould so that we could squash the 0.177 pellets out to 0.22 size with a little tap from a hammer. Being smaller in mass than the proper size of slug meant that each shot had a greater muzzle velocity than originally intended and this gave the rifle exceptional penetrating power with pellets easily going through both sides of a tin can before burying themselves well into the wooden coal bunker. It was even so powerful as to be able to make a hole straight through an electric light bulb without shattering the whole of the glass. Dad made a very good rear sight from a piece of aluminium from a German plane and I practiced every day, getting more and more accurate until I could put a pellet through the hole in the centre of a gramophone record at ten paces. My other secret weapon against the Germans, should they invade, was to make throwing knives from umbrella stays. By hammering a small block of wood onto one end of a twelve inch long stay and sharpening the other, I could make an effective knife looking like a giant hatpin which could be thrown to stick into the wooden coalbin, which after all my military attention looked as though it was suffering from a severe attack of woodworm. Mother got fed up with all these warlike activities and made her feelings felt, so I compromised and gave up the knife-throwing circus act and shot down the length of the garden instead. One day I seriously upset her and dad. She had been out at work and I got home from school earlier than her and decided to be a good boy and light the gas/coke fire for when they got home. We always put a fireguard over the front of the fire and covered it with a large sheet of newspaper to make the fire draw more vigorously. So having lit the gas poker and stuck it into the coke, this is what I did. I had just done this when I heard a friend calling me and went out into the garden to talk to him and completely lost track of time. Mother came home and was horrified to see smoke billowing out of the open back kitchen door. The newspaper had caught fire, fallen away from the guard and set light to the rug in front of the fire and the wallpaper on either side too.

In those days, we spent most of our evening time in the back room which served as dining room and convenient sitting room, rather than light up the fire in the front lounge, which, in view of the coal rationing, we couldn't afford to do unnecessarily. Our nice mahogany extending dining table made a very good general purpose table. It was fine for me to do my homework on, mum and dad did their glass painting on it and I also used it to set up my chemistry set with sheets of Daily Mirror newspaper spread out to catch any wayward drips. Apart from the simple experiments as set out in beginners' handbooks, I experimented with making gunpowder. Carbon powder, sulphur and saltpetre mixed in the right proportions gave an excellent result and with some iron filings mixed in for good measure would make the ensuing explosion sparkle. Rolled tightly into a tube of paper, they made good fireworks, even if a little unpredictable in their performance. Another explosive mixture I discovered was hydrochloric acid, sugar and Condy's crystals heated in a crucible to a critical temperature. I was doing this one evening when it all went off with a bang while mum and dad were sitting either reading or listening to Dick Barton on the radio. It was necessary to go round carefully picking up the bits of broken glass and while doing so, dad cut his fingertip on a piece of the glass and until the day he died, every year in the cold weather, that cut would re-appear. No doubt the hydrochloric acid had burned the tissues of his cut flesh, preventing it from ever properly healing.

* * *

PAST INTERROGATIVE

My mental trowel picks gently at memory's faded treasures.
Inquisitive fingers sensitively search, brushing, reshaping shadows –
seeking hidden fragments to restore him from half a century of sleep.

A few sepia scenes remain: of acid-cut thumb skin cracking wide
each winter – my faulty chemistry test to blame;
on his first hearing Rachmaninov's sumptuous melodies
murmuring 'Music of Angels . . .' smiling through affected eyes.

Too soon I grew, my khaki call, not be at home, to marry and serve
abroad.
What other treasures may yet be locked deep inside
my gentle father, so little known or understood?

Gurkhas and a Grand Piano

* * *

As part of our war effort, we kept some Aylesbury ducks, letting them use part of the garden and the fishpond. Dad built a nice hut for them with a ramp leading down to the water and they were ably looked after by a self-appointed leader whom we called Bill. Each time the air raid warning had sounded, Bill uncannily made them all troop up into their house while he stood guard at the entrance. It was quite amazing how he would know when the danger had passed, cocking one eye skywards to check before encouraging them all out again to swim round the pond, waggling their tails and gossiping away to one another. From time to time or as food and money became short, we had to resort to killing them one by one and eventually only Bill was left. Neither mum nor dad had the heart to kill him off, so he was given to mum's sister Vi who kept him in her tiny garden with a tin bath for him to swim in, which wasn't up to the luxury he had been used to with us. As time passed, however, Bill revealed his true sexual identity by laying an egg, much to everybody's surprise and he continued to lay eggs until too old, several years later.

In the later war years, mother decided to enter me into local talent competitions, the first of which took place in the open air in Bruce Castle Park in Tottenham, but I simply can't remember a single thing about it now. But the next, and my biggest, was held in the Regal Cinema by The Angel roundabout in Edmonton, now regrettably a Bingo hall as are so many of the great pre-war cinemas. The Regal seated about two thousand people and had been built in the 1920's when Art Deco was all the rage. The architecture was in The Egyptian style with great columns and palms, huge feathery fans and murals depicting the Pyramids and Sphinx decorating the auditorium in gilt and a green known as Eau de Nile being the main colours. In front of the screen was an orchestra pit out of which would rise a "Mighty Wurlitzer" organ, blazing with coloured glass lit up from within and I believe the organist of the day was Sidney Torch, later to become a famous band leader and conductor, who could swivel round on his seat to face his adoring audience. This organ had about four keyboards at least, plus a pedal keyboard and could make as much noise as a symphony orchestra playing at full tilt. One Saturday morning, I got the opportunity to play it when the cinema was empty, the only trouble was I was so small that as I leaned forward to play the topmost keyboard, I leaned too close to the bottom one, playing a whole bellyful of notes. It was obviously for adults only. The competition was to be held during the extended interval between the supporting film and the main feature and in that half hour period, four or five acts would compete for a place in the finals on Saturday night. One of the most popular films of the whole of the wartime that had been showing was called "Dangerous Moonlight" with Anton Walbrook as the Polish Count who was also a fighter pilot and Sally Grey his genteel English lady lover. The music had been especially composed for the film by Richard Addinsell and was known as "The Warsaw Concerto", still popular today among the older generation and guaranteed to bring back memories of 1944. It so happened that the Polish Count was also a concert pianist and the film showed him playing the concerto in the ruins of either his home or concert hall after a German air raid. I bought the piano score and memorizing it made it my competition piece and on the appointed evening walked onto the stage in my short trousers to be introduced as "London's Youngest Organist", the result of having played for cousin John and Doreen Pichowski's wedding a short while earlier. I sat in front of a very large Challen concert grand piano and suffered a complete memory blackout. I just couldn't remember the opening chords. If I got it wrong, I would be doomed as they were very loud and very determined. There would be no covering up my mistake. I had to trust to luck or what is called "muscle memory" and fortunately it didn't let me down. The audience liked it and I won my heat. When it was all over, I went up to the circle seats where mum and dad were and tucked into a sandwich during the main feature film.

On the Saturday night the finals were held and I found that a lady had won her heat during the week also playing the same piece. The Talent Scout who was organising the whole affair was a large Canadian gentleman by the name of Brian Mickey who smoked an equally large cigar in between generous sips of gin. He suggested we toss up to see who would go on first and I won, but being a good, polite boy, I said she could go first - you know, ladies before gentlemen and all that stuff. She did well and got a lot of applause. I went on last and thought that as the audience had heard it once they wouldn't want to hear it again, so changed my act without reference to Brian Mickey, playing instead a medley of popular tunes like La Paloma, Yours, There'll be Bluebirds over the White Cliffs of Dover and so on. I did well, but not well enough. Neither the lady nor I won. The winners were two men, one who played the piano and the other sang. When the curtains opened, the pianist was already seated, but the singer had to hobble onto the stage with a crutch and wrestling with a large, heavy microphone on a stand which took him some time to get into place and adjust without help from anyone back stage. When their performance was over, he had to repeat the whole business by dragging the mike off stage again, tangling it up with his crutch and nearly falling over. Naturally, they got an enormous response and without a clapometer, Brian Mickey declared messrs. Porter and Fairbrass to be this week's winners, handing over to them the first prize of ten pounds. A few weeks later, mother entered me again in the same competition, but this time at The Empire, another cinema in upper Edmonton. Much the same thing happened on the night of the finals with Mr. Mickey saying he had never seen Porter and Fairbrass before their spectacular success in winning their heat earlier that week and he was sure everyone would take them to their hearts. They did, of course, and once again won their ten pounds. I seem to recall hearing of them appearing more than once again on the Brian Mickey circuit, so it is not beyond the realms of possibility that they travelled together for mutual benefit, splitting the prize money. His £5 would buy him at least two bottles of gin.

Eventually the war came to an end in Europe and to everyone's joy, the 8th. of May became Victory in Europe (VE) Day. Huge street parties were organised with flags and bunting of all kinds strung from house to house and across the streets between the lampposts. Roads were closed and long trestle tables were lined up, covered with sheets to be loaded with cakes and jellies, sandwiches and ice cream, tea and lemonade. There was singing and dancing until late into the evening. Some streets also organised concert parties with Morrison shelters being placed together to make steel topped stages and in our street, someone played the piano while Stan somebody or other dressed up as a French Foreign Legionnaire to sing "Le Rêve Passait" and as dramatically required had to swoon at the end of it and in doing so, fell so realistically that he knocked himself unconscious on the steel stage. Gradually, our soldiers began

62

to come home from Europe, equipped with their new "Demob suit" and a few pounds in their pockets to try to find work in our shattered economy. The war in the Far East was still raging and it wasn't until the Americans dropped two atomic bombs on the Japanese the following July that they finally surrendered. When our soldiers came home from that side of the world, there was no spectacular partying for them; everyone had played that out a few months earlier. They were still the "Forgotten Army" and were left pretty much to get on with it as best they could. Jobs were even more difficult to find. The ex-soldiers from Europe had taken all the best ones.

The immediate post war election saw, much to our surprise, Winston Churchill deposed as Prime Minister in favour of Clement Atlee and his Labour Government. Britain had spent just about all of its gold and bullion reserves and had borrowed large sums of money from the Americans under the Lend Lease Scheme, putting us into severe debt with the U.S.A. This meant that the post-war reconstruction took much longer and was more painful than expected, with food rationing continuing and the days of austerity prolonged for another four or five years. Things became so critical that bread rationing, something that we hadn't even had during the war, was introduced and rationing lasted until well into the early 1950's. We could no longer go on propping up the economies of some of our poorer dominions and political troubles began to break out with them agitating for independence. In India, millions lost their lives when in 1947 India was hastily and incompetently divided from what is now Pakistan, leading to Hindus and Moslems massacring one another in a bloody civil war. We had won the war, but lost the peace, with Communist Russia dominating the east of Europe and America getting hysterical about finding Reds under their beds during the McCarthy period of political purges. Two years after the war ended, I was to leave the Tottenham Grammar School and find a job. I was not yet sixteen years old.

CHAPTER FIVE

A JOB FOR THE BOY

During the war we had been introduced to rationing. Everyone was issued with a Ration Book containing pages of coupons for various commodities to cover successive weeks. Every time food, clothing, furniture or any other rationed item was bought, you handed over a number of coupons. If you wanted to make a larger purchase than normal you had to save your coupons or swap them with someone else who could do an exchange with you and this led to a lot of bartering. If you had run out of coupons and had the money, you could still nevertheless buy a lot of things on "The Black Market" if you knew the right person.

Genuine "Utility" furniture and clothing carried a government label not unlike two black rounds of cheese with a slice cut out of each and the number 41 in one of the cut out sections. There were clothing and food coupons, petrol and furniture coupons and everything was really very well controlled. The remarkable thing about those years was that on the whole, everybody was well nourished on a small, but well balanced diet. Statistics have shown that cases of obesity fell and with people eating more fresh vegetables than they do today we were all healthier. Also, everybody either walked or cycled to work, unless they had to travel fairly long distances, when they would go by bus. Children all walked to school. We had no such thing as "E" numbers or chemicals and additives added to our food, it was all plain straight forward natural – organic in other words. Although the war ended in 1945, it wasn't until about 1952 that we finally saw the end of rationing. Even as a young subaltern coming home on leave I was still issued with a ration card if I came home for 72 hours or more.

During 1945/6 I got my first sports bike with drop handlebars and an "Oppy" derailleur three speed gear. I used it to do my paper round between 6.30 and 7.30 every morning and during weekdays after my breakfast I walked the two or so miles to school with one or two other chums who had also been at Rainham with me. Some afternoons after school, we used to cycle down to the gasworks on

the Tottenham Marshes where, a couple of hundred yards past the
huge green gasometers, ran the river Lea and L.N.E.R. mainline out
of Kings Cross. The gasometers were giant circular storage tanks,
about forty or so meters in diameter and height – similar to today's
oil storage tanks - which rose and fell into pits dependent upon the
amount of gas in them and the pressure that was required to maintain
industrial and domestic supplies. If these were hit by bombs, the
fires raged sometimes for days, providing good aiming marks for
successive bomber raids at night. I could fish, train spot and watch
the barges on the canal all at the same time. We could also just lie
about in bomb craters hidden in sweet smelling grass, talking or
watching and listening to the skylarks high above us while
surrounded by all manner of butterflies flitting between the grasses
and wild flowers. As we walked through the long grass, we disturbed
clouds of grasshoppers which flickered away for about ten feet
before losing themselves in another clump of grass. They are now
sadly almost extinct. The craters gave us wonderful hideyholes for
illicit smoking parties when we youngsters were experimenting with
tobacco. One or two boys usually "found" a couple of their dad's
fags which we would all share, taking one or two sickmaking draws
and often choking and vowing never to do it again. If lucky, we
managed to get our hands on a pipe or two and passed those around
like Indians at a pow-wow, being even more violently sick than with
the cigarettes. Although dad used to roll his own cigarettes using
Golden Virginia tobacco, he had one or two pipes, although I never
saw him smoke them, probably because he might not be able to grip
them properly between his false teeth. There was no spare Golden
Virginia to be found at home, so I took some dry geranium leaves
along with me as the next best substitute. When lit, the pipe gave off
pungent smoke which naturally smelled just like a garden bonfire
and tasted absolutely foul. The leaves smouldered at such a high
temperature that any of us who sampled this natural "tobacco" were
left with not only reeling heads and feeling sick, but suffering from
burned tongues that felt as though they were upholstered with old
carpet.

Opposite the gasometers were the tar pits, a natural by-
product of making domestic gas by converting coal to coke, and the
ground for yards around was saturated in a black, sticky deposit with
a mixed aroma of tar and gas, simultaneously pleasant and yet not

pleasant and with an underlying, throat-gripping taste of mustard. It was around this area that The Home Guard had practiced with their P.I.A.T. guns, the acronym coming from the initials of the full military name of Projectile, Infantry, Anti-Tank. As I was to find in considerably more detail in later years, the Military have a wonderful way of cataloguing their items of equipment which makes a lot of sense, by using the main noun first, then adding the necessary adjectives in descending order of importance or logicality, so our present car is a Vehicle, Civilian, Mercedes, Smart, 0.690c.c., Petrol, Black, 2002. There's absolutely no mistaking what we are talking about - I hope. So, the PIAT was like a turnip on a stick with fins at the end, fired from a spring loaded launcher held at the shoulder, somewhat similar to an ancient cross-bow. The bomb could only be catapulted about fifty or so yards at most, which meant that whoever the poor chap was who had to shoot it at an oncoming tank had to get suicidally close to stand any chance of a direct hit - with every bomb fired at least worth a medal for Gallantry I would have thought. As a matter of interesting digression, Jeremy Clarkson's (TV motoring show "Top Gear") father-in-law was a major in the army and during one battle had single-handedly put two, if not three, German tanks out of action by standing in the road and firing PIATs at them, despite being badly wounded. This very brave action enabled his Company to achieve their objective, for which he won the coveted Victoria Cross, the highest possibly Military award for bravery in the face of the enemy. Victoria Crosses are reputedly made from the bronze canons captured during the Battle of Balaclava during the Crimean War on 25th. October 1854 and since their inception in 1855 only 1300 or so have been awarded and each is today worth around £400,000.

I enjoyed watching the various trains which thundered by alongside the River Lea, sometimes even travelling up to London with friends to go to all the main line stations like King's Cross, Waterloo, Euston, Paddington and St. Pancras to see the various classes of expresses, resplendent in their own particular livery of maroons, light and dark greens and blue, dependent on whether they belonged to London, Midland Scottish; London, North Eastern; Southern or Great Western. Our local line sometimes gave us the opportunity of seeing Sir Nigel Gresley's famous "Mallard" which set the new rail speed record for a steam locomotive in the 1930's between Grantham and Peterborough with a top speed of 128 miles and hour. That one record-breaking run, however, was never to be repeated by Mallard, as she suffered so badly from the stress of the effort involved in the name of publicity for the L.N.E.R. Thereafter, she was relegated to pulling standard passenger trains, which I can't help feeling is a somewhat ignominious end for such a great engine. She is currently in the Railway Museum at York, alongside other famous engines. At the main line stations we also saw the wheel-tappers checking that no cracks had developed in the wheels by tapping them with a long handled hammer and listening for the ringing of the steel to ensure all was well, similar to tapping a piece of china or glass for that clear ringing note. When they reached the engines, they were dwarfed by the size of the driving wheels which were about eight feet high, coupled together with giant driving and connecting rods to the pistons. The atmosphere of any station was pervaded by the combined smell of smoke and soot, especially the main line stations which were all covered in with glass, apart from a small opening running down the length of the platform over the train lines and which was intended to let the smoke and steam out into the air above. Platform tickets allowed anyone for the price of one penny to wander round at will while slot machines dispensed small bars of chocolate at the same cost.

At weekends, we sometimes cycled off "en famille" or went by bus for an afternoon or day's fishing when we went as far as Ponders End or Waltham Cross to meet up with other members of the family circle. If we got everyone organised, there were enough of us to take up about a quarter of a mile of river bank with the huge cooling towers of the Brimsdown Power Station in the background looking like giant upturned flower pots, belching out continuous plumes of steam which finally evaporated in the upper air. Any decent sized fish we caught would be carefully carried back home in tins with ventilated lids, where they would add to the stock of goldfish in the pond.

One weekend, Dad and I cycled off early on Sunday morning to a very quiet backwater stretch of the river Lea we had spotted on one of our previous outings. It was still early morning when we arrived in the mist with the gently dripping weeping willows and sweetly damp earth of the river bank setting a scene of wonderful tranquillity. In the early morning silence, broken only by the occasional squawk of a coot or moorhen we set about getting our tackle ready and had only just started to plumb the depth of the water when a bailiff came along asking for our club permits, which of course we didn't have. Before leaving we were made very envious by being shown the wonderful catches that had already been made from the deep, slow-flowing reedy water. Neither of us had ever seen such championship catches, even the smallest of which made our best look like tiddlers.

I joined the Sea Scouts and our "Skipper Paul" taught us how to tie all manner of nautical knots. One year we went away to camp and pitched our tents on an open area of land alongside the river Lea at Waltham Cross where we all had to take turns at cooking. I got my Cooking Proficiency badge for cooking baked beans, sausages and fried eggs over a wood fire in a billycan lid and felt justifiably proud of myself when I stitched the badge onto my sleeve. Skipper Paul also showed us, not very successfully, how to bake a jam roll over the fire. This meant making the pastry, rolling it out and spreading it with jam, then rolling it round a stick that had been stripped of its bark, and supported at either end over the fire to cook. Either his fire was too high or the stick too low, but the end result was that the pastry burst, the jam dripped onto the fire and caught fire. Eventually, the whole thing burst into flames and dropped into the fire to disappear in a rich black smoke, ending up as a blackened ragged sleeve round what was left of the stick. On another weekend, he took us all to the Thames Embankment to go aboard Captain Scott's Antarctic vessel, The Discovery. It still smelled strongly of the tar and pitch which had been used to caulk the timbers and it was very interesting to see the cramped quarters the crew and explorers had to endure on the voyage beyond Cape Horn to the ice shelf prior to their tragic journey to the Pole. Discovery had remained locked into the ice in McMurdo Sound from 1902-4, when it was freed and towed back home to Portsmouth. It was then given to the Boy Scout movement as a sail training ship and permanently berthed at The Thames Embankment, London.

Roller-skating was fun, our skates having metal wheels with ball bearing axle liners. Plastics such as we have today were simply not yet in general use. After a few months of determined skating up and down the pavements, the wheels wore out and were reduced just to skeletons and as the holes appeared around the rims, we called these holes 'windows'. Anyone owning a full set of windows was considered an expert and their skates made a particular clacking sound as the wheels span round on the paving stones. Braking, by dragging one foot at right angles behind the other hasn't changed much over the intervening sixty or more years I don't suppose, except that now, you do have the added advantage of brake pads on the fronts, or is the backs of your skates? With ours, we had to strap them onto our ordinary shoes, so once again, the fancy ankle-reinforced boots today are something new as are the elbow and knee pads. We just had to grin and bear it if we fell over, which we did – often, especially if a small stone got in the way of a skate wheel.

Our streets were lit at night by gas lamps on tall cast iron posts and when lit gave quite a mellow atmosphere to the night. During the daytime, the base of the post made an ideal cricket wicket, but the hazard was if you were tempted to hit out for a full blooded six, there was a distinct danger that somebody's front room window was likely to get smashed, bringing the game to an untimely end.

There was a chemist's shop in Dalston which specialised in selling chemistry equipment to schools and aspiring young scientists like me and I got myself a Saturday job there helping assemble the various orders and even serving behind the counter if we got very busy. I got to know my Bunsen burners from my Leibig condensers, but it didn't help me understand the properties of chemicals with such long names as phenolphthalein.

From quite an early age, mother had sent me to the local Sunday School and when I was too old for that, it seemed natural that I should go to church proper now and again, the nearest being the Snell's Park Congregational Church and somehow one day I met the organist, a septuagenarian by the name of David Warwick. Mother must have told him I was learning the piano and he suggested I try the organ, a nice electrically pumped, two manual instrument. He hoped, no doubt, I would be able to stand in for him later. For my audition with him I played a couple of popular melodies and he said he would like to teach me and so became my tutor for both the piano and the organ. When he came to our house for my piano lessons, he would set me something to play and then quite often fall asleep, so I can't say that I was learning a lot, but somehow I improved. I did in fact take over a lot of organ playing for him on Sundays, playing the customary four or five hymns for the elderly congregation. To help me practice, he arranged that I should have a spare key to the Vestry so that I could get in whenever I wanted. I also used it to get one or two girlfriends into the Vestry for a kiss and cuddle after I had showed off the organ to them - the musical instrument one, I mean!

By 1943 I had just started at the Tottenham Grammar School and got the opportunity to sit for an Entrance Examination to Trinity College of Music in London to go as a weekend part-time student. After I had sat the exam, I forgot all about it and several weeks later, mum and dad had managed to afford to send me away for a month during the summer holidays to Swanage to get me away from the bombing. One weekend, mother took the train from Waterloo and came to see me at Mr. and Mrs. Goodey's, the boarding house in Victoria Road where I was staying. We strolled along the promenade and then sat gazing out to sea through the forest of concrete and scaffolding anti-tank defences which had been erected all along the beach about fifty yards out to sea. Mother suddenly said "How would you like to go to a real school of music and learn properly." I couldn't think what she was talking about, there was no way they could afford to do such a thing. It had probably cost her a couple of month's savings for the fare to just to come and see me, so I knew it was a financial impossibility. Then she told me that I had gained an "Exhibition" place at Trinity by doing so well in the exam I had sat earlier and that the next term was due to start as soon as I got back from holidays. This meant travelling by Underground from Manor House, not far from Rosie and George's garage to King's Cross, changing onto the Central Line for Bond Street or Marble Arch then walking the remaining quarter mile to Trinity College in Mandeville Place. This was a journey I did for the next four and a half years, every Saturday and the only reason I left when I did was because of Mother and Father's business venture with the Bretts.

When I first went to the College we were still suffering air raids and naturally, London was a prime target. The exposed sides of the buildings which had been hit were propped up with huge wooden triangular supports and where the dangerous parts had been cleared away, fireplaces and chimney breasts were now suddenly nakedly exposed for every passer-by to see. What, I wondered, had happened to the people who only a few days before had lived or

70

worked there? My walk to the college was often past newly damaged buildings and never knowing whether Trinity had escaped yet again unscathed until I actually got there. It was a tall, three or four storied Georgian building which had no doubt been the London home of a very wealthy merchant. From the outside on either side of the central front doors were a series of identical windows and from the upper ones came the gentle cacophony of all different kinds of instruments, playing different tunes in different keys, all rather similar to hearing a symphony orchestra tuning up before the start of a concert. It was exciting to me to know that I was to be a part of this world of sound before long. Usually my afternoon started with an hour long class of theory, which I never did quite get to understand at that time. After this we all went off to our individual teachers for another hour of strict instrumental teaching. After my first year, I had the opportunity to take a second instrument and chose the organ, but after only a few months or so I decided to give it up in favour of extra piano lessons with my teacher, Professor Audrey Ayliffe and this probably turned out, on the one hand to be a good decision, but on the other left me totally ignorant of string, brass or woodwind instruments. She soon introduced me to some of the great composers' music and before long I was playing Beethoven, Chopin, Schubert and Debussy, none of whom I had ever played before. It was a new world and one where her ever vigilant ear and eye didn't allow reading errors very often, so I couldn't bodge my way through pieces any more.

Unfortunately, circumstances over which I had no control were to bring my education at Tottenham Grammar to an early close and the pity of it was that in my last year there, I had sat the pre-matriculation examinations. I learned that if I passed the "Intermediate" examination at Trinity, I could gain an exemption in Music as a subject. So the next Saturday at Trinity I made enquiries, only to be told that I was too late. No more applications were being accepted as the examination was too close. Somehow, I managed to get the college office to accept me with Miss Ayliffe and I working very hard on the set pieces, knowing that I had only about six or eight weeks to learn them. I played the first movement of a Beethoven sonata, a Schubert impromptu and Chopin's Waltz in C sharp minor and as far as I remember, almost gained a distinction.

The H.M.V. studios were not far away in Oxford Street and

one day I went there with mother to make a twelve inch recording of Debussy's Claire de Lune and a Latin-American piece called Malaguena by Ernesto Lecuona. During the following few months, I made one or two other recordings there, but as they are all on the old 78 rpm format, there are few record players today that will play them. I've still got them "in the hopes" that one day I might be able to get them transferred to CD. Ironically, having got my Intermediate, no-one, including me, thought to enter music as one of the subjects in my Matriculation Exemption. Although I had done well enough to go on to higher education and possibly at University, thanks to this business venture I mentioned, I had to leave school at the age of fifteen and a half with no worthwhile qualifications.

By the time I was about twelve, I had been at Trinity for nearly a year and my playing had improved no end. I was making a useful contribution to playing the organ on Sundays at my local church and was flattered to be asked by cousin John (Pichowski) and his bride to be, Doreen, if I would play the organ for them at their wedding to be held at St. Mary's Church, Tottenham, the same church mother and father had been married at. I jumped at the chance to play their three manual organ and soon learned the wedding music by Wagner and Mendelssohn and it was as a result of this that a reporter from The Tottenham Herald afforded me the soubriquet "London's Youngest Organist", but the newspaper cutting has since been lost. I was still dressed in short trousers then and could only just reach the pedal keyboard with my feet.

During my first year or two at the Grammar school, I also began to find out what girls were all about and at a birthday party of a school chum, met his cousin Pat who lived in Catford in Kent and we seemed to get on well together. The first time I remember being actually physically aroused with a girl from those days occurred when I invited Pat to a party of some sort at home. I took her on a conducted tour of the house - such as it was, my bedroom, parents' bedroom (which I dared not show her into) and the bathroom cum lavatory upstairs. Standing on the tiny landing at the top of the stairs, I kissed this rather attractive willowy blonde of twelve and felt a stirring between my legs. She must have felt it too. We kissed again - for a long time, until mother's voice calling out 'Where are you Pete? Are you alright?' broke the spell. Mother's sense of timing was impeccable! Due to my pedal-car escapade a few years earlier

Gurkhas and a Grand Piano

Mother had invested in a telephone at home, one of those heavy black bakelite instruments with a rotary dial on the front and we had it installed at the foot of the stairs, in the tiny hall just inside the front door. Edmonton didn't qualify as important enough to have its own area exchange in those days, so we became Tottenham 6840. The phone was only about ten feet away from the piano so it was quite convenient for me to have a chat with Pat and finish up playing her some music before hanging up. This went on for several weeks before we ran out of things to say (or me play) to one another. At that time, of course, my knowledge of sex could quite easily be written on a pinhead and even through into my early teens, I had no parental preparation for the subject which, handled properly, I have no doubt could be one of life's greatest joys. I had to find out for myself and probably like most boys of this early age, I found pleasure in getting an erection and gratifying myself by masturbating. There was no such thing as "Girlie Mags", so the female body was a mystery. Both father and mother went out to work in those days, and the house would be empty when I got back from school. I took a secret delight in going up to my bedroom, taking off my trousers (short ones, then), laying on the bed face down with my hands beneath my legs to slightly raise me off the mattress, then slide my body gently backwards and forwards until climaxing. Usually I took the precaution of putting a handkerchief beneath me. This surreptitious indulgence was usually completed with a sense of double satisfaction - first that I had given myself this pleasure and secondly that I had managed to do so before mother came home. But the day came when I miscalculated and was at the point of ejaculation when mother came into my bedroom. She had obviously heard the gently rhythmic rocking sound of the bed and quietly come to investigate. She was furious and punished me physically, giving vent to her temper with one of father's belts. Rather than deter me, I became determined to not be found out on future occasions. It would have been a glorious opportunity for her to explain to me what the sex act was all about. Instead, she referred to what I had been doing as "wriggling" and "filthy", absolutely forbidding me from doing it ever again as it would weaken me. Thereafter, whenever she came home from work and I happened to be in my bedroom - for whatever reason, it was always a shout up the stairs of 'Pete, you're not wriggling, are you?' How silly. I only hope that in parenthood, I have behaved a little more reasonably, although in truth, I can't recall any actual instances when I talked about the sex act to Mark, so I hope I have not placed myself in a similar situation for future criticism.

This censorious attitude did nothing to cultivate any kind of warm bonding between us. If I went out for a bike ride with dad, he was more of a chum than a loving dad. Neither of them seemed to want to hug and kiss me, except perhaps when I was very small, when I would climb into their bed on a Sunday morning to lay between them and with the aid of the alarm clock learning to tell the time until it was time to get up. The pity is that this lack of warmth was manifested in other ways. I'm sure that mother and father were proud of me, but there was never any excess of praise for things really well done. If I did ever do anything worthy enough of praise, the parental response was always the same - "Well, we expected you to do well, anyway". Perhaps this apparent lack of reward from Mum and Dad was at the root of me not inviting them to my Passing Out Parade ceremony at Mons Officer Cadet School. We were definitely not a 'hands-on' family when it came to hugging and kissing and praising - more's the pity.

My first 'serious' friendship with a girl was as the result of an 'excuse me' dance at The Royalty Ballrooms at Southgate. I met her towards the end of the evening and was very attracted to her. We danced a foxtrot to one of the old dance tunes of the 1940's, "I'd like to get you on a slow boat to China". She was slim and lovely to hold and smelled deliciously of perfume, which I later discovered was called "June". I took her to her home in Cockfosters that night and kissed her a lot. Subsequent visits to her home resulted in meeting her parents and her older sister and everyone was very understanding when Betty and I went off to sit in the front room together. I even took time off from work when I was with The Canadian and General Finance Company to take Betty sight-seeing in London and when chastised by one of the directors for being absent, had the temerity to present him with a photograph of Betty together with some lame excuse. After a handful of fitful letters passing between us when I eventually moved to Bournemouth, the friendship fizzled out. I thought I would be heart-broken, but I survived and no doubt so did she.

During the ensuing eight to ten years, I met several girls, but nothing earth-shattering ever became of our friendships. We kissed, petted and parted as many couples did then. I remember one tall, pretty brunette who worked in Reception at The Cumberland. I took her out a few times when I had the Austin Healey, which was not an ideal passion wagon. Parked down beside The Serpentine one night, we petted and she kept screaming and I found this most disconcerting, especially as the Healey was a soft-top and not exactly sound-proof. I was certain that the local 'Bobby' on his evening beat round the lake would hear, or at least those other people in their cars nearby must have heard her. In the absence of knowing why she was screaming, and she never said, I felt it best to avoid a repetition, so never asked her out again.

My twenty-first birthday party was a small one at the Norfolk Hotel on Richmond Hill with just Mum and Dad, Aunt Dee, Godfrey, and Ben and Dodie Woodard. The other guest was a girl I had met in Torquay during a visit there as a guest of Godfrey's at the Holly Ball. She was the daughter of one of town's hoteliers and quite pretty, with short, almost 'frizzy' hair, strong jaw and good figure. It was a quiet party with mum and dad splashing out on a set dinner and two or three bottles of champagne. We got back to Knyveton and eventually all retired to bed. As I have said in another chapter, the house had seven bedrooms and mother had given Alma the single at the back of the house, at the far end of the corridor which also contained the bathroom and toilet. When I judged all was quiet and everyone (except, I hoped, Alma) was asleep, I crept down to her room and let myself in. 'Is that you, Pete?' came almost dead on cue and I realised to my dismay my mother was keeping an ear out.

I never did get on very well with the idea of playing rugby or cricket to any great extent, but once introduced to athletics, I found my sporting metier. By the time I was fifteen, I had developed into a good sprinter and long-jumper, setting a school record for the latter and this aptitude enabled me to set yet another, more impressive record on 31st. May 1947, when at The Henry Barrass Sports Centre I won the Middlesex County Junior Long Jump with a best leap of only a fraction of an inch short of 19 feet – or was it 20 feet? (Damned memory again)! When I arrived home and told mum and dad, mum's response was as enthusiastic as ever, with Mum as the spokesperson, 'of course I expected you to do well'. What was I to do to get her to say 'Well done' and give me a hug? They did, however, pay for a special pair of hand- made spiked running shoes for me though.

My early departure from the Grammar was brought about by mum and dad becoming involved in a business venture with a couple named Brett. They were neighbours and had become friendly during the war years. Bill appeared to be very much a "man of the world", always well dressed and sporting a pearl tie pin but his wife Anna was a very undernourished looking Italian lady who everyone thought was his refugee wife. We later found out this wasn't the case - she was more like a housekeeper to him, attending to his every need, although I can't imagine the sexual ones being very well satisfied. Maybe this is why he took a fancy to mother. The four of them discussed going into business and thoughts revolved around a small hotel somewhere and one weekend, we all went to Bournemouth to have a look at something which had come up. The Kings Langley hotel on West Cliff Road was up for sale. It occupied a corner site and had about twenty letting rooms and seemed to be what the Bretts and mum and dad wanted. So back in London, notice was given to Trinity College and the Tottenham Grammar that I would be leaving because we were all moving down to Bournemouth. After a while the deal fell through, so the Bretts bought a restaurant in Potters Bar and mum and dad bought a new house in Palmers Green. I therefore had to leave school and find a job; and so ended my education at both Tottenham Grammar school and Trinity College.

Number 68 Tottenhall Road was a very nice house, much larger than the one I had known for so long in Middleham Gardens. Mum had sold Silverlea to Johnny Green, the local greengrocer for £2,200 and they had bought Tottenhall for just an additional £750. The couple they bought it from had a son of about seventeen and during one of our visits to see the house before it actually became ours, I met the son's girlfriend, Norma Forrest, who lived off the Great Cambridge Road a mile or two away. My legs turned to jelly, she was such a beautiful blonde girl, but being about two or three years older, she was obviously too old for me, so I had to forget her. Anyway, she was his girlfriend and that was that. At the main road end of Tottenhall Road was the Palmers Green Dancing Academy and soon after I started work and could afford it, I had some dancing lessons. This meant I was then able to go to The Royalty Ballroom in

Southgate on a Saturday evening and not feel a complete beginner. Before leaving the Grammar, I had seen the "School Leaving Officer" who had asked what I wanted to do. When I told him that I wanted to be a concert pianist, he looked as though someone had hit him between the eyes and could only respond by saying "You had better start off getting yourself a job in a music shop, then". Some help he was! During my athletics days at school and setting new records for the Long Jump and the one hundred yards sprint, I was awarded my School Colours as a result. I had teamed up with another sprinter, Ronnie Dowling. Together we had joined The Highgate Harriers who met at Parliament Hill Fields near Hampstead. In the summer of 1947, I represented my school in those events at the Middlesex Junior County Championships, setting yet more records. It was later that year, running in the 4 x 110 yard relay race at the White City Stadium that when the baton was being handed over to me for the final leg of 110 yards by the third runner, he accidentally stepped onto my right foot with his spiked left shoe, tearing open both my special shoe and my foot into the bargain. Somehow, I still managed to cross the line in first place, although as I was slowing down, I felt my leg suddenly go out of control and I fell. I suffered for several weeks after with not only a badly damaged foot, but severely torn muscles in my right leg which put me out of all athletics for quite some time. I travelled up to Harley Street in London to see Dr. Christopher Woodard about my injuries. He was then the official doctor to the Amateur Athletic Association and took an interest in me, saying that in view of the records I had set and bearing in mind my age, he suggested I could be a possible member of the British Olympic team in the 1952 Games, at which time I would then be twenty years old. Comparing what I did in those days, with little or no professional coaching, with previous Olympics results is very interesting. At age fifteen, I had jumped to within a quarter of an inch (6mm) of nineteen feet (5.79m) (shall we say), so an additional five years of body and muscular growth and with the right training may have brought me into the lower 8m jumps of athletes of the day. In fact, by 1952, at the time of my projected team membership, the world record long jump was held by Jesse Owens with a jump of 8.13m, a shade under ten feet longer (28ft. 11.5 inches) than I had achieved as a fifteen year-old. Looking at my sprinting figures is also interesting. In 1947 at age fifteen, I was running the 100 yards in around 10.6 seconds, which translated into a time for the 100 metres of today would be about 11.6 seconds. Again, Jesse Owens held the record for the 100m. in 10.2 seconds; so theoretically, I was just 1.4 seconds slower than him at age fifteen. Reading this again, I reckon this Olympics business has blossomed into a bit of self-indulgent bombast, but then, there's no way of confirming or denying it now – it was simply an exercise in self-justification. With the absence of parental praise, I'm making up for that by doing it myself.

Fortunately though, when the coach to the Highgate Harriers, Ken Stagg, found out that both Ronnie and I were leaving school and would be looking for jobs, he introduced us to a friend of his who worked in The City and as a result, we both found employment with The Canadian and General Finance Company in Leadenhall Street. Ronnie was taken into the Shipping Department and me into the Accounts. This firm was the London subsidiary of a huge multinational which controlled national transport and electricity supplies in several South American countries, so we had to deal with companies such as The Brazilian Traction, Light and Power Company; Sao Paulo Railways, San Paulo Gas Company all of which I found utterly incomprehensible. I was just the junior office boy, doing odd jobs here and there and probably nothing of vital importance. Such jobs were done by the likes of Mr. Jones, the Accounts Office manager, who seemed quite a lonely figure. He was quite small with close cropped grey hair and a small brown nicotine halo at each end of his mouth where he used to hold the glowing stub of his cigarette in his mouth until the very last moment before burning himself; squinting and tilting his head to one side to stop the smoke from getting in his eyes. He would have been the ideal candidate for a pin to hold the smouldering stub on if it meant he could get one more teeny weenie puff out of it. A tall, fair man named Smith, in his early to mid-twenties' took take me under his wing and in doing so introduced me to pipe smoking. During our lunchtimes, we would walk down to Ludgate Circus to buy John Hardnam's Negrohead pipe tobacco from their shop which had a large, colourful wooden cut-out of an Indian Chief propped up on the pavement outside. This tobacco was thick and coarse and jet black and it burned very slowly, giving off a delightful aroma, a blend of cedar and tar with a slightly honeyed undertone. Once lit, I was very reluctant to put my pipe down. It was a million miles from the geranium leaves I had smoked in the bomb crater only a few years earlier. Another member of the department was Basil, a man with a wooden leg who told of the time he was in hospital having it amputated. His nurse had taken his fancy and when she came to renew his dressings, she obviously excited him. Seeing his erection, she dismissed it by giving him a glass of water, telling him to "Stick it in this, Basil", much to his disappointment. I was paid a quite generous wage of four pounds ten shillings a week (£4.50) for whatever it was I was supposed to be doing. On that 1947 Christmas, every employee received a food parcel from Canada with lots of goodies in including such things as canned butter, chocolate, tinned peaches and tinned ham. Everything came in very handy, supplementing the meagre range of foods that were available on ration, including bread, biscuits and cakes. One thing I did become quite good at was copying the signatures of two or three of the directors. I used to practice for hours - for no good reason other than to satisfy myself. Perhaps it was some form of frustration I was releasing. I had got a Distinction in Art during the Matriculation Exemption examination and at home also used to copy cartoon characters in pen and Indian ink - just for something extra to do in the long winter evenings. To think, I might have studied Art at University had I got there. Another senior member of staff was George Brozel, a chubby, cheerful Jew with whom I got on very well, even going home with him to his house in Lea Green to have supper with his wife, Paula. I don't know whether it was really George's fault or not, but it was certainly he who uttered the fateful and, for me, never-to-be-forgotten words,

"To do well in life, Peter, you've got to do one of three things - clothe people, entertain people or feed people".

I was a highly impressionable fifteen year old, fresh out of grammar school - far too early of course. So here I was; now working in Leadenhall Street in the City, bang opposite the famous and now restored Leadenhall Market, as a very junior junior in the accounts department of the London office of this large Canadian finance company. George became my mentor, introducing me to such arcane wizardries as how to work the little Burroughs hand operated mechanical calculating machine, looking like a miniature typewriter or hand-operated cash register, hardly any larger than the kind of crank operated pencil sharpener we used to screw onto the edges of desks. After setting the key tabs, by winding the handle clockwise, the machine multiplied or added and by turning it anti-clockwise, it subtracted or divided. Incidentally, Burroughs later became a producer of super-size computers for business use, each taking up a whole air-conditioned room with metal, glass-fronted cabinets containing large spools of magnetic tape which jerked round one way or another absorbing or dispensing bits or bites of data. I came across one such beast later on when we had SNS, as you will read. It also comes to mind that aunt Dee had the paper-punch data record system in her offices at the Middlesex County Council, so Burroughs was a well-known American firm in the data control business. Soon after joining, I was to learn my first lesson in banking. The Chief Accountant, the above Mr. Jones called me to his presence and handed me a bank paying-in book stuffed with cheques in it totalling something like a quarter of a million pounds.

'Peter, pop down the road and pay this in.' he said, inspecting the minute dog-end of his cigarette. Stupidly, I neglected to clarify with him exactly where "down the road" was. Mr. Jones wasn't one of those men who you engage in idle chatter. Having given me the book, bulging with cheques, he returned his attention to his tiny cigarette butt delicately held between his nicotine-stained fingertips and obviously gauging there were at least another two small puffs left, gingerly replaced it between his equally brown tinged lips. Screwing up his right eye as the smoke curled up towards his iron grey hair, he buried himself in his ledgers once more. Assuming I was dismissed and not daring to show my ignorance - in fact, not even realising that I *was* ignorant, I took him at his word and went down the stairs and out into busy Leadenhall Street. Nonplussed, I stood for several minutes among the throng of City Gents going about their business. Their uniform, unlike mine which was a sports jacket and grey flannels, seemed to be almost entirely dark striped suits, bowler hats and carrying pencil-thin rolled umbrellas and leather brief cases. Those who didn't have rolled umbrellas sported a pink rolled up copy of the Financial Times. Others, who looked as though they were going to the races and who I later discovered were bank messengers, were dressed in grey suits, some frocked with striped shirts and usually complete with grey or black silk cockaded top hats. These were the various bank runners or messengers who carried sorted cheques worth huge amounts of money between their own parent bank and the destination bank. I had no idea whether "down the road" was to the left, or the right and clutching my bulging book of paper treasure, spent some minutes considering the situation. Immediately next door was the newly opened London office of The Bank of China. Perhaps Mr. Jones meant I should go to that one. Not much farther on down, or up the road, whichever way one looked at it, was Martin's Bank with their distinctive golden grasshopper easily noticeable over the hatted (almost everyone wore hats then) heads of the steady stream of people bustling along the narrow City pavements, each going about his clerical or her secretarial business. There was also Barclays, Midland, for sure, probably also Cox' and King's and maybe the banks of Hong Kong and Timbuctoo for all I knew. Every twenty yards or so of Leadenhall Street was a bank of some sort. Round the corner was The Bank of Scotland. I knew that one because I passed it every day when I walked to the office from the bus stop near Liverpool Street Station. Now standing bewildered in my own oasis of total ignorance, I was aware of this, my first important assignment in the world of high finance and I was not enjoying the feeling of apprehension which swept over me. By "down the road", he surely couldn't have meant more than a few steps away, could he? No, of course not. Steeling my nerves, I walked into the bank next door, which I was sure was the one he must have meant. Would the staff all look like Sidney Greenstreet playing the part of Fu Manchu? What if any female staff had bound feet and conical straw hats? I didn't know - I'd only seen Chinamen and women with Ronald Coleman in snowy Shangri-La at the cinema, so only had them to go by. I found it was quite like any other bank, not that I had all that much experience to draw upon. Everybody was dressed in dark City suits, just like their English counterparts. They just had different facial features. I was encouraged to approach a cashier and hand across my package. In case he didn't understand, I bashfully muttered something about wanting to pay this in, please. His impassive Oriental face changed not one iota as he picked up his date-stamp and opened the book. Addressing his colleague at the next counter in his mother tongue, he no doubt found the equivalent expression for "We've got a right one 'ere". With centuries of training to suppress his bursting desire to laugh, he politely suggested that I go a little farther down the road to Rroyds Bank, as they might be able to help me . . . Looking back on it with the benefit of over sixty years hindsight, this experience should have been enough to teach me that finance and I were never meant to be perfect bed-fellows and Time has indeed confirmed just that.

My earnings encouraged me to behave like a proper adult and open a bank account, which I did at the Bank of Scotland in Gracechurch Street, just round the corner from our offices. I paid mother a weekly "rent" for my board and lodging, paid my own fares and saved what was left. When I had saved enough, I bought a Lovat green Harris tweed hacking jacket from a very high class City tailors, by the name of Thresher and Glenney. It cost me ten guineas and I was very proud of it. When I took it home and showed it off to mum and dad, mother thought it was "very nice, dear", but dad couldn't raise even that much enthusiasm, saying that he could have bought a whole three piece suit for the same amount of money. I got much about the same response, but in reverse, when I took home a very handsome .177 air rifle and eventually had to take it back to the City gunsmiths where I had bought it, eat humble pie and ask them to take it back. The opposition to that had been just too much. My next extravagance was accepted, however. We had managed to buy a Collaro electric portable gramophone, the cabinet of which was made from plywood and finished in imitation grey lizardskin hide. It was quite heavy; as was the pickup which used steel needles. Fibre needlcs were just being introduced at that time and were considered better as they didn't wear out the records as quickly as the steel ones. I splashed out and bought the HMV set of five twelve inch records of the Rachmaninov 2nd. Piano Concerto, which at that time was just becoming popular. Each record had cost ten shilliings and sixpence, so the set cost two pounds, twelve shillings and sixpence, (£2.65p) over half a week's pay. It would be like paying, say, one hundred and fifty pounds today if related to a week's wage. The score of the concerto for two pianos had cost one pound seven shillings and sixpence, (£1.40p) which was also quite expensive in those days. My savings also enabled me to go for a few days holiday with Ronnie Dowling, so we went off fishing on The Fens to Earith on the river Ouse between Huntingdon and Cambridge. I had been there earlier that year with mum and dad, staying at the same guest house. 1947 had seen some awful weather and when Ronnie and I got there, the fishing was just about wiped out as The Fens had flooded. Instead of there being a latticework of canals, everywhere was just one sheet of water covering several square miles. The trees we had moored our boat to earlier on were now standing in so much floodwater that we had to tie the mooring rope up to the branches. Although the fishing was a failure, we enjoyed ourselves at the local barndances.

For over a year, in the front room over Bill and Anna's café in Potter's Bar, they and Mum and Dad had talked about going into their joint venture with Bill insisting that Bournemouth was the El Dorado of the south coast. Their first attempt to go into business together had led to them making sandwiches, getting Day Returns and catching the train from Waterloo one Sunday (the café closed on Sundays) and to inspect the chosen property which I have already described. The hotel had looked very prosperous and although nobody admitted it, no doubt the asking price was more than "the partners" could afford. So Project No. 1 was therefore aborted.

Almost in desperation now that their intention to go into business had been formulated and their first sally forth into the hospitality industry thwarted, with Bournemouth still the prime target the partners turned their attention to finding an alternative business and The Elite Restaurant had become their next best substitute. After many months of talking with the Bretts, the business seed eventually bore fruit. The Bretts agreed to sell their cafe in Potters Bar and our house was put up for sale and when everything was completed, dad and I handed in our respective notices and we all moved down to Boscombe to take over "The Elite Restaurant" in Palmerston Road, opposite Hendy's the main Ford dealers. Next door to the restaurant was the local ballroom from which almost every evening the sound of music and smell of perfumes of varying degrees of allure would waft through the ventilation fans. Girls in tight skirts, Dirndl skirts and cotton dresses, many with cigarettes dangling from their mouths or fingers, would hang around the main entrance assessing the unaccompanied boys as they arrived. During the interval, groups would go off to The Palmerston pub just opposite for further assessments before making final choices as to who would take whom home that night. Bill was no longer able to be the suave, cigar smoking Mein Host, being relegated to offering chairs and paper napkins to the two and sixpenny diners. Anna was now sweating as full-time cook. My father peeled the potatoes on the back step each evening, having put in a full day's work as a printing machine operator at the Carillon Press in Roumelia Lane and mother was the full time waitress instead of being housekeeper/receptionist. It was all a far cry from what they had initially hoped and dreamed of. Meanwhile, day after day I surveyed the "Bournemouth Echo" in the hope of finding that "once in a lifetime" job, preferably not connected to a factory broom, but without success. What job was there for a sixteen year old in this town? There must be something other than making tea or sweeping a factory floor.

Connecting Palmerston Road with the main Christchurch Road was Boscombe Arcade, "L" shaped and glass roofed, with a variety of shops each overflowing onto the covered pavement with wicker baskets, benches on wheels and collapsible tables displaying what there wasn't room for inside. In the corner of the "L" was a balcony and small organ which the resident organist would play on a Saturday morning for the entertainment of the shoppers. He was also no doubt the resident organist of The Hippodrome theatre next door which belonged to Harry Mears, who also owned The Chine Hotel. Shippey's Antiques was an Aladdin's cave of new and second-hand items of bric-a-brac; small furniture, jewellery, glass and porcelain ornaments, earrings, Ronson lighters and silver cigarette cases with gilt insides and blue elastic to hold the cigarettes in position, monogrammed and crested spoons, some from Bournemouth but mostly from other seaside towns; and pearl tie pins clustered onto velvet pads to look like some exotic hedgehog. Edwardian table lamps with shades like cloche hats, glass and brass candlesticks were crammed into every available spare level space. Everything was tagged with a small label marked with the price in some arcane hieroglyphic, the formula of which was known only to the shop assistants. The shop opposite sold second hand gramophone records. Outside on the pavement were large wooden boxes on wheels containing hundreds of ten and twelve inch records in their creased paper or bent cardboard jackets. Red and gold labels with a dog called "Nipper" with its ear cocked almost inside an old gramophone horn were from H.M.V. Decca had gold lettering on dark blue and Capitol were gold on black labels – or vice versa. The choice was eclectic. Harry Roy and his band, Geraldo and his, Flannegan and Allen singing "Underneath the Arches", Vera Lynn, "The Forces

Sweetheart", Dorothy Squires, Rubinstein's Melody in F - they were all there for the sorting.

Now that I had left London and "CanGen" I was faced with the prospect of finding another job - preferably one that paid equally well. The Employment Exchange was in Post Office Road in Bournemouth and had a special section for "Youths". I told the man behind the counter what I had been doing and what my expectations were, at which he gave me an old-fashioned look of pity offering a job as a "tea boy" in the Southern Electricity Board offices not far away. The job, such as it was, paid one pound ten shillings a week. This was financial ruin. I had been getting three times that in London. I declined his offer only to be told that that's all there was, take it or leave it. I left it, concluding that I would have to find myself a job rather than rely on officialdom. He wished me "good luck", failing to quite hide his smirk and no doubt thinking what a bumptious little prat I was. 'Try the Situations Vacant column in "The Echo",' he called across the counter as I made my way out of the office, which bore a resemblance to a railway booking office. I think he was trying to be helpful. I bought a tuppeny "Evening Echo" and a glanced through the "Situations Vacant" columns quickly confirming the paucity of highly paid jobs for someone of my age. There seemed little problem getting a job sweeping up in a factory for a pound a week. This made the tea-boy's job at thirty bob seem well paid but I was determined to do better than that. After all, my London pay had been four pounds ten shillings a week, plus a very welcome food parcel from Canada at Christmas. I felt I was worth at least four pounds of somebody's money, but whose?

The "Evening Echo" each day brought no comfort and I began to fear that officialdom would be proved right after all. Days went by without a glimmer of hope until one Sunday afternoon. We had finished clearing up at The Elite after Sunday's three course lunch with roast meat and two veg. which cost about three and sixpence (now about eighteen pence) and mum, dad and I went for a walk. We intended going through Boscombe Gardens down to the sea. It was a very pleasing gentle stroll through the pine trees, down Boscombe Chine to the pier. At the main road end of the gardens was a very large, grand-looking hotel with the equally impressive name of Linden Hall Hydro, a large, late Victorian/early Edwardian building complete with a cupola over the central part of the main roof. The Hydro part of the name stemmed from the fact that it had its own indoor swimming pool which the hotel operated as a club, open to outsiders as well as the residents of the hotel. The main entrance to the hotel had a revolving glass door, with a normal door to one side and as we passed, we noticed a very dapper gentleman dressed in evening tails and white bow tie standing by the door. We felt he must be something to do with the hotel as surely it was a bit too early for any guests to be dressed in evening clothes. I took a chance and crossing the main road asked him if he was the Manager.

"Well, not exactly. What can I do for you?"

"I was wondering if there might be any good jobs going here."

"What are you looking for?"

"I don't know really, anything interesting, I suppose."

He asked me what I had done so far and I told him.

"Come back in a couple of days. I'll see what I can do for you."

"Who should I ask for?"

"Mr. Fitzsimmonds. I'm the Head Waiter."

The next few days passed in a cloud of anticipation. I was fearful Mr. Fitz wouldn't be able to get me anything and that I would be forced to eat humble pie at the Junior Labour Exchange. When I returned, he told me that he had spoken with Miss Sharpe, the Manager, (she was never called Manageress) and the offer was for me to join the kitchen brigade as a commis chef at four pounds a week if I was suitable, three while on probation. I was at once delighted with the wages and keen to try my hand at cooking. On the appointed day, I arrived at the hotel and entered through the revolving door. Not seeing my friend Mr. Fitz anywhere, it hadn't occurred to me that he might be busy in the dining room supervising the breakfast service, I approached the Reception desk. 'Can I help you?' the prim looking lady asked. I told her the reason for my arrival and was promptly directed to the rear staff entrance, 'Where the dustbins are,' she added sourly, making sure that I fully understood the location of the "Staff" entrance, especially the "Back of House" staff who never, but never, ever came in the front door. I reported to the Head Chef in his office, a tiny, cramped area in one corner of the hot, steamy kitchen. He looked up from his hard-backed daily menu book and small collection of grease-stained duplicate order books in which he was pencilling the next day's requirements, pushed his pencil behind his ear and adjusted his tall white hat. He was a thin-faced, pleasant man, known to all as "Pat", not that that was his name, but because he had been, until recently promoted, the patissier, or pastry chef. I never did get to know his proper name. I told him who I was and hoped he was expecting me. Pat quickly discovered I was an absolute beginner and introduced me to his brigade - well, not so much a brigade, more a diminished platoon. His number two was "Jock", a powerfully built man in his mid-thirties who had been a cook in the Royal Navy. When he walked, he rolled as though in sympathy with his lately departed ship arguing with the waves. "Charlie" was the breakfast and veg. cook, who also stood in for "Little Billy" who did the washing up. The kitchen porter was "Jimmy", an olive-skinned young man, always whistling or singing Neapolitan love songs and who lusted after Miss Pelosi, daughter of the owner of the local Italian ice cream parlour at the top of Sea Road. I was put to work under Henry Royle, the new patissier, who was single and lived in. Henry's domain was a cramped narrow kitchen off the main kitchen and adjacent to the vegetable preparation and refrigeration area, because this was deemed to be the 'cool' area of the kitchen and therefore suitable for the making of pastry. To my mind it was still as hot as Hades. Henry, about ten years my senior soon put me at ease, explaining what I would be expected to do as time passed and my experience grew. Never in a million years did I expect to work so hard helping feed the hundred and forty guests. Within a few months, I was producing about four hundred fancy cakes every day for afternoon teas, making cold sweets such as bavarois for the evening meal, taking my turn at being the breakfast and vegetable cook, scrubbing down, washing up if Jimmy was inundated, helping serve the meals from the fiercely hot service counter. A normal day's hours would be from 8am to about 3pm, and then back again at 5pm until dinner was finished at 9pm. By the time we had cleared up and done our preparation for the following day, we usually finished somewhere round about 10pm. With just one day off a week, this represented a punishing seventy-two hour week, spent in temperatures of Arabian proportions and learning quite a few new expletives in the process. Charlie cut himself badly one day which meant that I and another young commis, Reggie Beauchamp had to also take turns at doing breakfast and veg and cooking bacon, egg, sausage and tomatoes for a hundred and fifty, single handed, was quite an initiation into the pressures of volume cooking. These were still days of rationing, so recipes reflected the austerity of the times. Powdered egg was used in almost all our recipes for cakes and scrambled eggs and amazingly enough, it is still in use today in hospitals due to the salmonella poisoning epidemic of the 1980's. Sauces and gravies were not given quite the same degree of care and creativity as they are today. Jock's recipe for an all-embracing sauce which would do duty as white sauce, brown sauce and even Brown Windsor Soup was simple. Whisk some flour into cold water, whisk that into boiling water and cook until it thickened - et voila, sauce. Add sugar for white sauce, gravy browning for brown sauce and some H.P. sauce to the brown for it to become Brown Windsor soup. He called it "Jazey" for some incomprehensible reason, doing duty also as sauces for pies and puddings, roasts and many other purposes which might have included pasting up wallpaper! I was not yet seventeen and such was my introduction to this business of "Feeding People".

Dear George, why couldn't you have suggested three other vocations such as wine, women and song?

I had passed my driving test in London and the licensing authorities deemed that if I could drive a car, I could also drive a motorcycle. In fact, I could drive anything except a road roller for flattening Tarmac or a track laying vehicle – i.e. a bulldozer or tank! Never having ridden a motorcycle before, Henry nevertheless allowed me to borrow his Royal Enfield and dressed in an ordinary sports jacket and trousers and borrowed goggles, I set off somewhat uncertainly for a ride through the New Forest. As my confidence grew, so did my speed and soon I was flashing along through the dappled sunlight at sixty miles an hour with a frisson of excited danger lying in the pit of my stomach, telling me, ineffectively, to slow down. But I was reluctant to twist the throttle closed until tight bends forced me to do so. I rode almost into Southampton and shaking with excitement, I stopped at a pub for a drink before turning back for Boscombe.

During our split-shift afternoons, Henry and I sometimes went down to the beach for a swim. We also used the indoor pool after our evening shift, sometimes swimming and sometimes just watching other people swimming. One evening, trying to do a backstroke start, my right foot slipped on the slippery wall of the pool and I experienced a severe pain in my knee as my leg straightened out. I managed to climb out of the pool and sit down to rest it. After a while, the pain subsided and I was able to walk again. A few days later, having dismissed the event from my memory, I went to the beach with Henry and after a swim, we lay on our towels in the sun. As I turned over, my leg must have bent on the uneven sand and without warning, my knee locked in a spasm of pain. When I did manage to stand, I was unable to walk properly. With Henry's help, I managed to hobble from the beach up Sea Road and eventually to the Elite where mother saw me to bed and went for the St. John Ambulance man. Their Centre was only a hundred yards away along Palmerston Road toward the railway line. Resplendent in his black pullover and badges, the ambulance man asked me what had happened and diagnosed a trapped cartilage. At his request, I straightened my leg as best I could before yelping with pain. He said he would have to help me get it straight, so with me sitting on the bed, he got me to stretch it out and rest my foot on a nearby chair, whereupon he sat on my knee. I passed out. After several days of having my knee wrapped in cold compresses, the swelling eventually went down enough for me to return to work, but standing on it for hours on end soon made it painful again. Eventually, I learned how to manipulate the cartilage back into place if I twisted my knee and everything was O.K. so long as I was careful.

As time went by, I became a useful member of the kitchen brigade, was given a pay rise to four pounds a week and was offered the chance to live-in. This came at an opportune time. The Slaney/Brett quartet was hitting the rocks. What dad had failed to realise was that for the past few years, Bill Brett had been surreptitiously wooing mother and now they were all under the same roof he was buying her gifts of jewellery in the hope of furthering his cause. They had been meeting clandestinely while "out shopping", but exactly how far matters went, we shall never know. I do know that mother had been very impressed by Bill; but then, she did rather have an eye for men anyway. Her trouble was that she would allow them to go just so far, then expect them to turn everything off like a tap if matters threatened to get out of hand or go farther than she had wanted. (Listen to her comments on the matter on the CD). In later years, she suffered physical abuse from one of

89

her partners - no doubt when he couldn't get sexual satisfaction on demand. Dad had probably got the message in the end. After all, his place in the business arrangement was to go out to work at the Carillon Press, the local printers during the day and come back at night to do the washing up and peel the potatoes for the next day. I can clearly remember him sitting by the back door up to his elbows in potatoes, deriving no satisfaction whatsoever from being a partner in a restaurant. Bill was the book-keeper, Anna the cook, mother the waitress and dad did the other jobs. Eventually the crunch came and they all split up after the restaurant was sold. What happened to the Bretts I don't know, but mother and father went their separate ways, both into guest houses in Boscombe to live lonely independent lives.

I now lived in the tower room over the front entrance of the hotel and had a splendid view from my semi-circular window right over the top of Boscombe Gardens which in the summer evenings were aglow with the hundreds of fairy lights made from night lights in small jars strung between the trees. I was comfortable and self-contained, able to do as I pleased, going to the cinema or to the Chine hotel for a drink and a chat with Millie, the buxom, motherly barmaid - but missing a home life. One day dad came to see me in my room. He was in a very depressed mood and told me how desperately unhappy he was. He confessed that no-matter what she had done, he still loved mother and had been missing her so much that he had made an abortive attempt to commit suicide. He had decided to swim out to sea as far as he could and then just simply give up and drown, but before he had gone more than a few yards, a wave had caught him in the face and half choked him. In his spluttering and coughing, he had ejected his dentures into the water and this made him feel so foolish that he had given up the idea of suicide. I think he had spent some time duck-diving in the hope of groping around on the sandy bottom to find his teeth, but without much success. He was brought face to face with reality once more and having unloaded his sorrows trudged back to his small boarding house utterly dejected. I can't recall whether my mother ever came to see me in my room.

Towards the end of 1949 I was amazed one day to see mother and father walking arm in arm along Christchurch Road. They said that they had both made it up and were back together again, even having left their old "digs" and moved into another small hotel to share a room with one another. They had decided they were going to buy another house, large enough to run as a bed and breakfast business. They found Knyveton, no. 4, Wharncliffe Road in Boscombe. It was a quite nice semi-detached house, one of a group of three which lay well back from the road inside their own private parking area. It had three storeys with seven bedrooms. Downstairs was a long entrance hall off which came the front lounge, then the guest dining room, private sitting cum dining room and kitchen. At the rear was a small, but neat garden backing onto a bakery belonging to the cake shop in the main road. Once they had bought 'Knyveton', they asked if I would like to "come home and do a bit of cooking for them" while I was waiting for my National Service call-up. Having to reduce the quantities of recipes was a bit tricky and no doubt I wasted a lot of food, but it was nice to be in a proper home environment once again - so long as I had my own independence.

They put a lot of effort into improving Knyveton. Partly at my suggestion a ton of Purbeck stone was delivered outside the front of the house and between them, they built a stone hearth and fireplace, putting in the latest Baxi fire with an underfloor flue and sunken ashpit and this turned out to be one of the most efficient fires I can ever remember. They constructed the hearth with log boxes built into either side and every lump of stone had to be handed through the front room window. Gradually, business began to grow with them taking in groups of employees from the newly emerging Hurn airport where some of the latest planes were being built. The British Aircraft Corporation ran courses there for specialists engaged in building their BAC 111's and Knyveton was one of the local places offering good, comfortable accommodation at a sensible price. Mum and dad did quite well out of that connection.

In the Spring of 1950 I received my Call-up papers for National Service and was ordered to report to my nearest Employment Exchange to register. As I recall, I was asked my job experience to date and educational standard, but this was to make little difference as I was told I could join the Medical Corps as an orderly or the Catering Corps as a cook. Faced with this somewhat restricted selection, I chose the latter. At least I did know something about cooking. Apart from getting a Credit in Biology at school, my only medical knowledge had come from my recently damaged cartilage and I hadn't really learned much of any value from that experience. A few weeks later I received a single third class rail warrant and instructions to report to the Army Catering Corps Training Centre, Ramillies Barracks, Aldershot on the 25th. May 1950. I left home with a small suitcase containing a few personal possessions and with a tearful mother kissing me goodbye boarded the train at Bournemouth Central bound for Woking where I would change to a small, three-carriage electric train for the last part of the journey to Aldershot - "Home of the British Army". The journey to Woking was ordinary enough with my fellow passengers being businessmen on their way to London, or holidaymakers on the way home. But once on the electric train to Aldershot, the company changed radically. Each carriage was populated almost entirely by nervous eighteen year olds similar to me, each carrying parcels or suitcases and all heading into the unknown. It was like being evacuated all over again. But this time the civilian boy was about to become the soldier man.

CHAPTER SIX

ARMYDAYS 1- ROOKIE TO ONE PIPPER

The train clattered through the Surrey countryside, past Brookwood Necropolis (arcane language for cemetary) and Brooklands, the old motor racing circuit, by then closed and getting overgrown, with grass tufts spreading along the cracks in the concrete surface, eventually arriving at Aldershot. In contrast to the other stations we had passed, Aldershot was a buzzing hive of activity. Considering there was only one "UP" and one "DOWN" platform it seemed as though the entire station had been sold to the Army. There were khaki uniforms everywhere. As we all got out of the train in the dying minutes of civilian life, we were all carrying the common identity; a suitcase or parcel of spare belongings. Quite suddenly we had all become blood brothers, bonded to one another, each awaiting a common fate, to segue from casual clothing to khaki. Like short-tempered shepherds, the "real" soldiers set about gathering us into flocks for transportation to the military abattoirs which would sooner or later snuff out the remaining vestiges of civilian existence. For us the National Service juggernaut was now under way and would relentlessly grind on, brooking no argument or resistance.

A fearsome Warrant Officer gestured with his huge brass bound cane.

'For Christ's sake, what a bloody shower. Right, now listen you lot. I'm only goin' ter tell yer once. Service Corps 'ere, Medics 'ere and cooks over there.'

As we began to move in the intended directions, his minions harried us into manageable groups to be "embussed". My education in things military, vernacular in particular, had begun.

The lorries were huge canvas covered affairs with tail gates, which even when dropped down, were still several storeys above ground level. Climbing aboard was a minor feat of mountaineering as holding our precious luggage, we had to grasp a rope to help us get one foot into the "D" shaped cut-out footrest which was at least at waist height. Unless someone gave you a leg up or pulled you aboard, there was more than a distinct possibility that you would be

93

left dangling from the rope unable to obey the obscene orders to "get a fuckin' move on". This injunction suffixed by "you dam'd dozey, idle lot" became a familiar expression in the weeks to follow. Once aboard, I found myself sitting among total strangers all bound for the same destination. I had been one of the last to climb this metal Matterhorn, so sat nearest the tailgate, inhaling the hazy pale blue fumes of exhaust smoke as we waited for the remainder of the convoy to form up on the station concourse. The shouting and cajoling continued until everyone from the train was suitably penned into their correct vehicle and at an unseen signal we began to move off. Some of my fellow passengers were brave enough to chance a last cigarette, like the condemned men they were. Some sat silently, tight lipped and lost in thought while others garrulously introduced themselves in an attempt to chase away the dragons of foreboding locked in their guts. Aldershot Town revealed itself to me as it unfolded during our journey; cinemas, pubs, the Police Station and various shops which in time I would get to know. Up the long hill out of the town with The Prince Consort's Library at its crest, where in years to come I was to sit with other officers listening to Field Marshal Lord Montgomery of Alamein deliver his Autumn lecture in his particularly nasal twangy voice. After we had all stood to acknowledge the great man's arrival on the platform, we were invited to be seated. Montgomery's first words to the assembly which ranged from second lieutenants to Generals was 'Right, gentlemen. I will give you just thirty seconds to get your coughing over and done with before I start to talk. Then I want total silence until question time!' Such is the power of a Field Marshal no less . . .

From there, the convoy rumbled down the long straight hill known as Queen's Avenue which stretched from the Library some mile or so to North Camp and which apart from the area of huge level fields opposite the Military Sports Stadium was flanked by barracks all suitably named after famous battles and each with its parade ground and regimental flag. Past the two Garrison churches, St. George's for Anglicans and St. Andrew's for the Scots. Over the Basingstoke Canal by Buller Barracks, the Sports Stadium was followed by more barracks until we turned right into Ramillies, home of the Army Catering Corps Training Battalion. Our period of growing anxiety was about to end. At any moment now, life as we knew it would stop to give way to a new regime, which for some, whether they yet knew it, would become intolerable. The lorries turned off the road onto the main gravel surfaced parade ground, the size of two football pitches and surrounded by grim, single storey barrack blocks in which we "squaddies" were to live and sleep, squabble and laugh for the next two weeks. At the north end of the parade ground was a huge, rambling Victorian officers' mess and at the other, an even less welcoming building - The Guardroom, complete with its complement of ruthless looking Regimental Policemen. Their red armbands with the initials RP could have easily been replaced by one with a Swastika, or at the very least with a lower case "i" between the R and the P. They looked frightening, very frightening indeed.

'Right. Get yer arses off them seats. Let's 'ave yer down 'ere so we can see wot we got this time.' 'Come on, yer lazy buggers, jump!' and other similar suggestions were bellowed in our direction. We did as bid. Some using the dangling rope lost their grip, falling the six feet to the ground, parcels bursting from their wrapping, much to the amusement of the NCO's watching. They'd seen it all before. Soon, with the sheepdog corporals snapping at our heels, we and our pathetic luggage bundles were assembled in some kind of orderly fashion to await the Head Shepherd, the Regimental Sergeant Major Livingstone. He was not as huge as I had expected, but made up for this by having a fine waxed moustache and whom, we were soon to discover, was on permanent attachment from The Royal Scots. Tucked under his arm he carried a 'pace stick', fully three feet long and brass tipped, which when opened was used like a pair of giant dividers to measure the length of pace to be used when marching. His stature had nothing to do with his ferocity. In a Scottish brogue, he addressed us.

'As from this minute, it's ma job tae turn you wee laddies into soldiers and may the guid God help anyone who doesna' do what he's told.' His moustache trembled like an antenna, sending out vibrations of disgust. 'It's nae been ma guid fortune to greet any intake I ever liked, but you lot hae just aboot reached the bottom. I've ne'er seen such a load of rubbish. Ye disgust me. Where the bluidy hell did they find ye lot? Look at ye. They expect me t'perform miracles...' and so he went on, doing his best to welcome us to his fold, pacing backwards and forwards, glaring at each of us in turn, prodding here and there with his pace stick, humiliating each

95

and every one of us right from the start.

We were formed up into lines, three ranks deep and for the first time all facing in the same direction. There must have been a hundred of us in the dusty heat of that May afternoon, each clutching our precious belongings our Mums had given us when we left home. Now we looked and felt like refugees awaiting the gas chambers. This was going to be a total shock to every one of us, nomatter what our cultural background. Our names were called out and unless we answered 'Sir', pronounced "Sah!" in immediate response, we were ridiculed in front of our peers. This was no time for rebellion. Having answered to our names, we were, by some mystical formula, divided into groups of about twenty five when we assumed the group names of "Number One Platoon, Number Two Platoon" and so on. The Platoon was to be the working unit which for the next two weeks would sweat, heave and strain together - like it or not. Starting as an utter shambles we were marched off to the Reception Centre where we would be given our new Military identity. By the time we reached the long wooden shed, our own special corporal had somehow got us all more or less marching in step, even though some of us managed to swing the wrong arm with the wrong leg. With our bundles and suitcases swinging we tramped along, attempting to swing our free arm to shoulder height without punching the person in front in the back of his neck or tripping ourselves up with our luggage. We soon learned that losing our step would bring down a deadly hail of verbal fire upon us whether we were to blame or not. I had learned a few swear words at school and at the Linden Hall, but nothing like those I was rapidly learning now. This was an entirely new vocabulary and most impressive it was too.

Everyone was given a small brown covered booklet with unintelligible pages of grids of information which would later show the results of SCHICK, PULHEEMS and various other tests, showing to the military world who I was and that I was physically fit to be a soldier. On the front page were spaces to show Rank and Name and Number, an eight digit label which once given dare not be forgotten. So I became 22369239 SLANEY, P. Private, Army Catering Corps – see, it's still indelibly printed onto my memory! The last three digits of the number were all important and highly significant should there be other persons with the same name when all were gathered together. There was no such person as just plain, good old Smith. All Smiths were Smith 123, or Smith 234, or Smith 999, the last three numbers readily identifying just exactly which Smith it was being referred to. Likewise all the Browns, Greens and Jones's. This was a useful tool when dealing with Welsh regiments when it was almost a dead certain bet that one in every five would be a Thomas. My Army Record of Service went on to show how much I weighed, whether I had any scars or not by which my (dead) body could be more easily identified, the colour of my hair and eyes, whether I wore glasses *and* how well I could see, whether I wore them or not. This booklet was to be my Passport, to be carried at all times and produced on demand for scrutiny by just about anyone "in authority".

Having now officially enlisted, we were again marched off to the Quartermaster's Stores to be issued with our army kit. The Quartermaster was not unlike a decidedly unfriendly shopkeeper who guessed your size for your two suits of battledress "for best", your suit of denim overalls (presumably "for worst") and other items of clothing. The denims were heavy duty cotton replicas of our battledresses and were worn for everyday work. Among our toiletries were the regulation number of towels including white huckabacks which resembled pimply cardboard, khaki cotton vests and pants which had a drawstring waistband so they would fit just about anybody and grey woollen socks. Apart from our boots, which came as two pairs, everything else was issued in threes on the assumption that you had one on, one in the wash and one on show on your bed for inspection. As we passed along the rows of benches, we were by now festooned with the items and finally arrived at the last bench where an assistant would guess the size of your feet and drop two pairs of incredibly heavy, black, greasy boots in front of you.

'You'd better try 'em on. Yer goin' ter 'ave 'em on yer feet for quite a time. No bleedin' good bringin' 'em back 'ere in a few days sayin' they don't fit.'

We tried them on, for what good it did us. Once I had threaded the yard of sticky leather lace through the holes and done them up, my feet felt as though they were encased in loose-fitting concrete boxes. Dressed in one of the suits of battledress, or BD for short, we were then scrutinised by "The Military Tailor" who dabbed at the fabric with his flat piece of chalk. If he felt that the quartermaster's guestimate of our size was too wildly out for him to correct, the item was changed. Having chalked up the other uniform, we then changed into our denims, whether they fitted properly or not, while our BD's were labelled and taken away to the tailor's workshop. A week or so later, we were re-issued with them, suitably altered and pressed.

Loaded up with our new kit, we had to march off to our allocated billets and for the first time see the inside of the barrack room which was to be our home for the next two weeks while we underwent our induction training. Immediately inside the front doors were two small rooms where the NCO in charge slept. The main room was about sixty feet long by twenty feet wide, a single area of polished floorboards with fifteen beds down each side and in the centre of the room was a solitary coal-burning stove with a tubular metal chimney rising up through the ceiling. Beside each bed was a steel upright locker which served as wardrobe, tallboy, dressing table, gun cabinet, toiletries cabinet and much else. For those in more secure positions of rank, they often housed a variety of contraband pin-ups. We were allocated a bedspace and locker each and told to pack up all our civilian clothes into parcels for sending home. We would not be needing them again for quite some time to come. It was at this stage that our own Platoon CO introduced himself to us. As far as he was concerned, for the next two weeks he was to be given the status of a god, although in the ensuing days I was to learn that there were other, greater gods than he. But for now, he, Corporal Pulford, Green Howards, MM (Military Medal – the equivalent of an officer's Military Cross for extreme bravery), was to be obeyed in all things and his row of medal ribbons identified him as someone who had accumulated quite a lot of military experience. He left us in no doubt that he was accustomed to his platoon being judged the best in all passing out parades and we were not going to let him down. On that final day of judgement in two weeks time, it was we who would win for him yet another tick for merit, or die in the attempt. To start with, we would learn to polish everything in sight from the floorboards to the light shades and everything in between. The flooring was almost daily treated to re-anointing with polish by a "Bumper", a large heavy metal brick swathed in an old blanket and hinged to the end of a broom handle. It could develop a satisfying rhythm as it swung backwards and forwards. With the blanket replaced by a cleaner one, it did the actual polishing. At this, we all took our turn. Corporal Pulford told us that our ghastly greasy boots would become lustrous deep black mirrors, the toecaps of which would dazzle the eyes of the inspecting officers. Just how we were to achieve this miraculous transformation was to remain a mystery for the remainder of that day. All the brass items of kit were to be similarly transformed, again by some strange magic, known at present only to the gods. Everything metal was going to be made to shine, including our mess tins and combination knives, forks and spoons. The floorboards were to be so shiny that if god bent down to see beneath the rows of beds, he expected nothing less than a complete and unbroken mirror of wood, right to the far end of the last bed. Even the Victorian stove was to shine like a lighthouse. Corporal Pulford advised us that he occupied the two end rooms and once in these, he was not to be disturbed. The reverse was not true however, as we were to discover.

With our regulation issue of sheets, pillows, pillowslips and blankets we were shown with great precision how to make our beds. This done, we had to strip them and do it all over again - and again until everyone made the identical hospital corner tuck and displayed the same precise length of sheet turned back over the blankets. When we had learned to make our beds to his satisfaction, god then showed us how to unmake them and display the various items to the required military method. Sheets and blankets were to be folded into identical sizes and laid on top of one another in alternating layers, finally being wrapped around with a blanket to make the entire assembly resemble a multi-layered sandwich wrapped in thick grey paper. This was placed at the head of the bed and on top of the fabric sandwich were to be displayed our mess tins and cutlery, razors and enamel mugs. The bare mattress would then be covered with our neatly arranged webbing haversacks, ammunition pouches and belts. Locker doors were to be opened to show hanging items and neatly folded on a shelf, our underwear and socks. God inspected our first attempts, and our subsequent ones until expressing himself reasonably satisfied - for now. I was forever to remember the adage "A place for everything and everything in its place" and if Norma moves anything I have got used to being in a certain place, it takes a time for it to sink in. I find myself automatically going to where I think it is, not where it now is.

Our first evening was spent polishing according to god's

99

instructions. An earlier visit to the NAAFI had enabled us to buy Brasso, Blanco, black Cherry Blossom boot polish and yellow dusters. From the vast quantities purchased in the time of National Service, those fortunate people with shares in the various companies which manufactured the Army's cleaning materials must have seen them leap in value. Back in the barrack room our boots were given their first session of cleaning. With the handle of a spoon, we liberally spread the Cherry Blossom all over the boots - this practically used up the whole tin in one go! Then, standing the boots on sheets of paper, we set them alight with matches held against the waxy polish and the moment the flames died away wiped off the bubbling preservative grease. Before the boots could cool down, they were anointed with a further coating of polish which was rubbed well into the purified leather with the ever useful spoon. This first coating was brush polished and for the time being considered sufficient for our working boots. But the pair chosen for "Best" was given further attention which involved wrapping an index finger in yellow duster and rubbing small amounts of polish in tiny circles all over the toecaps and uppers, moistened with frequent amounts of spit. As the depth of polish began to build up, the leather began to shine like thick French polish and the longer we continued, the deeper, richer and harder the shine became. This wasn't all achieved in one night, of course. It took several hours a day of laborious spitting and polishing in tiny ringlets to get anywhere near the desired end result. In fact the entire process was reduced to being called "small ringing". Brasses received their own special treatment. Corporal Pulford handed out pieces of brown cardboard and some brown parcel paper to us. Following his demonstration, we poured small puddles of polish onto the cardboard and by laboriously rubbing the brasses backwards and forwards through this ever darkening puddle, a motion not dissimilar to preparing a toboggan for its run, the orange peel effect on the metal's surfaces began to be smoothed away. After a long time of continuous sledging backwards and forwards, we could transfer the pieces of brass to similar puddles of polish, this time on the brown paper which would give them a finer finish. Finally, the yellow duster did its duty - if we could find an area which was not already blackened and stiff with boot polish. By "Lights Out" at 11pm that first night, we fell exhausted into our beds.

Reveille at 6am the next morning came as something of a shock as Corporal Pulford marched up and down the barrack room clouting a fire bucket with his cane. Crash, Bang, 'Wakey, wakey.' Crash, Bang, 'Wakey, wakey.' Crash Bang, 'Hands off cocks, hands on socks.' Crash, Bang, 'Come on you lot, bloody move - NOW!'

Within a minute, the entire room was like a seething can of maggots as we fumbled to get into enough clothing to allow us to get to the ablutions for a quick pee or more, breaking wind from both ends, a wash and shave and teeth-clean. As we queued on the puddled floor around the washbasins and latrines, god was on the warpath, shouting, harrying, cursing and urging us to go faster and ever faster. Stumbling into our denims, hopping on one leg trying to get socks on over damp feet and struggling to lace up boots took its toll of good humour as we began cursing everybody and everything we thought was to blame for our present predicament.

'Get fell in outside with yer breakfast kit'. We did and were marched off to "The Five Hundred" (obviously named due to its seating capacity) dining hall for our first breakfast. There in the clamour of several other squads queuing for breakfast we moved in single file past the line of hotplates where cooks, some already looking fatigued, dolloped out scrambled egg and baked beans and a slice of cold, hard toast into our mess tins. Each platoon corporal seemed intent on getting his charges to eat faster than the rest. Time, it seemed, was at a premium. Outside, we had to queue once more at the "Wash, Rinse and Sterilise" tanks, each one containing progressively hotter water and into which we had to sluice our mess tins and cutlery and God help anyone who was daft enough to drop them into the water! We marched back to the billet to prepare for morning inspection, laying out all our kit in the previously prescribed manner. A young officer, a second lieutenant, accompanied by the Company sergeant major and Coporal Pulford in attendance, complete with notebook and pencil at the ready, walked slowly down the room gazing at the exhibition of kit. In a very polite manner, the officer spoke,

'Sergeant Major, would you kindly ask this man why his underwear is not folded correctly?'

'Sah! You lad, what the bloody 'ell do you call this 'eap of shit?' and before he could answer, the offending display was torn apart by the sergeant major's cane. 'Come on, speak up!'

'Sorry.' he was interrupted fiercely.
'Officer on parade. Say "Sir" when you speak to me!'
'Sir'.
'Well, get on with it then, I've never seen such a 'eap of rubbish. Corporal Pulford, take 'is name'.
'Name?' demanded Pulford, although he knew it perfectly well. This was sheepishly given, only to be cursed again and told to give his "last three" as well - and answer "Sir", yet again. The name and number were entered into the notebook for future reference. The offender started to rearrange his belongings only to be cursed yet again and ordered to stand still until told to move. A tear of humiliation crept down his cheek and was ignored by the visitors. He would have to endure more than this if he was to become a soldier. Such inspections followed daily, with increasing vindictiveness and if a recruit's name was taken three times, he was placed on a charge to appear in front of the Officer Commanding the company.

Outside once again, we were marched off to the Medical Centre to be measured and weighed, listened to, back and front, knees and elbows rubber hammer-tapped, tongues pressed with wooden spatulas and eyes and ears peered at with a tiny torch. Then we were questioned so that Forms could be duly filled in recording all past remembered illnesses.

'Cough' said the Medical Officer, cradling my one testicle in his hand and nodding in affirmation of some internal movement, diagnosing to him, at least, that all was well in that department of my physical body.

'And what's happened to the other one?'

'I was born with a rupture and hydrocele, sir', I responded, 'the other one hasn't fully come down yet.'

'So I see. Well if stamping around the parade ground and jumping over assault courses doesn't do it, nothing will.'

Adolph Hitler, our recent arch-enemy of the Second World War was similarly afflicted, although I did not know this at the time and neither, I suppose, did the doctor or else I may have been arrested as a distant relative perhaps.

After our various checks and examinations, we were lined up to receive our complement of vaccinations and inoculations, our Army Records of Service being entered up accordingly, but no reference being made to those unfortunate recipients who fainted during the proceedings. That evening and the following day we each felt the after-effects of the jabs. But swollen, painful arms and feelings of nausea didn't slow the relentless rhythm of the training programme however.

The Dental Officer viewed and probed into our open mouths, expressing dismay at some of the cavities long ignored, pronouncing sentences of death on "upper right sixes" or "lower left fours" and commenting on any emergency treatments he would have to perform. Following our visit, we were gathered into the camp cinema to see a film on Hygiene in which a caveman was shown biting a special measuring device which showed the enormous pressure he could apply with his jaws, the commentator revealing to us that it was many times more than we creatures of the 20th. Century could ever hope to apply. Why we were being told this was a mystery, unless it was a portent for the future diet we were to live on. I recall we were also introduced to the varieties of sexually transmitted diseases we could encounter in the future, but whether they had Aldershot in mind, I can't say.

Our next visit was to The Armoury where we all had to sign for the receipt of a point 303 calibre Short Lee Enfield rifle, webbing shoulder strap and a 'pig-sticker' bayonet in its black scabbard. Later, during our drill training, once we had learned to march reasonably properly, we were instructed how to drill with our rifles and immediately learned how cumbersome and unruly they were, falling with a frightening clatter to the ground at the least provocation and bringing with it another hail of abuse from our own god.

'That's no way to treat yer rifle – it's gonna save yer life one day. Pick it up, you dozey bastard'

As with so many other things, our rifles also needed their loving care and attention, polishing and nursing. Inset into the brass butt plate was a small trapdoor which, when opened, revealed a tube which ran down inside the butt and was home to a brass flask of rifle oil and a cord pull-through on a corded brass weight, plus a small quantity of red and white flannelette material. The flannelette was to be torn into small narrow lengths and fitted into the loop at the end of the cord. By removing the bolt from the breech, the weight could be allowed to slide down through the barrel and the cord gently pulled through to clean any foreign objects out. When done enough times to make the interior of the barrel shine like a silvered corkscrew, the results were inspected. With your thumbnail inserted into the breech, the person inspecting could look down from the foresight end and see the light reflecting off your nail and quite easily able to see any dirt which might be lurking in the rifling - a punishable offence. This cleaning routine was repeated every day whether we used our rifles or not. Gradually, all the various routines began to slot into place, as did our ability to respond properly to the various orders shouted at us on the parade ground. "Sloping and Ordering Arms" were almost mastered, "Presenting Arms" was a bit more difficult, but we were getting the hang of things. As our second week was about to start, Corporal Pulford gave us the exciting news that the following day we were going to go out onto the ranges for some real live firing practice. Once again, we had to scale the heights of those dreaded tailgates on the lorries, but with our increasing fitness found that they were not quite so fearsome as on that first day. Sitting in the backs of the lorries clutching our rifles and wearing skeleton order of just our belts and ammunition pouches over our denims, we headed out for the Ash Ranges some five miles away. We debussed at the six hundred yard firing point of our allocated range and another young officer gave us strict safety instructions which we were to follow without deviation at all times. Just for good measure, we were fallen in and made to march down to the twenty five yard firing point. Corporal Pulford chose a group of boys who would be the first lot of butt markers whose job it would be to operate the targets and they were packed off under the wing of a lance corporal to do their duty and before long, four foot square canvas targets on frames began to appear above the parapet in front of us. We who were left were instructed in the correct procedure for loading our rifles with ammunition by Corporal Pulford, watched by the Range Officer whose responsibility it was that nobody got accidentally shot.

It all looked pretty simple stuff, until, in groups of eight it was our turn to advance to the actual firing point and do it. With the safety catches applied, we were shown how to lie down with the rifle held properly into the shoulder and take aim; how to take up the first pressure on the trigger and then how to squeeze the trigger gently until it tripped and fired the bullet. We were also shown how to eject the spent cartridge and reload with another and how to apply the safety catch until told to fire. In theory, it again looked pretty easy stuff. Now came the real thing. We each took a clip of five rounds and placed it into our ammunition pouch, then went and stood in front of our allocated target twenty five yards away. The black semi-circular bulls-eye looked quite large from where we were. We were commanded to lie down and load. When it came to trying to slide the first five bullets out of the clip into the magazine, many of us suffered broken thumbnails and grazed knuckles. It wasn't so easy after all. We were then directed to fire, in our own time, five shots, each at exactly the same point on the target. With my heart pounding in my ears and excitement constricting my throat, I took aim for the first time with a real rifle, about to fire a real, killer bullet. We had got used to feeling the first pressure on the trigger in dry practice - and even the second before the sear tripped the firing pin, but the actual sensation of firing a real bullet was entirely new. As the bullet fired, so a hidden mule in the butt lashed out at my shoulder, making me gasp with shock and pain. The entire complement of Rachmaninov's Bells was donging away inside my head. I could see peoples' mouths opening, but couldn't hear a thing. As the pain in my shoulder subsided, I ventured another shot and suffered almost the same results. God, if shooting a real rifle was always going to be like this, every soldier in the army must have a permanently bruised arm. At last I held up my hand to show I had finished firing my five shots and the officer came to inspect my rifle, making sure I had not miscounted, leaving the one rogue shot "up the spout". Eventually, my hearing returned sufficiently for me to hear that we were being commanded to stand up and, still carrying our rifles, advance down to the targets. As we stood in front of them, we could see the results of our endeavours. Some had their five shots - or less, scattered all over the four foot face of the target. Although mine were not in the bulls-eye, they were all neatly grouped into a tight pattern which would comfortably fit under a saucer. This "zeroing" enabled the Armourer to adjust our sights to bring the groups of shots into the centre of the bull - in theory.

"That's a very good group you've got there, Slaney. Have you done this before?" I admitted I had had an air gun which might have helped.

Once the holes in the targets were pasted and patched up, we each had to fire another five round group. I was lucky, getting another tight group right in the bull this time, to more compliments from the officer. After a midday meal and taking our turn in the butts to the accompaniment of bullets zipping and smacking into the high earth bank behind the targets whilst we sheltered under a concrete ledge, we returned to barracks to clean our rifles and carry on with the rest of the day's work. Once back in the barrack room, I took off my shirt to inspect the green and mauve bruise now spreading out from my shoulder, to the admiration of those not so badly marked.

'Bloody 'ell mate, that's a bramah you've got there,' smirked one of my comrades. I was still having some difficulty with my hearing and wondered whether I had heard his "bramah" properly; where had he got that word from? My hearing did slowly seem to recover, but God, my shoulder hurt. Lesson no. 1 – don't pussyfoot around with the rifle as though you're scared of the recoil as I had done after the mulish response to my first shot, pull the butt tightly into your shoulder. Later, I found this was the solution to technicolour shoulder syndrome.

Gradually, as our two week's induction training continued, with parading, marching, cleaning and polishing, mopping out the latrines, being bullied and harassed and made to conform, we began to work as a cohesive body of people, responding to the words of command shouted at us by our various gods. We worked so hard during the days and cleaned so hard at night that the common cry was 'What about time for some 'Egyptian PT'? – or 'blanket pressing' as having a bit of a rest on your bed was called. Our BD's were returned duly tailored and pressed and with best boots now polished to look like black glass, we assembled outside for Sunday Church Parade, when we progressed, like the Duke of York's men, up the hill to the local Garrison church. On reaching it we had to break ranks to pass through the doors into the hallowed interior, still supervised, as ever, by our own god watchdogs. In his excitement, or total bewilderment, the recruit beside me forgot to take off his beret as he entered, being reminded by a Corporal in a stage whisper through clenched teeth to 'Take yer 'at orf in the 'ouse of the Lord, cunt!'

In the last two days, we were subjected to interviews by the Personnel Selection Officer who, in conjunction with our record sheet, would divine our future for the remainder of our two years of National Service. Having enquired about parentage, schooling, hobbies, previous work done (if any) since leaving school, he informed me that I would make "a good hospital cook".

'But sir,' I protested, 'I want to be an officer.'

This led to him scoffing and puffing heavily on his pipe and to asking what on earth gave me the impression I was good enough. I must have given him some reasonably acceptable answers, as he reluctantly capitulated and agreed he would recommend me to become an OR 1 (Other Rank, First Class). This meant that unlike all the others who would be shipped off to various parts of the country to undergo a further thirteen weeks of cookery training, I would join the other OR 1s at St. Omer Barracks, the headquarters of the Army Catering Corps and home of the Technical School, not far away in another part of Aldershot, there to await further tests, which could almost be likened to trial by combat.

A day or so later, we all paraded on the square to be inspected by the chief god of all, Lieutenant Colonel David Holder, who commanded the entire A.C.C. Training Battalion and where our squad gained top marks, placing yet another feather in the cap of Corporal Pulford. As my newly found colleagues packed their kitbags bound for Catterick, Blandford, Woolwich or other Cookery Instruction Centres, I prepared for my comparatively short walk to St. Omer Barracks to report to Headquarters Company. On arrival at the Guard Room, I was directed to the Company Office where I reported to the Officer Commanding. Following my interview with him, I was granted my new status of OR 1 and sent down to the hutment which was to be my new home for the next few weeks while I awaited my summons to attend a three day War Office Selection Board. While still subject to military discipline, my life suddenly changed for the better. Either a white disc behind the corps badge on my beret and/or white flashes on my epaulettes identified me as a superior being, excused from the rigours of normal daily routine, enabling me to become more relaxed, getting to know my handful of fellow OR 1s. As time went by, they were summoned to their W.O.S.B., returning to await their fate. Those who failed were packed off to Cookery Instruction Centres, there to become just ordinary soldier cooks and the task of readjusting to the old way of life. The lucky ones were sent off on a few days leave prior to reporting to their respective Officer Cadet School.

My turn came to attend the Selection Board at Lingfield, not far from Tunbridge Wells and from the moment I entered the camp, I was under intense scrutiny, even while in the Candidates' Mess. There was always someone with a clipboard noting down things about me - all of us in fact. What did we eat, how did we eat it, what did we talk about, what papers did we read, how did we behave generally, were we always smart and tidy? The catalogue grew larger by the day. They might have even spied on us in the lavatory for all I knew. During those packed three days, we were taken out to various sites to be physically and mentally tested, asked to perform seemingly impossibly stupid tasks like crossing a ravine with only one plank of wood that was too short anyway and crossing a swamp using one length of rope and an oil drum. At each task, a leader was chosen by the invigilating officer. If he retained control of his group without any one of them challenging his decisions, he did quite well. If he allowed others to take control, he did not. Neither did he do so well if he retained control but made the wrong decisions. Was he a leader? Could he inspire his men to perform these ridiculous tasks? Could he consult with his peers, but still retain the leadership? Could he "think on his feet"? On the final day, we were all subjected to an in depth interview by a very senior officer who fired all manner of questions at us, some of which were nothing to do with the army at all. Once we were done, we were instructed to return to our units to await the final judgement.

It was a lonely journey back to St. Omer and once there, it was harrowing waiting for the news. I had seen what happened to the failures and prayed it would not happen to me. Had I done well enough? I kept asking myself whether I had made the grade and as the days passed, didn't know whether to just relax and leave it all in the hands of fate or what to do. About a week or so later, I was summoned to see the Company Commander and guessed "this was it". Full of trepidation, I marched into his office where with a broad smile he told me I had passed. I was to pack my bags, go on leave for a few days and report to Mons Officer Cadet School, almost in the neighbouring barracks to St. Omer on a certain date to embark upon my next period of four month's training. I can't recall those few days of leave - they were totally blotted out of my memory by that four months which followed! Surely, I reasoned, learning how to be an officer was going to be a gentlemanly affair. How wrong I was...

At Mons, I was issued with further identity of being an

Officer cadet to affix to my uniform, this time, white georgettes to go on my lapels, in addition to the white discs behind my badge. Having been allocated my new barrack room for the next sixteen weeks, civilisation suddenly and savagely terminated. We were barely given time to unpack and settle in and get to know one another before our new god arrived. Corporal Pulford was, by comparison, a pleasant, benign, gentleman compared with this one. Ramrod backed, huge and evil in the extreme, this god was fresh from The Brigade of Guards. We were not unique. Every platoon had one. They could have easily been at home in the death camps of Eastern Europe under the Nazis. Incapable of speaking in a normal, modulated voice, they would stand just inches away, screaming into our faces and it was difficult not to flinch. The cursing and swearing was of a different kind, but even more effective. From now on, life was lived "at the double". If we were not actually marching as a group, we ran to wherever we were going. The slightest misdemeanour such as having your beret anything other than the regulation distance above your eyebrows, a scuffed toecap, button not done up properly, dirty nails, virtually anything that offended brought down a sentence of near-death on us by way of extra punishment drills, all carried out "at the double" and with rifles carried aloft over our heads. They were out to break us and in this, succeeded in many cases, with the result that the offender who cracked up was immediately "Returned to Unit" as not being worthy officer material. During these weeks, we were at least given the doubtful honour of being called 'Gentlemen' collectively and "Sir" individually by them, but even this title was made to seem like so much shit if said with a mocking tone as was often the case. Discipline was so strict that had we been ordered to march straight over the edge of a cliff, we would have done so without a moment's hesitation. It was their job to mould us into shape and if we broke in pieces in the process, hard luck!

In charge of all the drill sergeants was none other than the famous Guards Regimental Sergeant Major "Tibby" Brittain, a giant of a man and built like a house, whose voice when on the parade ground could be heard at least a mile away. As we progressed through our torment, he would be more in evidence at parades, taking charge, when his faithful pack of Dobermans would snarl and snap at our heels, insult us "Sir", bellow into our faces, ridicule our mistakes and generally make life intolerable - almost. That was the art of survival - the almost bit. To break under the strain was an ignominy not to be forgotten, providing a spectacle for all to see. Skidding to a halt one day on the slippery concrete surface of a large transport hanger we were drilling in, a cadet nearby slipped over, dropping his rifle with a deathly clatter for all to see and hear. He was immediately pounced upon by a drill sergeant and ridiculed. He couldn't stand it and picked up his rifle and marching a couple of steps clear of the front rank laid his rifle on the ground and announced he would "Soldier no more". At this, he was doubled off the parade ground with his rifle at the high port above his head, straight into the Guard Room and from there, within the hour, out of the barracks and off in disgrace to his unit. These were hard times with hard lessons to be learned. It was of no matter to Mons Officer Cadet School that his father was a Lord. He had failed the test. His walk on hot coals was over.

I was never any good at tactics. I was not born to be an infantry officer. I could understand what it was all about, but somehow was unable to grasp the niceties of the subject and when it came to our finals examinations, I failed my Tactics. This meant I was to be relegated for a further period of four weeks, during which time I was to have the opportunity of putting matters right, or else I would fail and become just an ordinary private cook. It was like Cinderella losing her shoe - today a cadet, tomorrow a cook. The benefit of this extra four weeks also gave me an added opportunity to become even better at drill with the result that at our final Passing Out Parade I was appointed Right Marker, a place of honour on the parade ground. It meant that everyone on parade took their positions from me and followed my movements, using me as a pivot. The parade was taken by Field Marshal Sir William Slim of Burma, then Chief of the Imperial General Staff and holding the highest military appointment in the land. As he passed down the ranks, inspecting, he stopped by me and in his gruff voice complimented me, saying how bloody marvellous it was to see a cook in such a worthy position, (he too had come up "the hard way" from being a boy soldier, I believe, so appreciated the effort it had taken for me to get such an appointment on that all-important parade). I had shown everyone that cooks were soldiers too. I had scraped home with a pass at tactics and so was now set to embark on my last lap of officer training at St. Omer where for the next twelve weeks would study ration planning, food storage, accounting, menu planning, basic cooking and a number of other duties which would come my way as a second lieutenant.

After yet another short spell of leave, I reported back to St.Omer to share a hutment with three or four other young potential officers undergoing the same training programme. My immediate buddy was "Sandy" Brown, son and heir of a Birmingham chocolate manufacturer. We became the best of friends throughout the remainder of our National Service, training and having fun together. The main ACC Training Centre housed both the Technical School and the Headquarters for the whole ACC organisation including the Training Battalion. The whole building had been specially designed during the 1930's and 1940's as the perfect cookery school being recognised as such throughout the culinary world. It was staffed by brilliant technicians brought in from the highest echelons of the civil catering trade, assisted by selected military technical training staff, one or two of whom could not quite live up to the highest demands being made upon them. I recall being given a talk by one such warrant officer on the subject of vegetables and their correct storage. He may well have been a wizard on the stove, but his knowledge of horticulture was very suspect. We asked him why it was that some potatoes had a black crack through the centre, which in hindsight, we now know to be caused by frost during storage.

'That's 'cos of the fertilizer they use nowadays, see?'

'No, sorry, we don't.'

'Well, this fertilizer they use is so strong that it makes the skins grow faster than the inside can fill 'em out.'

Our cadet mealtimes were a dream. We had a private dining room to ourselves just off the kitchen in which the meals for the officers' mess were produced. Cooks undergoing the highest qualification which could be achieved were attached there for final training, producing luxury meals such as would be required when they returned to their final postings, such as in the service of Army Commanders and Generals commanding prestigious areas. It was not unusual for us to dine off the finest steaks and fish, accompanied by exotic French classic sauces and finish the meal with home made ice creams and bombes using the very best of ingredients. We were waited upon by W.R.A.C. waitresses undergoing training for the

111

staffing of important officers' messes and these were under the expert guidance of Michael Miles, the Maitre d'Hotel of the Headquarters Mess. In civilian life he had been Maitre D at one of London's finest hotels, Claridges or The Ritz or the Savoy, I can't recall which. Under his tutelage, the WRAC girls would become proficient at silver service and all other aspects of waiting at banqueting tables and from this, we benefitted. As opposed to when they were serving the officers, they could relax with us, but still give us wonderful service. Some of them were very, very pretty, too, flirting with us when Michael wasn't watching.

This was a time of great change in army catering. Here were the officers eating the best of food, whilst the soldiers were getting indifferent food dolloped out on their plates in colossal dining halls, large enough to seat a battalion at one sitting. The post war Army Catering Corps was slowly influencing the pattern of feeding throughout the army, but it would all take time to filter through the system and that time was yet to come. It was up to us up and coming youngsters to spread the gospel, but for now, we were ignorant of that fact. It was enough for us to learn how to fill in the necessary Ration Indent forms and compile easy-to-cook menus which our semi-trained cooks could cope with. In the greater scheme of things, the ACC was also training Royal Navy cooks to become better able to cope with the demands of the Fleet both at home on dry land and on board. We ourselves benefitted from attachments to various training departments, such as Butchery under the inimitable Tom Selby, a Cockney butcher of enormous knowledge and resource. Learning from him the difference between the periosteum and ligamentum nucae was a lesson in anatomy many a surgeon would have been pleased to have attended. With him we also learned how to sharpen our knives properly. 'Gentlemen,' he said, 'you never cut yourself with a properly sharpened knife. Why? Because it always goes where you aim it.' We learned how to dissect whole hind and fore quarters of beef, whole sheep and pigs and while my work at The Linden Hall had been invaluable, this training was something else! Our visit to the Royal Army Service Corps abattoir was a bloody induction to the slaughtering of beef in particular and one I shall not enlarge on.

Eventually, Sandy Brown and I reached the end of our training and shedding our skins as Other Ranks, we passed out to become Second Lieutenants with an effective date in my case of the 20th. of January 1951, only sixteen days after my nineteenth birthday. We immediately caught the train for London to celebrate, Sandy suggesting we called upon his "Uncle Bill" who had a penthouse flat in Lancaster Gate overlooking Hyde Park. He had got back home from Plumpton Races not long before and was still in his pinstriped morning dress trousers and grey waistcoat when the maid showed us into his flat. He had obviously had a good day and was seated in a huge armchair with a large glass of whisky. He had forgotten to do up his trousers after his last visit to the loo and was in an expansive mood. "Sandy, my boy, how are you?" Sandy said he was well and introduced me and told him that we were in London to celebrate our commissions. We were waved toward the decanter of whisky and told to help ourselves, then sat by him to talk about the army, he about the racing that day. After a while, Sandy said we should be on our way. Uncle Bill pulled a wad of notes from his pocket, peeled off several and stuffed them into Sandy's hand saying that we should go out on the Town and have a bloody good time with his blessing. As neither of us was arrested and we got back safely to Aldershot in the small hours, I can only presume we did. But I can't remember a thing about what we did, except for that visit to "Uncle", who turned out to be William Hill, the Bookmaker.

Back at St. Omer it was now a case of packing up all our belongings and collecting our new uniforms from the Military Tailor' shop in Aldershot. These were our Number One uniforms in dark blue barathea, the trousers of which had two dove grey stripes running down the legs. Our caps were also dark blue with a grey banding. Our badges were now gilt and silver instead of common brass and on the epaulettes were single "pips" denoting our new rank. We each sported a leather covered cane and Sam Browne belt to complete the ensemble. Our instructions were to take two weeks leave and report back to Ramillies Barracks (of all places), where we were both to become Training Officers, taking our places in the heirarchy of gods above such people as Corporal Pulford and even the Regimental Sergeant Major, both of whom would now be answerable to us, rather than the other way round. I suppose they must have become used to this reversal of authority. It does seem strange though to think of WWII battle-hardened, be-medalled soldiers now having to answer to young kids who only weeks before

113

had been their daily bread.

My two weeks at home was mostly spent in London, being exhibited to all the family, when their "Oo's" and "Ah's" must have been music to mother's ears.

'Oh, Micky, doesn't he look lovely in his uniform. So smart. He's a credit to you.' and so on.

Although the details are lost to me, I can remember mother taking me to see Grandpa's grave in the Tottenham Cemetery in White Hart Lane, not far from my old School, the Tottenham Grammar. I felt very self-conscious, standing in front of his gravestone as I gave him a salute in farewell. It impressed mother and the few other people attending their own dearly departeds' graves nearby but I got the distinct feeling that she still hadn't forgiven me for failing to invite her and father to my Passing Out Parade at Mons, four months earlier. Somehow, I excused my unforgivable lack of thought by assuming that neither of them would be able to afford to take the time off, nor the cost of the train fare from Bournemouth. It hadn't really dawned on me that they might be proud of me. In the past, whenever I had achieved something of note, mother had always said it was the least she had expected of me. I had become accustomed to not receiving praise. She excused her lack of recognition by saying that she didn't want me to get a swollen head. And so between us, we had a stalemate situation which I regretted in later life, as I was never able to really get close to her. Perhaps I should have given her and father the benefit of the doubt and at least asked them. After all, they could always have said "Yes", rather than "No".

CHAPTER SEVEN

ARMY DAYS II - NS TO SS

Leave over, I reported back to Ramillies Barracks and went to see Captain Tony Gibson, the Adjutant of the Training Battalion I had so recently joined as a raw recruit. He gave me a list of do's and don'ts and allocated me to one of the companies as a Training Officer under the command of Captain Walter (Wally) Watney, MC who was himself on attachment to the ACC from an infantry regiment. Having reported to him in the Company Office, I went off to the officers' mess to find my new bedroom. It was a typical sprawling old Victorian cavalry mess built on just two floors. On either side of the front entrance hall were the Ante Room and the Dining Room with its vast polished mahogany table which could seat forty in comfort. To the right of the main staircase was the billiard room and the bar and to the left, the servants' mess room, near the kitchens. On the ground floor beyond these rooms to either side were senior officers' quarters and upstairs were the bedrooms for the junior officers. The entire mess had about six bathrooms. It was necessary for very junior officers like me to share a large bedroom with two or three others and I joined up once again with Sandy Brown, plus Bobby Butlin, son of Sir Billy (the uncrowned king of holiday camps) and Martin Heath, son of Ted the Big Band leader. How Martin became involved with the ACC I never found out. Our bedroom had one minute coal fire and we had a daily ration of one bucket of coal. As it was February 1951 and bitterly cold at night, we all slept in our underwear and socks and draped our greatcoats over our beds for good measure. It was no great hardship getting out of bed at 6.30 each morning as it was warmer to be up and dressed!

All our meals were of a very high standard as we now lived off the full army rations, supplemented by daily "extra messing" for which we were charged on our mess bills. This little bit of extra money in the kitty meant that the Committee "Food Member" officer could spend it on comparative luxuries. All our meals were waiter service and breakfast was at 07.30 so that we youngsters could be on parade or in our offices by about 8am. The bar was open each day before lunch and during the evenings until the last senior officer present decided enough was enough and ordered the steward to close it. There was a very strict hierarchy in the mess. All junior officers had to stand if any officer of field rank (Major or above) entered the room and we could not occupy the armchairs nearest the fire, nor stand in front of it basking with the warmth on our backs, as the senior officers did. It was all very new, but eventually I settled into my new way of life, making some very good friends. A lot of the more senior officers were on attachment, serving out their time on extended wartime commissions, so it was fascinating hearing them telling stories of their past exploits in Germany, Italy, France, India, Africa, the Far East and wherever else the war had taken them.

During the daytime, my time was spent with my new recruits, checking on their training, inspecting their barrack rooms and doing my best not to ask such damaging questions of the sergeant major as "Why is that soldier's kit not correctly laid out". I preferred to show rather than tell and the same went for watching them doing their drill. I could well have been accused of showing off, I suppose. I knew my ability to drill was better than any of the NCO's such as Corporal Pulford and his fellow instructors and if I saw anyone having difficulty in getting the hang of a particular movement, I was more inclined to take him on one side and give him one-to-one tuition. This might well have flouted convention, but I found it worked better than all the shouting and ridiculing. I could also take command of entire parades, and often did. I enjoyed taking squads of recruits onto the live firing ranges, getting closely involved in their introduction to firing their rifles. Two or three evenings a week, I would also go down to the indoor miniature rifle range to shoot .22 calibre rifles at tiny targets, the bulls-eye of which was not as big as the diameter of a pencil. Competition targets were laid out in groups of five on a single card of about 12" x 10" with two at the top and bottom and one in the centre. Each one was a black disc inscribed with thin white circles to denote the scoring areas, from five points on the outside to ten in the centre. Inside the smallest centre circle was another circle of dots and this was called a "carton bull" which if you clipped it scored 10.1, so theoretically a maximum score could be 101 out of 100. Through proper breath control it was possible to set yourself up on the firing point with a telescope alongside and your ammunition within hand's reach so that once settled, you need

116

hardly move to fire, spot your shot and reload. Eventually, I was scoring 99's and 100's quite regularly and often clocking up 100.3's and 100.4's. My very best in one competition was 100.7, but I ever only did it that once. My silver spoons were my prizes, together with the odd mugs, rosebowl and medals for my full bore, Sten gun and pistol shooting.

The pay of a National Service second lieutenant was just £16.16.0. per *month* (£16.80) and out of that we had to pay our mess charges including the extra messing charges for the "luxuries" and any special charges which came along. If we were lucky, the one or two or three pounds we had left each week took us to the cinema in Aldershot, local dance at Farnborough Town Hall or pub. Unless given one by some family benefactor, to own a car was unthinkable, so it was the bus or walk, dependent on our destination.

Once a month would be a special Mess Dinner Night when all the officers including those who lived out in married quarters or hirings would come to dinner. On these occasions, it was the custom to invite very senior officers such as The Garrison Commander, or even the General Officer commanding the whole district or area as guests of the mess. As the A.C.C. was then considered to be the little cousin of the Royal Army Service Corps, our own Controller, Colonel Richard Byford, CBE, MVO would sometimes invite the General who commanded the R.A.S.C. These were very strict affairs, following ancient rules of military etiquette. The dinner was presided over by the Mess President, usually a senior major and from the junior officers, a Mr. Vice would be chosen to sit opposite him and it was Mr. Vice's job to respond to The Loyal Toast and ensure that the port which was usually of good quality was correctly passed round. Dinners were usually a four or five course meal, with wines. In my ignorance in those days, I was unable to appreciate whether the wines were good or bad and from my few experiences of attending dinners after I had left the Army, I'm inclined to think they may well have been inferior. After dinner it was the custom to return to the Ante Room for drinks and a chat and sometimes to be introduced to the visitors. If the more senior ones went off to the billiard room, as they often did, we juniors would clear the floor of the ante room and play stupid games like piggyback fighting and high-cockalorum. Others would gather in small groups for cards or games of Liar Dice. Once, on one such evening, the Director

R.A.S.C., a major general came into the toilets to find me in the middle of having a pee, laughing with Sandy and wearing the General's No. 1 Dress cap with its ornate gold wired General's badge of rank and loads of scrambled egg on the peak. Fortunately, Sir Robin was in a good mood and passed it off by saying something such as "Which one of us should be standing to attention?" He was a charming man, thank heaven.

I spent about six months as a Training Officer at Ramillies and in that time did my fair share of being Orderly Officer. This was a regular 24 hour duty for young officers, supported by a major appointed "Field Officer of the week", to whom we could report if anything very serious occurred. If you were the Orderly officer, your day started with a visit to the Guard Room at 08.00 hrs to inspect the prisoners and check on any events which were scheduled for the day. You also visited the men's' dining halls to check on their lunches and suppers. At 6pm. you mounted the Guard for the night and checked on them at least once after midnight to see that everything in the guardroom was in order and that the prisoners were locked up safely in their cells. You slept in a special Spartan bedroom allocated solely for the purpose so that your Orderly Sergeant knew where to find you at night if need be and it was also your duty to close the Warrant Officers and Sergeants Mess at 11pm, unless it was a Saturday night, when it would be midnight. Closing their mess was always a tricky time, as there would almost inevitably be at least one NCO who was drunk enough to want you to stay and have a drink with him, almost forcing himself on you, much to his comrades' amusement and your discomfort. Saturday nights were worse still, as then, the NCO's could invite their wives into their mess. Sometimes they were wives in name only and if they too had had too much to drink could come on very strong, making life extremely embarrassing for we pink cheeked nineteen year olds. The Old Guard was inspected and dismounted at 06.30 when the Guardroom was handed over to the Regimental Police for normal daytime duties. Then it was time for a check on the men's' breakfasts, a quick bath back at the mess, breakfast and off to work again. As we averaged only about four or five hours sleep for the night, it was quite tiring.

At Easter time, I found I had drawn the short straw to be Orderly Officer over the entire holiday, which meant going on duty at 8am on the Thursday and not standing down again until 8am the

118

following Tuesday. Over the Good Friday, Saturday and Sunday I played myself sick at solo snooker and billiards and finally in desperation on the Easter Monday evening took myself off to The Queen's Hotel in Farnborough for a drink in the big outside world. As I was standing at the bar enjoying a pint of Flowers, I caught a whiff of a particular cologne which I instantly recognised. Lieutenant Colonel Holder, my Commanding Officer, dressed in civilian clothes was standing behind me, still in my uniform, buying himself and his wife a drink.

'Hello, Peter. What brings you here?' It was an innocent enough question - or was it?

'Good evening, Sir. Well, after four days confined to the barracks, I just felt like getting out and having a bit of a break, but the Orderly Sergeant does know where I am if he needs me.'

'Oh, thank goodness for that. Would you be good enough to call in to see
Tony Gibson (his Adjutant) tomorrow morning?'

'Yes, sir, of course.'

'Well, goodnight then, Peter.'

'Goodnight, Sir.' I drank up and left the bar, cursing my luck.

After I had dismounted the guard the following morning, I duly reported to the Adjutant who left me in no doubt as to the seriousness of my transgression, rewarding me with a continuous block of *fourteen* extra Orderly officer duties. And dammit, just to make matters worse, I happened to have a fund of dirty stories which went on for almost an hour and getting carried away one night in the mess, someone reported my unseemly behaviour to Tony Gibson who promptly awarded me yet another fourteen duties, which made me favourite among all the other junior officers as they knew they would not be orderly officer for at least another four or five weeks. Shortly after these extra duties were all over, I was just getting back to a normal daily routine when I was again summoned to the Adjutant's office. Bloody hell, I thought, I wonder what the hell I've done now? But someone higher up had decided that it was time to remove me from my present surroundings. I shall never know whether it was intended as a punishment or a reward, but I found that I was being posted to Tactical Wing of The School of Infantry at Warminster as their Specialist Messing Officer in the rank of Temporary Lieutenant where I was to be in charge of the catering for two men's' messes, one huge NCO's mess and two officers' messes, so I had almost a thousand mouths to feed every day.

The entire School of Infantry was spread over three or four areas of the country and commanded by a Brigadier Richard Goodwin DSO, later to become Lieut.General Sir Richard KCB, CBE, DSO who was resident at The Tactical School, to which I was attached as part of his headquarters organisation. The Demonstration Infantry, The Bedfordshire and Hertfordshire Regiment were at Knook Camp, a few miles away towards Salisbury, Support Weapons Wing and Signals Wing were at Netheravon elsewhere on the vast Salisbury Plain and The Small Arms School was at Hythe, right down in Kent. At Warminster Camp itself was the demonstration Armour made up from a squadron of tanks from the 6th. Royal Tank Regiment, all the Tactical Wing training staff and all the various officers and NCO's who were attending the courses being run at that part of the school. The Chief Instructor of the School was a Colonel Peters, the Commandant was Lt. Col. P.V.V. Guy and my headquarters company commander was Major Roland Ingleby-Mackenzie, of the Seaforth Highlanders. The purpose of the school was to train officers and NCO's from all the infantry regiments in the latest battle techniques and weaponry, so this meant that we had an ever changing population bringing into my world officers from all the illustrious and romantic regiments imaginable, including those from the Indian Army and the Commonwealth and U.S.A. I met some fascinating people, some of whom rose to become very senior Brigadiers and Generals later on in their careers.

The colourful ones were from old cavalry regiments and the Brigade of Guards and it was from them that I copied my mode of dress. I felt deeply underprivileged in my ordinary battledress uniform and regulation shirt and tie. And my service dress cap was no match for theirs. I went to London and sought out Herbert Johnson's, the military hatters for a new SD cap. I never knew there were so many different styles. I plumped for a cavalry style. I bought new fine poplin shirts complete with epaulettes in pale coffee coloured khaki and a dark brown knitted silk tie for good measure. I changed my black boots and gaiters for brown brogues, turned back the cuffs on my BD jacket and acquired a dog. If The Guards and Cavalry could do it, why not me?

One of the Guards officers attached to our HQ staff was Lt.

David Naylor-Leyland, to me an aristocrat and obvious role model. He had a beautiful 2.5 litre Alvis Grey Lady saloon in which he would sweep out of the drive of the mess to visit in London. He wore golden yellow suede gloves to drive in and was always impeccably dressed in beautifully cut suits and cut-away collared shirts. He must have been incredibly well connected, as he was chosen to be the officer in charge of the late king George VI th's coffin bearing party. Regrettably, some of the upstart nouveau riche young officers who had got into The Guards purely as a result of their parents' wealth were not so nice, one or two of them mocking my Corps to my face quite openly in the mess. These were some of the people I had been associated with as cadets not so long ago and who felt they could now show their true colours. I did my best to ignore them and in my heart of hearts knew I was equally as good as they were - maybe even better at my job too.

    I got my dog Pavlo, a yellow Labrador, from Peter Bowden, a lieutenant in the Bedfordshire and Hertfordshire Regiment who was attached to the HQ. He had had a most unfortunate accident when on manoeuvres one day; he had thrown himself down to take cover while in a cornfield and stabbed himself in the face with a corn stalk, which cost him his eye. He had bought Pavlo as a puppy but now wanted to get rid of him. I should have asked why. I thought Pavlo would be just the thing if I also bought a sporting gun and did a bit of shooting out on The Salisbury Plain. I bought my gun, an elderly Midland Gun Company 12 bore from Captain Tom Casey, MC, who was the Transport Officer and currently on detachment from The South Staffords. I think I paid about £10.00 for it. While it was of an old design with exposed hammers which needed cocking by hand, it fitted me beautifully. From the mess, I also bought boxes of surplus WD cartridges fairly cheaply, so with the addition of a hand-made leather cartridge belt, felt fully equipped to do the country squire act. By day, Pavlo would behave himself reasonably well on the leash, although if I let him off, he was an unruly dog. In the evenings, when I took him out shooting on that part of the Plain which lay behind the mess and which was used as a military training battle ground, he behaved like a mad steamroller. He ran absolutely wild, charging up and down, putting up every rabbit and pheasant for miles around. I thought of a brilliant way to control his exuberance. Get a long length of washing line. Tie one end round my waist and place the other end, tied in a noose round his neck. If he pulled, he would throttle himself and I felt that would deter him in time. But no such luck. On my first try out, he tore off after a rabbit and despite my calls wouldn't stop. The line was paying out rapidly and I braced myself only just in time as this canine hurricane was jerked into the air by his neck and I found myself almost pulled over by his strength as he tried to charge on after the fast disappearing rabbit. I wound him in like a leaping shark and tried to quieten him down. I tried again - with the same result. And again and again. Each time, he just jolted into the air as the line tightened. My patent dog-training system was obviously not going to work. I resorted to something I had heard from an old gamekeeper. He had said "it were bein' cruel to be kind". Without the rope on him, I let him get to what I judged to be a safe enough distance and then fired both barrels at his backside. Even that didn't bring him to heel. The final ignominy was being invited out on a shoot with the Brigadier and some other senior officers, all with their beautifully trained spaniels and Labrador gundogs and watching helplessly as Pavlo outstripped the Brigadier's dog and fetched the pheasant back to within twenty feet of us and then lay in the grass happily eating the bloody thing!

Mother and father were doing fairly well with Knyveton as a guest house and at weekends I took home my bag of rabbits and pigeons. Catching the bus in Warminster I would travel upstairs with Pavlo and a tennis holdall containing the rabbits and birds to Salisbury where I could change onto another bus for Bournemouth. Even then, the dog would be forever snuffling into the holdall trying to get at them. I could buy special WD 12 bore cartridges which had a magnesium tracer pellet mixed in with the lead shot and which had been originally intended for use by RAF air gunners to show how much they had to aim off to hit a moving target. They were just the job for me, too. I spent hours practising, throwing tin cans in the air and snap-shooting at them as they fell. I even learned to shoot my twelve bore well from the hip - a most unorthodox thing to do. As a result of all this learning, my best ever day's shooting resulted in thirty three kills with thirty two shots.

Bird tumbling down,

feathers floating in the air.

The bang comes later.

(Japanese Haiku form – 5, 7, 5 syllables)

Pavlo managed to get his own back on me though. I always took him to my office where he would lie down beneath my desk. One afternoon, he must have slipped out without me noticing. When it was time to pack up and go back to the mess, he was nowhere to be found. I tramped all over the barracks looking for him, but without success. Finally, in desperation, my search took me towards the stables, where I saw him coming back down the lane. As it was getting near dinnertime, I hurriedly took him back to my room, shut him in and went for dinner. Later that evening, I went back to get him to take him out for his last walk and when I went into the room, he was lying on my bed with the room smelling of horse dung. When we got back from our walk, I got undressed and went to bed, thinking the whole affair was over. But the following morning, I woke early with a hot tingling sensation all over my body and when I really became fully awake, saw that the bed was alive with fleas. I had broken out in lumps and bumps all over from the flea bites in the night and of course at that time, I was still having bouts of urticarea from time to time, but never as badly as my father. I took Pavlo along to the bathroom and shoved him into a tub of hot soapy water and was amazed at the army of fleas which floated struggling out of his fur. He was lousy with them - and so was my bed, carpet and bedroom in general. As soon as I could, I went along to see the Medical Officer who burst out laughing at my misfortune when he saw the state I was in and prescribed a massive dose of anti-histamine for me. Within a day or so, the fiery swellings had begun to disappear and the miracle of it was that the drugs totally cured me of urticarea, so there was also a good side to the saga. My bedroom needed the full treatment with liberal doses of flea powder brushed into the carpet and all my bedding had to be sent to the laundry, so I reckoned the score between Pavlo and me stood at "Deuce".

I quickly became a member of the Tactical Wing Small Arms team and having our own rifle range within the camp, we all did a lot of practice. Each year, the School held a small arms competition called The Luckock Cup, with each Wing taking it in turns to host the event. The first year I took part, it was the turn of the Small

Arms School at Hythe in Kent. Our team travelled down from Warminster by coach, arriving the day prior to the actual meeting and stayed as guests in our respective messes. The competition itself was quite a marathon, involving firing off a whole magazine of Bren machine gun at six hundred yards in thirty seconds, then on the appearance of the rifle targets, running down to the five hundred yard firing point, laying down and loading with five rounds and firing them off before the targets disappeared. This was repeated for the four hundred, again to the three hundred, where this time we knelt to fire, the same at two hundred and finally to the one hundred where we stood to fire. No sooner had we done this, than we had to run to the thirty yard point with our Sten guns, load them and fire at Slim Jim targets. These were edgewise on to us, turning to face us for only two seconds in which time we had to get in two shots, doing this five times in all. By then, everyone would be just about knackered. So much for the theory.

That previous evening, on arrival, we had been invited to be mess guests and attend a Dinner Night, which led to lots of drinking. The officers of the Small Arms School were magnificent hosts, plying us with a never ending river of gin, whisky, beer, whatever we wanted. The evening went on till past midnight, by which time I had consumed practically a whole bottle of gin alone. I dimly recall saying something cheeky to the Brigadier before stumbling off to bed to be rudely awoken at 06.30 by a batman with a steaming mug of tea, saying that breakfast would be served at 7am, so that everybody could be away to the ranges by 8am. I felt dreadful and couldn't face anything to eat and as soon as I went out into the fresh air, began to feel even worse, so stumbled back to the mess and settled for a slice of dry toast after all. Dressed in my shooting gear, I climbed aboard the lorry which bounced and rumbled out to the ranges, doing nothing for my rebellious stomach and splitting headache. The ranges were on the coast facing the sea with the butts built into the shingle, but the sea air was no comfort to me. The distant targets almost half a mile away were barely in focus, let alone hittable.

For the Bren gun part of the competition, we were allowed a spotter who could lie behind us with binoculars watching the whorl of the bullets as they travelled through the air towards the targets and he could guide you if necessary. My spotter was Tony Cranstoun,

124

the Assistant Adjutant of Tactical Wing, whom I knew very well by now. He did his best to settle me down with soothing words of comfort, knowing how awful I felt, but probably not really having that much sympathy for me.

'Take your places on the firing point gentlemen. On the appearance of the targets you will adopt the prone position, load your gun with a magazine of twenty eight rounds and complete the practice. You will cease firing when the targets disappear, secure your weapons and lie still until you are told to move. Any questions? Good luck.' The senior range officer retired to a safe place.

'Come on now, Peter, relax. Remember how we practiced this one. Get the gun balanced nicely, then get into a rhythm of two shots, re-aim, two shots, re-aim. I'll be watching and guiding you if necessary.'

A friendly pat on the shoulder from Tony left me standing there wanting to vomit at any moment.

The targets suddenly appeared and I fell down, rather than 'adopting the prone position', fumbled the magazine out of my pouch, couldn't get it loaded onto the gun properly and panicked. Time was tearing past. Finally, I got it on, thought I had taken aim well enough and started firing. All my previous training went by the board and despite Tony's shouted instructions which I could only dimly hear above the noise all round, kept my finger on the trigger until the magazine was empty. I could vaguely see dust from the shingle flying up all over the place down the far end where my bullets were tearing into the stones and I saw later that my target was absolutely lacerated with holes all over it, peppered by the stone fragments rather than any neat round bullet holes. Apparently I had created mayhem down in the butts with everyone ducking for cover.

By the time we had completed the whole exercise of running and firing down to thirty yards, I was just about on my knees and knew I was a disgrace to the team. But fortunately, most people took the competition as a bit of fun and it was soon forgotten. But not by me. I vowed that the next year the same thing wouldn't happen a second time and for weeks before the competition, I went into strict training, including not visiting the bar so frequently. That following year the competition was held at Tactical Wing and we were the hosts. I had a good night's sleep in my own bed and awoke bright and refreshed on the day of the competition. Although my two sighting shots with the Bren at six hundred yards were off the target, this was due to my not allowing sufficient aim off for the strong cross wind, but my spotter had given me a very good idea of where they had struck. At that range, a stiff cross-wind can blow a bullet several feet well off target. I judged exactly where to aim and once we started, I dropped into a sweet rhythm of bang, bang - re-aim, bang, bang - re-aim and so on. I felt confident I had done well and with my morale high, did well in the rifle 'fire and movement' practice. Finally, I could see my hits on the Slim Jims when I fired my Sten, hitting the 'enemy' target right in the centre of his chest. When the scores were totted up, I had made the highest score of the day, beating even the Bisley Queen's Medallist for that year who was shooting for the Small Arms School team. What was more, I seem to recall that I had even set a new record for the competition, but I can't remember whether I received any special prize or not.

After this success, I began to feel that The Army wasn't such a bad place to be after all and my thoughts turned to applying for a "Short Service" commission which would extend my National Service by three years. That would give me time to find out whether I really did enjoy the life and perhaps even make a career out of it. To get a Short Service extension, I would need several recommendations from senior officers. The first step was to apply to my immediate superior, the District Catering Advisor, Major Charles Minardi, who had recently taken over the district and whom I had met once or twice before, but never really knew. I remembered him as a short, waspish man, but that was all. He telephoned to say that he would come over to The School for a visit before making his decision whether to recommend me or not. When he arrived, he looked at me in horror.

'Where on earth did you get that cap?' I told him.
'Who gave you permission to wear such a thing?'
'No-one, Sir, I just did it.'
'It's certainly not an A.C.C. regulation cap, is it?'
'No, Sir.'
'Does the Brigadier know you are wearing such unauthorised headdress?'
'Yes, Sir, he does.'
'Hasn't he said anything to you about it?'
'No, Sir. He doesn't mind a bit what we wear, so long as we

126

do our jobs efficiently and to his satisfaction.'

'Look at those cuffs of yours and your shoes. You've got half your buttons undone. Do you expect me to give you a recommendation if you go on like this, letting the Corps down? And especially that damned cap.'

'No, Sir, I don't suppose you will.'

'Well then, as far as I'm concerned you will get yourself properly dressed. Understand'

'Yes, Sir, But if I may say so, the cap is a lot smarter than the one we're supposed to wear, don't you think?'

Somehow or other, I got my recommendations for my Short Service Commission, which appeared in the London Gazette on the 1st. of July, 1952, backdated to the 25th.of May, exactly two years from the day I joined the Army.

CHAPTER EIGHT

ARMY DAYS III - SS TO REGULAR ACA

In all, I spent fifteen months at the School of Infantry, from the 19th. June, 1951 to the 28th. September the following year. Not long as postings went, but I enjoyed every moment of my time there. For most of that, my spare time was spent out shooting over the rough countryside of The Salisbury Plain which lay behind The School and practising on the ranges. Thanks to Pavlo's antics when we were out together, most of the rabbits, pigeons and game required all long range shots, which was good for my aim. After all, anyone can hit a target with a shotgun at close range.

Our milk supply for the school was from a local family milkman, a Mr. Smith who delivered it in churns in a battered old Morris Eight tourer. It was dented and all the seats were torn by the churns with only the driver's seat fully intact, the brakes were nearly worn out and the clutch slipped if it was overloaded on a hill, but apart from that, it worked - well, it was better than walking. One weekend, I invited dad to come out for the day shooting and borrowed Smithy's car, picking dad up in Warminster at the main bus stop from Salisbury and driving him out to the Plain. I had sandwiches and a flask of tea for our lunch. We went as far as the deserted Imber Village which was now a ghost village, taken over by the military for training during the war and never returned to the civil population. We spent a good day together with him, I hope, sharing the shooting and came back with a reasonable bag which we took back to Bournemouth for the guest house.

It was in and around Imber that the school staged its annual "Battalion in Attack" demonstration to visiting Service Chiefs and visiting foreign dignitaries. The demonstration consisted of showing off the firepower and latest techniques and tactics, including shooting at tanks, breaking through wire fortifications, calling in an air strike, infantry fire and movement and eventually house clearing. A large 'visitors' stand was erected on a hillside and on the other side of the valley were some tank hulls. Nearer to the stands were the barbed wire fortifications. As the demonstration proceeded, the

visitors were shown how to breach the wire using Bangalore
Torpedoes, lengths of metal tubing packed with explosives and
which could be fitted together like the joints of a fishing rod. These
were pushed under the wire and when detonated would blow a gap in
it for the infantry to get through. Remember, this was only six years
or so after the Second World War had ended, so was then the latest
"state of the art". Next, anti-tank guns shot up the old hulls opposite,
with the Meteor tanks of the 6th. Royal Tanks careering forward,
stopping every now and then to fire. The Meteors were the
forerunner of the Centurion, and were smaller, lighter and not so
heavily armed and not having the main gun gyro-controlled, they did
not have the ability to fire on the move. The air strike consisted of a
flight of rocket-firing Typhoons called in to hit the so-called enemy
armour and it was rumoured that one year in the not too distant past,
one of the pilots had mistaken his target and fired off his rockets at
the V.I.P. stand with devastating results. Then "The Funnies" were
brought on. Churchill flails to clear the mines, Arcs to lay wire
netting or bridges and other Churchills mounted with petards which
fired huge mortar bombs over shortish distances. These were known
affectionately as "The Flying Dustbins". It was all very impressive -
and noisy.

The time came to leave and so in the September of 1952 I
reported back to Aldershot to once more become a Regimental
Officer, being attached to Headquarters Company of The Technical
School at St, Omer Barracks. I retained my temporary rank of
Lieutenant and had a bedroom all to myself in Ramillies Mess. With
the Korean War at its height, we had officers coming back and
others going out to take their places with the United Nations troops
out there. Keith Hudson came back as did Humphrey Marlowe who
had collected an M.B.E. for his efforts. There were also some newly
commissioned officers and among these was Barry Perkins, a
charming arty-crafty type of chap who had trained at R.A.D.A.
before becoming enlisted as a National Serviceman. Graham Kerr
was there too, later to become "The Galloping Gourmet" after he had
left the British Army and joined the New Zealand or Australian Air
Force as a catering officer. Tony Roe became a very good friend, as
did David Archer, another Korean veteran who was my Best Man at
our wedding seven years later. The Commandant at that time was
Colonel Reginald Wolstencroft, who had twin blonde daughters who

were mad keen to go on the stage. He used to bring them along to informal affairs in the mess and we all got to know them quite well. Unlike Noel Coward's Mrs. Worthington, he positively encouraged them to 'go on the stage'.

In the early months of 1953, Coronation Year, Keith Hudson by now a junior captain, Barry Perkins and I got together and decided it would be fun if we put on a Review for that year's Corps Week celebrations in the summer. Colonel Reggie gave us his backing and we auditioned loads of people who said they could sing, dance, tell funny stories or act a bit. Keith had an excellent baritone voice and Barry was a splendid actor, camp as hell if need be. I, naturally, played the piano for all the music and with Keith writing the lyrics, composed the opening number for the show and which became our signature tune for "Too Many Cooks". Colonel Reggie's two girls were the only real females in the show and we all had a wonderful time playing to packed houses in the NAAFI for three nights, then transferring some of the sketches to the stage in the main hall of the technical School for the Officers' Dinner Night and Grand Ball. Keith sang "Mud, Mud, Glorious Mud" to much applause and Barry dressed up as a very drunken old Scot, looking very bedraggled in his kilt and dragging behind him a moth-eaten set of bagpipes to render a wonderful Noel Coward skit which started off "I've been north of the Border with old Alex Korda", (a famous Hungarian film director of the time). His accent and timing were perfect and he had the audience literally holding their sides with laughter. The whole evening was a huge success. Everyone was having such a good time that over a glass of gin and tonic I found myself being offered the job of Assistant Adjutant to Jumbo Williams, who was then the Adjutant and feared by every young officer on the establishment. It was about this time when I was also influenced by my colleagues, resulting in me becoming very particular about my laundry, to the extent that at Keith Hudson's suggestion I started sending my shirts for special laundering to an exclusive firm of dry cleaners up to Hawick in the Scottish Borders. My bedroom in the mess also sported a champagne bottle on either side of the fireplace each with a single perfect red carnation. My soaps and aftershave changed too. I now washed and bathed with Roger et Gallet Mignardise and massaged my newly shaved face with Prince Gourielli aftershave. How absorbent is the mind to the right kind of message – or even the wrong one come to that? Where had I got this 'other world me' from? Was this to last a lifetime, resulting in fast cars, eventual love of good wines, fantastical ideas of being a successful entrepreneur?

Jumbo was a paper-work and systems man and a fanatical disciplinarian when it suited him. I was daunted by working with such a man, but decided to accept and from him, I learned an enormous amount about organising and military paperwork. One day I was given the job of writing a very lengthy, complicated report on a new item of equipment which was being tested under field conditions and when I submitted my report found that it went out virtually unaltered, but under his signature. I was hopping mad at that plagiarism. He was married to Stella and they had two sons, one of whom was called 'Pip, as I recall. I also seem to remember that they also had, at Jumbo's insistence, two Bull Terriers, which when he got mad with them were in danger of being thrown down the stairs. His Welsh temper made him very difficult to be with especially if he had had a few drinks. Although he was a sod to work with at times, he was an extremely good golfer with a handicap of four, not far short of professional standard and teaching me a lot about the game.

During Corps Weeks, all manner of sporting activities were arranged and naturally, I found myself a member of the shooting team and no doubt fired hundreds of rounds in practice every week leading up to a week of competition shooting, when hundreds more were fired. Without proper ear defences, it's little wonder that with just little bits of flannel stuffed into my ears to protect them from all the banging, I finished up damaging my hearing. It was not until several years later when we were getting S.N.S.Bournemouth running that a visit to the Department of Audiology at Southampton University to sell them an intercom system that my trouble was first detected. The doctor who headed the department explained that lying on the firing point alongside other shooters, the rifle on my left side would have been exhausting its excess gasses supersonically directly into my left ear, hence my particular deafness on that side. The Tinnitus, a persistent whistling in my head was caused by all the banging noises, so this was called "noise induced" tinnitus. Likewise, I would have been damaging not only my own ears, but to an even greater extent the ear of the shooter on my right, so we were indulging in an orgy of mutual deafening. I did this for year after year. No wonder I and lots of others suffer now.

During this period at the Technical School, we junior officers had to all take part in what were known as "The Junior Officers' Efficiency Tests" (JOETs for short). These were a cunning device dreamed up by some zealot at District HQ to subject all we young officers to a two day marathon involving a forced march in full battle order, cross country run, battle assault course, bivouacking out overnight, riding motor cycles cross country and swimming a length of the baths which involved undressing at one end, wrapping all our clothes in our groundsheets to make a floating bundle, resting our machine guns on top and swimming the length of the pool pushing the bundle ahead of us, then getting dressed at the far end - all against the clock.

As the weeks of rigorous training went by, we were whittled down to two teams of four and learned to work together counterbalancing one another's strengths and weaknesses. We began to become like a well-oiled machine, reducing our times for completion of the various stages until everything was done really slickly and efficiently. We were even taken off some of our normal regimental duties to make sure that we did as much training as Captain Andie Silk, our trainer wanted. I was the only team member who had previous motor cycling experience - and that wasn't much. But it meant that I was supposed to be able to show the others how to do things. Our cross-country motorcycling training was carried out with the help of experienced despatch riders from the Royal Military Police from their depot at Woking, a unit I would get to know better a year or so later. We had to wear battle order and ride with a Sten sub-machine gun slung over our shoulders for good measure. The bikes were incredibly heavy old Royal Enfields and were not really intended for anything much more than going on roads, but we were expected to ride them up hills and over rough country as part of our tests. With only a couple of weeks to go to the date set for the tests in which teams from every regiment and unit in the Aldershot District would compete, I came a cropper. We were practising riding over some very rough hilly ground and I was in the lead going as fast as I could, when going up a shale hill, my denim trouser leg came out of my gaiter and flapping away got drawn into the air intake of the carburettor, causing the engine to stall. That might not have been too bad, I could have kick-started the bike again, but as the bike began to topple over on the side of the hill, I found that the metal cut-out butt of the Sten gun had got trapped in a saddle spring, so I couldn't get my right leg free. The incredibly heavy old bike fell over, taking me with it and completely trapping my right leg underneath with the hot engine burning into my bare leg. It seemed like an age before I could be got out from under it, by which time I had a very severe second degree burn on my calf which meant I was taken straight back to the unit for dressing. A Medical Orderly cleaned me up and put some special powder on the burn to dry it up, but it turned septic and so I had to spend some weeks in Cambridge Military Hospital having treatment. They decided not to give me a skin graft, and opted for nature to take its own time, which was a long, painful process as the burn had removed all the skin over quite a large area, exposing the raw flesh which had to be treated for the infection before any healing could take place. Naturally, I missed the actually competition, but with a reserve from our other team we, the A.C.C. won, beating all the other units including the much vaunted Paras.

Neither did I have any better luck the following year. Again riding a motorcycle cross country, I gave myself another injury by hitting an unseen clump of obstinate grass hidden in the ground at about forty miles an hour. This time, I was unseated and lost my right foothold on the footrest. The jolting of the bike caused my foot to touch the ground in front of the footrest which immediately dislocated my ankle, throwing me off the bike completely headfirst into a tree trunk which knocked me out despite wearing a crash helmet. Again, it was another spell in hospital and missing out yet again on the actual contest, which once again the ACC won, much to the upset of all the other units in the District. So I never did make it to the final contest and was ever only the bridesmaid and never "the blushing bride".

On the 1st. of June 1954 I was again promoted, this time to the rank of Temporary Captain and posted to the Royal Military Police Depot at Inkerman Barracks just outside Woking to be their Specialist messing Officer, taking over from Len Bishop. Here, the job was almost a sinecure as I had only about five hundred troops to feed, plus one Sergeants' Mess and one Officers' Mess. They were very keen on small bore rifle shooting and I joined their team, which allowed me to integrate with them as a unit quite quickly, especially when they found out that I could hold my own in competitions. The actual job has faded in my memory, but two things I can remember with startling clarity. The first is that I bought my first car - with a loan from mother and father. It was a beautiful, black one and a half litre Jaguar saloon, made in 1939 with seats the size of armchairs and a lovely walnut dashboard. It also had spats for the rear wheels to enclose them if wanted. As it had chromium wire wheels, I wanted to show them off, so opted to leave the spats off most of the time. Jaguars also made a two and a half litre version with the same styling which was a slightly bigger, faster brother. Both models had huge chromed radiators flanked by giant headlamps and the bonnet cover had louvres all down the sides and opened up along its centre to expose either the left or the right side of the engine. Mine wasn't particularly fast, but it would cruise incredibly comfortably at about sixty miles an hour. It turned out to be an ideal "passion wagon". But after a while, hankered after other, even more exotic cars and was sorely tempted one day when I saw a beautiful Railton in a garage. I simply had to have a look, sit in it and imagine all the society life such a car must have known. But somehow, common sense prevailed, just as it did when at another time I was again tempted by the latest Daimler SP250 or "Dart" as it was also known.

The second memory was of meeting Irmgard, the brand new German wife of Captain John Betty, the senior motorcycle instructor at the depot. He was a famous Scrambles champion of the times, having his own special bikes which he took to events abroad as well as at home in Britain. In fact, he was very well known on the Continent and through his championship riding had wooed Irmgard, the daughter of the Mayor of Dusseldorf, I believe. She was incredibly beautiful and worked as an air hostess for Lufthansa, the German airline. I took John in the Jaguar to meet her at London Airport when she arrived to live with him in their army hiring in Woking, a lovely bungalow in a quiet close somewhere between the barracks and Woking town itself. When she came down the stairway from the plane, it was like looking at a Hollywood star and I couldn't help feeling absolutely stunned by her.

Perhaps it was just as well that my posting to the Military Police was a short one. Only five months later, in the November of 1954, I was posted to the Royal Army Medical Corps Depot at

Church Crookham. This was a much more arduous job involving feeding between fifteen hundred and two thousand a day including two senior NCOs' messes and two officers' messes. I had to draw up the daily menus for the twelve to fifteen hundred men who fed in three or four mess halls and make sure that the senior messes received their daily rations with such further advice as I could give them to help plan their menus. My work there brought me into contact with the Garrison vicar, Joe Gooch who had an adopted Chinese son. Joe was the most way out vicar I have ever met and one of his manifestations of way outness was to drive a brand new ivory white Austin Healey 100 sports car. But one day, he told me he was thinking about selling it. "Thou shall't not covet thy neighbours wife", but his car is O.K. and I certainly coveted it. I said I would do a part exchange for it with my Jaguar and a cash settlement - if I could have the cash part of the deal on HP with him. We set up the financial arrangements and the swap was made. I think I agreed to pay him something like £5-600 plus the Jaguar. Although he was a vicar, he was no pushover. I later learned he was also a property developer, so was no doubt used to driving hard bargains. Never mind, I was ecstatic with my new car. A twin carburettor, two litre engine, three forward gears with overdrive on middle and top gave it a top speed of I don't know what - 110 mph, 120 mph. maybe. I never had the courage to drive it at more than about 105 or so and felt that was fast enough on the ordinary roads. There were no motorways then. I did lose it one evening though showing it off to Tony Roe who had an MG TD which could only do about eighty-five flat out. Driving him back to London on the North Circular Road, I went into a roundabout fast, changed down into middle gear, switched out of overdrive into normal direct drive and really accelerated hard on the way out. Unfortunately, at full power I hit a patch of oil and went into a spin at about sixty. There was no barrier separating the two dual carriageways and by good fortune we span three times and came out of it going backwards across into the oncoming two lanes of cars managing, miraculously and quite by accident, to skid through a gap between cars. We finished up parked backwards on the grass verge with our bonnet out over the kerb and able to see the astonishment on the faces of the passing drivers. When we both got out to see if there was any damage, Tony's door would only open halfway due to us being so close to a concrete lamp standard and the same with mine thanks to the poles of a road traffic sign. Two feet either way and we would have finished up crumpling the whole of the boot. So we didn't even get a scratch on ourselves or the car. When I took it home for the first time, I was so proud of it. But mother told me in later years after he had died that dad had said to her "Oh yes, he's become the typical selfish bachelor. Only wants room for a girl-friend. No other passengers." After his motor cycling, fishing and shooting days, I find it a bit hard to reconcile those remarks as coming from him. Still, my aunt Dee thoroughly enjoyed being hurtled through the New Forest at over a hundred miles an hour one weekend.

During 1954 I had decided to try for a regular commission and following another of those three day trials of strength at a Selection Board, I was accepted as a proper career soldier - in for life. Well, until age fifty five if I kept my nose clean. I was allowed to stay with the Medics for only one year because as part of my continuation training I was required to attend the ACC Long Civil Catering Course. This was a one year attachment to one of the three big Lyons hotels in London. Sir Isadore Salmon, one of the original Lyons founders had been asked by the Government sometime in the late 1930s to be Honorary Catering Adviser to the Army. It was he who was responsible for the founding of the Army Catering Corps and later, the institution of the Young Regular Officers' Course for one year duration at one of his group hotels, the Cumberland, Strand Palace and Regent Palace. I went to the Cumberland at Marble Arch, teaming up with Nick Carter, another captain. My regular commission had been backdated to my 21st. birthday, the 4th.of January 1953 and this course was the next step up the rungs of the ladder of eventual promotion. I went to lodge with aunt Dee in her flat in Palmers Green and drove in with her each day to Marble Arch in the Healey, dropping her off in Baker Street from where she went on to her offices in Victoria. I could park the car quite safely for nothing in any of the back streets round Bryanston Square near the hotel. How times change! Mr. Vincent, the Staff Manager had my training programme all mapped out for me and this was to take me into all the various preparation departments, then The Grill Room kitchens.

While in the Preparation kitchens, each department received its produce through the Buyers at the various markets and this meant that I was expected to be at the markets by five in the morning, meet up with the buyer and go round the dealers' shops doing the buying with him. At Smithfield I learned how to tell good meat from not so good, cow beef from steer, lamb from mutton and so forth. My two weeks at Billingsgate taught me about fish and I learned a lot about fruit and vegetables from the buyer at Covent Garden. Apart from getting to see the obvious and not so obvious telltale quality signs to look for, I learned that every fruit and vegetable had its season. Air freight was not yet a commercial proposition, so most of our imported foods came by boat. With journeys taking several weeks in some cases, the degree of ripeness when fruits were picked was all important and suppliers prided themselves on selling it at almost the peak of perfection. Naturally grown and naturally ripened. No additives and pesticides to worry about then. You could eat an apple without even washing it. After market, I would have a pub breakfast and pint of beer with the Buyer. I would get back to the hotel at about 9.30am then get down to that department I was attached to. Usually, the chef of each would greet me with the same old thing, "O.K. Captain, you bought 'em, you prepare 'em". This would mean skinning and filleting several boxes of Dover soles, plaice or whatever other fish had been ordered for the day's menus; boning out fore or hindquarters of beef, carcases of lamb and cleaning and preparing boxes of vegetables and fruit. In the catering colleges of those days, a student would be lucky to be given one Dover sole to prepare in his whole period of training. I was doing hundreds and not having to hang about in the process, either. The Lyons way of on-costing their food was to charge the base cost of it on arrival and every department which handled it added their charges for doing so as they passed it on to the next. So the butcher's shop would charge the Grill kitchen an elevated cost (on paper) for the work involved in preparing the various cuts of meat asked for, leaving the end user to sell it to the actual customer for a total charge which covered every single departmental transaction in the chain. It seemed a fairly fool-proof method to me, but it did mean that for strict portion control purposes, it meant that every fillet steak, for example, had to be exactly the right weight. Too light and it would be rejected by the Grill kitchen, too heavy and the butcher's shop would not make its full mark up of profit - and so on. This meant that portioning the various cuts and joints of meat was a precise business, so being able to judge the weight of the steaks etc. I was cutting was a distinct asset. Underweight steaks would merit a kick up the backside as they couldn't be "sold on" and overweight ones meant that they had to be trimmed, producing too much pie meat and that merited another kick up the backside.

Following my indoctrination in the Preparation kitchen, I was then attached to the various corners of the main Grill kitchen under the ever watchful eye of the head Chef de Cuisine himself, Monsieur Charles Douarret, an explosive little Frenchman whose toque was almost as tall as he was. His second was Henri – that's all I ever knew him as, Monsieur Henri, a huge bear of a man who had seen service as a Corporal in the French Foreign Legion and he brooked no nonsense from anyone - Non! The chefs in charge of each of the corners made up a motley crew. Jan from Hungary and with an uncertain temper ran the roast, Raoul, a scruffy Frenchman who used his fingers for everything the fish, Charles of almost aristocratic bearing compared with the others the sauces, Jimmy the Indian Curry cook and several others I can't now remember. They each had their idiosyncracies to say the least. With no cling-film, keeping prepared foods in fridges was something of a cyclic art. Bread-crumbed fillets of fish would be washed off and re-bread-crumbed for two or three days if they hadn't sold, after which they would have to be sacrificed and made up into something else, or sent for staff meals. Poor Jimmy the curry chef had a very bad accident one day. He ever only wore a pair of chupris (open sandals) and having made an enormous pot of curry sauce, he lifted it bubbling off the stove and for convenience put it down on the floor – I suppose because he hadn't cleared the space for it elsewhere. He then had to climb up on a step stool for some reason, I think to a high shelf, and, coming down put one foot right into his pot of near boiling sauce. Live trout and lobsters were kept in tanks of water ready for selection by Raoul when necessary. He showed me how to gut a trout without cutting its belly open, especially useful for truite au bleu orders.

All orders were called in French and at the height of meal service, the whole kitchen was a madhouse, with M. Douarret and Henri pacing up and down the hotplates sniffing, tasting, inspecting and occasionally rejecting the various dishes being presented. We worked split shifts but the few hours off we had each afternoon were not really enough to do a great deal with. Some of the young commis played merry hell in the kitchen if they got back before everyone else, as they were supposed to get stoves lit and basics out of the fridges. On one occasion, a group of them were playing tennis using a "spider" (a long handled wire tool used for lifting fish out of the fryer) and raw peeled potatoes. Standing at each end of the kitchen, they were throwing the potatoes for the others to bat back. One potato was substituted by a raw egg and just as the batsman hit it, Monsieur Henri the Deuxième walked in to be spattered by the pulverised egg. He nearly killed the commis, ending up by sitting him on a nearby hot stove and giving him a well burned backside. So no Health and Safety there, then.

Although I was on a captain's pay and London Allowance, and living almost rent free with Dee, I was still finding the repayments on the Healey a struggle and reluctantly came to the conclusion that I would have to hand it back to Joe Gooch. I got the Jaguar back, but he had driven it into the ground and on the way back through central London to Dee's flat, the exhaust fell off, making it sound like an old Sherman tank. The engine hadn't had too much oil and loving care either, so I had to have that completely overhauled, which cost me a small fortune. With all that extra expense, I could have kept the Healey! One afternoon, during a split shift, I was walking down Park Lane and just as I passed The Dorchester caught sight of a girl in a passing taxi. Our eyes met for a brief instant of recognition and I realised it was Norma Forrest, the girl I had been introduced to once when Mother and father were buying the house in Palmers Green, when I was sixteen and she a very adult eighteen. Out of curiosity, I looked her up in the London phone book and found her parents listed at the same address as I had remembered from those earlier days. I rang, she was unattached and we met. She had grown into a very alluring blonde with an hourglass figure and she told me that she was now doing some modelling and film extra work. In fact, she was doing a modelling session that next Saturday in Brighton - would I like to run her down there and back? The obvious answer was "yes", so I picked her up in the Jaguar from her home. On the way down to Brighton, I noticed she was doing something behind her back through her sweater and when I asked if she was uncomfortable, she said that she was undoing her bra straps so that the marks wouldn't show on her skin during the modelling session. Beneath her sweater, her breasts were so firm and beautifully shaped that even without the support of her bra, her chest profile didn't change one iota. I envied the photographer his job - if you could call it that. While I was waiting for her my mind was imagining all sorts of erotic scenes. During the journey back to London she was dressed in a short skirt and chose to sit on the ample front passenger seat as though it was an armchair, with her legs drawn up beneath her, putting her knees very close to the gear lever which meant every time I changed gear, my hand touched her knees. When we got back to her house in the late afternoon, she told me that her parents were not coming back until very late that night so the house was empty if I wanted to come in for a cup of tea.

The next day I had a euphoric feeling of being absolutely head over heels in love for the first time in my life. I was walking on clouds, singing and full of happiness for everybody and with everything in life. It didn't last. Dee had nothing good to say about Norma and I allowed myself to be influenced by that and things quickly fizzled out between us.

As if to compensate for this tragic turn of events and the loss of the Healey, I happened to drive past a large corner garage site at Staples Corner one day with Dee and saw on the forecourt a superb red open touring car and naturally went to have a look at it. It was a Triumph 1800 Roadster, a comparative rarity, as it was an experimental model which Triumph had fitted with a Jaguar 1.5 litre engine - an updated version of the one I already had in my saloon. Their next model produced a few years later was the Triumph 2000 which became well known in the Bergerac detective TV series set in Jersey and which was shown in the late 1980's. The all aluminium bodywork was painted tomato red and so was very light and would never rust. Behind the front bench seat was a special compartment which opened up with a separate windscreen and two dickey seats. This car I simply had to have so borrowed a hundred pounds from Dee and did the part exchange on the spot. It wasn't as fast as the Healey, but my god, it certainly was a head turner.

With the Long Course barely ended, I was posted back to the Technical School on standby for Suez, which I enlarge upon in Chapter 10. Then on the 12th November 1956 I reported to Aldershot once more to take up my new duties as a Technical Training Officer which brought me into contact with a WRAC (Women's Royal Army Corps) officer, Mary Moore, who was on a six month training course prior to becoming a specialist catering officer with her WRAC depot over at Liphook, just outside Guildford. She was ten years older than me and at thirty five was a very attractive, mature woman and although Welsh, had hardly any accent to accompany her Celtic, olive-toned skin. She looked almost more a mixture of French and Spanish than British. She was living in her own two roomed quarters in the QARANC (Queen Alexandra's Royal Army Nursing Corps) officers mess for nurses on the outskirts of the Garrison and we started going to the cinema together seeing all the hits of the time such as Oklahoma and High Society and when we got back to her quarters, she had a Pye Black Box hi-fi on which she played the wonderful selection of romantic tunes we had in those days. We soon began kissing and petting. Who wouldn't have under the circumstances? We went away together for the Whitsun Bank Holiday weekend, touring through The Cotswolds on our way to her parents' home in Cardiff. I learned that Mary had been married to a very good painter and although now divorced still moved in very arty circles whenever she could. We stayed the first night in a hotel in Burford or some such similar little town and the following night we stayed at another Cotswold town. We got to Cardiff in time for the Cardiff Arms Rugby Club Ball on the Saturday night. Mary dressed herself in a wonderful silk and taffeta ball gown and I wore my Mess Kit and any idea of petting when we got back to her home was a non-starter, as her parents appeared to be strict Churchgoers and in any case, we had separate bedrooms. But we made up for it the next morning, going for lunch to some friends of Mary's. After a very fulsome meal with plenty to drink, they suggested we all have a nap before going out and bless their hearts gave us a spare bedroom with a double bed for the next couple of hours. Some few weeks later, I took Mary down to Bournemouth to stay at Knyveton for the weekend. She had a miniature black poodle she called Louis and when we arrived, I carried him up the front garden path. That did it. When mother saw me with a woman ten years older than me and me carrying her dog, she immediately exploded to dad saying I was nothing but a bloody gigolo now. Mary's visit was not an auspicious occasion and I was glad to get back to Aldershot.

    Sure enough, my financial situation deteriorated once more which meant that the Triumph had to go the way of all things and was sold to repay my debt to Dee, so for the first time in three or four years was car-less again. It was during this period that the War Office made what was to become for me a significant decision, although I didn't know it at the time. Due to the shortage of regular officers in the ACC, they decided to open the doors to other officers to transfer in from other regiments and arms, provided they passed a three month transfer course with us at the Training Centre. They arrived in their droves and we had to set up a series of technical courses to deal with them, with me in charge of one such course. Naturally, I got to know them all well. Some were interesting and were likely to become suitable for transfer, but most were just out for an easy ride. At the time, one of my colleagues was Dennis O'Reilly, a giant of some six foot three inches and who was also another technical officer. One of our transferees was Harry Williamson a Lieutenant in the South Staffords who had a black eye patch. He was getting married to a naval officer's daughter in Portsmouth and asked Dennis and me if we would like to be part of his Guard of Honour and we accepted. This meant travelling down to Portsmouth in Dennis's minute Austin A30, which belonged to his sister anyway, and staying the night in the Officers' Club in the centre of Portsmouth so that we would be on hand the following morning for the church ceremony. That Friday night, we were invited on board the frigate commanded by the bride's father and the evening passed in a blur of pink gins. I awoke early on the Saturday morning and even though I was suffering the after effects, suddenly became quite clear headed when I discovered that I had forgotten to bring the trousers of my No. 1 uniform. Dennis rose to the occasion and not without some loss of humour, drove me all the way back to Aldershot so that I could get them from my room in the mess. Thank heaven it was an afternoon wedding as being a Saturday, the roads were quite busy. Wanting to save time, I elected to get dressed into my No. 1's while we were travelling on the way back down to Portsmouth and doing that in an Austin A30 which was no bigger than a sardine tin was no mean feat. I had just stripped off to my underpants and was struggling to get my trousers from the back seat when we hit a traffic-jam with a bus pulling up alongside us so that the passengers could all look down at me sitting almost naked in the car. Eventually, we arrived at the church just as the bridal car was drawing up. We screeched to a halt and tumbled out with me still doing up my buttons and fumbling to get my Sam Browne and sword

142

on. Sprinting to the church entrance to get there before the bride and her father, we thought that we had just made it until walking up the aisle with me still trying to do up my Sam Browne, the tip of the sword scabbard jammed in one of the curlicue holes in the central heating grating, dragging me to a standstill halfway up the aisle and with the Bridal March from Lohengrin announcing the arrival of the bride and her father. Everybody turned to watch their procession up the aisle to see me struggling to unhook my bloody sword from its iron trap!

I can't believe that was anything to do with it, or whether it was anything to do with my association with Mary, but the powers that be decided it was time to move Slaney on yet again and so on the 20th. September 1957 I found myself being posted as Area Catering Adviser to Home Counties District, based in Shorncliffe assisting Major Rodney Monk, the District Catering Adviser.

CHAPTER NINE

ARMY DAYS IV - ON BEING AN ADJUTANT

Rodney Monk, was an easy-going boss who let me get on with doing my own job more or less the way I thought fit. Naturally, from time to time he asked me to do various jobs, but these were never too onerous and life was sweet. Luckily, he had a very dry, keen sense of humour which made him an ideal senior officer to work for as far as I was concerned. I lived in the Royal Army Service Corps officers mess in Shorncliffe garrison and had a very nice room there on the ground floor. My fellow officers were all very pleasant, including the Commander, R.A.S.C., to whom both Rodney and I reported. The Colonel had a very attractive young daughter to whom I felt drawn, but never more than friendly hand-holding when circumstances allowed. I think this upset the Colonel a bit - whether he expected more to develop or felt I was out of line, I don't know. I was allowed to draw up my own itineraries to cover all the thirty-four or so units within the District and my farthest flung unit to the west was, ironically, the Women's Royal Army Corps Depot in Liphook, where Mary Moore was now the Catering Officer. So although separated from her in Aldershot, we were brought together again almost immediately. My territory took in the whole of the south east of England bounded by The Medway in the north as far as Woolwich to the north-west, then down through Guildford to Liphook and from there back to the coast at Chichester. As I had to travel almost every day to get round seeing all the units, it was again necessary for me to get a car. Although I could have used military transport, it was not always readily available, nor was it as comfortable and convenient as going by car for which I could claim petrol allowance. So with another loan from Mother and Father, I bought myself a little black Morris Minor 800 saloon, a dear little car which took me thousands of miles round the Home Counties and when fitted with Dunlop All Weather tread tyres through deep snows in winter.

When I went westwards on visits, I might make Mary's unit the last for that day so that I could stay in their Guest Room and have dinner with her in the Mess. On one occasion, my visit coincided with an official dinner, to which I was invited. The Commanding Officer of the Depot was a very well-adjusted woman in her middle age. She had a wonderful sense of "occasion" and on this particular evening, once everybody present had ordered what they wanted to drink for cocktails and the wine they wanted with their dinner, quite out of the blue, she said that she would pick up the bill for everyone's' drinks, which I thought was extremely generous and in a way, quite clever as everyone had exactly what they wanted and had she announced it beforehand, there would have been some who might wel
l have held back and others who would have gone overboard - at her expense. Gradually, however, my visits to see Mary tailed away. The ten year gap was, at that time, too daunting to me.

Each year, Home Counties District held their competition for the "Festing Trophy", a cup awarded to the unit in the district which had achieved the highest standard of catering, based on a set number of visits by the Catering Adviser and it was part of my job to visit every unit three times to assess them. With over thirty units to visit, this amounted to making at least two inspection visits a week for a start, plus a day to complete all the paperwork. Add to this my other routine visits and other jobs which cropped up and the job was certainly a full time occupation. In summertime, I had to take on the organisation and supervision of the catering for almost two thousand Army Cadets who came camping on the permanent site just outside Shorncliffe. There was such a lot to do that I *had* to put in hours and hours of work and after doing one whole day and night, I decided to just go on to see how long I could endure without sleep. I managed the second day and night, returning to the mess at lunchtime on the third morning, fell into bed and slept the clock round until the next morning. Whether I had been fully effective on that last morning or not, I don't know, but it wasn't an experiment I tried a second time. It wasn't until years later, when at around age seventy that I sent away to the MOD for copies of my Record of Service and discovered that for the period I was looking after those cadets I was assumed to be a temporary major. This was something I never knew at the time. Some of my units were fascinating to visit, especially the Bomb Disposal Unit at Horsham and the Intelligence Centre. I met Major Bob Hartley RE of the Bomb Disposal unit who had been awarded The George Medal for one of his more dangerous jobs – among many. How much more dangerous any one disposal job is than another, I never found out, but Bob was a very nice, humorous, family man who certainly would not have stood out in a crowd as being the superhuman he was. The Intelligence Corps was always a very quiet, seemingly placid unit where nothing ever seemed to happen, yet underneath that smooth surface lurked all the intelligence gathering systems which supplied the Military and the Government of the day with a never ending stream of information.

One day, Rodney and I were summoned to a meeting which was to take place at the Royal Artillery Depot at Woolwich where Bill Herbert, the ACC officer was carrying out a pilot scheme of a new, logical style of catering for the troops. It was based upon producing whichever main courses were best suited to the kind of meats being supplied on the ration scale. So sirloin or rump steak was grilled or fried and the lesser cuts of meat were used to make roasts, puddings and Shepherds pies etc. Instead of just one or at most two main course options, there were now five or six on offer, plus a selection of vegetables and about four sweets to choose from. Where the initiative for this radical change had come from, I don't know, but it marked the start of "the Cafeteria System" which was to become the norm and now my new bible to preach from. I now had to ensure that every unit adopted this new style of feeding and this meant introducing and supervising a whole new raft of training sessions. My recently gained knowledge of butchery and fish preparation was now really being put to the test, as was my knowledge of more sophisticated menu planning. It was a challenge I enjoyed. It was the beginning of "The New Wave" of catering which was to eventually sweep through not only the Army, but the RAF and Royal Navy as well and I was glad to be at the forefront of this most beneficial change.

One weekend in November 1958, I went home to Bournemouth and was invited out to a party by Peter Robinson who used to run the little TV repair shop just round the corner from Knyveton. Peter said he could get his girlfriend to find another girl for me, but by the time the evening was over, his girlfriend, Norma Powers and I found ourselves attracted towards one another and so began our whirlwind romance. From that weekend onwards, I drove home to Bournemouth in the Morris Minor almost every Friday night, returning to Folkestone very, very late on Sunday nights, even the early hours of Monday mornings. It was a long, tedious journey in the Minor, taking four or five hours and I simply had to get a quicker car. Eventually, the ideal car came on the market. The British Motor Corporation launched their new Wolseley 1500 and Riley 1.5 models. These were based on a Morris Minor chassis, but with very much larger 1500cc engines, the Riley even having twin carburettors, giving it an alarming turn of speed. I chose a rich red Riley and found it so fast that I wore out the first set of tyres within 8000 miles. I replaced the standard factory Dunlop crossplies with Michelin radials and got both better mileage and road handling as a result. The journey time home to Bournemouth was cut by 25% and was much more exhilarating. One weekend, I took it to a boatyard in Christchurch and got them to measure up the exhaust piping so they could make me a copper replacement for a richer exhaust sound. It was a great success, the engine now sounding more like the Austin Healey, a full, rich, throaty burble. The only trouble was that the tail end which protruded from the back end needed constant polishing with Brasso to keep it looking attractive. Norma's parents, Norman and Maymie owned The Fircroft Hotel, a forty or more bedroomed

146

place in Owls Road, not far from Knyveton. Fircroft had grown out of a family house which had been originally built in Victorian times and had been added to as its years of being an hotel had passed by, resulting in its corridors of bedrooms being at all different levels, quite like a rabbit warren. Until you got to know the layout, finding your way round was quite confusing, especially as the bedrooms had been given their numbers as and when they had been added, irrespective of exactly where they were within the building. Before Norma's father owned it, it had belonged to his mother, who I came to know as "Granny Chadda" as a result of her second marriage to Lakme Chadda, an Indian or Pakistani cricketer. She was also known as "Burley Momma" as she owned "Burley Manor" in the New Forest and at one time had asked her two sons, Norman and his brother Horace, which of the two places they wanted to take over. Horace said he wanted to be a chemist and Norman said he was content to stay at Fircroft. So she sold Burley Manor, which in the property boom of the late 1980's was to become worth about £5million. Norma's mother, Maymie also came from a property owning family. Her mother, who we knew as "Sue Momma" owned several properties in Bournemouth and as a present to Maymie, bought her "Netheravon", the huge semi-detached house next door to the Fircroft in which she and Norman now lived with Norma and her younger sister, Phyllis, a sylph-like pretty girl with an unfortunate caste in her eye which was corrected later. During our courting days, Norma had her own flat on the top floor of Netheravon and most weekends, we either ate up there, or with Norman, Maymie, Phyllis and her boyfriend Brian Webb in the hotel dining room. It was a wonderfully cosy family atmosphere, quite unlike anything I had ever experienced before. Their standard of living was so different from that of my own mother and father, it was quite another world.

One day, I developed a rather nasty toothache and went along to see the Dental officer at Shorncliffe. Quite unusually, he had the very exalted rank of lieutenant colonel and when he saw my tooth, said it couldn't be repaired and took it out on the spot. After my gum had healed, I went back to see him about having a small plate made with just that one missing tooth on, but he said that couldn't be done unless I had one other suspect one out on the opposite side of my mouth. This would then at least give the plate sufficient anchorage to stay put. I agreed and when the plate had been made and fitted, I tried my best to live with it, but found this smooth bit of plastic up inside the roof of my mouth was not at all pleasing. It felt so hard and unnatural to my tongue that I knew it would not be a very nice experience for Norma when she kissed me deeply, so went back to see him yet again to see whether anything else could be done for me. Although he was very reluctant to get involved in such expensive orthodontics, he was eventually persuaded to get a special cobalt steel skeleton-framed plate made for me. This was a thin band of high tensile steel moulded to fit behind my top teeth and holding the two false ones in place. It was bridged across just in front of the soft palate in the roof of my mouth and so resembled a domed, jagged "D" shaped lightweight structure with single teeth mounted on either side of the curve of the "D". At least I could once again feel my soft palate and hoped that it would be more acceptable to Norma, as well as me.

'Captain Slaney, this is going to be the most expensive piece of dentistry you are ever likely to be given. Please take care of it.'

I must admit, my earlier tooth gap had caused me to develop a self-conscious lop-sided smile and this new contraption would enable me to once more smile naturally. I gave him a straight smile and said I would. The trouble was, that despite its expense to the Army Exchequer, I still felt it was an intrusion in my mouth and bound to cause some offence, no-matter how small to Norma in our more intimate moments, so on those occasions, I would take it out and this was to be my downfall and the demise of the ultimate in military dental bridge-building. One Friday evening we had supper upstairs in Norma's flat and I took out my bridge and wrapped it into a paper napkin, but instead of putting it in my pocket, left the napkin too near my supper tray. Maymie, acting the loving mum came to clear away our trays. When I couldn't find my paper parcel, I realised what had happened and went searching for it in the dustbin, only to be told by Maymie that she had thrown everything into the Aga. When I took the lid off the firebox, there among the orange coloured coke was my bridge, glowing incandescently, but minus the two plastic teeth, which had long since melted. I retrieved what was left of my precious mouth jewellery and ran it sizzling under the cold tap. That next Monday I took it, nervously, to the Colonel and with some trepidation showed him the blackened chassis.

'What the bloody hell have you done to it?' he asked, not

without some venom in his voice.

'Well, I'm terribly sorry, sir, but you see I had a very hot curry over the
weekend and...'

He cut me short. 'Don't come the bloody fool with me man, I told you to look after it.'

I tried to apologise by telling him what had happened and when he calmed down said he supposed I wanted a replacement, which I said I did, please.

'Well, this is the last time I want to see you over this matter. Is that clear?'

As our courtship progressed, I received invitations to join the family at various hoteliers' and Masonic functions, one of which was at the old Grand Hotel in Bournemouth, now regrettably demolished, but at one time run by a retired ACC officer, 'Dusty' Miller, who I knew of, but never really had met. Norman and Maymie, Norma and I, Phyllis and Brian all shared a table with Marcel and Phyl Clouzy who owned The Whitehall Hotel overlooking Bournemouth Gardens and Gwen and Charles Webb, Brian's parents who were minor partners in the hotel. Gwen Webb and Phyl Clouzy were sisters and were chalk and cheese. Phyl was of a quite different class from Gwen, just as my own aunt Dee had been different from all her other sisters. Brian's uncle Marcel was an "old school" French hotelier and ran a very good, higher class hotel than average. At this one table then were sitting two of Bournemouth's long standing and much respected hotelier families. Notwithstanding this conjunction of family enterprises, my love for Norma spurred me on to propose to her that very night, writing my proposal on the Dinner Menu with a ball point pen borrowed for the occasion. She responded in the affirmative on the same menu and the pen responsible for those fateful messages has since been framed. When we broke the news, both sets of parents were overcome with sudden sickness caused by the shock that such a thing could have happened with such alarming speed. We had known one another barely two months and here we were wanting to get married. At first, I thought of saving Norman and Maymie a great second expense by joining Phyllis and Brian on their wedding day and making it a double occasion, but that idea was dumped as being impracticable. They were getting married in the February of 1959 at St. Peter's Church just off Bournemouth Square, near Beale's and J.J. Allen's department stores. All their invitations had gone out some time ago and the arrangements now made. We set our date for the 14th. of March at Richmond Hill Congregational Church on the opposite side of The Square and started to make plans accordingly. I had taken Norma to Meaders, a long established jewellers in Boscombe and there we chose an engagement ring. It was a marquise setting of diamonds and Mr. Meader offered us the opportunity to have an emerald he had selected set in the centre. It made a beautiful engagement ring. I had our wedding cake made by Gerry Watcheous, one of the civilian master patissiers at the ACC Training Centre and it was an undoubted three-tiered masterpiece and in its short history, the most difficult part of its life was transporting it safely to Bournemouth for the great occasion. I was delighted to get six army friends to be our Guard of Honour with Keith Hudson in charge and with David Archer, now a very dear friend as my Best Man. David was probably my very closest friend and I was enormously saddened when I learned of his death from a heart attack in the street while running to catch a bus one day when he was working at The War Office. He would have made a fine Director ACC, as did Keith when he was chosen for the job in 1983, collecting his C.B.E. (Commander of the British Empire) from The Queen the following year, as had become the customary award for all Directors of our Corps at that time.

I did not have the customary spectacularly drunken stag night and so woke in good fettle on the morning of the 14th., only to find that it was wet and windy with no hope of the sun breaking through whatsoever. Mother had been to decorate the church the day before and had made silk posies for the ends of each of the pews. She had also made herself a very smart outfit for the occasion while dad hired a tail suit from Moss Bros. and did his best not to look too uncomfortable in it. I had asked my department of The War Office if I might be allowed to wear Ceremonial Dress for the occasion, which would have consisted of a gold and red silk swordbelt, sword with a silver scabbard and epaulettes of plaited gold braid, but was told that I was not of sufficiently high rank. So I had to make do with my best Number One Dress of navy blue barathea, blue and dove grey trousers, blue and dove grey hat, leather Sam Browne and ordinary leather scabbarded sword, which is exactly what our Guard of Honour wore too. The Rolls Royce collected me and David from

Knyveton and delivered us to the church to await the arrival of
Norma and her father. She looked a picture in her pearl white dress
and train with her veil held in place by a pearl bandeau and pendant
pearls across her brow, making her look like a Tudor princess. We
were both so overwhelmed by the occasion that neither of us can
really remember any detail of what happened during the wedding
ceremony, other than The Reverend Trevor Davies giving us some
advice about marriage and its joys - and no doubt some of its pitfalls.
The ceremony over, we assembled on the steps of the church for
photographs in the drizzle and although Norma put on a good show,
her lovely headdress slowly wilted in the rain. Our Reception was at
the Highcliff Hotel, just the other side of The Square, up on the West
Cliff overlooking the sea and at one time had been owned by
Auguste Wilde, the author of "Mixed Grill in Cairo". Our wedding
car got delayed, then took all the wrong roads and so we finished up
being late for our own Reception. Despite our tardy arrival, I asked
David and Keith to hold up the proceedings while Norma and I went
to our booked bedroom to tidy up from the rain and to have a private
celebratory glass or two of champagne. All of this caused us to make
a very late entrance on stage, but when we did, everything, the
buffet, speeches and more photographs seemed to go like clockwork,
thanks to David. When it was all over, we got changed into our
"going away" clothes, found the Riley which David had parked away
somewhere safe and we drove off for our honeymoon in Cornwall
where we had booked to spend a week at the Budock Vean Hotel,
near Frenchman's Creek on the Helford River. On our first night, we
stayed at The Exeter Motel. The next morning was bright and sunny
and we set out in good heart for Budock Vean in its romantic setting
made famous by Daphne DuMaurier's "Frenchman's Creek". During
our time there, we explored one another and parts of Cornwall,
flying over to the Scilly Isles one day in a DeHavilland Rapide and
visiting the main island of St. Mary's where Harold Wilson (Socialist
Prime Minister) used to spend most of his holidays during his
political life. On another day we visited Mevagissey, a quaint little
seaside town and bought a bottle of Premier Cru Meursault from a
wine merchant who opened it for us, then sold us just one large
brandy glass so we could sit on the beach and share the wine, which
was fabulous, inducing us to fall asleep in the sunshine in the shelter
of the sea wall. It was surprising that we got back to the airport just

in time to catch our return flight.

I had applied for and been granted a fairly new married quarter in New Broadlees on the hills on the eastern side of Dover just beyond the castle and this three-bedroomed house was to be our married home for the first eight months. As a captain, I was entitled to the part-time services of a "bat-woman" cum cleaner and Mrs. Pickett was certainly a cleaner. She positively revelled in getting on her knees and with a hairpin pricking out the dust and fluff from between the floorboards. If there was anything which didn't move, it got polished. And poor Norma had to cope with this lady for three mornings a week, while I was out at the office. Not only had she got to come to terms with Mrs. Pickett, but she also had to now become a Cordon Bleu cook overnight to meet my culinary requirements - at least, so she told me in later years. I always thought my food requirements were elegantly simple. I was quite happy to eat baked beans on toast - so long as the toast was cooked to perfection! She got her laugh on me the weekend that Phyllis and Brian came to see us though. On the Sunday morning, I asked Norma where was the leg of lamb we were going to have for lunch only to be reminded that I had not picked it up from the butchers the previous day. I had to set to and make a Quiche Lorraine from scratch from the bits and pieces we had in the fridge to make up for the missing joint.

On the 16th November 1959 I was posted back to the Technical School once more, this time to become the Adjutant, which was a job usually given to those who were destined for greater things. It was a very responsible and demanding job and my Commanding Officer was again Rodney Monk, who had been only recently my Catering Adviser boss. He had been chosen for promotion to Lieutenant Colonel and to command the Technical School of the Training Centre and he in turn had chosen me, with the approval of War Office, to be his Adjutant. I think we continued to be a good team. I was his eyes and ears and voice as far as the running of the School was concerned and in my new position had had the good fortune to take over from David Archer, who was going on to his next move up the ladder by being Staff Officer at our branch of the War Office. In those days of National Service, the incidence of Absence Without Leave was high and for those absentees who persistently offended or stayed away for over a certain length of time, the punishment was a trial by Court Martial, the result of which would almost inevitably be a term of imprisonment in the Military Prison at Colchester, wonderously referred to as "The Glasshouse". As Adjutant, it was always my job to prosecute at the trial and I attended over fifty courts martial in this capacity. The paperwork leading up to the trial had to be 100% accurate and I was lucky to have Staff Sergeant Goodall as my Chief Clerk who had done so many of these cases that he knew exactly what to do, which is just as well. Naturally I had to make a great study of Military Law and quite enjoyed it as a subject. Not all the cases I had to deal with were for absence. Those involving violence and theft were additionally interesting because it brought me into contact with the local Police force and I got to know several of the Hampshire Constabulary quite well. The problems came when I was up against civil lawyers, but in very serious cases, the Military had its own Judge Advocate's Department who would take over the difficult parts.

Our new home in the Aldershot area was known as a 'hiring'. It was a flat in a lovely Queen Anne house in Frimley and called "Tomlinscote", owned by Colonel and Mrs. Walton. Colonel Freddy was an RO2 (Retired Officer 2nd. grade) attached to our ACC Training Battalion in Ramillies Barracks. The house stood in several acres of grounds bounded on three sides by heathland and on the fourth by a quite large lake. Near the lakeside was a mushroom farm from which we could buy an ever ready supply of freshly picked mushrooms at dirt cheap price. The front lawn of the house had a most wonderful display of Rhododendrons and Azaleas which some people said were better than those in one of the historic houses famous for its rhododendrons (and whose name I can't remember). Among our varieties was a glorious one called "Sappho" which had creamy white petals with a mauve eye in the centre and unusually, some of them had a rich scent which in spring and early summer gave the house an atmosphere and all pervading perfume of the archetypal 1920's gentleman's country house. Our flat was on the upper floor and looked out over the front and the rear gardens. In the kitchen was a small coal stove for cooking and which heated just the water and our one and only fridge was a contraption called an "Osocool". This was a small, insulated metal cabinet, the top surface of which had a depression in it, which was partially absorbent and by pouring a small puddle of water into the depression, the cabinet was kept cool as the water evaporated. In winter, we didn't bother pouring the water in as we had no decent working central heating and the water froze anyway! But in summer, it was a joy to be in such beautiful rural surroundings, going for walks round the lake with "Buttons", Norma's cat from Fircroft following us. We also had a pear tree growing up outside our lounge windows which meant we could pick the fruits when they ripened simply by reaching out of the open window. It was here that Norma introduced me to music that was other than just piano music. All my life till then, I had concentrated more or less on piano music and now we listened to Tschaikovsky's Romeo and Juliet, his violin concerto played by David Oistrach and we both sat entranced as we listened to Mahler under the baton of Bruno Walter together for the very first time. It was at Tomlinscote that I swatted for my Promotion Examination for my Majority. So in addition to my very demanding job and being newly married, I also had to find or make time to study such things as Military Law, King's Regulations, Current Affairs and the military campaigns of World War II, covering in particular those from Alamein to the River Sangro in Italy, which took in the Sicilian Invasion along the way. I did a correspondence course with St. Alban's College for my Miltary Law which required a comprehensive knowledge of The Manual of Military Law and of King's Regulations (good foundation for being called to the Bar, perhaps). I passed my exams with flying colours, although when I later attended an Adjutants' Course I again made heavy weather of Tactics. Here I was at the age of 28 now fully qualified for my promotion to Major as soon as I reached the age of 32 or a suitable vacancy arose earlier. Thereafter, promotion was by recommendation and seniority. I had successfully jumped the last fixed hurdle, everything after would depend upon my own individual achievements.

Living as we now were in Surrey, we were that much nearer Bournemouth so could get back to Netheravon to see our mums and dads quite frequently. Phyl's husband, Brian, was not yet in the family business, but was a policeman stationed just outside Blandford. One Saturday we went over to see them in their cottage and at that time they had a little Austin Healey Sprite, a tiny green two seater with frog-eye headlamps and after supper, they said they would come back to Bournemouth with us in their car. By now it was dark and we set off in the lead in our Riley. As we went through the stretch known as Badbury Rings where the road undulates a lot, I thought it would be a bit of fun to put my foot down and see whether we could leave them behind. We hadn't gone far along this switchback bit of road when we crested one of the hills at about eighty miles an hour only to see a car parked on our side at the bottom of the dip, about a hundred yards ahead. The trouble was that another car was coming towards us quite fast and I sensed immediately that we would both arrive at the parked car simultaneously. I braked and on the damp evening road started to skid. Our car then started to slowly tip over and in doing so, it careered up onto the nearside grass verge. Because the verge was about a foot higher than the road surface, the inside edges of our offside wheels were unable to climb the verge and that had the effect of putting us back on an even keel - so thank heaven we stopped rolling over. But now we did climb up onto the grass, still skidding and slithered all the way along a picket fence, taking the thin little posts out of the ground like snapping teeth out of a comb. Fortunately none of them flipped through the windscreen. When we finally came to rest almost into a screen of trees, we were pretty shaken, even more so when Brian and Phyl arrived to tell us that they had been able to see the underneath of our chassis in their headlights as we began to roll over. I know I should not have been so stupid as to race on such a dangerous piece of road, but somehow thought it would be clear. The other silly thing was also that the people in the other car chose an incredibly blind, dangerous place to stop. And it wasn't as though they had conked out - they hadn't, because they drove off when they saw the result of their car parking. Fortunately, all we suffered was a slight dent on the front bumper from our de-fencing operation and a bit of grass sticking out from under the car when we went agricultural motoring!

During the early part of 1960, it again became apparent that we didn't have enough money coming in to maintain our payments on the Riley, despite Norma having a part-time job as secretary to Christopher Buxton, a nascent property developer who later went on to become something of a tycoon in the higher end of the property development market. She had a little moped to go to and fro on and she became very handy with a bent hairpin when it was necessary to clean out the carburettor from time to time. So we put the Riley up for auction at the Frimley Car Mart and it sold instantly for a good price. We cleared our debts and then went looking around for something to replace it and in a garage in Camberley, I found a beautiful black 1.5 litre Alvis saloon dating from about 1947. A very stately affair and in impeccable condition. I knew how good Alvis cars were, partly from knowing the Grey Lady at the School of Infantry some years earlier. It meant we had virtually no H.P. It was no rocket, but would go along very smoothly at about sixty and as long as you overtook with plenty of room to spare. All in all, it was a very sedate motor car. But not the sort of car I really wanted.

After we had had it for a few weeks, we went down to Bournemouth to see the folks and on the Saturday while Norma was with her mother and father, I went for a little drive and found myself going down Pokesdown Hill towards Iford. On the way, I passed Swanmore Motors who dealt in classic sports cars and the like and on their forecourt stood a gleaming ivory white Jaguar XK120 roadster. I simply had to pull in and see it. I fell in love with it - instantly, and asked if I could take it out for a drive. It was immaculate and had only 55,000 miles on the clock. The acceleration was like being in a Titan rocket and the snarl of the six cylinders through the Stage One tuned twin exhaust system was intoxicating. I had to have it. It was marked up at £495. I traded the Alvis in for about £350 and drove it away with my heart beating like a steam-hammer. Norma was thrilled with it too, which was half the battle. Our mutual parents were unsure, although Norman had to give us best when we raced him in his Bentley one day. We even took Buttons, Norma's black cat backwards and forwards between Camberley and Bournemouth at weekends. She didn't seem to mind having the wind blowing onto her in the cockpit. A few weeks later, I got a letter from the new owner of the Alvis asking why I had sold it so soon after having bought it. He wondered whether there was something direly wrong with it that the garage hadn't told him about. But I reassured him that had I not seen the new motor love of my life, I would have still had it.

It was a car to remain in our memories for ever. To thunder along at over a hundred miles and hour with the twin exhausts roaring in your ears was motoring heaven on earth. Not quite on earth, either, when we developed total brake fade at almost 120 mph one night coming back across the Blackbushe Airport road towards

Camberley. Thank heaven there was little or no traffic on the road that night otherwise we might have been killed - or at least killed someone else. I marvelled at how the gearbox stayed in one piece as I crashed down through the gears to slow the car down to a manageable speed as we hurtled into the village of Blackbushe. Never again would we go so quickly. The Mike Hawthorn Tourist Trophy Garage in Farnham told me it was the best 120 they had ever worked on and gave me a quotation for fitting some new-fangled disc brakes that Stirling Moss had just proved to be the safest in the world of motor racing when his little Coventry Climax Cooper out-cornered the bigger Ferraris, Mercedes, Astons, Auto Unions and BRM's at Goodwood. But I couldn't afford them - more's the pity. Later, I learned that brake fade was a notorious feature of the 120's and although the previous owner had had the latest Alfin oversized drums fitted, they still couldn't cope with stopping the car safely at 120 mph. Apart from the brakes, which I accepted, the Jag. gave me only two other spots of bother. One was when I learned the hard way not to accelerate too viciously on a normal road - that merely had the habit of tearing the valves out of the two rear tyres giving me instant twin punctures; the other was to do with the throttle linkage. I used to drive it to the office every day from our hiring in Frimley, often taking Colonel Freddy with me as far as Ramillies. Then at St. Omer, I would park it on the main parade ground in front of the Technical School building where my office was. One day, the accelerator felt sticky and the revs were reluctant to drop back to a normal tickover. I had a look under the bonnet and saw that the linkage was in need of lubrication. I had some graphite grease in a tube and decided that I would do the job after lunch that day. To do the job properly, I had to dismantle the linkage so that I could get the grease into the ball and socket joints. The dismantling was easy. Putting it all back together again was a nightmare. The harder I tried, the greasier I got and the more bloody minded the little rods of brass became. It wasn't until I heard the band strike up somewhere off the square that I realised there was a big parade starting at 2pm and here it was 1.50 and me up to my elbows under the bonnet of the only car left on the parade ground. Fortunately a final, desperate effort did the trick and I managed to drive the jag off the square just as the first platoons started marching onto the parade ground. Then I had to sprint to my office, get myself properly dressed in cap and best boots, putting my gloves on to hide my greasy hands and hurl myself downstairs and walk out of the front doors of the main building all cool, calm and collected to take over the parade from the Regimental Sergeant Major prior to Rodney Monk taking command. A close call was that one. With Colonel Reggie Owens' (the Commandant) office overlooking the parade ground, I felt his eyes were upon me. Sure enough, the following day in the mess he said that he didn't think I should have such an ostentatious car, but Colonel Freddy came to my rescue, saying that it wasn't really any of his business and if I enjoyed it, why shouldn't I have it?

That November gave us a sad insight into the life of a disillusioned old soldier. On Bonfire Night, Colonel Freddy lit a huge bonfire in the garden of Tomlinscote and we and some friends enjoyed potatoes baked in the ashes. Sadly, those ashes contained the remains of his Indian Army uniform which he had decided to burn, so breaking his last links with his old Frontier regiment, the Guides Cavalry. He must have been terribly dejected about something, because he dressed the Guy in his uniform and sadly watched it as the flames consumed it. He never did say what had brought on this fit of depression, but I suspect it might have been something to do with the fact that Tomlinscote was scheduled for demolition to make way for some modern housing estate. Many years later, Norma and I went to see the site of the lovely old house and all we found was a piece of ceramic tiling from our old fireplace half buried in the earth somewhere along what used to be the main drive. As for the gardens and azaleas, these were now covered by modern two-bedroomed rabbit hutches. But Sod's Law was at work even then, and after only one month of ownership brought the news which was to deprive us of all further enjoyment of the Jaguar. We received six month's notice of posting overseas, leaving us with the dilemma of what to do with the car, let alone our household furniture etc. We could either put it up on blocks somewhere for the three years we were to be away, take it to Bournemouth and let somebody drive it to keep it roadworthy or sell it to give us the money to buy another car in our new home - Malaya. Reluctantly we decided to sell it and with only about two weeks to go before our Embarkation Leave was due to start, managed to get £425, a good price, for it which enabled us to clear the remaining HP penalty with a fair bit in hand. Little did we realise what it would eventually be worth had we kept it.

158

CHAPTER TEN

ARMYDAYS V - MALAYA

It's amazing how quickly you can lose track of time. While we were in Frimley, Norma had worked for Christopher Buxton for several months and had got to know the Buxton family quite well. They were the descendants of William Wilberforce, who was instrumental in getting slavery abolished around 1840, and were highly respected people in the community. They were very active Christians, spending much of their time and resources on promoting the Faith, particularly behind the Iron Curtain and in China, both of which countries they had visited when younger. Christopher had taken himself off to Harvard Business School and come back the cleverer for it, becoming a highly successful entrepreneur in the property development field. His speciality was particularly that of restoring historic houses, creating beautiful apartments within them for letting or selling off. "Period and Country Houses" went from strength to strength, as did he, becoming involved in all kinds of charities such as The Abbeyfield Society. He was also connected with a very similar concurrent project to Roger Smith of Highnam Court when he became involved in the development of an opera house within a country house called Compton Verney. One main difference was that his architect was a famous Swede who had won a prestigious international competition for his design for the opera house. Roger's was not quite so famous.

I suppose it must have been fairly early on in 1961 that we became due to go to Malaya. I had to hand over my job as Adjutant, pack up our home and possessions, separating those things we wanted to take out with us into large black wooden packing boxes, labelling them with "Not wanted on voyage", plus our name, port of disembarkation (Singapore) and our final address c/o HQ 63 Gurkha Brigade, Kluang, Malaya. It gave me quite a frisson of excitement knowing that I was to be joining such illustrious soldiers and we were both looking forward to our voyage out to the Far East. We had a succession of vaccinations and injections of all kinds. The vaccination I had in my upper left arm went septic and it wasn't until about eighteen months later in the tropical heat that the septicaemia finally broke through the skin, oozing puss, after which it quite rapidly healed. Our embarkation leave was naturally spent in Bournemouth with our parents before finally catching the train to Southampton Docks where we reported to the Embarkation Officer prior to boarding the S.S. Nevasa, a British India Line passenger ship being used as a troop ship. She was built only six years earlier in 1955 and commissioned as a troopship, quite large, something over 20,000 tons, was fitted with stabilizers and in addition to her own crew (mainly Laskars) could carry about 1000 troops, plus perhaps 150 officers and 250 warrant officers and sergeants. She later went on to become an educational cruise ship before being laid up in the River Fal in the eighties. We were incredibly lucky to go by boat as they were being phased out in favour of going by air. The journey took twenty six days which not only gave us time to acclimatize, but was a very leisurely way to travel, stopping off at various ports along the way, dressing for dinner and so forth. By air, we would have been crammed into our seats for about two days, seeing nothing but clouds and being totally unprepared for the climatic conditions we were about to encounter. Our farewells to our parents were strange. I can't recall saying good bye to Norman or Maymie at all. My mother came to the station with us and gave me a long, passionate kiss on the mouth, rather than a tender kiss of farewell. As far as I can remember, dad couldn't get the time off, so I said goodbye to him at breakfast and I was never to see him again. We climbed the gangway to an open doorway set into the side of the ship where the white hull was bisected by the wide blue-painted stripe of the B.I. (British India) Line. Carrying our hand luggage, we were allocated our cabin and I was told to report for an officers' briefing at a certain time. Our cabin was not exactly over-large, but was quite pleasant with built-in furniture and a large porthole. The officers' dining room was in fact the first class restaurant and was extremely well laid out and comfortable, with tables for fours, sixes and eights with The Captain's Table for ten taking pride of place. The ship was like a floating industrial estate, having its own laundry, printing works, kitchens (galleys), freezer plant, refrigeration, hospital, tailors shop, chemist shop and so forth. So once we set sail, everything that we needed done was done on board. Naturally, all the drink was duty free, which was also a bonus.

As instructed, I reported for briefing to the Ship Commandant and was immediately made Ship Catering Officer. I didn't actually have that much to do, as the Purser's department looked after all the provisioning of the ship and the working out of the menus and the cooking. My responsibility was really to make sure that everyone on board (except the crew) was well catered for and this meant being present in the various messes from time to time. I was allowed to go into the galleys and stores, which were otherwise out of bounds to everybody else and I found the galleys fascinating, especially during heavy weather, when the large cooking pots would slither around on the stoves, only arrested at the extremities by a high bar like a metal fence which ran around all the cooking stoves. I can't recall whether these were only raised during rough weather, but I expect so as it might have been a bit of a nuisance during other circumstances. Almost imperceptibly, we slipped from our mooring at Southampton and were heading out into Southampton Water in the early evening before we realised we had left port. We had been busy getting our cabin sorted out and unpacking our clothes which were to last us the next four weeks. As it was growing dusk, we passed the twinkling lights of the Isle of Wight and Bournemouth and headed out for Cape Finnisterre off the western coast of Portugal in quite calm conditions. On deck, the last of the English weather was overcast and chilly, so as the lights faded, we went back below to our cabin to prepare for our first dinner on board. Our route was to take us down the west coast of the Iberian peninsular, through the Straits of Gibraltar and into the Mediterranean, out of the far end of the Med. via the Suez Canal and into the Red Sea, past Aden and on to Somalia. From there, on across the Arabian Sea round the southern tip of India and up to Ceylon. From Ceylon, across the Bay of Bengal, past the Nicobar Islands and the northern tip of Sumatra to the tiny island of Penang off the north western coast of Malaya, then for the final 500 mile journey down the west coast of Malaya to Singapore.

Whether we dressed for dinner on that first night or not, I can't remember. But certainly every night thereafter, we did, either in full mess uniform or DJ and it wasn't until we got well into the tropical waters of the Red Sea that the order was finally given for us to dress in tropical dress at night. Our hot barathea was exchanged for much cooler sharkskin and the ladies were no doubt thankful to be able to dress in shorter cotton dresses. During the daytime, we could wear anything we liked, so this meant that shorts and sandals were the most favoured clothes. Shirts in the dining room for lunch had to be smart with the sleeves rolled to the regulation height, observing the traditional Military "shirtsleeve order". We slowly began to find our way round the ship. Norma had at least been on the French liner "Normandie" and the Italian cruise ship "Homeric" when she went to Canada, whereas I could only boast of a day trip on a paddle steamer from Bournemouth Pier to the Isle of Wight and a four berth cabin cruiser on the Norfolk broads.

The often dreaded journey through the Bay of Biscay passed without incident and by the time we got to Gibraltar, it was beautifully warm and sunny and passing through the Straits we could see Cadiz on our left and Tangiers and the Atlas mountains on our right and our first view of The Rock was duly impressive. We made a short stop at Tripoli (this was several years before Colonel Gaddafi became dictator, declaring the country an Islamic Republic) for fuel and water and then went on past Alexandria to Port Said where we dropped anchor to take on more supplies and wait for other ships to join us to make up a convoy to go through the Suez Canal. As I mentioned earlier, in the October of 1956, Colonel Gamal Abdul Nasser, the President of Egypt decided that he would nationalize the Suez Canal and charge every nation using it a toll for doing so. Israel, who had a long term hate relationship with Egypt, France who had a major interest in The Canal (De Lesseps had built it in the late 1800's) and Britain as perhaps the major user decided they would not put up with this and chose to clandestinely provoke an Israeli invasion of Egypt rather than see the Canal come under solely Egyptian control. France and Britain were then supposedly to go to war against Egypt in defence of Israel. While the Israelis advanced by land, Britain and France mounted an airborne invasion. Nasser's first action had been to block the Canal with old sunken shipping. The whole episode became known as "The Suez Campaign", for which I had been on standby. I had been sent home on leave to await a telegram which would instruct me where and when to report. At the time, I didn't know where I was likely to go, until the Suez invasion was launched. Later, I found out that I was intended to go to Kano in Nigeria. Kano was to be used as a staging post for reinforcements coming up to Egypt from the south. But after only a

162

few days, the Americans really leaned on our Government and we had to find some excuse, together with the French for calling the invasion off, leaving Israel to settle her own differences with Colonel Nasser. Now here we were actually about to see the battle site for ourselves from the safety of our ship. By now, the weather was really hot both by day and by night and as we were not yet into tropical dress, our formal uniforms were getting rather uncomfortable at dinnertimes.

Almost as soon as the anchor chains had stopped rumbling out, the bumboats came flocking round, with traders offering to sell us practically anything and everything, but all at ridiculously inflated prices. They swarmed up the gangways like a horde of marauding pirates, jabbering away in Arabic or fractured Eengleesh. Everyone was expected to barter. I had badly scratched the glass in my wristwatch and asked how much for a replacement. The price started at about five pounds and finished at about five shillings. We were treated to a quite astonishing show of magic by a "Gully-gully Man" whose catchphrase was 'Look, nudding in ma hent, nudding up ma sliv'. He then produced the most amazing number of articles seemingly out of thin air, including several items of personal belongings of the people standing watching him. How he had relieved them of their watches, wallets, earrings, combs, handkerchiefs without them feeling was a tribute to his skills as a pickpocket, let alone a conjuror. That night, with Port Said lit up, and standing on deck in the balmy tropical air drinks in hand, we looked across the shimmering water to see the huge illuminated cut-out advertising figure of the eponymous Johnny Walker (of whisky fame) striding across the rooftops of the main hotel, and enjoyed being tourists at the expense of HM Government. Meanwhile, back down below, our cabin was being invaded by seemingly millions of tiny red flying insects. When we opened the cabin door to go to bed, we were surrounded by clouds of these little bugs which had settled everywhere, including our beds. They had come in through the open porthole and we now had to spend ages swatting them with towels, killing them in vast numbers and smearing their red body juice all over the cabin and ourselves before being able to get into bed. If this was what cruising in the tropics was going to be like, we were singularly unimpressed! Although the Suez war had been over four or five years by now, little progress had been made in clearing away

Nasser's sunken boats. This meant that shipping had to form up into convoys to be led through the maze of wrecks by a skilled pilot, who also navigated us through the narrows of the Canal into the Bitter Lakes, which were at about the halfway point. The Canal operated on a "one-way system", so The Lakes were used as a meeting place for convoys to pass one another in opposite directions. Once in the actual canal passage, ships as large as the Nevasa pretty nearly filled it, with precious little room to spare on either side and because of the danger of erosion, the speed of the ships had to be dead slow. Eventually, we arrived at Port Tewfik at the southern end, which is where I took one of my favourite photographs of a small trading dhow with its triangular lateen sail. How I wish I had had the good fortune to have a zoom lens.

   We left Tewfik and sailed into the blazing Arabian heat of the Red Sea and it was now that we were told over the public address system that we would have to lose a day due to berthing delays at Aden. So the message from the bridge to the engine room was "dead slow". It was also now that the captain decided it would be a good time for his officers to give us a tour of the ship - for something to do and pass the time. The conducted tours were great - until it came to visiting the engine room. I had become fairly accustomed to the exceptional temperatures of hotel kitchens such as at The Cumberland where temperatures would climb to over 100 degrees every day, so was not unduly affected. Not so some of the ladies, who passed out, having to be carried to any shady part of the deck where they could recover. Some of the men didn't do so well either! It was decided that another good way of passing the time would be by having shooting practice at balloons released over the stern of the ship.

   At last we arrived at Aden. An ochre-coloured bleak, barren, jagged and mountainous piece of country and a more depressing, desolate place would be hard to imagine. This place was hot, really hot and its saving grace was that it was absolutely bone dry with hardly any humidity at all, which made it just about tolerable for the few hours we were ashore. A few years later, watching Peter O'Toole as Lawrence crossing "The Forbidden Land", I was reminded of conditions in Aden. The whole area had been volcanic aeons ago and the capital was, suitably enough, called "Crater". Although it looked so inhospitable, the walls of the rockfaces were

164

pitted with Troglodite caves, all inhabited. Aden was an Entrepôt and Duty Free port. We had changed some money into local currency and gone off on an expedition with a Gurkha officer and his wife who had been there before and knew the ropes. We made for the camera shop area, little more than a succession of holes in the rock with steel link shutters and canvas awnings to keep the sun off the goods on display. We haggled our way through the market and I finished up with a Sankyo Zoom 8 cine camera with zoom lens and some film. Both the trader and I were happy with our transaction, which took quite a long time to agree upon, with our friend chipping in his bit from time to time to lower the price even more. With the first fifty foot of film loaded, we set off back to the docks where I later discovered when we had the film developed, that I had not quite got my panning speeds quite right, having zipped from one end of the Nevasa to the other in one quick roller-coaster shot. I filmed my way round the ship as we proceeded through the Arabian Sea, catching glimpses of flying fish as they leapt and fluttered their way across the waves like huge dragonflies.

One morning at breakfast, a couple of days out from Aden, the public address announced that we were approaching a typhoon and we had about half an hour to get to our cabins and secure all movable objects, then proceed to an area of the ship where we felt we would be most comfortable. This was followed by the now familiar Lascar call for "all hands on deck" which sounded like "Angle, jangle, peecha jay sore-eye". Soon, the deck crew were scurrying round securing loose bits and pieces and closing various hatches and doors. Out on deck, I could detect nothing untoward, although I did spot what I thought was a bit of mist on the horizon, but that was quite a long way off. Gradually the breeze stiffened into a wind which grew stronger and stronger with every passing minute. The delicate tracery of mist I had seen was now becoming a swirling mass of steaming, heaving water, with the waves getting higher and steeper. The order came for the stabilizers to be run out and these had the immediate effect of calming the corkscrewing motion of the ship. But before long, conditions worsened still more, combining huge waves and a howling, searing, hot wind which whipped the tops off them, slamming them straight into the ship from all directions. We bucked and ploughed, rolled and pitched our way through this maelstrom, with the stabilizers doing their best to

165

counteract the lurching of the ship and as we rolled, I could catch glimpses through the blue-green water of them paddling away below, twisting and turning in their gyro-controlled efforts to hold us steady. It was an amazing experience which simultaneously held me enthralled, excited and apprehensive. Some years later I felt really sorry for the characters in the disaster movie "The Poseidon Adventure" in which a cruise ship is hit by a tsunami. After about an hour, the wind dropped, the sea calmed and we sailed out of the veil of mistiness into the full, brassy glare of the sun. During the whole of this time, Norma had found herself a seat midships where theoretically, she would experience the minimum of movement. The humid wind and watery sun had nevertheless given her an instant tan, the depth of which a Tamil would have been proud of. She could have spoken Indian and got away with being a Ranee. As the days passed, her darkened skin began to flake off like strips of brown clingfilm.

A very hot journey across the Arabian Sea brought us to our next port of call, Ceylon, where we docked at the capital, Colombo. This was quite different from anything we had seen before. Everywhere was so green and the main streets were wide and lined with palm trees which provided lovely patches of shade, lots of beautiful shops with interesting window displays, rickshaws and trishaws mixed up with cars and buses, Indian traders bustling everywhere. We went ashore with more of our precious money in local currency and spent some time window shopping. Foods of all kinds spilled out onto the pavements in colourful displays of reds, yellows, greens and mauves in every conceivable shade. Clothing and materials, saris in their brilliant hues and above all, jewellery greeted shoppers everywhere. Gold, filligree silverwork and gemstones, flashing rubies, diamonds emeralds and sapphires beckoned from numerous jewellers' shop windows. It seemed that all the plunder of the Spanish Main was on offer. We were seduced into stepping into one such shop as a result of seeing a huge topaz on display, stepping out, ten minutes of haggling later, with it and a considerably thinner wallet. It was the sort of impulse buy that overtakes you once or twice in a lifetime and thirty five years later I can still see us going back out onto the pavement into the heat and palm trees, thrilled with our acquisition. I surprised Norma later on when I took it to Singapore one time and had it mounted in a gold frame, capable of being worn as either a brooch or a pendant on a necklace. I thought about having it also made so it could be worn as a ring, but for some reason this never happened. While we bought it as a topaz, we have since had it valued and it is now described as a citrine, worth £500-750, which must be ten times what we paid for it all that time ago.

Back on board it was "Angle, jangle, etc." and after crossing the Bay of Bengal, we arrived at Penang a few days later. Penang is an island about the same size as the Isle of Wight, lying off the top-most part of the north-west coast of the Malay peninsular. Its old Colonial history is clear to see from the architecture and like Colombo, it is busy, clean and teeming with Chinese, Malays and Indians who all seemed to intermingle quite happily. As with the mainland, we were to find that it was the Chinese and Indians who were the clever traders, while the Malays tended to sit around watching the grass grow. There were restaurants everywhere, including down on the beaches among the palm trees. It was a tropical island par excellence and very beautiful and nowadays, this could be said to be either its making or its downfall, being one of the major tourist spots in the Far East. No doubt the "Raffles" type of Colonial hotels have all disappeared in favour of high-rise tower blocks and the dug-out canoes with outriggers have given way to high powered luxury cruisers. We spent the afternoon and evening on the island and the next morning took on a fresh contingent of Gurkhas who were moving out to Hong Kong, the Nevasa's final destination. When they and their equipment were safely aboard, we cast off for the final leg of the journey down the west coast to Singapore.

As we approached it through "The Roads", Singapore was all lit up for the evening, looking like a necklace of diamonds twinkling on the horizon and we dropped anchor a mile or two out in The Roads to wait overnight for our berth to become vacant the next morning. The evening air was oppressively humid and the offshore breeze brought with it all the smells which over the next two or more years we were later to associate with "The Tropics". We packed ready for disembarkation and went to bed on board for the last time. Next morning, we found ourselves moored alongside rows and rows of "Godowns" or warehouses with Chinese dockworkers carrying huge bundles at each end of their simple springy bamboo yokes across their shoulders, the bundles gently bouncing in rhythm to their steps as they padded along in their vests, shorts and flip-flops and of course, their conical straw hats. The heavier items of commerce were being craned over the side into waiting lorries to go off to the warehouses. As we watched, our noses were assaulted by the myriad new smells. Heavy, solid bundles of cured raw rubber smelling of burnt elastic bands, the fetid stink of durian fruits and nail varnish smell of bananas straight from the trees and the sweet, syrupy tang of freshly harvested pineapples piled high in the backs of open lorries, already warming up in the morning sun. Looking down from the rails, I spotted Lieutenant Colonel George Anderson, the Chief Catering Adviser Far East Land Forces and with him was none other than Jumbo Williams, my erstwhile Adjutant from six years earlier, whom I could have done without! He was the Catering Adviser to the 17th. Gurkha Division and once again, my new immediate boss. We were to spend the night with George Anderson and his wife who made us very comfortable in their large house and Jumbo stayed too. For the rest of that day we were given a whirlwind tour of Singapore by George, including his own ACC HQ which was in Nee Soon, where the Far East Cookery Instructional Centre was based and where I met several other ACC people I knew. We were to set off the following day for Kluang where we were to be based with the HQ of 63 Brigade of the 17th. Gurkha Division.

George's quarters were on high ground and the following morning we woke early and looking down out of the bedroom windows were entranced to see a delicate mist enveloping everywhere, except that poking through the top surface of the white veil, were the tops of coconut palms and other tropical trees. This was, of course, a daily phenomenon due to the high humidity. As soon as the sun rose into the sky, which, being Equatorial it did very quickly, the mist evaporated, leaving behind just a very hot, humid atmosphere which was guaranteed to have you sweating within minutes. We breakfasted on the verandah with cereals and fresh fruits including not only pineapple, which we had eaten in England, but also a selection of mangoes, mangosteens, papaya with fresh lime, rambutans and lychees, all of which were new to us. Then Tony Roe arrived in a staff car in which he was going to accompany us back up-country almost a hundred miles to Kluang where I was to be based at 63 Brigade Headquarters. He had been accompanied by a small lorry driven by two Gurkhas who were now down at the docks loading our heavy baggage with instructions to return to Kluang independently, leaving us to bring just our hand luggage in the car. The plan was that I was to spend the next three weeks or so taking over my area from Tony before he left to return to U.K.

By now it was about mid-morning and before leaving for Kluang, Tony thought it would be a good idea if we visited the main shopping area of Singapore so we could buy some extra lightweight clothes. From an Indian tailor, I ordered a pale grey made-to-measure suit with two pairs of trousers and was told it would be ready that afternoon if Sahib cared to call back in two or three hours. Tony advised that I should have my olive green uniforms made by the Gurkha military tailor in Kluang, as apart from anything else, such as getting the necessary style right, he would be on the spot in case any alterations were needed. So after our shopping session and return to the tailors for my suit, we set out for our novel drive to Kluang, well up towards the northern border of Johore State. We crossed The Causeway which separates Singapore from the Malay peninsular, passed through Malay Customs and for the first time set foot in our new home country - at least for the next two or three years. The main road north took us past the Sultan of Johore's palace and out of Johore town into the country where the road surface became just solid-packed red laterite, a crystalline gritty earth with very deep monsoon ditches on either side. We passed through plantation after plantation with Chinese peasant workers in their conical straw hats busily cutting and scraping new sap channels round the trunks of the rubber trees and collecting the latex in cups which when full were transferred to five gallon drums which they suspended from their bamboo shoulder poles. Others, further on were cutting ripe pineapples, coconuts or palm oil seeds. The Malays shunned the conical hats, preferring to wear a variety of caps and cast-off army jungle hats, or nothing at all on their heads. I discovered later that the more elevated social strata of Malayan male society wore handsome fore-and-aft caps of velvet called 'songhok' (I wish I had bought one as a memento). These, according to rank, could be very elaborate affairs with gold braiding round them or formed into exquisite patterns. After about an hour of this, we saw ahead of us what looked like a small army lorry up-ended in the monsoon drain and as we got closer saw that it was all our luggage, with the driver and his mate standing forlornly beside the wreck, waiting for help to arrive - from somewhere – heaven only knows where as they had no means of communication with the outside world. Tony told them not to leave the lorry unattended. He would arrange for a relief vehicle to be sent from Kluang for the luggage and a breakdown vehicle to take care of the damaged lorry. Amazingly enough, when we did finally unpack our belongings some weeks later, the fact that we found nothing broken was testament as to how well we had packed it before leaving Frimley.

We had already made arrangements to stay with Meg and Mike Parrish, whom we had known during our days at Tomlinscote. Mike was a captain in the Medical Corps, specialising in paediatrics and was now attached to the British Military Hospital in Kluang. We could have stayed at the local Government Rest House overlooking the golf course, but decided to stick with the original plan of staying with Meg and Mike - which as it turned out, was not such a good idea after all. With their two little girls to look after, their daily life was quite busy enough, let alone having us both getting in the way, especially when it came to bathing or showering. I felt Mike's temper getting shorter and shorter and the more we did to try to help, the worse matters became. One evening, Norma volunteered to help get supper ready by cutting up some fresh chillies and got her fingers well soaked in hot chilli juice. The effect was as though she had held them in a flame and the pain was excruciating for her. Mike, with just enough good grace, provided her with a bowl of cold water with some ice cubes in it suggesting she sat with her hand immersed in the cold water for the next few hours. Eventually, and none too soon as far as we were concerned, a hiring became free just down the road a little and so after about four weeks, we moved into a very nice, furnished, two bedroomed bungalow with front and back gardens and car-port. In the front garden was a coarse lawn (all grass in the tropics is coarse, unless specially sown lawn seed is used, such as for the greens on the golf courses) bordered by a variety of local shrubs including Rose of Sharon, the blooms of which were white in the mornings and by evening had turned a beautiful soft pink; frangipani which gave off an intense, heady vanilla perfume in the calm of evening; poinsettias with their red leaves; crotons with their yellow blade shaped leaves (and nicknamed "Mother-in-Law's tongue") and pinky-mauve bougainvillea along the fencing. The Rose of Sharon made a fascinating floral table decoration in the evenings, as when picked in the morning while still pure white, they could be put into a plastic bag in the fridge until the evening when they would make a centrepiece which slowly changed from white to pink in a period of about two hours. On the verandah we had a large pot with a Keng Wha plant which bloomed only one day a year and which the Chinese valued for its healing properties, and other pots containing Moonflowers, a heavenly scented climber of the columbine family, but which bloomed only in the early evening. It was possible to actually watch its umbrella-like bloom open in the time it took to drink a large gin and tonic! In the back garden, was a papaya tree which provided us with plenty of fruit for breakfast.

I went to the Public Works Office in town and got us an amah to help with the washing and housekeeping and a kebun to do the gardening. These were all part of our entitlement as married officers. Our Chinese amah's proper name was Ah Phoon, but she asked us to call her Ah Moon for some reason I never did manage to discover. She was in her middle twenties and number two wife of a local Straits Chinese Police officer who lived in a kampong (native village) just outside Kluang town. She was a wonderful help to Norma in getting the house sorted out, although she perhaps had difficulty in understanding why Norma wanted to DO SOMETHING, like cooking etc. in her own home unlike many of the other Memsahibs who were content to spend their time at "the club" or swimming pool. Although she did all our washing in cold water in the little washroom out the back of the bungalow, everything was spotlessly clean, impeccably laundered, including my new olive greens, which were starched and ironed to within an inch of their lives. Often, thanks to the incredibly high humidity, I had to change into a set of fresh clothing in the afternoons, especially if I had been sitting for a long time in a car, which even with the windows open became like mobile ovens. Ah Moon was lucky. She lived with the rest of her family including number one wife, all the children and grandparents in a proper house her husband actually owned, just out on the road to Malacca. It was a typical wooden house built on stilts on a patch of land rescued from the jungle. Strictly speaking, her husband couldn't actually own any land as a Straits Chinese until he had been resident in Malaya for twenty years. But he was different from all the others. Whether it was his

171

luck or business acumen, I don't know, but he had bought a tiny old 1930-something Austin Seven and one day, driving through Johore town, he had been spotted by one of the Sultan's sons who was dotty about old cars. He had Ah Moon's husband stopped by the police and brought to the palace where the prince had told him he wanted the car and would buy it from him. After the usual haggling, which might well have been royally one sided, Ah Moon's husband struck a deal which enabled him to become a landowner much more quickly than waiting for the twenty year period, giving him both some cash and a plot of land on which to build his house in Kluang.

We settled into our new bungalow fairly quickly. It was in a quiet cul-de-sac just off the main road which ran from Singapore right up north to the Burmese border and followed almost parallel alongside the single line railway through the jungle. For most of its distance, whenever it rained the dull red crystal-like laterite earth road surface bled a rich orange custard into the monsoon drains which were anything up to four feet deep - and very necessary if the road was not to be totally flooded. From our number 7 Jalan Ria, we could look out to Bukit Lambak, our local mini-mountain, so called because of its silhouette which resembled the outstretched wings of a flying fox, the indigenous fruit eating bat. These bats were quite large, with a wingspan of perhaps two or more feet and one of their favourite perches were the telegraph lines alongside the road, from which they would hang head downwards during the daytime. Sometimes, they would die while hanging there, becoming first like old tattered umbrellas, then skeletons which would eventually drop off when sufficiently decayed. At the summit of Bukit Lambak at a height of about a thousand feet, was a radio relay station and from up on the top, we could look out over hundreds of square miles of jungle and plantations. Every evening we heard the chorus of thousands of cicadas in the surrounding rubber plantation. Cicadas live for anything up to seventeen years underground and when they finally do emerge, by inflating and deflating their lower body rapidly create a clicking sound which when magnified by the many thousands of insects makes an incredibly noisy rasping screech. Much more musical was the morning chorus of bul-buls, a cousin of the sparrow family, but unlike our domestic sparrow is a wonderful singer, its bell-like melodies rivalling the nightingale, blackbird or song thrush.

My office at Garrison HQ was about a mile from home and each day I passed the very hilly little nine hole golf course, carved out of the jungle by a group of very determined planters several years earlier and of which I later became a member. Then followed the Kluang Club itself, a rambling colonial style clubhouse in the style of Somerset Maugham, with equally Somerset Maugham type characters drinking their "minim (small) whisky, panjang (large) sodas". Alongside the clubhouse were tennis courts and behind it were quite good squash and badminton courts. Inside, the bar and lounge took up most of the space and the walls were adorned with a variety of trophies including heads of "sladang", the ferocious wild jungle buffalo as well as the almost obligatory heads of tigers and other lesser jungle animals. Kluang town was a very busy little place with the shops and stalls mostly being run by Indians or Chinese. The Malays were quite lazy as businessmen. In fact, only a few years earlier, the Government had tried to improve the Malay status by clearing areas of jungle and giving them to pure Malays on condition that they farmed them. All that happened was that within a year, most areas had reverted to jungle. On the far side of the town was the Kluang airport, a military landing strip with a small clubhouse and control tower. The main strip was very long and able to take the Hercules transporters, the largest of military supply planes. Talking to one of the pilots I asked what it was like flying one of these giants, only to be told that it "was like driving a block of flats while looking out of the lavatory window". Apart from a few lessons from a local Indian driving instructor, I taught Norma to drive using the airstrip as our "main road". At least, she couldn't come to any harm on such a large area. Brigade HQ was a wooden hutted complex of buildings a little way past the airport. More of that later. On my staff, I had the services of Peter Nuttall, not only a jolly, rotund, Pickwickian Warrant Officer Supervisory Travelling Instructor whom I could send to any unit I felt needed a bit of help, but a brilliant cook; plus an Indian Staff Sergeant by the name of Baskaran Shankar. Baskaran seemed to make it his periodic mission to arrive at the office with a brown paper bag of fresh curry powder, made by his wife squatting on her hunkers grinding the spices on a flat stone and which smelt and tasted divine. Quite unlike any curry powder I have had elsewhere anytime since.

    The Garrison Quartermaster turned out to be an old colleague of mine from Aldershot and one day, soon after our arrival, he asked me if I played golf and duly recommended me for membership of the Kluang Golf Club. On my next visit to Singapore, I bought myself a set of clubs and some very comfortable lightweight spiked shoes and started to practise. It wasn't long before I was joining in the tournaments. As we were also now members of The Kluang Club itself, Norma was able to join some of the other wives to play tennis while I was on the course. Soon I was playing four rounds a week and got to know all the members, civilian planters as well as the military who were mostly officers from the Garrison. All this playing with some practise thrown in for good measure, my handicap was coming down and quite quickly became a respectable sixteen. Most of the planters had lived through the terrorist days of the mid-fifties, when General Sir Gerald Templar was GOC of Malaya. The bandits had known whenever it was pay day on the plantations and often chose those days to carry out their raids, killing as many tappers as possible and quite often the planter and his family before making off with the money. Thanks to General Templar, this was just about all over by the time Norma and I got to Malaya, so everyone was in a more peaceful frame of mind. The planters' conversation now tended towards what they were going to do in retirement with one of the oldest declaring he was going to retire to the Seychelles and sit on the beach all day long with "bloody great gins and tonics and pretty girls." By about 1962, the Malays were getting quite keen on independence, introducing a "Speak Malay day" once a week. This meant you were buggered if you had to ask a telephone operator to get you a number you didn't know. I was having enough trouble trying to pick up Gurkhali, let alone Malay as well.

The ninth hole of our little course was built high up on the hillside looking towards the clubhouse and running diagonally across the fairway was an incredibly deep concrete lined monsoon drain needing a bridge to cross it and which acted as a magnet for every reasonably long hitter in the club. With monotonous regularity good drives would gently arc through the air and either the first or second bounce would land in the drain, ricocheting straight out again. Quite often, if the ball struck at exactly the right angle, it would bounce back almost a hundred yards towards the tee. Unless you got it right, the results would have been the same if you had just nudged the ball over the front edge of the tee and let gravity do the rest. The hillside was so steep that climbing puffing up to the tee invariably caused "Snakey" Donald to curse the geography.

'I hate this hole - bloody cardiac heights! Be glad when I've had enough of golf. So much for my retirement to the Seychelles - if I last that long. I want my dusky
maidens to fan me for pleasure not while I'm recovering from a heart attack!'

I hope he made it.

One day, it was announced that the King of Malaya was paying us a visit for a game of golf. For no other reason. He just felt like seeing part of his domaine and receiving some local hospitality in the process. He was a tubby gentleman with a smooth olivey-brown face which was almost nearly always smiling. Our Club Captain, John Allen, a major in the Gurkha Engineers, organised a match in which the King could take part. John had to make the correct political choices of players, of course. He was a very good player and controlled the game so well that as they came to the last hole, the King and his partner were on level score with John and his partner. John contrived to miss a ridiculously short putt which allowed the King to make the winning stroke, which pleased his majesty enormously of course.

Apart from Ah Moon, our amah, we also acquired the services of a "kebun" (gardener). Batu worked for us part-time. He was a lithe, handsome, near black-skinned Tamil. Although we had no lawn mower (hardly anyone did), Batu was brilliant with the small scythe which he would whirl round and round, skimming the grass with the blade, trimming it to just the right height. He could keep this up for ages, slowly walking barefoot up and down the front and back lawns, almost without a break - and in that cloying heat, too. He also cleaned the car every week and made a perfect job of it. We had bought the car from the couple who were moving out of the bungalow to return to UK and fortunately, although it was more than I had wanted to spend, he had agreed to me paying for it over an extended period. So we now became the proud owners of a duck egg blue Sunbeam Rapier, with overdrive and with windows that all wound right down, giving the car all the attributes of either a proper saloon, or a hard topped sports car. It was perfect for the climate. The one problem was that the electric overdrive unit had never been properly designed for use in the tropics. Every now and again, because of the humidity, it would fail and remarkably enough, the main agents in Singapore, (The Singapore Carriage and Wagon Company) (there's a colonial enough name for you) would fit a new one free of charge, as the failed one was always within its own warranty!

I spent the first three or four weeks taking over my area from Tony Roe who I knew very well from Aldershot. We had both been on holiday together in Cornwall a few years earlier when we were junior subalterns. His father had bought him a brand new MG TD for his birthday and that summer we had gone away in it to stay on a farm near Helford. Tony's grandfather who had served "under sail" in his younger days had a beautiful little pink-washed cottage at Gillan Creek not far away and we visited him during the two weeks to hear some of his stories of what the old sailing ships had been like, including his various passages round the Horn. We shared that two weeks on the farm with the young Tollemache family (of brewing fame) who were also there with their children. The weather was perfect and it was so new to me to wake in the mornings to the accompaniment of all the farmyard noises, chickens clucking as they pecked over the grass and cows gently mooing as they went for milking. We borrowed a small motor boat with an inboard engine and went mackerel fishing off The Manacles, a dangerous reef of rocks about a half-mile or so off the coast. While we were out, a south-westerly squall blew up quite suddenly and we found ourselves drifting towards the rocks. By the time we got the engine going, we were dangerously close to them and the sea had roughened up a lot with eight foot waves threatening to break over the boat. We managed to make very slow progress back to Gillan Creek, soaked to the skin, but with a whole load of mackerel, most of which we had to give away. That night, in the local pub, we heard that the Coastguard had been alerted because a small boat had been spotted in difficulties off the Manacles earlier that day. We hoped we hadn't put too many people to too much trouble.

Apart from a visit to Divisional HQ to pay our respects to Jumbo Williams, our ACC boss, Tony was left to arrange the handover as we saw fit. The territory I would have to cover was quite vast, taking in just about the whole of the bottom third of the Malay peninsular, plus those units of 63 Brigade which were stationed on Singapore island itself. Altogether, I was nominally responsible for about thirty or so mixed units which between them comprised not only Gurkhas, but Chinese and Malay, Indian and Commonwealth such as Australians and New Zealanders, as well as British. My philosophy soon became "if there ain't a problem, don't fix it." It was pointless trying to get nationals to change their way of doing things if what you wanted them to do was no better than the way they were already doing it. Tony hadn't quite seen it this way and had spent a lot of time getting some of the Gurkha units to prepare their food in our more cultured, European way, such as filleting and boning meat and fish before cooking it. An example of his "missionary zeal" occurred during his handover. We were going to see one of the Gurkha Army Service Corps units up country and our journey took us through mile after mile of rubber plantations (several sporting the name "Bata", the name of a well known British shoe manufacturer). We also passed areas where countless acres had been felled and burned to make way for new rubber trees to be planted as saplings. The old trees were never cut right down low to the earth, so the scene was similar to those often seen of the French countryside after a period of bombardment during World War I with thousands of blackened stumps sticking six feet or more out of equally blackened earth. Some were still wreathed in smoke, curling up into the heavy moist atmosphere and everywhere that smell of damp burnt wood. Eventually the rubber estates gave way to oil plantations with the palmoil trees resembling the tops of huge pineapples growing in straight lines for mile after mile, each tree bearing its crop of palmoil kernels clustered between its yellowy-green fronds. Eventually, we reached an area of pineapple plantations. At ground level, the plants looked like big brother versions of the little tuft of spikey leaves which grow at the top of each fruit. The fruits themselves grew at the ends of long, coarse stalks. Everywhere was dull green, as this local variety of pineapple produced dark green fruits with a most wonderful flavour from the luscious near-white flesh.

We arrived at the unit, saw the Adjutant and went off to the cookhouse. Tony said how pleased he was with this particular unit, as the Gurkha cook sergeant really had tried very hard to put into practise this new-fangled way of cooking. As we stepped into the cookhouse, a cook spotted us and shouted "British Sahib". Everyone in the kitchen froze on the spot. The sergeant did a smart turn towards us and saluted. Tony asked him how things were going (in English, with the odd word of Gurkhali thrown in here and there) and was told things were fine. The main ration for the day was fish and the cooks were preparing it the way Sahib had shown them. The trouble was that sahib had shown them on ikan tinggeri, a fish about the size of a salmon, whereas today's ration was ikan merau which resembled sardines. The two hours of preparation had so far produced a small heap of spines and bones which would just about fill a respectable 7lb jam tin and the cooks were expected to then make a stock from these before getting down to the real job of cooking about a hundredweight of rice and curry for the main meal of the day - enough to feed three or four hundred hungry men. Unless they went back to their old ways of cooking everything on the bone, there was no way they would be ready in time on that day. I vowed then and there to myself that I certainly wouldn't interfere in traditional ways of doing things. If, during eating, they were content to have to pick out the bones and fragments of them if they had chopped through them, who was I to change things. After all, they had been making curry for centuries so should know how to go about things by now. Tradition required them to behead a beast (in one clean chop while it was still alive), gut and skin it and chop it up into bits for cooking, including all the bones. It was as simple as that. They preferred sucking the bones and spitting them out rather than have them removed in advance. Their cooking equipment was equally simple. If you imagine a Chinese wok and multiply its size by about ten to the size of a small round fishpond, that's it. That is all they use. That and a wooden lid. Their complete daily diet is curry for breakfast at about 6.30am and curry for lunch at about 3pm. Only the main ingredients altered, ranging between fish, chicken, goat or jutkha (carcases ready beheaded in the correct religious way) mutton and beef or buffalo. Side dishes were always timbals of dhal (curried lentils).

Once I had taken over from Tony, I allowed the traditional methods to creep back and the resulting quiet life was very welcome. From time to time, I took Norma with me when visiting units, as much as anything to get her out of the bungalow and see something of the countryside. Actually, as south Malaya is fairly flat, there was very little to see by way of changing scenery as it was either plantations, paddy fields of rice or jungle. Only the villages (kampongs) varied and then only between mainly Malay or mainly Chinese, dependent upon the predominant inhabitants. The two most interesting places were Malacca in the north west of my area which was strongly influenced by the Dutch settlers and which showed in the architecture, and Singapore. A day's visit to Singapore was never long enough; there was so much to see. One of the things which we noticed most were the vegetable stalls which displayed everything so neatly, and all scrubbed clean. Rows and rows of long white Chinese radish, pak choy (chinese leaves), mangoes, lemon grass and shiny green limes, heaps of onions and garlic and heaven knows what. All laid out for the haggling over and frequently sprinkled with water to keep everything fresh. Throughout the day, mobile food stalls fried a variety of foods, offering plates of curried this and that, sticks of satie (skewered chicken or pork marinaded in ground peanuts and spices), Indian chappatis filled with all kinds of curried ingredients. The Chinese food stalls were often no more than a bicycle hitched up to a barrow with an umbrella to keep the sun off the food and hanging from a string would be whole steamed, plucked chickens looking all waxen in the heat of the day and fanned at from time to time to keep the flies off. Then there were the various market areas where you could buy silks or bric-a-brac, clothes or handmade shoes, jewellery of gold and silver, gems of all sorts, the "Flea market", the camera market, and the jade market. Everywhere a market specialising in something or other. They were in addition to the regular shops. The roads were constantly choked with cars, buses and lorries all hooting away at one another and the pedestrians who weaved in among them, the Chinese dressed in brilliantly coloured cheongsams or plain white shifts and black trousers and mostly half hidden beneath coolie hats and waxed paper umbrellas. All the Chinese women did their best to keep the sun off their skin, although the men were not so worried, their faces often resembling dark brown wrinkled paper. Pedal rickshaws careered among the pedestrians and all the traffic and motorized ones just simply joined the throng, they adding their hoots and bells to the general hubbub. The noise was an inescapable cacophony. Constant and fascinating. It seemed that the Chinese couldn't talk without shouting while the traffic policemen on road intersection duty took delight in blowing their whistles (which were a permanent feature of their mouths) and pointing and gesticulating at the queuing vehicles in an authoritative attempt to keep the traffic flowing. Down by the sea front and docks area, there was just as much activity on the water as there was on the roads in the middle of the city. Junks and sampans chugged and paddled between the waiting ships, mostly loaded down to the gunwales with goods of all kinds - including highly stinking durian fruit. As the Chinese lived on board their junks and the larger sampans, there would be rank upon rank of them moored in the mouth of the river with planks between each to provide access from the farthermost to the shore and it seemed that no-matter what time of day, there were always people running lightly across the plank bridges with bundles bouncing from the ends of their bamboo shoulder poles. One of the main roads in Singapore was Orchard Road and for shopping this was the equivalent of Oxford Street in London. C.K. Tang was the main air-conditioned super store, rather like a slightly smaller version of Selfridges and the Singapore Cold Storage was the equivalent of Fortnum and Masons, the food shop to end all food shops. Opposite these was the Ngee An block of flats where Rodney Short, a colleague of mine from the ACC Cookery School at Nee Soon lived with his wife Moira. We sometimes called to see them when we visited Singapore and from their balcony we could look down on the teeming life of Orchard Road. Not far from them were the famous Raffles Hotel and the Hong Kong and Shanghai Bank where I had my account. The guardian of the bank was an enormous Sikh dressed in a scarlet robe and turban and sporting a huge waxed moustache in best Victorian style and armed with a shotgun. As officers approached the doors of the bank he would come to attention and give a wonderful salute accompanied by "Good Mahrrning (of Arrfterrnoon) Sahib" and beaming smile. Field officers got a "Present Arms" from him.

After we had been there a few months, we almost began to get used to seeing mangy pi-dogs roaming the streets, but the distressing tales we heard of Chinese eating puppies were hard to dismiss. Local government did its best to restrict the number of strays by enacting a law which required all dog owners to register their animals, receiving a large triangular brass medallion to hang from their collars. Dog catchers employed by the local department of health toured the areas armed with long bamboo poles with a wire lariat on one end to round up all dogs which had no identity tags. If they were not claimed within a few days, the dogs were destroyed - probably none too humanely, either. Often, if the dogs were in poor condition, they were shot out of hand on the spot. So when one day a stray dog nervously dared to come into my office begging for affection, I was hard put not to show it pity. She was a poor skinny thing with patches of mange showing through her otherwise attractive coat. She had such appealing eyes and a winning way that I took her to the local vet, an Indian, who said she was treatable and gave me some ointment to rub into the affected areas of her skin. I then took her to the local "Polis" station, got her identity tag and took her home. We named her "Tingey" and she became a wonderful companion and house guard dog. She appeared to have a pathological hatred of dark skinned people. The darker they were, the more she bared her fangs at them, so Tamils tended to come off worst. Our next door neighbours also had a dog, a cross between a labrador and a boxer, quite a biggish dog with the golden fur of labrador, but the squarish head of boxer. Tingey however, was built more along large whippet cum small greyhound lines and when she had her first heat with us, she was immediately 'got at' by the dog next door. A couple of months later, she was swollen with pups and getting listless. Eventually the time came for her to give birth and we made her comfortable for the great event. This turned out to be more of a marathon than we expected. The pups kept arriving and after the third, we decided to give them the names of numbers in Malay, so they became Satu, Dua, Tiga, Umpat, Lima and so on up to nine at which point they stopped arriving. We quickly realised that she could never cope with a family of that size, nor were we likely to be able to find really suitable homes for all of them. So the unenviable task began of deciding which ones I would have to take to the vet for putting down. They were all so adorable, but eventually we decided to take them in strict rotation and kept only the first three. I hated the job of taking the others to the vet, but knew that it was the only thing to do and only hoped that he would despatch them quickly and efficiently. Knowing the Chinese penchant for puppies and not wanting any shady deals done with the local restaurants, I insisted on staying to watch him kill them, which he did with an injection of strychnine directly into the hearts, with horrendous results, especially when he missed their hearts and injected into their lungs. Although it was quite quick, it was nevertheless unpleasant to watch them squealing and foaming at the mouth until the strychnine took effect. Still, better that than being boiled alive next door!

When we had taken over the bungalow, we had also inherited the cat which went with it. A red point Siamese by the name of "Blossom" who very much had a mind of his own and loved curry and cornflakes. If Blossom thought that you were spending too long on the telephone (and therefore ignoring him), he would quite simply gnaw your ankle. He was also a fearless snake fighter around the house. We came across him one day involved in a duel with a cobra and rather than see him come off second best, I intervened with a garden spade and decapitated the snake. In the matter of snakes, we really didn't see too many although Norma did ring me at the office one day and ask if I could come home quickly as there were two cobras in the front garden and she was rather apprehensive about them. I gave them the same treatment with the spade and was amazed to see that although chopped in half, the head half was still rearing up and striking as I hosed them down the monsoon drain. One evening we went to a party at Brian Self's house. He was the headmaster of the British children's' school in Kluang and they had a nice bungalow not too far away from us. They had two cocker spaniels as their pets and during the course of the evening, these two dogs kept on sniffing at a rattan armchair, getting quite excited in the process. Eventually, Brian asked the person sitting in the chair to let him see what it was they were smelling and to everyones' consternation found a rather large cobra coiled up beneath it. He got a golf club and despatched the snake with a well-aimed shot. There was also a report of a huge python found in one of the local buses. It had gone to sleep in the bus overnight and the early morning passengers had disturbed it when the bus set off for its usual journey. I also seem to remember coming back late one evening and feeling two distinct bumps as I turned into Jalan Ria. The next morning, I saw that I had driven over a large python which had been crossing the road. We also had a bronzeback racer in the bourgainvillea which grew up our front garden fence, but I don't know if it was a poisonous variety or not. On the whole, we did not suffer too badly from any of the local fevers and creepy-crawlies, although I did develop denghi fever early on and this must have been as a result of an infected insect bite. A few days after a visit to the War Dog unit which was situated out in the more jungly area of Johore, I began to feel a bit off colour and went home to bed, where I began to run a temperature. As it got worse, I was eventually admitted to the local military hospital for observation. Before long, I went into a coma and was put into an isolation ward with extra special care. I think I was unconscious for about two days and when I came to, I ached like hell all over and it took quite some months before I was back to normal. Malaria was almost a thing of the past in Malaya, thanks to the regular spray treatment given to the monsoon drains and any patches of open water. On another occasion, Norma woke up one night and when she switched on the bedside light found a huge poisonous centipede on her pillow, but thank heaven for us such occurrences were fairly rare.

When I was back to normal and playing golf once more, I entered an annual competition. My handicap was about sixteen and my game was getting better and better due to the amount of practise I was doing. As a serious part of my practise, I had set up the cine camera on slow motion and got Norma to film me playing certain shots, which gave a very good indication of what I was doing right or wrong. After the first round, with handicaps taken into consideration, I was in the lead by quite a large margin, so the handicap committee cut mine to fourteen for the next round. I won that too by a large margin, so they cut it again to twelve. But I still won the semi finals by another large margin, so they cut it again for the final which I played off ten - and still won. I think my total margin over the entire competition was by about 21 holes over my next nearest runner up. The prize was to be a silver rose bowl, but I already had one of those for shooting and asked if I might have something else to the same value and chose a Selangor pewter jug (which over the years of moving house has become slightly dented and the protective varnish has now begun to deteriorate. But both Norma and I love the shape).

It was about this time that I became involved in K.A.D.S., our Kluang Amateur Dramatic Society and was given the very small title part in Mike Parrish's production of Noel Coward's "Dear Charles". My main involvement, however, was to write some incidental music for the play in the style of Rachmaninov (we didn't want to get involved in paying Royalties, after all). We had a Doctor Kulescha who lived at the end of Jalan Ria, our road, who had a piano and I went there a few times to compose this piece of music.

For the play, the garrison carpenter constructed a plywood and cardboard grand piano which looked very lifelike when on the stage. When I was satisfied with my composition, I recorded it onto tape so that I could pretend to play it at the required time in whichever scene it was intended for. A Hungarian or some such nationality character was supposed to make his entrance through the French window and in a loud voice say 'Ah, Rachmanninoff, I luuuffe Rrrrraackmaaarrrrnnninoffff. He writes such a good tune!!!' (You can say that again!).Apart from the background music when the audiences were coming in and during the interval and exit as being the then currently popular Edith Piaf, and that's about all I remember of the whole production – other than my hair being powder puffed at the temples to look impressively silvery grey, which I quite liked.

About half way through our tour of duty, we became eligible for a "change of air", which meant spending two weeks virtual holiday up in the Cameron Highlands, about three hundred miles farther north. This period was not considered to be part of our annual leave entitlement as I was supposed to be 'on duty' while there. We drove through Kuala Lumpur the capital on our way there and after another hour or two, the countryside began to become hillier - just like driving into the Borders of Scotland. Eventually we saw this mountain range on the horizon and as we reached it, began to climb. As we reached two or three thousand feet, the atmosphere noticeably changed, the air less oppressive and the flora and fauna altered. We stopped for a break at about 3500 feet, pulling in to a secluded area where a cool waterfall fell out of the rocks above. Within moments, we were surrounded by wonderful black and irridescent green Rajah Brookes butterflies. I got the movie camera from the car and photographed them settling on Norma's hands and fingers. Eventually, knowing we still had some way to go, we drove on until we reached the change of air station at a height of about 6500 ft. We were still not at the summit which was wreathed in mist above us. We were in brilliant sunshine in an atmosphere which was crystal clear with the air like champagne, well above the humidity of the lowlands. I reported to the main office and was given the run-down on what to expect for the next two weeks. This amounted to doing one day's Orderly Officer duty, but nobody minded what I did on that day, so long as they knew where to find me - even if it meant scouring the golf course for me - that was only to be expected, it seemed.

We were allocated a holiday bungalow named "Moonlight" for the next two weeks which actually belonged to a rich Chinese tycoon who had built it as a holiday home and let it out to the military for most of the year. On the first night, we were surprised to find the maid servant had lit a huge log fire and soon discovered why as the temperature dropped to a frost outside beneath a brilliantly starlit black sky. Our neighbours were another couple from Kluang who lived just opposite us in Jalan Ria. Bernard McGibbon was the obstetrician attached to the British Military Hospital in Kluang. He and his wife Lynne were going through a difficult time and eventually separated. But while they were there with us, Bernard, a brilliant player himself, coached Norma at tennis. I played golf for the whole fortnight. Alongside the eighteenth fairway was a beamed and thatched pub in true Olde English tradition called The Smokehouse which was a much used venue by us Brits during the chilly evenings. Unfortunately, something or someone had given Norma a streaming cold, so for several days, she was sitting on the verandah, swathed in blankets, shivering and looking very sorry for herself, poor girl. Her change of air wasn't quite the holiday it should have been. Bernard and Lynne and Norma and I teamed up for a stroll through the high altitude jungle, which was nowhere near as dense as down below. We came across huge trees smothered in lianas and great moths fluttering through the glades, waterfalls, screeching monkeys and brightly coloured birds. In the shady places were wild orchids growing among the branches of the trees and among the ferns were pitcher plants shaped like saxophones with an open lid over the bell of the plant, each with a pool of enticing nectar in the bottom to lure insects inside and from which there was no escape. We also found a dead Atlas moth, just about the largest moth in the world. If you hold your hands together as though reading a book, that's about the size of the moth. During our holiday, we also went out to the Boh Tea Plantation which covered hundreds of acres of hillside with tea bushes planted in regular, terraced lines like the vines of France. Everywhere among them were Indian women in their colourful saris, who from a distance looked every bit like exotic insects among the foliage. With their baskets on their backs, they moved down the rows of bushes expertly plucking just the tips of each twig, each a cluster of no more than three tender green leaves.

When they got back to the main warehouse, their baskets were weighed and the tips sent for dehumidifying and gently rolling to set free the essential oils and flavours. When the leaves were sufficiently dried they were broken up by machine and sent for packing. Each of the visitors received a special wooden presentation box lined with metal foil containing about half a pound of tea and we were told that the Boh tea was at that time one of the main ingredients of the tea drunk in England under the name Typhoo. Drinking it neat was to our way of thinking by far the best. Our change of air over, we drove back down the mountainside and not far from where we had stopped to film the butterflies, we saw a small group of four or five Aborigines coming out of the jungle. They made a strange sight as one or two of them were dressed in the centuries old fashion of just a loin cloth and carrying the traditional eight foot long blowpipe. At the other end of the scale, one was dressed in tee shirt and shorts and carried an elderly shotgun. They were quite small in stature - the tallest being only about 5ft. 3ins. but it was obvious that they were well muscled and physically fit. Whether they were medically fit, we don't know. Many years later, at the height of "the Cold War" we heard of "Moonlight" again in a much more unpleasant setting, when a news report said that a CIA agent who had been staying at the house had been abducted and murdered. But who was responsible was not known, although it was believed that it could have been either the Indo-Chinese drug barons or Communists.

Back in Kluang, we became involved in an agreeable social round, visiting various people for parties and going out to see some of the local planters and one couple we met were Geoff and Judy Rothwell. Geoff was a "Visiting Agent". His job was to be an area supervisor, responsible for the smooth running of several rubber plantations; each looked after by a junior planter. Just for good measure, his employers gave him a small (600 acre) plantation of his own to run. They invited Norma and me to go and stay with them for a long weekend and when we arrived, we discovered that United Artists had hired his plantation to shoot various scenes of a new film "The Seventh Dawn". The stars were Capucine and William Holden without whose "help" the Malays and British army were, of course, unable to beat the CT's (Communist Terrorists). The studio set designers were obviously not satisfied with Geoff's rubber trees, so set about creating jungle in place of some of them, no doubt so that no-one would actually have to be so in-covenienced as having to go into the jungle for those scenes which required a jungle setting. How much the uprooting of some of Geoff's trees cost them I don't know, but they imported growing bamboo etc. and carried out a quick planting scheme where necessary. We never saw the opening shots of the film shown during the rolling credit titles were of Geoff paying out his tappers on the verandah of his offices, when suddenly a group of terrorists with sub-machine guns appeared to attack, killing Geoff and several tappers and stealing the payroll. The weekend Norma and I arrived coincided with them filming a sequence of Holden crossing a rope bridge, carrying a rifle with a white handkerchief tied to the muzzle, to parley with the CT leader who was supposed to rip it off in disgust or anger before giving Holden a bad time. This little sequence had to filmed countless times because either the hankie wouldn't come off, or Holden lost his grip on the rifle, or between them they got the timing wrong. Eventually, the Director seemed satisfied and called for a break. Everyone of importance sat around in those dinky little folding "Directors" chairs with their names on while it was agreed how the next sequence would be done. Wardrobe must have agreed, but now it was decided to give Holden's hair a once over. The next sequence is duly set up and this is supposed to show Holden calling down an air strike on the CT camp. A spotter plane has to be filmed flying above the jungle clearing, from where its engine can be heard. Firstly, the plane had to fly on an exact bearing over the cameras; otherwise they would not be able to see it through the canopy of the surrounding trees. This takes several attempts, including retakes for the wrong cloud formation being filmed and because Slaney talks during the shot. When the big scene of the airstrike is set to be filmed, it has to be a one-off because of all the pyrotechnic demolitions which will be used and due to the vast expense, can be shot only the once. With everyone in place, the Director shouts for "Action", whereupon the demolitions experts start going through their routine of blowing up this and that, including demolishing several trees. The idea is that the number 1 camera team are to film the overall thing from a little way off, while the no. 2 team are to do the close-ups. When all the dust and debris had settled after the "Cut", the no. 2 team appeared looking the worse for wear and letting everyone know in no uncertain terms that they and their fucking camera had nearly been blown sky-high because of the fucking stupid lack of sandbag protection they had been given.

Back at Brigade Headquarters, our social life moved smoothly on, Mess Dinner nights, cocktail parties and so forth. One evening we were invited to attend a special evening function when the Band of the Royal Marines came to Kluang to perform the ceremony of The Last Post. There was much marching by the Gurkhas accompanied by not only the Marines Band, but their own Pipe Band based upon the Scottish Pipe Bands. It was quite like being at the Edinburgh Festival – without the Castle. Eventually when all the troops on parade were properly formed up on the square in front of the Union Flag, the Commanding Officer made his appearance to take the salute. His arrival was by open Landrover specially adapted for the purpose with a set of steps fixed to the back end and a hand rail for him to hold during the short ride. His uniform had been so stiffly starched that I had the feeling it would crack rather than crease. Maybe a bit of an exaggeration, but I think he was even lifted down the steps so as not to damage the creasing so carefully ironed into the trousers. Everybody stood stock still while the Union Jack was reverently lowered to the accompaniment of a single bugler playing the much revered "Last Post" call, used at every Armistice Day Service. On another evening occasion, Norma and I were invited to the ceremony of the Gurkha Dashera at which they celebrated their Gods and Blessed their Weapons. This ceremony opened with their chosen champion soldier stripped to the waist ritually chopping the ends off ever increasing sizes of vegetables using a normal size Kukri (their standard battle knife for which they are greatly feared by any and all opponents) and culminating in him severing the head of a young bullock with a much larger ceremonial Kukri, preferably in one clean stroke, which, from my knowledge of butchery, couldn't have been very easy. This was followed by a session of dancing by a group of Gurkhas dressed as barefooted maidens complete with facial make-up and in brightly patterned red and gold dresses and with anklets of little bells which jingled rhythmically to the dance steps as they slowly got themselves worked up into a wild dance with much foot stamping. Gurkha Flamenco, perhaps? The rest of the evening was spent with the soldiers drinking copious amounts of rum, their favourite drink apparently. We guests did likewise as a polite accompaniment to the Colonel's short celebratory speech to his men, plus the usual G&Ts and whiskies. There wasn't much wine around in Malaya in those days; it didn't keep too well in the heat. Even the shops didn't have much in the way of stocks, although I do recall that a few Australian wines were just being imported around then.

Towards the end of 1962, trouble broke out in Indonesia when the Communists started creating problems and before long, it had spread to Borneo. Sheik Azahari, a dissident but charismatic Muslim school teacher challenged the ruling dynasty of Brunei and tried to set up his own Peoples' Democratic Party. This may well have been reasonable in view of the fact that the Royal Family owned and controlled just about everybody and everything in that tiny little State. With oil having been found in great quantities, revenues were pouring in and a lot of it was going into the Royal purses. Azahari and his supporters were all for it being shared out, but this wasn't the way the Sultan wanted the cookie to crumble, so he invoked his Dependency treaty with Great Britain and asked for some military support - which he duly got. This help was given also due to the Indonesian Communists poking their nasty political noses into the pie and it was quite a few years before our combined support could safely be withdrawn. Azahari's supporters turned nasty and started a shooting match which the British put down in a comparatively short, but bloody time, as it seems we didn't want to see the oilfields being taken over by revolutionaries with consequential loss of oil to the Empire. COMBRITBOR was born. The acronym stood for COMmonwealth and BRITish Forces BORneo and was made up more from British than others, give or take the Gurkha units who made up a substantial portion of the force and was supported by Royal Marines, RAF and Royal Navy. Command on the ground was by a brigadier with General Sir Walter Walker in overall command. A few days before Christmas, I was called to Brigade HQ and given my instructions to report to Changi Airport on the 20th. of December to fly out to Borneo and take up duties as Catering Adviser Combritbor. Sylvia and Norman Hyson a couple of very dear friends a few doors down from our bungalow offered to drive me down to Singapore with Norma and we got there on the afternoon of the 20th which allowed me to do some last minute shopping in Raffles Place. I bought a tiny Sharp radio/record player and two or three EP records. The record player was about the size of a thick paperback book and cleverly designed so that when opened, the lid could be arranged to rest back on the record on a tiny rubber wheel and an equivalent drive wheel in the body of the player turned the record round at the correct speed. A small pickup arm swung out to rest on the record and with a pair of earplug headphones it played in stereo. My record choice was of some Chopin études played by Alexander Uninski, a Russian pianist I had heard play the Rachmaninov 2nd.Piano Concerto at the Harringay Summer Concerts in 1947 when I was still a fifteen year old and studying at Trinity College; some Beethoven Romances and a 10" recording of the Brahms 3rd. Symphony in F played by the Concertgebouw Orchestra conducted by Eduard Van Beinum and this became my "Borneo Symphony" reducing me to tears when I first heard the slow movement.

I duly reported to the RAF control and was told to be at Changi by 03.40 the next morning, the 21st. So I grabbed a few hours sleep in the mess, getting up at about 2am to catch the RAF bus to the airport. The plane we were to fly in was an RAF Hastings transport, very similar to the old Dakota DC3 and scheduled to take off at 06.15. There were fourteen passengers in all and we climbed aboard at five past six and took off right on time. The flight was at 11,000 feet and at 8am we were served hot coffee and at 9am some orangeade and for the first couple of hours, we flew totally blind in the clouds. The flight took just over three and a half hours at a ground speed of 240 mph, which put Brunei at about 850 miles out into the South China Sea from Singapore. As we began the descent, the crew said it had been the bumpiest trip yet, due to the monsoon conditions. On arrival at Brunei airport, there were plenty of signs of a battle which had taken place only a day or so earlier. The control tower and buildings were pock-marked with bullet holes and some of the damaged vehicles and one or two planes were looking a bit worse for wear. I eventually found some transport to take me to the Sultan Omar Ali bin Saifuddin school where Force HQ had been established initially and where I had to wait nearly four hours before I could see the DQ (Deputy Quartermaster) to let him know I had arrived. I found somewhere to sleep for the night on a mattress on the floor of a crowded classroom and after listening to my new records, crashed out for the night. My first day of duty was the 22nd.

of December which was spent familiarising myself with the situation in Brunei Town and discovering what and where things were meant to happen. I had to find out where all the main rations had got to and what the various detachments had to eat for the next day or so. I also had to get Force HQ organised pretty quickly, as the feeding was something of a shambles - in all the messes irrespective of rank. I went to see the local Civil Chief Engineer and gave him a design for some improvised cookers I wanted built pronto, then went into the main shopping area to see about setting up some local purchase for the Officers' Mess. I also got the complete picture on supplies from the Brigade supplies officer, an RASC chap I knew from a few years earlier.

My few notes that I made at the time show that I was pretty busy. Here's what I recorded:

Sunday the 23rd.
Up early. 08.00hrs. flew by Beaver to Anduki and saw the Quartermaster of the 1st. Queens Own Highlanders. Promised to visit all units of the QOH with him on the 27th. on his ration run. 10.15 flew back to Brunei and at 11.00 hrs boarded a Twin Pioneer for the 25 minute flight to Labuan Island, our main supply depot where we landed after two attempts. Saw 31 Company Gurkha Army Service Corps re supplies. Went for some egg and bacon sandwiches and a couple of glasses of Tiger beer and a sit down in the Labuan Hotel.

15.00 hrs returned to the airport for more sandwiches and coffee before catching the Twin Pioneer back to Brunei at 16.00hrs. Flew at 1100 feet at 90 knots (about 110 mph).

Got back to Brigade HQ in time to find the prototype cooker nearing completion. Made a few modifications to it, but otherwise very satisfied so far. It looks good and it only remains to see whether it works! Spent the evening talking to Cook Corporal Hann of 20 Regiment Royal Artillery who has come to join Brigade HQ as officers' mess cook.

Monday 24th.
Up at 7am. Breakfast at 7.45 - the first decent one due to the improvements in the ration system. Left for Force HQ at 08.50 to hear "Prayers" (nick-name given to the Brigadier's daily briefing). Met G.1 and RAF Catering officer. Force HQ to come under RAF

supervision (for catering and convenience) and spent most of the morning on the Force HQ problem due to mixed Army, RAF feeding and only one RAF cook and four local Chinese kitchen hands. RAF to move in more NCO's and equipment. This happened by 16.00 hrs. Lunchtime drink at airport and back for lunch where the arrangements are still not good.

2pm left for round trip of Brunei units. Called into St. Andrew's Church to try the organ (electronic) and very impressed. Canon Paul, a Chinese runs the church. Sympathetic about the pistol (obviously I was still wearing my revolver in church), which I assured him was purely for self-defence.

Back for supper - still organisation breaks down due to Gurkha orderlies and the language problem. BM (Brigade Major) agrees to me going back to Kluang, but getting ACC NCO/WO in for Brigade HQ and units. (this must refer to me getting an early return to Kluang for some reason?) Attended prayers at 8pm. Christmas Day blow-up (what this refers to I simply can't recall – certainly not an actual explosion, that's for sure).

Tuesday 25th. Christmas Day.
"Blessed be the Child, born Son of man, but Father of us all."
Busy day. Good breakfast - egg, sausage, beans, cereal, coffee. Wrote brief to ADACC (Assistant Director, ACC back in Singapore). Checked on buffet lunches for Brigade HQ and Force B Squadron Queen's Royal Irish Hussars.

Petrol burners not very good (a piece of standard issue equipment for cooking).

Went to church and played organ (6 carols and lessons) but only about fifty people there, including HE the Governor and General Walker.

Sandwich lunch. Out at 2pm until 4.45 seeing all the local British units. Some were having Christmas lunches and others having it as a main evening meal. People helpful. Local Chinese baker cooked Turkeys and chickens for Brigade for $54.00 (about £6.50). HMS Dartingford (minesweeper of 250 tons) cooked for 42 Commando unit. All had good meals and brigade HQ all happy. Officers Mess dinner good, but half an hour late (7.30pm). Thoughtless people kept cook (Paul) hanging around.

10pm checked and signed Brief and despatched it through SDS (this

must have been the Signals unit).
Wrote letter to Norma. Bed by 11.30pm.

Boxing Day, 26th.
Up at 06.45, breakfast by 07.30, airport by 08.00, Took off in Beaver
08.30 (piloted by Conan Kerry) for Anduki and on to Lutong to
spend 4-5 hours with the Greenjackets. Mike Cowan (BRASCO)
(Brigade Royal Army Service Corps Officer - Supplies)
accompanying. We both plan to spend tomorrow with 1QOH
(Queen's Own Highlanders). Jungle looks very swampy from above.
Fly along coast and sea looks a bit muddy along the beach. Very
pleasant above the clouds. Conan now has us going along the beach
at about 40-50 feet - below the tops of the coconut palm trees. Bit
bumpy, but very interesting (that's an understatement!). Touch down
at Anduki for ten minutes, saw Ian Nason and arranged a visit for
tomorrow. Now on the way to Lutong. Shell Oil installation at Seria
very interesting (I should think so, a fairly respectable pitched battle
had been fought there only about a week earlier to secure the
oilfields). From above, the jungle looks like huge, flat cauliflower.
Nearly everywhere, water sparkles through the mass of greenery –
very swampy, I expect.
Pleasant stop off with Greenjackets some 8 miles away from the
airstrip. Returned to airstrip at 14.30. Helped refuel Conan's Beaver
and waited until 15.30 for him to return.
Went to Anduki and there got a lift in a Beaver to Brunei. Called
into BAA(?) who are moving tomorrow to PWD (Public Works
Department) yard. Supper 8.30pm. Letter to Norma and bed by
10pm.

Thursday 27th.
Took off in courier (Beaver or Auster monoplane) 08.00 for Anduki.
Went on the ration run round to all areas of QOH with Bill Tait, the
Quartermaster. Saw the Istana (like a mini Town Hall) where several
rebels were killed and the Penaga Police Station where quite a battle
ensued with the rebels using a human wall. Saw the grave of the
Shell Oil signaller and a rebel Vauxhall which was shot up just
outside Anduki airport. Saw Highlanders and Hussars doing "cordon
and search" of Kuala Belait (local small township).
Returned to courier piloted by Conan who after take-off let me fly

the Beaver all the way back to Brunei, right up to the downwind end of the runway. He says I have a natural aptitude for flying.
After supper, wrote Journal notes (for the quarterly ACC Journal).

Friday 28th.
Brunei airport 08.15. Reported to first Whirlwind helicopter. But after two attempts to start, the engine failed altogether. Went to second one and am now on way to Bangar.
Arrived Bangar safely - good trip. Bangar is on the River Temburong - all muddy and mangroves etc. Quartermaster Charles Morgan very hospitable. Saw kitchens and discussed rations. Visited the detachment at the ferry and picked out large shotgun bullet from the wheelhouse of the boat. Was given a "working parang" from a jungle clearing where a few Marines were guarding the ferry.
After lunch, boarded a "Z" craft lighter at 14.15 hrs for a monotonous three and a half hour journey down the rivers and through the jungle to Brunei harbour. Saw no wild life, not even any crocodiles – they had probably taken fright at the sound of the engine.
Returned to Brigade HQ, attended prayers at 8.30pm at which the Brigadier gave us a complete picture of the situation. Bed by 10.30pm.

Saturday 29th.
Moved my bedroom this morning (this was to a large classroom within the college and which I shared with three other officers, The Paymaster, The Postmaster and the Doctor. We announced on the door who we were by writing "Pennies, Poundage, Pills and Pastries."
Spent the day locally seeing the State Engineer about alterations to the ovens (the ones he started building before Christmas). Work started on the one for brigade HQ in the early afternoon. Stood over them (the Chinese engineers) giving them hand signals etc. re the alterations. During my half an hour off for tea, they went wrong! Hope to put it right tomorrow.
Good lunch and supper (chicken). Talked catering to the Brigadier at lunch and gave him my plan for British and Brigade HQ Gurkha feeding. He is in agreement, i.e. combined GOR (Gurkha Other Ranks) feeding (Brigade HQ, BAA, Gurkha Engineers, Gurkha

194

Signals and "odds and sods"). The British unit messes and Brigade HQ have an ACC Staff Sergeant to supervise them, with one Supervisory Travelling Instructor out visiting the units. The Area Catering Adviser needed to visit periodically, i.e. once a month.
I drew a plan of the GOR cookhouse layout and made an appreciation of the requirements of Gurkha feeding.
Went to the camp cinema for half an hour during the evening. Appalling behaviour from one of the QRIH (Queen's Royal Irish Hussars) soldiers.
No water supply since 4pm.

Sunday 30th.
Still no water, but managed to wash in what I found in a fire bucket. Duty Staff Officer tonight. Played organ in church 11am . Very happy day. Got a letter from Norma. Oh, what a joy. After church did tour of inspection of brigade HQ with DQ.
After lunch, did shopping for officer's mess. Booked plane for Lawas tomorrow. Later in the afternoon planned administrative organisation.
During the evening, wrote to Norma then spent from 11pm to 2.30am writing a brief for Works Services, together with drawings and diagrams of what I wanted.
Final wash at 2.50am, then bed.

Monday 31st.
Up at 7am, breakfasted by 8am. Catch 10.30 courier for Lawas. I was the only passenger, so flew the plane myself. On the return trip did some banks and turns and reckon I am getting the feel of flying now. The plane was a Beaver piloted by an Army Air Corps sergeant major.
Back in time for lunch. Spent the afternoon planning new temporary kitchens for Admin. Force.
After a very bad dinner due to the organisation breaking down and the Gurkhas cooking rice in the boilers, I went to a film, but stayed only about 20 minutes as the sound was so bad. Wrote a quickie letter, then bed, glorious bed – even if it was only a canvas camping one!
Have booked a seat on Friday's plane from Labuan to Singapore.

Tuesday 1st. January 1963.
Happy New Year - for some!
A REME corporal attached to B Squadron, QRIH was killed last night in a road accident. A requisitioned landrover, overloaded with party revellers, hit a kerb, overturned and caught fire. 1 dead, 1 seriously ill with burns and 3-4 injured. What a start to 1963. Did not discover until 7pm that one of my cooks was in the landrover. Spent the morning driving round all the Brunei units and after lunch drove through the jungle to Tutong with an armed escort to see 1 company of the 1st/2nd. Gurkha Rifles. The O.C. "wasn't quite with us" (what I meant by that, I really don't know).
On the way back, I escorted two prisoners of war, who were no trouble. Went to the other side of Brunei Town to the main POW compound to see how the War Dog unit was getting on. They themselves were OK, but the 1200 prisoners made the place smell like a zoo! They walk about with their hands up all the time. Contract feeding has been arranged for them.
Saw half an hour of a bad film in the evening. Have not written to Norma, as I shall be home before the letter arrives.

Wednesday 2nd. January
How I loathe the bloody Army. Damned Gurkha orderlies have really upset me at lunch. Pre-lunch was all happy. I had managed to buy some nice Camembert, butter and biscuits from the local Chinese stores in town. Now I have cussed, sworn and generally behaved like a spoilt child because I was kept waiting for 20 minutes for my lunch during which time at least eight other people were served and to make matters worse, when I got there, the cheese had all gone. Helped compile a letter to GHQ for cook replacements (who did I help? Can't remember).
The "Puffing Billie" (custom built cooker) works a treat, but is better burning wood than using a petrol burner.
Most people now know that I am going home on Friday, but I shall NOT be happy until I am back at 7 Jalan Ria.
Visited a few local units today including the Marines at the docks. Wonderful - got Norma's second letter xxxxx.

Thursday 3rd. January.
Spent most of the morning on two things, (a) my passage home, and
196

(b) the improvised ovens. Terrible disappointment - no passengers AT ALL tomorrow, so have made sure of the next flight on Saturday as there are no more after that until Monday. Terribly anxious time getting Force HQ to agree to my passage. However - won the day(?!) - I hope.

14.00hrs. attended conference at the Detention Camp, where I was made secretary of the conference, despite the fact that I had only been invited as specialist adviser on prisoners' feeding. Spent until 6.30pm writing up the minutes as copies would be going to HE (His Excellency, the Governor), Director of Operations, etc. Made friends with Captain John Van Gelder of The Intelligence Corps and went to supper with him at the Brunei Hotel where I met some of his Special Branch associates and the Deputy Commissioner asked me for guidance daily menus for feeding the prisoners. During supper with John, he told me that he had locked away a wide range of weapons which had been taken from the rebels and these included ancient Arabic rifles and krisses, the wavy edged swords favoured by the warlike tribes. He suggested I might like to have a look at them and take whatever I wanted. I simply cannot think why I did not, other than foreseeing problems with my military baggage on the flight back to Singapore.

Got back to HQ at about 10pm.

During the day sent Norma a telegram about coming home. The Telegraph Office in the town was still spattered with blood.

Friday 4th. January.
Many happy returns! Checked on my flight again and everything seems firm enough.

Spent most of the day checking on the building of the ovens and Gurkha quallies (wood-burning cookers. Other than getting wet as it rained nearly all day, nothing much to report today. Gave the Brigadier and Brigade Major a verbal report. Got clearance for two Chinese cooks to be employed as officer's mess cooks. Saw Robin Johnson who is coming over for a drink tonight. Robin gave me a letter for his wife Anne (they also lived in Kluang). Had about four beers, steak supper and a long talk with "the Mole" (Brigade Major). Briefed Geoffrey Lee, my replacement about messing. (as I recall, the Mole was one of the more senior staff officers at Brigade HQ, but can't recall Geoffrey Lee other than he was to take over from me).

Saturday 5th.
Pack up, clear up and buzz off. (So my flight back to Singapore seems to have taken place as scheduled).

I can't remember anything about the flight back to Changi, but must have sent a telegram to Norma to let her know what time I was expected to arrive. When I checked into "Arrivals", I was given a message to ring Norma at some strange telephone number.
    'Darling, thank goodness. I'm at the Polis Station in this little kampong I'm O.K., don't worry. Just a problem on the way down to meet you.' She gave me the name of the kampong about forty miles up from Singapore. But worry I did and grabbed a taxi and told the driver to get going. About an hour later, I arrived at the Polis Station and marched in, in jungle green uniform and still wearing my revolver. The officer in charge took me to his office where Norma was waiting. She had driven down in the Sunbeam to meet me and some little while after leaving Kluang, she found she was being tailed by some Chinese in a Mercedes Benz. She had tried to shake them off at 100 mph, highly dangerous on those laterite roads, but she couldn't get rid of them. Every time she slowed down, so did they. With one of the wives in Kluang having recently been raped, Norma was understandably upset and so sensibly had stopped at the next Polis Station for safety. We drove back to Kluang with me not sure whether I would have used my revolver on the Chinese or not.
    Now follows a "dark ages" period in my memory. I think that not long after, perhaps a period of two or three weeks, I was ordered back to Brunei and spent about another month or two there before coming back to Kluang to pack up our things prior to coming home to England and early retirement. There was a whole package of letters from me to Norma written during this time from Brunei, but they were accidentally thrown out some thirty years later. There is a period of some five months between the end of my first period in Brunei and our return home and I am damned if I can remember anything about that time, other than quite a large portion of it must have been back in Brunei - otherwise I might not have qualified for my campaign medal. From the diary notes I have written however, there are several episodes in Brunei which I can quite clearly

198

remember and these lead me to be certain that I did in fact spend a second, longer attachment out there. Due to the all-surrounding dense jungle, travel between places was possible only by the very occasional, maybe even solitary road, by water or by air and I experienced each during my time there, but mostly air and water. For example, my first boat ride in a dugout canoe. That was hair-raising. The canoe was one huge hollowed out log, about forty feet long and four feet wide with simple cross benches for seats. At the back end was a 50hp Johnson outboard. The canoe belonged to a Sea Dyak with great pendulous earlobes weighed down to his shoulders with heavy brass earrings and with his tattooed throat, short, business-like parang at his waist and black hand-rolled cigar, he looked a frightening prospect. He understood where I wanted to go and indicated that "Tuan" should sit down and hold on, which Tuan did - and just as well. With the sides of the canoe only a few inches above the water level, he backed out from the jetty, got us facing in the right direction and opened the throttle. Under such a surge of power, the stern of the canoe was actually below water level as we catapulted to about 25mph. All along the banks of the river were mangrove swamps and we disturbed several crocodiles which slithered off the mud into the water. Perish the thought of what might have been the outcome if we had capsized. Going in a straight line eventually became tolerable, but when we came to a tributary, we banked right over to one side as we swept round the corner and the feeling was not unlike riding pillion on a motorcycle and having to trust the person actually doing the driving. My "skipper" was quite unconcerned, puffing away on his home-made cheroot. After that first journey, all the others were a similar routine to get used to. Another new experience I had to get used to was landing and taking off again in the jungle. As the airstrips had to be cleared by hand and cut from prime jungle, the effort involved demanded that the strip was no bigger than absolutely necessary. This meant that landing was like coming down into a very short, green, blind alley. Taking off again was equally dangerous as the plane had to climb fast enough to clear the 25 metre high trees at the far end and it churned your stomach up a bit when on occasions the wheels clattered through the topmost branches. Take off usually involved the pilot almost standing on the foot brakes while opening the throttle to full power. The plane was doing its best to move with the shuddering becoming almost frightening until the brakes were released, the plane charging full tilt down the bumpy earth runway, bouncing into the air and then having to almost stand on its tail to get up above the treetops. But again, I got used to it and ended up almost enjoying the rush of adrenalin and the Beaver planes with their large twelve cylinder radial engines were a little better suited to this treatment than the smaller engined Austers . I certainly enjoyed being allowed to fly the planes myself, following the radio compass bearings back to Brunei. During this second tour, we had requisitioned the Sultan's personal yacht, the "Bolkiah". It was not the ultra sleek luxury yacht you would expect to see today, but was a sturdy sea-going cruiser of about fifty feet in length, capable of carrying about twenty people and plenty of stores, so it acted as both taxi to Labuan island, the supply depot and a small time freighter bringing back supplies which couldn't or were not necessary to go by air to Brunei. That strip of water between Brunei and Labuan was well inhabited by sharks. When flying to the island, we could often look down into the clear water and see schools of them. I never enquired whether they were man-eaters! As I said earlier on, one of the trips I made by air was by Whirlwind helicopter. I boarded the plane and sat up front with the pilot who told me that he had been having a spot of bother with the aircraft recently. Starting the engine to get the rotors going entailed the pilot firing starter capsules that resembled blank sporting-gun cartridges. He had to insert each cartridge into a special chamber and when fired, the explosion should have been enough to spin the rotors. When everyone was on board, he fired the first cartridge. There was a loud bang followed by a clatter, clatter, clatter of the rotors gradually dying away. He tried the second. Bang – clatter, clatter, clatter as the rotors whirled round, only to die away a second time. 'Bugger. Third time lucky', he said and tried yet another. Having fired three without success, he turned to me with a look of exasperation and said 'If I were you, I would hop out and get on that one over there – it's going to the same place as I am anyway.' So I did, taking off quite happily a few minutes later, followed by an uneventful trip out over the jungle to my destination, perhaps about forty miles away. I learned the next day that the engine of the first helicopter had eventually started, but had conked out again when the helicopter was well out over the jungle, coming down in some remote area never to be seen again. We must presume that everyone on board was killed or died trying to find their way out of the jungle. Any attempts to find them from the air would have been frustrated as the tree canopies were so dense that they would have simply closed back over the helicopter after it had crashed. As the years went by, I began to think that I had dreamed this accident and that it was all a fantasy until one day at Ettrickshaws hotel, I got talking to one of our guests who had been in Brunei at that time and he confirmed the whole story. So in this instance my memory had not let me down after all.

On another occasion, I decided to visit a unit which had been sent down to Kuching, the capital of Sarawak, so caught a civil Dakota DC6 from Brunei for the flight down. We got caught up in an electrical storm which tossed the plane about like a toy and for the first time I experienced what it was like to hit an air pocket. One moment we were flying along quite normally, the next dropping like a stone - literally falling out of the sky. Fortunately it was very brief, but it caught the stewardess unawares as she was carrying a tray of coffees which flew out of her hands as she momentarily experienced zero gravity! We flew over the Baram River and could see a great muddy delta belching a huge cloud of yellow-brown, dirty water miles out into the ocean where the river had flooded in the severe monsoon which struck a day or two before - and from which we had not long ago felt the after effects in the plane. The pity was that traditional village communities in Sarawak lived in Longhouses built on stilts alongside the banks of rivers so that the villagers can fish and grow simple crops. One such longhouse had grown to such an enormous length that it was reckoned to be the largest in existence, stretching over a quarter of a mile as one continuous building. It had been built over several generations, each carving its own legends onto the stilts it was built on. It was of great historic importance. When the Baram had flooded a day or two before, it had destroyed this community completely, washing away the longhouse and much else downstream and out into the South China Sea. I called to see the Curator of the National Museum in Kuching and he was totally demoralized on behalf of the lost community. I saw my unit of Sarawak Rangers, went back to the museum and bought a beautifully woven Kanowit basket as a memento of my visit. The flight back was luxury compared to the journey down, as it was in a Viscount, one of the latest turbo-prop. engined planes, able to fly smoothly well above the clouds. It was from the window of this plane that I took one of my better photographs of the wing with the clouds as background.

Perhaps the reason I was so anxious to get back to Kluang the first time (and utterly pissed off having to go out a second time) was that I had come to the conclusion that the promotion prospects in the Corps were now so lousy that I was unlikely to get to any rank higher than major, let alone half-colonel. This had all come about through the decision by War Office to allow officers from other arms to transfer into the Corps and retain their existing seniority. I mentioned this in an earlier chapter as at the time I was one of the senior training officers helping these people to become transferees. At the time, the implications of what was happening never dawned on me or some of my colleagues. But by the end of 1962 it became a blinding revelation when I was told that Jumbo Williams was going home to England and a new Divisional Catering Adviser was coming out to take over and thereby become my new boss. As far as I can recall, this new officer was a chap who had transferred in from the Royal Engineers and until only a few years ago hadn't the first clue about catering. This really got up my nose and I scoured The Army List to read the seniority list of regular ACC officers. It made dismal reading as I found my name fairly well down the list now. Having been so young when I was first commissioned all these people had now jumped over me. I reckoned that now my chances of ever becoming a really senior officer were not worth a candle. I was blocked. So in a fit of pique I told Norma that I was thinking of getting out. She confirmed that she too was not really happy to be an army wife for much longer - and certainly not for the rest of her life. That did it. I put in my application for an early retirement. But in those days, no-one went to the trouble to explain the financial implications of such a move. Two more years of service would have secured me a pension payable from the age of 55 and index-linked. As it was, I was given a straight lump sum gratuity of £1840 for my thirteen years of service. But I thought that at least we would be alright back in Civvy Street as it was fairly certain that we would both be employed at Fircroft. It wasn't until several years later, perhaps as late as the mid 80's, that I was tempted to go back to a Corps Week reunion and during the cocktail party before lunch, I met up with Harry Scarisbrick, who had been Commandant during the 1950's. He subsequently finished up as Director ACC, by then a Brigadier's appointment. He asked me why I had left the Corps and I told him what I had thought about the transfer scheme. He agreed, saying that he had warned War Office that defections (such as in my case) would occur and had thought it was a bad short term decision to have made. Following that decision, they had made drastic alterations to the structure of the Corps by increasing the upper echelons from one full colonel to two brigadiers, several full colonels and so on downward. He made matters worse by telling me that I had been already earmarked for future Director and that I would have followed Keith Hudson as Director ACC, with the obligatory CBE and an indexed and very generous pension. I can't help thinking about that nugget of information in two lights. The first is regret at having thrown away such a career opportunity and the second is that without the benefit of having had such a varied lifestyle since then, I might have finished up a boring old military fuddy-duddy.

When we had only about two or three weeks to go before leaving Kluang, we advertised the Rapier in the Singapore Straits Times and it was bought by a young Chinese banker. With about £550 in our pockets, we went shopping in Singapore for the last time and fell in love with three rugs in an Indian shop. The owner, Mr. Qureshi, spent ages selling them to us, buying us lunch and eventually driving us all the way back to Kluang in his Jaguar Mark VII. He did a brilliant sales job on us, leaving us thinking we had bought the three most treasured rugs in the world. I'm sure now that we paid through the nose for them. Come to think of it, I don't recall us having done any haggling whatsoever, just become mesmerised by his sales technique and paid what he asked for them. He had them packed for export to U.K. and we didn't see them again until we had been home about a month or more. With our flight instructions and hand luggage, Sylvia and Norman again drove us to Singapore where we were to stay one night in a transit hotel before reporting to Changi airport to catch the flight home. But our flight was delayed and we had to stay an extra night or two. Our plane was a B.O.A.C. Comet jet, newly in service in those days. We boarded and took off and during the climb to cruising height, the air conditioning began to chill the atmosphere inside the plane. Reading the newspaper, it was noticeable how the paper itself dried out, making quite a loud crackling noise when folded or turned over. Our first stop was the remote island of Gan in the middle of the Indian Ocean where it was hot. Very hot. We were allowed to get out and stretch our legs, but Norma by now was feeling lousy. She had developed very weepy eyes, as though suffering from some evil conjunctivitis. These continued to get worse as the flight progressed. The next stop was Aden, where we had stopped on the way out and was by far the hottest place we had ever experienced, and then Tripoli, which being in the desert was almost as hot as Gan and by now Norma's eyes were really causing her considerable distress. The final leg of our homeward journey took us to RAF Lyneham in Wiltshire, where we landed twenty seven hours after leaving Singapore, twenty two of which we had been sitting in the plane. Norman, Maymie and my mother were waiting for us at "Arrivals" and so we had a joyful reunion. Norman had bought a Bentley sports saloon and let me drive it back to Bournemouth where the cherry trees in front of Fircroft were still in full bloom. When Norma saw the doctor, he said she had a classic case of "pink-eye", whatever that was – probably some virulent form of conjunctivitis. It certainly caused her some distress until it cleared up.

At the time and throughout my Army training, it never occurred to me what a psychological change was taking place within my mind. It is only in later life that I realise and have recently admitted to Norma that I have become a 'control freak' (as they say in current jargon). Little wonder really. Listening to my mother's tape recordings (of which more later), I can see how narrow was her point of view on things and how touchy she got whenever I 'with my superior education (thanks to her)' made certain comments on her speech or behaviour. It is an understandably uncomfortable feeling to be criticised by one's own children – even if they are right and you are wrong; those who do not mind are very few and far between. As a consequence, although I did not appear to have a restrictive childhood, I was somewhat limited as to how I might behave and think. I think I may have mentioned earlier that we had no books in our house other than maybe an occasional women's magazine or knitting magazine – hardly mentally uplifting. Therefore it was not until I got to Grammar School that my literary horizons began to widen, only to be cut off again when I was taken away from school at such an early stage in my learning. My early Army life, as you will have gathered, was all discipline, discipline and more discipline, especially during my officer training at Mons, and my mindset was no doubt very malleable at that time. There was no doubt about it, the Army machine ground you to pieces then reconstructed you into the required shape. I can't say that my life as an officer was hard, but it was still totally enclosed in the disciplinary envelope. Now this may affect some people in different ways to others and I do honestly feel that whilst it might have been good in many ways, it left me with set ideas on behaviour and a misplaced ability to criticise that are not perhaps less of an asset and more of a liability in civilian life. It's a wonder Norma has not hit me or walked out on many an occasion.

CHAPTER ELEVEN

FIRCROFT

My first introduction to Fircroft was through Peter Robinson when he invited me to a party, where I met his girlfriend Norma Powers that evening, and eventually married her. From then on, I was always a guest in the hotel, never interfering in any way, but enjoying the fruits of forthcoming marriage by way of being made to feel one of the family by Norman and Maymie, joining them and Norma in their dining room for meals. After we married, we were both looked after in the same way whenever we drove to Bournemouth to see our parents. It always seemed a loving atmosphere that permeated the hotel and Netheravon, the very large house next door where Norman and Maymie lived. But beneath this tranquil surface ran an unseen tension caused by a number of subtle factors. Netheravon was Maymie's house, bought for her by her mother, yet Norman managed to devote one of the prime front rooms to his ageing mother, who was by then an extremely crabby old woman who demanded a lot and gave very little. Maymie hardly ever ventured in to see her and Norman had to stop whatever he was doing at certain times of the day to go and visit his mother and take tea with her. In another room looking out towards the hotel was Norman's Aunt Ada. She was a sweet woman who imposed nothing on anyone, coming and going, so long as she was able, like a ghost. But again, yet another person in Maymie's house. Then there was Phyllis and Brian upstairs with baby Laura and so long as Phyl was working in the hotel reception, it seemed that Maymie felt almost duty bound to do as much of her personal washing as possible, including Laura's nappies. Maybe I'm wrong, but it was my impression that Maymie spent the greater part of her day in the laundry room in Netheravon and always managing to look harassed by it all. She even managed to do some of the hotel's laundry as well. What angered me rather more than somewhat was when Brian came home from cricket, he would dump his dirty laundry somewhere and Maymie almost made it her quest in life to do it for him - then complain about it after, but not to him.

Now here I was, back home in Bournemouth and with a

different relationship with the family and the hotel. My resignation from the Army was made that much easier in the knowledge that I was going to help continue running the "family" business. I am reminded in later years by Phyllis, Norma's sister that I was told it would not be a good idea to get involved in Fircroft and perhaps thereby equally, I should have listened and remained in the Army. Bearing in mind that Phyllis and her husband Brian were already in the management team of the hotel, it is perhaps not unexpected that they may have had second thoughts about sharing the responsibilities and rewards with us. But my disillusionment with the Army had been so strong over this promotion block which had so needlessly been created, that it is possible I might have ignored *any* advice, nomatter from which quarter. Fircroft or no Fircroft, being the impetuous person I was (and perhaps still am to a certain extent), I may well have chucked the Army even if I had not got a job to go to. After all, I "fell" into the Army. I could as easily "fall out" again. At least, that was likely to be my attitude. But there it was, my die had been cast and here was my new life about to begin.

We came home with a one-off gratuity for my thirteen years of service amounting to £1840, plus some personal belongings currently on the high seas. We had sold the Sunbeam and bought two Persian and one Pakistan rug with the proceeds. We could have just banked the money until we got home, which in hindsight would no doubt have been by far the wiser thing to have done. One alternative which I, more than Norma, did consider was to bring home a brand new Sunbeam "Tiger", the latest sports car from the Sunbeam Talbot stable which I could have bought free of Purchase Tax. But had I sold it in the UK within three years, I would have had to pay the tax in arrears. That, plus the cost of shipment by sea put such a scheme out of court as far as I was concerned. So it was rugs, which we were assured were a brilliant investment and saleable in UK for much more than we paid for them in Singapore. As it turned out, either we paid too much for them, or the market value of them in UK was much, much lower than we had been led to believe. With nowhere to live of our own, my mother had offered to provide us with a flat within Knyveton and said at a later date that she had even "gone to the expense of having our own electricity meter installed". But it wasn't to work out. It was not long before she and Norma began to cross swords. Finally, one day Norma came to me desperately unhappy saying she couldn't go on living under the same roof as my mother and was moving back to Netheravon - which left me with no choice but to follow suit. When I broke the news to mother, she flew into a rage and left us in no doubt what she thought of Norma, that it was breaking her heart and reiterated the cost of having made whatever alterations she had to provide us with our own home. To my recollection, these were not very much in evidence. Finally, she said that she had hoped that we would take over the mortgage on the house so that the whole thing could eventually become ours. But if we weren't going to live there, with Dad now dead, she couldn't possibly keep up the mortgage without us and would therefore sell the house and be done with it. This now smacks of emotional blackmail to me. As with most things, hindsight is a great teacher. When they had bought the house in 1948, it cost them £5250 which was quite a lot in those days but the mortgage was reasonably affordable, even to us. That house now might be worth around £350,000.

Norman came to the recue in double-quick time, saying that Fircroft Hotel Limited would lease a flat for us and that it would become part of our salary package, which was adjusted to take account of this. So off we went flat-hunting and found a very lovely two-bedroomed flat in a fairly new purpose-built block named "Guildford Court" in Surrey Road overlooking the Bournemouth Upper Pleasure Gardens and complete with its own dedicated garage space in the basement. We furnished it somehow with all new furniture and still managed to buy a Jaguar 2.4 saloon car out of our Gratuity and set up a very happy new home there where Mark was conceived on Norma's 30th. birthday in close proximity to the airing cupboard door which certainly gave him a warm start to life. Among the people we met in the flats were John and Delphine Etches, a charming couple. John was quite a few years older than Delphine and an industrial photographer who had his own studios in Holdenhurst Road very near to Bournemouth Central station. He was a perfectionist and the quality of his shots was incredibly good with total attention to detail and composition. Over the years we knew them while he remained in that business, he also specialised in marine photography, having his own fast boat for taking action shots out at sea. Later, during our SNS days, we were to engage his services for some of our products. He eventually retired to a cottage with a smallholding and some sheep in the village of Fiddleford near Sturminster Newton.

At Fircroft, Norma and Phyllis shared the Reception with one or two additional staff, Brian "looked after" the wet side of the business and I took on the catering. Regrettably, none of us was given a clear remit as to what we were to do and as a result, the business just "bumbled along" without any strong sense of direction. Brian's cricketing always managed to take prior claim to his time. He was also good at then going over to the hotel cocktail bar and acting "mein host" to the residents and guests for a few hours during the evening. My thoughts about the quality of the food led me into a rather tricky area. Chef Holmes had been with the hotel for donkey's years. He was a good old-fashioned chef, a little on the slapdash side and certainly not the kind of "whizz-kid" I had left behind in the A.C.C. But he was solidly reliable and had served the hotel extremely well over the years. I wanted to lift the quality of the catering beyond the comfortable plateau which it was currently grounded on and to do it I had to make life a bit tough for Chef. My problem was that I had absolutely no idea of handling civilians, expecting them to jump if I said so. I simply didn't see him in the same league as some of the chef instructors I knew in the Corps and so agitated for him to be replaced - much against Norman's wishes. Eventually, he acquiesced and Chef Holmes was allowed to retire earlier than planned, with Norman giving him one of his own gold watches for his years of loyal service. Later, I found this gesture so touching and typical of Norman. It simply wasn't in him to hurt anyone deliberately. Now it was up to me to get the kitchen running along the lines that I had said I wanted and ideally the first step was to find an ACC NCO or Warrant Officer who was prepared to move to Bournemouth on leaving the service. Eventually, after much advertising, 'phoning and fewer and fewer interviews and not finding a suitable replacement from within the normal civilian pool of chefs, I finally settled on a red haired short-service ex-corporal I had heard of from somewhere as being available and I took him. Unfortunately for me, he either didn't want to, or couldn't run the kitchens the way I expected and so the atmosphere between him and me became somewhat strained. But I had to put up with it as it was; I had made my own bed and now had to lie on it.

I was now also beginning to experience my first pangs of

frustration in my newly chosen career. Getting the new chef, Bill, to do things the way I wanted was proving difficult to the point of me settling for the quiet life and allowing him to do things more his way than mine and saying nothing. In effect, I regret to say that the catering had not really improved above Chef Holmes's standards. I was also becoming more and more angry at Brian's attitude towards the business. Norman had paid good money to send him (now as a son-in-law, of course) on a hotel management course to Bournemouth Technical College, but it made little or no appreciable difference to what he managed to achieve. During the summer season, when we were at our busiest, cricket was still his main occupation, with him being out of the hotel for hours on end for three or four afternoons a week. When Phyllis first married him, he was a policeman and I hate to think how he had applied his mind to his duties then. He certainly had no qualms about shirking his work now he was in the safety of a family business. Eventually, we found that he had developed the habit of opening the bar to his cronies and giving them drinks, followed by selling them bottles of drink at cut price, and even worse, fiddling the National Insurance stamps of the employees on the payroll. Later still, Phyllis discovered he was having a string of girlfriends around the town and finally, she divorced him, with Norman asking him to leave the business. Even then, Norman covered up his dishonesty, repaying all the deficits himself rather than have the scandal of taking Brian to court. But long before all this, I had my first taste of how difficult it was going to be to get some semblance of organisation into the management. I had kept on nagging Norman to hold regular management meetings and he eventually agreed to do so, with one or two provisos, such as it must be held upstairs in Phyllis's flat, so that she could break off and attend to Laura if she cried and that Maymie should still be able to keep the laundry room working as the machines finished their wash cycle and so forth. It was a compromise situation and so the first meeting was held, when I presented a list of things I wanted to see changed, or at least discussed and justified. With various interruptions for nappy changing, laundry and arrangements for cricket fixtures, we finally got to the disorganised end of the meeting and I got Norman to agree to the date for the next one, by which time we were supposed to have made whatever changes had been agreed upon. At the second meeting, I asked for us to say what changes had been made and how successful they were, only to find – not a great surprise - that not much had been changed. Because he judged it all a failure and waste of time, Norman was reluctant to hold any more "management" meetings, so we abandoned them, returning to the old tried and trusted "hope-for-the-best" methods.

My frustration was to get even more wound up after several evenings of doing bar relief. Often they were lonely, boring evenings with only one or two people coming down for a drink, particularly as the summer ended and we went into the autumn gloom of fewer and fewer customers. Going were the days of "the winter perm", when each year, almost as in a migration, the winter permanent residents would return to occupy their regular rooms and regular dining table and lounge chair. Paying next to nothing, they had just about helped hotels like Fircroft to break even over the long dreary winter months. But as the early 'sixties were to prove, they were a dying breed, becoming more and more scarce, meaning increasing overdrafts for hoteliers all over the south coast. It angered me intensely that Brian's luck should be so good that not only could he have all this time off for his evening pals, but that he was also so ineffective in the business. In my boredom, I resorted to putting the odd shilling or two into the one and only "one armed bandit" installed in the bar. I always lost. Once or twice, I would get so determined to prove my "bad" fairy wrong that I borrowed money from the till to feed the bandit in the uncertain hope that my notions of never having a good stroke of gambling fortune might, for once, be proved wrong. It never happened and having refunded the till, my fairy often teased me yet again when Brian would come down to the bar, saying 'It's time the machine paid out'. Within a few coins, sure enough, he would win a substantial prize- often the Jackpot. It was as if the Fates were conspiring to tell me something. The message seemed to be 'This is not for you'. As far as I was concerned, it all went to prove that I was one of the world's unluckiest gamblers. I should have known better than try to win. After all, my first introduction to gambling had been in Form 4S at Grammar School when I bought some raffle tickets and got the consolation prize of a lemon! On another occasion, watching a four horse race on TV, Norma said 'Go on, have a bet on on.' I chose a horse which promptly fell over! My mother's luck certainly hasn't rubbed off on me. She could bet on almost anything and win - except choosing a suitable husband for herself after dad died. She tried three and none of them gave her any real happiness. In fact, two of them knocked her about a bit for her tempting ways.

One day an electrician by the name of Derek Naylor came to do some work at the hotel. He was employed by Mr. Dacombe, a Rotarian friend of Norman's and the owner of an electrical shop in Old Christchurch Road. Apparently, Norman had been advised and convinced that the hotel needed re-wiring to bring it up to current safety standards. By the time Derek had finished installing the miles of metal trunking, main fuse boards, circuit breakers, control panels and heaven knows what, the basement of the hotel looked more like the control room of an ocean-going liner. The tree of trunking ran from the bowels of the building, up through floors and walls, reducing in diameter from about six inches square down to what seemed a mere two inches and I was certain that had the hotel been struck by an earthquake, it would have been entirely supported by this maze of metal thus surviving the worst that nature could throw at it. As the days of dockyard drilling and hammering progressed and the hotel became more and more festooned with miles of coloured electrical cables, yet to be encouraged into their metal sheaths, I got to know Derek, discovering that at heart, he was really a New Forest man. He lived and breathed "The Forest" and his greatest wish was to become a Verderer and to live in the depth of the forest with his wife, an equally ardent admirer of the forest, like a modern day Hansel and Gretel in their gingerbread house. During the course of conversation one day he told me that his boss held the agency for some kind of Norwegian intercom system, but wasn't doing much to promote the sales of it. He expected people to just come into the shop and suddenly find they needed such an item, as though it was just one of those things that from time to time get put on a shopping list. I had had some experience of intercoms when I was the Adjutant in St. Omer, back in the late 1950's. Ours had been a simple Siemens' system, but had proved much more convenient than having to go through the telephone exchange each time I wanted my Chief Clerk. It also had the advantage of allowing "hands-free" reply, unlike the telephone which had to be awkwardly cradled beneath the chin if both hands were wanted to look up documents. I asked Derek to bring in the "Demonstration kit" so I could see what the latest "state of the art" equipment was all about.

The next day, he put a heavy, rigid suitcase on my desk, plugged in the lead and uncurled two separate lengths of cables, each about twenty feet in length, with a highly sophisticated looking piece of grey plastic equipment with rows of numbered buttons, coloured lights and discreet loudspeaker grille at each end. Taking one of them to another room, Derek then called me from his unit and I was astonished at the splendid quality of speech given by this new system. He demonstrated various other facilities and my mind immediately went into overdrive, seeing how useful such a system could be in the hotel. Instead of tramping up and down corridors looking for staff, they could be paged without moving from the office and so long as they were within audible range, could reply without stopping what they were doing. I got Norman interested and as he was always fascinated by things electrical or scientific, he agreed we should have such a system. Derek went on to explain that this Stentofon equipment came in many guises, ranging from simple one-to-one sets right up through Master and multiple slave systems and on to fully intercommunicating, multi-channel, hands-free systems with perhaps a hundred or more units, even being so clever as to be voice operated, so that nobody needed to press any buttons at all! It seemed a miracle of modern technology and I was totally fascinated. If we could have one system for staff communication, why not one from Reception to all the bedrooms? With the ability to listen to what went on at the other end, unless the secrecy button was pressed in the bedroom, we could even offer a baby-listening service for guests without the Receptionist even having to leave her desk. This was a brilliant idea and once again, I "sold" it to Norman. So the order was placed with Dacombe. The only problem was that he had no stock whatsoever, only the demonstration kit. He would have to plan the system, price it, then get it ordered from Norway where it was made, if Norman agreed to the price. Delivery was running at several weeks and as he was such a small agent, he would have to pay for all the equipment up front with Derritron Electronics, the main UK importer. This would all take time and money to organise and because of the approaching summer season, it was all postponed to the early part of the next year, 1965. The seaside hotel trade was undergoing far reaching changes following the end of the war. Once the shackles of rationing had been shed, holidaymakers flocked to the coast for their annual holidays and in the 'fifties it was quite the usual thing for people to flood into towns such as Boscombe and Bournemouth in such vast numbers that the trains would be crowded with passengers standing in the corridors all the way from London. Flooding out from the stations, they would descend upon the hotels in their droves. Those who had booked in advance were sure of their accommodation, but many left it to chance, some ending up sleeping under the piers when everywhere was full. The pattern then was for guests to book full board, trooping down to the beach or shops after breakfast, returning to the hotels for lunch. Then they would go back down to the beach until tea-time, when everyone would come back again for their pots of tea and cake. Finally, following yet more beaching and shopping, it would be dinnertime, so back to the hotel, there to wait for a bathroom to come free, or settle for a wash in the hand basin in the bedroom before going down for the evening meal. Only the very top hotels had cocktail bars, very few of the lesser places even having table licenses. Those that did sold the odd bottle or two of German Hock which would be almost surreptitiously opened by a not very skilled waitress, a glass or two poured and the remainder re-corked for the following day or two. By the sixties, this pattern was beginning to alter, when thanks to air travel, foreign holidays was a growth industry. English hotels had to compete, particularly in the winter time when holiday makers were few and far between and winter "perms" were a dying, if not dead breed. The era of business functions was now having to fill the dimishing coffers of hoteliers, so the making of improvements to hotel businesses was like chasing your own tail. Make money during the summer, and possibly keep it for the rainy days which came in winter, or perhaps chance spending some of it on improvements. Maybe, perhaps, maybe not . . . caution all the time.

Fircroft had always prided itself on a very full programme of entertainment for its residents and in many ways had been well ahead of its competitors, having installed a petrol pump for those who were now enjoying the "Motoring" style of holiday. I remember hand-cranking the pump, resplendent with its illuminated glass head of Mercury denoting that the hotel sold National Benzole petroleum. The tennis courts were well used by day and in the evenings, Norman and Maymie held fancy dress parties, whist drives, dances and any other entertainment currently popular. In having its own cinema, however, Fircroft was unique. It was the first provincial hotel to do so. In the downstairs ballroom, Norman had had a small projection room built into one corner and diagonally opposite was a stage complete with a silver screen and sound system, plus electrically operated curtains and remote controlled lighting. The "cinema" seated about eighty and from the projection room, a gramophone turntable played the introductory and interval music. The films came from an agency in London on huge 24" reels which would be fitted onto the projector and laced into the array of sprockets and pulleys. By the Reception desk was an easel with a properly painted notice topped by "George" the wooden commissionaire announcing the film for that evening and as this was a very popular entertainment, the residents would "bag" their seats the moment the evening meal was finished. Despite all the good things about the hotel and its lovely family atmosphere, something still wrankled in my mind. I was still dissatisfied with the way things were done and most of all, Brian's attitude. My mind kept returning to that Stentofon equipment and what I perceived as its endless possibilities. Surely others who saw it would be bound to be attracted by it, as I was and as Norman was. It seemed a great pity that Mr. Dacombe was letting it all sit there doing nothing, hoping someone, anyone, would, as if by some miracle discover that it was he who had this magic piece of equipment in his care, want it and walk in off the street and buy it. Surely if I were to create a firm of some kind, I could go out and find heaps of people who would fall over themselves to have such a boon. Alongside such a system, the telephone looked a dying dinosaur; old fashioned and very limited in what it could do. Here was Modern Technology with all the knobs and bells you could ever want. With the right combination of bits and pieces, you could even install a system of loudspeakers in factories to play music, make announcements and still give the management their own fully-intercommunicating replacement telephone system. The telephone would be relagated to just making calls to and receiving calls from the outside world. Stentofon had to be a world beater. Nothing could stand in its way. The more I thought about it, the more fanciful my thoughts became. It would be rather nice to be Managing Director of my own business selling such sophisticated equipment instead of a hotel manager with no clear portfolio of responsibilities. I would suggest it to Norma when the time was right.

One day at Guildford Court, the moment seemed right when she was in the bath (and perhaps psychologically I chose that moment because she would be unable to get away?) and I broached the subject. I enthused about this Stentofon stuff and asked her whether she would like to be a director in our very own business. We could ask Derek Naylor to join us to look after the technical side of things, using the initials of our two surnames for the name of the company, SNS. Norma didn't disagree with what I had been saying, so I took it the next stage further, by asking Derek if he would join in such a venture and as he was getting a bit fed up with just being an electrician in a little shop, he agreed. I sounded out Norman to see whether he was prepared for us to slowly fade out of the hotel scene and whilst this was something of a surprise to him, he gallantly accepted that I wasn't happy and agreed to do all he could to help, introducing me to his own Solicitors (again, Rotarians) who would be instrumental in setting up the legalities of the new company. Norman also introduced me to some Accountants who would do the books for us. With a contribution of £250 each from Derek and ourselves, giving us a £500 capital, SNS (Bournemouth) Limited was formed.

Forming the company was the easy part, but what followed was a bit trickier. We had to convince Derritron that we were a thrusting, dynamic young firm, simply bursting with energy and well able to take over the agency in Hampshire and Dorset for Stentofon. The Domestic Sales manager for Derritron at that time was a very young executive by the name of John Robins, who I later found had been a subaltern in the Gurkha Rifles around the same time as I was with the Gurkhas in Malaya. He took Derek and me out to lunch at a nearby pub and we virtually agreed terms for the Agency over a pint of beer. We had to recompense Mr. Dacombe for his loss of the agency and this was eventually agreed to be the top slice of profit from the Fircroft job, as and when it was finished. At least that way, we didn't have to eat into our £500 capital which was used to buy the first consignment of equipment to do our first new job, a small system in a garage in New Milton. It soon became obvious that if this new venture of ours was going to get off the ground, we would have to devote all our time to meeting people and selling to them, other wise we would do no better than Mr. Dacombe. I couldn't do this sitting in the office at Fircroft, half doing hotel management. So

I asked Norman if he would agree to me leaving to do one job properly. To help us, he even put the use of some outhouses behind Netheravon at our disposal and let us use the second telephone line of the hotel for our business. The main problem with that arrangement was that dear old Harold, the kitchen porter would remain behind in the afternoons to wash down the kitchen when he had finished doing all the pots and pans. For donkey's years he had always answered the telephone then and it was some time before we found that we were losing incoming telephone calls. The 'phone would ring and in his particularly cracked voice, he would answer,

'Ello, Fircroft'.

'Is that SNS?'

'No, it's Fircroft.'

'Are you sure that isn't SNS?'

'No, this is Fircroft 'otel.' ... and put the phone down.

This gave us a bit of a communications problem until we could convince Harold that yes, we were *also* SNS Bournemouth Limited. By now, Norma was looking pregnant so after we had sorted out the outhouses into a stores and an office of sorts, she was our permanent secretary and telesales person. Here we were, a fully fledged limited company with little or no capital left, three directors who were already on next to no pay and one of whom was bearing a child, no orders on the books and about to have to quit Guildford Court, our home, unless Fircroft Hotel Limited could be extra generous and pay the rent for another month or two, which, in the end, was what happened. I sold the 2.4 Jaguar and bought a Mini 850, which gave us a little bit of spare capital to live on until "things improved".

CHAPTER TWELVE

SNS (BOURNEMOUTH) LIMITED

It soon became clear that without orders, we would hit disaster. Orders came from customers, who, if we were lucky enough to unearth them, ideally wanted to know of other successful jobs we had done. So far, one measly little garage job wasn't much of a sales portfolio. We had to get something more substantial under our belts. But what? I had the brainwave of asking Norman if we could get on with the Fircroft job and receive stage payments from him to keep us solvent. It was my first introduction to the phenomenon of "Cash Flow". Once more, bless him, he agreed and it gave us just enough money to pay for the equipment as we needed it from Derritron, plus a bit to live on. We struggled on living at Guildford Court for as long as we could, with Norma becoming more obviously pregnant by the week. Each day, we would drive into Fircroft from home so that Norma could hold the office for us and to give her the company of her parents and sister. The plan had been for Norma to have our baby in Tuckton Nursing Home, where Maymie had had both Norma and Phyllis. It is quite likely that Phyllis even planned to have Laura there, I'm not sure, so there was almost a degree of family commitment to using *only* that one nursing home. So when Norma went into labour, I took her there. A room had been booked within a guestimated period as to when it was likely to be required and when we arrived, it proved to be very Spartan and as I recall, there were areas of lino with holes in and certainly not much in the way of carpeting. Poor Norma was too pre-occupied to worry about such trivialities. Her labour was not running true to form and she was in a great deal of pain. It was some little time before the nursing home came to the conclusion that she wanted some expert help from the gynaecological department of Boscombe General Hospital, but eventually an ambulance was summoned. With bell ringing, the ambulance drove at quite high speed along Seabourne Road to Pokesdown, turned left down Christchurch Road, past all the Boscombe shops and eventually right into Shelley Road, with me following in the red Mini. On arrival at the hospital, I was told my

218

services would not be required and to go home. I did, more or less, to the bar at Fircroft, where with Norman and Maymie, Phyllis and Brian, I had a brandy or two. Later that day, the 20th. of May, 1964, I returned to the Maternity Ward to see Norma and our son, Mark, a healthy eight and threequarter pounder.

With the added responsibility now of a child, it was imperative that I got orders for SNS. Derek at least knew one end of a transistor from another. Norma at least knew how to use a telephone and a typewriter. What did I know? Only that we had a good product and I had to convince people that it would be good for them and their businesses. The difficulty was getting in to see people. I would drive to an industrial area, size up the factories and screw my courage up to go to see the Managing Director, Sales Director, Production Director, Financial Director - any bloody director would do so long as I at least saw someone. But it was nearly always the same response from the soulless young painted thing who sat at the Reception desk.

'Can I help you?'

'Yes please, may I see your (?) director' (whichever one I guessed might be the most appropriate for that particular occasion). If I saw a name on a door, I would choose that one, so giving the impression that I already knew him.

'Do you have an appointment?'

'No, sorry.....'

'Well, you can't see him then.'

'Oh, why's that?'

'Because you don't have an appointment.' (I would often hear the unspoken word 'stupid' added almost as if in parentheses).

'But I've just seen him go into his office and he hasn't got anyone else with him, so he's free, isn't he?'

'Yes, I know, but you still can't see him.'

'Well can you make me an appointment to see him?'

'No, I don't make appointments'.

'Well then, can I speak to someone who does?'

'No.'

'Why not?'

'You have to make an appointment by telephone.'

'What's the point of that if I'm already in the building? Who do I ask for?'

'Me.'

'Well why can't you just make one here and now to save us all some time?'

'You have to telephone first.'

This stupid stonewalling would go on and on in one form or another at most of the receptions I ever went to. Very rarely would they see whether they could get me in to see anyone. They were being paid to keep visitors out, not to allow them in. Nobody wanted to know. Didn't these stupid little girls know that if I didn't sell something today, my wife and child and my business partner and I wouldn't eat tomorrow? Didn't they care? No, I suppose so long as they had their painted nails to attend to and answer the telephone, the world ended there. Well, I would NOT be beaten. I bitterly hated cold canvassing, but it was the only way, even though it cost time and petrol, neither of which I could really afford. Thank god we had the economy now of a Mini. The trick there was not to park it out the front of the building in case anyone saw it and guessed we couldn't afford a *proper* company car. This business of getting sales was frighteningly tough. Far tougher than anything I had imagined. In the Army I got used to simply telling someone that I was going to be seeing them at a certain time and that was all there was to it. It happened. Now, I was having to learn a completely alien life where sheer guts and doggedness would have to pay off. I was neither a born nor trained salesman. My hope was that having finally been able to see someone, I could at least infect him with some degree of my enthusiasm for Stentofon. But even when I did succeed in getting past that certain female barrier, more often than not, the answers were always the same.

'No, we don't need anything like that'.

'Why should I spend £300 (or more) on that stuff when I've already got a
telephone system?'

When push came to shove, I had difficulty in finding a convincing enough answer. It was getting more and more difficult to screw up my courage to drive to Southampton, Winchester, Portsmouth, Salisbury – all bloody miles away - or wherever I thought I might be lucky. Often days would go by with me dithering and getting sick in the stomach at the thought of wasting yet another day, especially as our tiny reserve of money was running out. It was at least OK for Derek, he was plodding away in Fircroft, feeding his lengths of wire round the building and still receiving a salary from Mr. Dacombe. The responsibility of keeping the business and ourselves afloat was weighing unbearably heavy on my shoulders. I wondered how much longer I could avoid buckling under the burden.

Then I had a stroke of good fortune for a change. Driving out of Southampton one afternoon, I passed a very large Ford dealership and thought 'Fuck, let's give it a try.' I went to Reception and asked to see the MD. I was invited to take a seat while the Receptionist tried to find him by ringing around the offices. She smiled a wan smile and said he couldn't be found, but if I would care to wait . . . I waited. Then I saw a well dressed executive walking purposely through the showroom area where I sat, obviously on his way to the office block. He stopped by me to enquire if I was being attended to, obviously not wanting to see a potential customer go away empty-handed.

'I'm waiting to see the managing Director.'

'Really? That's me. Am I expecting you?'

'No.'

'Well what do you want to see me about?'

'I have a simply wonderful communications system that I'm sure could be of great benefit to your organisation.'

'Oh really. I might be able to spare you a minute or two, but you'll have to wait
for a bit till I've attended to one or two more urgent things.'

'No, it's OK, I'll wait.'

I sat down again with my stomach fluttering with excitement and anticipation of what the future would hold. Could this be my lucky day? I waited and waited. Perhaps an hour went by, by which time it was getting dangerously close to 5pm when I expected everywhere to shut down. Perhaps it was after another half an hour, by which time the Receptionist had gone home, he came out of his office and saw me still sitting there.

'Can I help you?' without the faintest glimmer of recognition in his eyes.

'Well, yes. I am waiting to see you.'

'What about?' he asked with genuine lack of the memory of our earlier brief meeting.

'My communications system.'

'Oh god, I'd forgotten all about you. Oh well, I suppose the least I can do now is to give you a few minutes, now that you've waited all this time.'

So I took my demonstration case into his office and started to go through my set piece. He liked the concepts I proposed of being able to speak to his mechanics actually working under the cars in their pits, the salesmen in their offices, having paging announcements round the garage for missing people and so on.

'Right. This is what I want. Give me a quote and I'll consider it.'

I went back to Boscombe elated with the prospect of such a potentially good sale. When I had worked out all the costings, it came to somewhere in the region of £700-800. We would make about £300 profit all being well; enough to keep us going for at least another two or three weeks or more once we got the money. But first of all we had to get the actual order and get the stuff installed. I rang him with the price. He bargained and haggled until unknown to him our profit had been cut to less than £200. This was not so good, but it was better than nothing after all this time. I agreed the price and sent him a firm quotation in the post. After a while, we agreed an installation date and did the job. It was the first major order that I had got and if I could get one, I could get another. And so I did, nothing monumental, but little bread and butter jobs which kept us going while Derek put the finishing touches to the Fircroft systems. Once these were commissioned and proved to work to everyone's satisfaction, they represented the largest installation of Stentofon in the country at that time. One system for staff use had about ten fully intercommunicating master units and the other was one master unit with over forty slave units, one in each bedroom for room communication with guests, plus baby-listening. It broke our hearts having to give a substantial chunk of our profit away to Dacombe, but the final payment from Norman was a healthy one which kept us going for quite some time and gave me breathing space to get more orders into the pipeline.

At least having such a flagship installation in Bournemouth gave me the courage to go to other hoteliers and try to interest them. Also, being Norman Powers' son-in-law helped quite a bit too, once I had convinced them of the fact that I was not actually working in the

222

hotel with him and only doing this communications thing purely as a part-time hobby. I had to work hard at getting them to understand that this was *my* company and nothing to do with Norman. Hoteliers are notorious businessmen and Bournemouth had its fill of them. As a breed, they usually want everything for nothing. The way some of them treated their staff was adequate demonstration of that. They were reluctant to spend money on their businesses unless they could see some immediate financial return. They were not an easy market to break into in the early 'sixties, but I kept chipping away and began to make some progress, using Fircroft as my reference point. Surely, what they would be doing was offering a better service and so on. Without it, they could expect Fircroft to steal a march on them in future years. They may have agreed, but the cost . . . They would have to wait until the end of the season. Then they would have the excuse that they would have to see how they had survived the winter and whether they had got enough money left. And so the prevarications went on. Always jam tomorrow.

In the meantime, Derek had been working on a new bit of circuitry which was to be of use to us. He had designed an amplifier which would do all the big Stentor one would do for paging systems at much less cost to us. I later found out what a pig of a thing it was inside, but at least it worked. Somehow or other, he had also got wind of something going on up in the city of Hull. Hull had its own private telephone system. Not constrained by all the rules and regulations imposed on the rest of the country by the then GPO system, it was possible to get agreement to the system being used for uses other than purely straightforward telephones. He had some electrical colleagues up there who had been murmuring on about a group of privately owned Bingo clubs wanting to play group Bingo. Instead of each club playing for its own house prizes, if they joined forces, they could pool their prizes and play for much larger stakes. But to do so, every club in the group would have to be able to take its turn as host for the night and every other club on the circuit would have to be able hear the numbers being called and capable of immediate response if someone claimed a winning number or line. With a bit of local inside information, we learned that there was anything up fifteen or twenty clubs wanting to be involved. Derek got his thinking cap on and designed a system which could be run over the Hull Telephone Company's lines. It was all theoretical and incapable of being proved until it was installed and commissioned. With this dangerous chance in mind, we both drove in the Mini up to Hull, leaving Bournemouth at about 4am, arriving sometime during the morning to discuss the details with his electrical shopkeeper friends who would be our local agents and installers. Having thrashed out the technicalities, we then went on a lightning tour of some of the clubs involved, convincing the owners of what we could do for them. It took a few more visits to finally convince them all, but when I felt it prudent, returned to Boscombe to draw up my own layman's version of a written contract each of the club owners would have to sign and by which we would also have to abide in completing the work. They each ran to several pages of "wherefors", "heretofores", "aforesaids" and I did my best to make it look as though it had all been drawn up "by our company solicitors", which was the least to be expected from such a highly respected company as ours. It was nonsense of course – any competent solicitor could have ripped it to bits in no time. I borrowed the hotel Gestetner duplicating machine and ran off twenty copies and sent them off for our "Agents" to get signed. The final order was for about seventeen clubs and gave us a total contract value of about £8,000. This was an astonishing deal to have pulled off and gave us a euphoric feeling that now nothing could stop us. We were on our way in the world. After all the equipment had been bought or manufactured and sub-contractors paid, we stood to make well over £1000 in sheer profit. Within a matter of two or three days, another miracle happened. Two other very large quotations I had submitted, one to another hotel and one to a factory were both accepted. The hotel not only wanted intercom with baby-listening to every bedroom, but three radio channels as well. I had gaily said we could do such a thing (on Derek's say-so) and now we were faced with living up to our promise. So yet another piece of circuit wizardry had to be invented and a sub-contract manufacturer found who could build the new style room units incorporating all that was necessary. Here we were with nearly £12,000 worth of orders tied up in just three jobs and not a single small pot-boiler on the books to keep the daily cash turning over. This now presented us with what was to be the biggest crisis we had yet encountered. To buy in all this equipment, we would need a lot of money - several thousands of pounds, carefully scheduled. We would also suddenly need our own installation team and a van to carry all the gear. Derek could no longer do all that work on his own, especially now that we had another hotel and a factory to be done. So we started looking for installation engineers. Meantime I visited the bank to see about some more money. I had banked with Lloyds ever since I had joined the Army, fifteen years earlier and had transferred my account to the Boscombe Branch, where Norman had the Fircroft account. As Mr. Toop the manager was also a Rotarian, I felt we were bound to get some help from him. I was shown into his office and made welcome. We talked about Fircroft and how things were going there for the season and so forth. Then I eventually managed to steer the conversation around to the real purpose of my visit, happily telling him about these three whopper contracts we had just landed and how we needed money for our unexpected expansion. He listened and said how nice it was to see me. After a few more minutes of this non-committal conversation, he said that I was welcome to come and see him at any time. As I was shown the door, I asked whether he was going to let SNS have the extra £2,500 I had asked for.

'Mr. Slaney, contracts can be broken. Nothing is certain until everything is paid for. So as far as your £12,000 worth of orders is concerned, they are just bits of paper. You have no assets to speak of so I am unable to place the bank at risk by lending you such a very large sum of money without proper security. Because you have banked at Lloyds yourself for several years and because I know your father-in-law, I will grant you an additional £250 unsecured overdraft.'

I left his office in a state of shock. What now? We were stuck. I was insufficiently schooled in financial matters to know where to go for venture funding such as this. Could we have come so far up the mountain to be caught in an avalanche which could totally destroy us?

The factory job I had picked up was for the fitting out of a new factory owned by another of Norman's lifelong friends, Cyril Bird. Cyril's father had been a clever entrepreneur who had founded an electronics company way back in the 'thirties and which had invented the front door bell chimes unit. He had done incredibly well out of it as bell chimes were all the rage of the time. No self-respecting house owner would be seen dead with just a common-or-garden electric bell if they could afford these lovely sonorous two-tone chimes. Having made his fortune from these, he sold out to Friedland who went on to improve them even further. Cyril, his son and Norman's friend was of a similar bent and discovered a system of powerful forced air heating suitable for factories and open spaces. He bought a run-down little engineering company with which he could do the metal fabricating of the heaters, bought in Swedish pump units from Danfoss and an ignition system from someone else and put together these portable space heaters which ran off industrial paraffin. His business had flourished and it was time to expand out of the little engineering works in Boscombe to a much larger factory in Wallisdown. We had been given the job of installing all the communications systems throughout the offices and covering the factory floor. By this time and through Norman, I had got to know him and his son, Donald, quite well, even going for drinks at his flat once or twoice with Norman and Maymie who was very friendly with his wife, June. As he was such a successful businessman, I thought it utterly reasonable to tell him of our present financial predicament, as it was eventually likely to affect our contract with him. He listened to what I had to say and weighed his thoughts carefully before making his suggestion for our salvation. If it was a case of 100% of nothing or a smaller share of something, he thought he could help. Would we be prepared to sell out a controlling interest in our little company, whereby we would become his subsidiary? He would then guarantee our overdraft at the bank, giving us all the money we needed to complete our present orders and anything else that came along. He could even give us some space for our own workshops and offices in his new factory. It sounded too good to be true. The problem was that he insisted on 51% of SNS and that Norma's one share should be relinquished. We had set up the company originally with Derek holding 250 shares, me 249 and for some peculiar reason, Norma one. We talked it over and saw little or no option and accepted, parting with 255 in all, leaving Derek and me holding 49% between us. The legalities were attended to; a new bank account set up for us at the Midland Bank, Westbourne under the shelter of his main company, our workshops and offices constructed by a firm of jobbing carpenters within the new factory and we felt safe enough with this new arrangement. After all, half a loaf was better than no bread at all! The financial support that we now had through Cyril enabled us to safely commit ourselves to getting on with these three big contracts. However, the firm which made the amplifiers for the seventeen bingo halls gave us a few problems. Not least when after the system was up and running we received an irate call from Yorkshire one day from one of the principal club owners.

'A'm bloody oopset ah am. Ye'd best get yerselves oop 'ere bloody quick before ye have a riot on yer 'ands'.

It seemed that the night before, someone at one of the clubs had got a winning line and when the club calling button had been pressed to stop the game centrally, nothing had happened and someone else went on to win that game. Derek had to be despatched pronto to sort it all out before the entire club network went on the warpath. A few years later, in the hands of a new in-house electronics wizard, the whole circuitry concept was redesigned and vastly improved making it a very useful system to sell on to other companies such as Westrex Sound Systems who were one of the biggest in the cinema sound world. We managed to find Keith, an ex-trawlerman from Poole who could do electrical wiring and so he became our "Installation Department" with the aid of one junior of about seventeen who was so tall and thin that we thought he should be capable of squeezing through the tiniest of spaces. He became known as "Dick the Duct". Keith was a bit of a "Jack-the-lad" and we had to keep our eye on him as he was of, what can I say, imaginative, to say the least. On one occasion, he had the electricity cut off to the cottage he was living in because of non-payment of the bill. That night, he managed to gain access to the S.E.B. main distribution box out in the road and replaced the removed main company fuse to his cottage with a suitable piece of *our* cable! To show that we meant business, we even bought a new Bedford van for them to use and had it painted with the company name.

But having got these three contracts was no guarantee for the future. The work wouldn't last for ever. We needed continuity of business now that we had got started. My mind kept turning to John Robins, this young Domestic Sales Manager Derek and I had met when we went to Derritron to negotiate our agency. To me, he seemed just the kind of chap we needed - someone who obviously knew his way around and who had connections in the world of electronics in particular and business in general. Not only that, as a

227

result of the increasing value of the various purchase orders we had placed with him over the past year or so he had obviously seen how we had taken off. With Derek's agreement, I went to London and wooed John Robins. Over lunch, I made him the offer of joining us as Sales Director. Like Cyril Bird, he too drove a hard bargain and I found myself having to agree to splitting Derek's and my equity three ways with John taking one third, making him equal to both Derek and me. But it was all I had to negotiate with. We certainly couldn't bribe him with a big salary, we simply hadn't got that kind of money. He worked out his notice with Derritron and with our local knowledge, found himself a small house in Ringwood and started work for us in our new factory unit within the main factory of Boscombe Precision Engineering Co. Ltd., Wallisdown Road, Northbourne, Bournemouth. He quickly set about re-organising the sales approach and found us a brilliant salesman. Derek Fisher was working for Olympia, a National typewriter/office equipment company and he could sell ice cream to Eskimos. We set him up with a car and a brochure of what we could make and sell, which included all the normal Stentofon equipment, plus a range of electronic equipment we could buy in for resale from Derritron such as high quality microphones and loudspeakers, highly specialised microphones from Shure, an American manufacturer, telephone amplifying equipment, typewriters and dictation systems from Olympia, thanks to Derek, and whatever else we could lay our hands on, even closed circuit TV cameras to make up a good sales catalogue. It certainly gave Derek enough to go out on the road with and unlike me, he revelled in it. To give him encouragement, John, Derek Naylor and I agreed to give Derek Fisher a good basic salary, plus car, plus a very attractive rate of commission on the principal that whatever he sold, we were *all* the beneficiaries. Such was this package that at times he even earned more in the month than any of us. The next task was to set about designing our own exclusive range of equipment which we could manufacture in-house so that we were not in the hands of sub-contractors. For that, we needed a good R&D engineer who could also design well. Almost through an act of providence, Donald Bird's secretary was married to just such a person and we took him on. His single qualification was a City and Guilds Certificate in electronics, but he was quite simply an electronics genius. Within a very short space of time, he was putting

Derek Naylor in the shade. They were in two entirely different leagues. It wasn't long before John Robins was champing at the bit telling me as MD that I was going to have to sack Derek. That was a difficult one to handle - after all, he had exactly the same number of shares as I did. I had to draw up a list of Derek's most recent errors of judgement as technical Director, some of which had cost us money to put right and then with John in my office, confronted him with the fact that we considered he was not up to the job of growing with the company. I felt awful – like an executioner beheading a friend.

'Derek, we, John and I, are terribly sorry, but you really seem to be a bit out of your depth a lot of the time. Here's some of your recent gaffs that have cost the company a fair bit of money to put right . . .' and I read off those on my 'black' list. 'Any comments?'

'Yeah, I'm sorry.' He looked like a scared rabbit sitting between two hunters. 'But I've done my best.'

'Well, sorry, mate, but we're in a different league now. Everything's got to be 100% professional. You must see that? 'Look,' I added quickly, afraid I might not be able to deliver the coup de grace, 'John and I will buy your shares at a sensible price and you can keep the Company Saab as your personal car. What do you say?'

'Well, I was thinking I could get myself a job as a Forest Verderer, it's something I've always wanted to do.'

We gave him his company car for nothing and John and I bought out his company shares, splitting them equally between us. It was not a happy time for me to see him go, but I knew he simply was of very limited technical knowledge. His circuit designs were like childish Meccano compared with Rob Jones's sophisticated state-of-the-art stuff.

With Derek now gone, Rob Jones, John Robins and Derek Fisher set about creating a totally re-designed range of products. I was already something of an outsider, knowing absolutely nothing about electronics. My worth at that time was no doubt as a figurehead, connected with the hotel industry (a huge market) and family connections to the owner of the company who in turn owned us. I was still an important cog who could pull strings when required. This new product range, when fully developed, led us into a variety of markets including the world of "Pop" when we sold amplification equipment to groups such as "Slade" and "Yes" who regularly performed at the Lyceum in London. In those days, the Pop groups would often finish up either physically smashing their equipment on stage, or driving it all to such enormous volume levels that they literally blew it up, with the electronic circuitry simply short circuiting under the strain. Rob Jones designed the very first amplifier circuit which was indestructible and we patented it. Although "Slade" and "Yes" loved it because they could drive it to the maximum, it was not so popular with some of the others who were firmly wedded to amplifiers made by a company called WEM, owned by Charlie Watkins. When driven to extreme they would produce a distorted sound preferred by the majority of bands, whereas ours remained crystal clear no-matter what was thrown at them by the various guitars. Hence we never really broke into the Pop world. Many years later at Flete, I met the lead singer of "Slade" again who, when we discovered our old connection, told me the group were mobbed on their American tours by groups over there wanting to know whose fabulous equipment they were using. Somehow, the USA never got to hear about SNS, nor vice versa, otherwise I'm sure Derek Fisher would have been over there like a shot.

We also unearthed a tiny two-man electronics business elsewhere in Boscombe who were struggling with perfecting a design for a radio-microphone which did away with the need to be connected to an amplifier by a length of wire, such as had been the tradition ever since the days of electrical recording started. Wolfendale Electronics were virtually stuck through lack of resources. Here they were with this brilliant new idea and yet unable to spend the cash necessary to develop and exploit it. It was SNS's first buy-out. We acquired their designs - and their development engineer, set him up in his own dedicated laboratory, funded his research, applied for and obtained all the necessary GPO licences to operate this kind of equipment and perfected the transmitter part of the system - not without some difficulties along the way. But when we had done so, it opened up new markets for us, including the unusual one of enabling building companies who were wanting newer, safer ways of guiding their tower crane operators when it came to them lowering their loads into areas which were out of sight. With a receiver high up in their cabins at the top of the cranes, often two hundred feet above the ground, a banksman on the ground could give directions to the operator quite simply by voice instead of a complicated series of relayed hand signals. I had the unusual experience of testing out our prototype at the top of such a crane belonging to Drewitts, the Builders when they were building a new Office block on Richmond Hill. The climb up to the cabin was exhausting and I thereafter had great respect for these chaps who made it a daily job. The cabin swayed alarmingly in the wind and from that high vantage point, I could see for miles, way out to the Isle of Wight and The Purbecks. I did a similar climb one day up the inside of a cooling tower belonging to the Southern Electricity Generating Board's power station at Fawley on the Southampton Water. That was even higher with wider views and the height was dizzying.

Our range of amplifiers and loudspeakers was proving very successful and Rob Jones, this time with my help, designed a new hotel communications system into a console which incorporated room intercom, baby listening, three channel radio distribution, public room paging, and fire detection. This proved to be a winner and was known as the SNS Flexicall system. It could be tailored in any conformation and to any size of hotel ranging from ten rooms to (at that time) several hundred rooms, with suitably powered amplifiers being slotted into place inside the console. Everything could be pre-wired and factory tested before the main equipment was taken out on site for the final commissioning. We got the Joinery Company from Drewitts the builders next door to make the consoles and loudspeaker cabinets for us and when eventually they couldn't keep up with our demand, we bought them out, including their joinery manager and set up our own joinery department within our factory space. We were growing so fast that BPE, our parent had to make additional space available for us in their factory. By now, our hotel equipment was being sold under "Own Labels" to nearly all the competing companies in the UK, including GEC Reliance, Rediffusion, Westrex and other lesser companies. This time, we drove the hard bargains, reserving the right to also go selling our equipment under our own name in the market-place. Nowadays, our equipment can still be seen in many guises in hotels up and down the country. Thanks to my dealings with Bowmaker Finance, we managed to set up a lease-purchase deal with them which enabled

Derek Fisher to offer our equipment fully installed on leasing terms, which avoided hoteliers having to stump up large sums of money to buy the systems outright and this gave our sales an even greater impetus.

Before long, we were turning out so much equipment that it was necessary for us to have even more space in the factory. At the same time, BPE were having an upturn in their business too, having themselves been taken over by a giant engineering conglomerate by the name of Firth Cleveland. This meant that we were now the subsidiary of a subsidiary, but so long as FC didn't interfere too much, we were free to run our own show pretty much as we pleased. From time to time, their management accountant experts would come down to see us, but they were a bit reluctant to get involved with electronics. I later found out why. Not too many years before, FC had acquired Solartron, a very sophisticated electronics company working within the aircraft industry and after pumping several millions into it, it had failed to 'take off', so they sold it to the French Banking organisation, Schlumberger. Seeing the possibilities, Schlumberger, who understood what avionics was all about had put just one more injection of money into them with the result that Solartron became one of the most successful aviation electronics companies of the 1960's, no doubt to FC's chagrin. After that, Firth Cleveland decided to keep to what they knew best - engineering. BPE moved out to new factory premises in Poole, leaving us to now occupy the whole of the old factory area. BPE's move to Poole also, almost by default, gave us yet another factory sound installation to do. Our new factory space now enabled us to set up our own proper production lines for everything we made and as we had also bought out Medgar, the light engineering company who did all our metalwork for us, we brought them into the new factory. This meant that we now had just over one hundred employees under one roof working in the main electronics areas, the joinery department, Medgar and offices. We even bought out the company who made all the hundreds of transformers we used in our various items of equipment, making us almost totally self-sufficient. About the only things we didn't make were the tiny resistors, diodes, capacitors and transistors which we still had to buy from specialist manufacturers.

One day I received a telephone call from a gentleman who introduced himself as Mr. Stonor.

'Good morning, Mr. Slaney. We haven't met, but I'm the Chairman of Sound Diffusion and I wonder whether you and I might meet to see whether we have anything we can offer one another.'

This sounded interesting and I went along to John's office.

'Hey,' I said, poking my head round the door, 'I've just had an interesting call,' and proceeded to tell him about it. We agreed that it might be interesting to pursue it and see what happened next. So I rang Mr. Stonor and made an appointment to visit him at his factory in Hove, near Brighton. Sound Diffusion was the manufacturers of "Radiotel", our biggest competitor in the hotel field. We were obviously a thorn in their side and he wanted to make us an offer. To start, he introduced me to his brother, Tim, who was their Company Secretary and Finance Director. The three of us went on a tour of his factory which took up about three floors of a large purpose-built unit. It was very impressive with technicians building and testing their electronic units of varying sizes and functions seemingly everywhere. Their testing bay was to me what NASA looked like, with TV monitors and coloured lights winking to the accompaniment of bleepers in various tones quietly peeping away in the background. After lunch, he put the question, 'Could I possibly come over to your place and see what it's like? I feel we may well be able to come to some arrangement.'

I quickly got his point and said I would like to consult with my Board of Directors before committing us. Back in Bournemouth, John and the others agreed and I fixed a time for Mr. Stonor to visit us. After seeing round and being suitably impressed, he popped the final question. 'Would we be interested in becoming *his* subsidiary if he bought us out from Firth Cleveland and BPE?' I said we would, but under certain conditions. I wanted to know what his offer was for John and me, as the shareholders and major directors of SNS. It was once again our turn to be hard-nosed. We didn't really need him, although it would be nicer for us to be wedded to a parent who thoroughly understood the market we were in. Before he left that day, the deal was agreed between us. It was now up to him and FC/BPE. For us, I had got a salary package for John and me of a basic £4000, plus 4% commission of audited profits, plus new cars for us both. In exchange, he would place one of his present directors on our Board as Non-Executive Chairman. We would go on doing what we wanted, the way we wanted to and he would not interfere in our marketing. What was more, we were to also now sell our products to *his* company including our hotel systems in addition to our present customers. The remaining final benefit to us was that we could take advantage of the financing arrangements he had and so set up our own company rental system, which was even more advantageous than the arrangement we had with Bowmakers. Paul Stonor pulled off his deal with Firth Cleveland and we became his subsidiary as planned. John and I moved onto our new salary packages, so that by the end of 1971 we were both earning in the region of £9000 a year. SNS by now was achieving in excess of three-quarters of a million pounds in annual turnover with three subsidiaries of its own, and an office in Germany to look after SNS Communications GmbH and the Common Market – one of John's not quite so brilliant ideas, I felt, as it subsequently produced very little business for us just at that time.

At John's insistence, as he now felt himself to be in an unassailable position, we restructured the company, creating John and myself Joint MD's, Derek Fisher as Sales Director, Rob Jones as Technical Director and an Australian accountant Financial Director. I knew that really, my role as figurehead was at best nominal, especially as the hotel market was now rolling so well with Derek Fisher at the sales helm. Again at John's insistence, we also found ourselves a supposedly highly qualified Works Director to look after a very special contract we had picked up from a firm called Mordaunt Short, who wanted us to make ultra high quality loudspeakers to their design and using their circuitry. Regrettably, this contract was short lived as our Works Manager at the time simply wasn't up to the high demands of quality control during the assembly of these luxury loudspeakers and we had to eat humble pie and compensate Mordaunt Short for the problems they had experienced. Mordaunt Short went on to become a leading name in their field and it is a great shame that we lost that contract. We also fought shy of an enormous contract with Plessey Electronics who were creating a highly sophisticated form of traffic control system worth millions of pounds for the Government. Having done all the calculations and costings, the financial dangers were such that we passed it all by, leaving Plessey to find someone else willing to take the risks. One major hiccup on such a contract would have killed us stone dead. Within about six months, I was beginning to feel insecure. John Robins had surrounded himself with people of his own choice and it was to him they owed their allegiance. I began to feel excluded from the decision-making, particularly when John began to throw his weight around a bit now that he was equal top dog. I knew that the only knowledge I had was what I had learned since setting up the company. I had no previous experience and so was now rapidly getting myself into the same situation as Derek Naylor had found himself in with Rob Jones. I had to have a job to do which was (a) important to the company, and (b) that I and I alone could do without advice from anyone else and finally (c) at which I could become the acknowledged expert. The opportunity came when it was suggested at a Board Meeting one day that we gradually put the entire company on a computerised Payroll and Stock and Production Control system. Although it was an area of expertise I knew nothing about, I gladly took it on and for the next year or more spent all day and every day going into the minutiae of all that was necessary. The Computer Bureau we employed undertook the Payroll system, because that was a set program which they could use for any firm anywhere at any time, as everybody paid Income Tax and National Health at the same rates, no-matter where they worked. But no two firms ran their stock and Production Control the same way; neither did they make identical products. So this aspect of the system had to be specially written for us in The States and sent back over to the bureau in Southampton.

It was necessary for me to itemize every single component we used in our manufacturing process, right down to the last microscopic nut, bolt and resistor. Every item had to be given its own unique six figure number, every type of printed circuit card given a unique number so that every product would reflect its own family tree of component numbers through every sub-assembly mounted on every sub-chassis, every group of sub-chassis mounted on every main chassis and so on until the whole complicated product was complete in its outer case and, where appropriate, cardboard transit box. The electronics industry even then was a highly complicated one with even quite small assemblies containing perhaps dozens of resistors, diodes, transistors and capacitors etc. So a large, complicated final assembly might contain a family tree containing hundreds, if not thousands of parts, all of which had to be capable of identification by its computer number. Quite often, assemblies we could call "son" may contain certain components which were identical to those found in its "father" and even "Grandfather" and this was why each of the generations had to have its own unique identity so that when added together, the computer could work out what were the *names* and *totals* of all those identical parts. This in turn produced a stock requirement schedule which the technical stores would have to assemble ready for issue to the production line. If any items were out of stock, ideally the computer system should also be able to predict from known forward orders placed by the Purchasing office when those missing items would come into stock. This would then determine what sort of delivery date could be offered to the customer. The system should also be able to say what work-in-progress was on the shop floor and what its component value was in terms of cost to the company and what stocks of finished products we were holding in stock and already free for despatch to complete any new orders received.

To set up this system was a monumental task and one I revelled in, especially as it was guaranteed to be a long-term project and sure enough, I did become the only person in the company who could speak about it knowledgably from A-Z. About a year later, as the time approached for the system to be put into use, the Computer Bureau in Southampton received regular visits from me to make sure that they were covering all the eventualities I saw arising, which they assured me they were. They were using a huge Burroughs computer in an air-conditioned suite of rooms and it looked to me like HAL, the computer in 2001 a Space Odyssey. They were also by now running a newly imported Stock and Production Control Program from America, also produced by Burroughs, and for us, they had amended the Burroughs program in consultation with Burroughs in The States so everything should be hunky-dory. It was part of our agreement with them that when we were approaching the final countdown, we should have two or three months of what was called "Playtime" when the system would be run alongside our own manual system and the results compared to make sure that both agreed with one another. Playtime could be extended, but it would cost us extra money to do so. We ran the first month's trial and I received back reams and reams of zigzag printouts smothered in numbers, some of which made sense, some of which didn't. I checked them over with the Bureau and they found some parts puzzling. The answers were not coming out correctly. We tried again the following month and the results were the same. We tried a third month and although various alterations had been made, the results were still disappointingly inaccurate, so they referred the matter to America for their assistance. Time was now dragging on and I could tell that now that I had broken the back of this computerization business and if all went well with it my presence was not going to be needed for much longer. As it was, John Robins was being thoroughly objectionable towards me and I knew I had little or no defence. What more could I bring to a million pound company that he and his cronies couldn't? Soon I began to suffer stomach ulcers from the stress of going in to work each day feeling isolated and it got so bad that I even began to get frightened at the thought of having to talk to him about something or other. I would sit in my office strung up with apprehension with my guts screwed up in knots. This was no way of life for me. I no longer fitted in. Bugger it. After all, *I* had brought this man into *my* company, *I* had promoted him. Dammit, I was even a few years his senior. I felt sick that he should respond this way. I should have realised what he would be like when one day he told me in what was to become a prophesy that when he was the Sales Manager of Derritron, he had visited one of their agents in Yorkshire only to find the boss, a Mr. John Smith sitting at a bench out the back of the premises repairing an electric kettle. He should have been out selling Derritron's products – that was why he was their agent, according to St. John. When he felt people were trying to operate beyond their capabilities, he called it the "John Smith" syndrome. The computer system didn't work. There was nothing else I could bury myself in as I had done for the past year. It was time to call it a day. I was another "John Smith".

I drove to the main factory and offices of Sound Diffusion in Hove and saw Paul Stonor. I told him that I thought my usefulness had reached its limit and felt it would be best for everyone if I left SNS. Would he buy out my shares? He said he would and would also want to buy out John's holdings at the same time, as he was cooking up some huge deal and wanted total control of what he was doing. He had his accountants value our shareholdings in SNS and offered to exchange each of our shareholdings for 78,498 of his Sound Diffusion shares which were listed on the Northern Stock Exchange at a market value of 47 pence each, a total sum well in excess of £30,000, a comparatively huge sum in those days. We were asked not to sell them in any quantity as this would upset his arrangements, but we could sell off small, un-noticeable parcels of them every now and then to suit ourselves. I felt that my next move would have to be back into catering as this was the one thing I did already know something about and where I could once more be my own boss. I resigned my Directorships with SNS and our subsidiaries and spent the next three months with the firm in a consultancy capacity, trying to clear up the mystery of the bum computer system, which eventually turned out to be someone's fault in writing a bug into the original program in America. It was going to be ages before the program could be run and trusted in this country and it cost the Bureau and Burroughs a lot of money before it was finally sorted out. Meanwhile, during my consultancy, I spent the time formulating a Business Plan for the creation of my own very special restaurant business and with the help of an accountant recommended by Eddie Moors, set up Opus Catering Limited with Norma and me as the two founding Directors. The name Opus came from the word "Opera" the only anagram I could make out of our two Christian names abbreviated. It seemed quite appropriate in that Opus was the singular of Opera and it meant that as the company grew into a chain of successful restaurants, we could at least have Opus One, Opus Two and so on as in music.

Having been bitten rather savagely through borrowing money to get us over a crisis in the early days of SNS, I was definitely very wary about tying up my capital in a property until I could see that it was safe to do so. So here I was with a very healthy portfolio of shares now, thanks to Paul Stonor's deals worth close on £50,000 on the open market, but little or no actual cash reserves. All our money had gone into making alterations and improvements to Netheravon where we lived with Norman and Maymie. We had moved into the ground floor flat and spent quite a lot of money on a teak woodblock floor in the lounge, very expensive curtains and furniture and building onto the back of the house an upstairs office for Norma to use for her writing. Below, we gutted the interiors the old outhouses and built a bedroom and walk-in shower room and bathroom for Mark. Fortunately, as part of my resignation deal, I had acquired my company car, a Renault 16TS for the princely sum of £1, which bought it legally from SNS. I went to various estate agents to see what properties were available for our new venture and found there were three sites which we could lease. One, on a prominent corner opposite the Midland Bank in Westbourne where we now banked and where by now I knew the Manager, Vaughan Thomas very well; another which was just an empty concrete shell right by The Winter Gardens in the centre of Bournemouth and finally another with a complete four-bedroomed flat above it in Southbourne. Because of the expense involved in setting up the first two, plus their much higher rentals, I chose the one in Southbourne. It was not ideal, having been at one time a fishmonger's shop, but it did have a large cellar below, a small garden out the back, just enough room for a kitchen to be built between it and next door, plus the four bedroomed flat above, all for £1800 a year lease. We took it on a twenty year lease and so in the very early spring of 1973 it became goodbye SNS, hello Opus One.

CHAPTER THIRTEEN

OPUS ONE

So here we were in February 1973 with a boy of not quite nine years of age, a Renault 16TS nowhere near as old, a brand new £10,000 overdraft facility at Midland Bank, Westbourne secured against my lovely big hand-out of SD shares, a Business Plan and a totally empty old shop with two floors of accommodation over. The Business Plan was beautifully drawn up and presented, but a rather inept attempt to justify us going into a restaurant business. Instead of it proving how tough it was going to be, I "adjusted" the figures to show that not only could we do better than break even in our first year, but would go on to make good profits subsequently, thereby ensuring the future birth of Opus Two. Utterly ridiculous, of course, but it was my anti-SNS medicine that was going to remedy all the problems I had encountered in the last year or so of being with John Robins and company. It simply *had* to work. Thanks to Norma and a small circle of her friends, we gathered together a team of young la dies who were prepared to come and work as waitresses, including Phyl, her sister. One of them, Maggie was an excellent dressmaker and under Norma's guidance designed and made all the long brown skirts and frilly aprons and in their cream blouses the girls all looked great. My mother pretty nearly wore out her sewing machine hemming all the gold and brown tablecloths and matching napkins from the dozens of yards of pure Irish linen I had bought.

I (note: not Norma and I, but I – the 'expert' now having loads of money to burn?) had decided that we would gut the shop, rip out the shop-front and create a Georgian-style dining room with a bow-fronted window, chandeliers and thick carpets. Fool – a few years later another now famous French chef came to another part of Southbourne and opened his restaurant in a shop just as he had taken it over, merely putting in tables and chairs at a fraction of our/my expense! Phyllis had a friend, Ray and his brother who had a small firm of interior decorators who looked after the inside, a specialist firm of shop-fitters did the frontage complete with the name Opus One in gilt lettering and I found a specialist electrician to supply and fit the chandeliers. But before we could open, I had to apply for a Licence without which we would be stuck with just a shop for the next twenty years. The Health Department had to approve the plans, insisting on the requisite number of sinks and toilets and the Fire Brigade had to also be satisfied. The main problem was going to be the kitchen. There simply wasn't room for one unless I could have it built in the empty space between the outside walls of our place and next door. I called in a Surveyor, who also drew up some plans for me to submit for approval to the Borough Engineer and we also had to nicely ask the Landlord of the adjacent property if we could fix joist hangers to his outside wall to support the roof of our kitchen. Fortunately, he and our Landlord Hector Vack and everybody else involved agreed and the necessary permissions were all given, so we were safe to proceed with the building, which included laying new drains, new electricity supply and heaven knows what else. From my SNS days, I called in Mike McLaughlin who owned a small firm of builders who had done all the factory alterations for us and he undertook this part of the work. Finding and buying all the kitchen equipment was a totally separate exercise. Clive Exton, whose family had owned the Linden Hall Hydro where I was commis back in 1949 also owned an equipment supply company with showrooms in Holdenhurst Road. I visited him there and with his manager drew up a list of all the heavy equipment needed, from the Garland double-oven cookers to the potato peeler and Crypto mixing machine, dining tables and chairs and the cutlery - all top quality silver plated stuff. Whilst on the one hand I knew that we would set an incredibly high standard of decor and appointments and that naturally we would also produce wonderful food, the overdraft was getting used up pretty quickly. I had planned to have a chef and advertised in The Caterer. Eventually, after getting him to produce a meal for us at Netheravon, I chose Peter and Irene, his wife who would be our Head Waitress. As part of their salary, they were to be given free accommodation above the restaurant and their food. This decision now required us to furnish the flat above and in doing so, we fully furnished it throughout, including the upstairs kitchen which I was convinced would make an ideal second kitchen if needed. By furnishing the whole flat, it did give us another option at a later date, which was to let it to theatre people such as Lulu and her "Second Generation", Derren Nesbitt and others who appeared for the season at the two or three theatres in Bournemouth.

Not long before our opening day, I suddenly woke up to the fact that we would need glasses - lots of them. I wasn't at all taken with the cheap old things that every other hotel and restaurant used and hunted for something in a class of its own. One day I went to Bournemouth and the main department stores. In Beales' glassware department I saw what I wanted. They were displaying hundreds of cut glasses which were going on sale in about five day's time or so, all at the one price of 60p each. I asked for the department manageress.

'I'd very much like to buy a quantity of these glasses. Can you please tell me the best way of getting them without having to try and fight my way through all the other people who might be in the department grabbing what they want first?'

'Yes, sir. If you can let me have a list of what you want at least one day before the sale opens, I can have them all packed up for you to collect. How many were you thinking of?'

I made a guess ranging from sherry to large wine, goblets to tumblers. I thought we would need quite a few, plus spares for breakages and said 'Oh, about five hundred or so.' She gulped and said she had better have forty-eight hours notice to cope with packing all that lot. In the end, I ordered six hundred assorted glasses.

She said 'If you could be in the department the moment the shop opens on the day of the sale, I will have them all packed up for you out the back. Simply hand me your official order and cheque and I will have them delivered within the week'.

On the day of the sale, I got up at about 5am and went to Beales, where at 5.45am I was already still about third in the queue. When the doors opened at 9am, I ran down to the glassware and staked my claim. As promised, dozens of boxes of fragile cut glasses arrived a week or so later, all of which had to be washed, dried and carefully stored away somewhere safe until needed for the grand opening. The cellar looked like a cut glass emporium with glasses everywhere. I then realised we would have another storage problem on our hands – where on earth do we keep them for daily use? The upstairs kitchen became the obvious place to keep our working stock until we could come up with something better and the reserve glasses kept down in the cellar in boxes until they were required.

Having the glasses was fine and dandy, but now I needed to consider what wines I was going to offer for sale. Really, I was quite ignorant about wines and I really only knew the few I had drunk in the Army, and then they were mostly run-of-the-mill hocks. Dammit, I knew more about beer, gin and Scotch than about wines! Even on Regimental Dinner Nights only the port remains in my memory. So I bought and read Hugh Johnson's "Wines of the World" for inspiration and knowledge. It became my Bible and served me well. I learned a hell of a lot, quickly. Almost all my opening stocks of wines were culled from this book and the Peter Dominic wine shop in Old Christchurch Road couldn't believe their luck when I walked in one day with my order. I had listed clarets from the finest vintages such as 1961, 64, 66, many of them Crus Classé, superb Burgundies, great Sauternes, classic estate wines from Germany, rare Tokays from Hungary and the best wines of South Africa, Austria and Italy, great vintage ports and wonderful vintage champagnes. In all, our opening wine list listed around a hundred wines and the "House Wine" was even a decent Beaujolais from a good year. I spent an enormous amount of money on 'my' cellar and in hindsight was astonished at how little our customers understood about the wines they drank. A few did and these stood out as being notable customers who enjoyed both their food and their wine. The cellar beneath the restaurant was racked out with hundreds of holes, all the racking also bought from Peter Dominic and all of which were now filled; with cases and cases of reserve wine still in cardboard boxes stacked neatly ready for use, all lying properly on their sides. One day, a young French salesman called, offering me a special deal on a red wine "Chateau du Plantier" and saying that it would become a great wine in time. I didn't understand such things yet as to how the tannins balanced the fruits, but believed what he said and bought *fifty* cases from him. When all six hundred bottles arrived, they presented me/us with yet more problems of storage and drinkability. The wine was as hard as nails and it stayed that way for years, so was not a good short term investment. The cellar was now almost totally filled with wines with hardly a square inch for the storage of other things such as surplus crockery and tables, let alone personal items brought with us. What Plantier we did sell, we had to sell at stupidly low prices. It definitely was not a favourite with the customers. It wasn't until eight or ten years later, when I had let Mark have the last case

243

or two for his birthday, that I discovered what the salesman had said was coming true. And to think - I had been selling it as House Wine at a stupid price and even lavishly cooking with it just to clear it to save any more drain on my cash-flow.

Eventually the time came to put away the shopping lists, stock up with food and open. I had decided that the best way to get everything running as smoothly as possible for the avalanche of public who were going to invade us was to send out about 100 invitations for friends to come for a free meal on two successive nights before the grand opening day. It would only cost them the price of their wines and drinks. The food was free. Those two rehearsal nights were sheer pandemonium. From doing nothing, the kitchen, i.e. Peter, was hit with an avalanche of orders from the short á la carte for about 30-35 starters and main courses and the temperature began to rise. Naturally, he couldn't cope with this sudden tidal wave of orders and as panic stations took over, the systems went into overload. Poor Aubrey had dirty crockery stacked everywhere, pots and pans were flying, because I had insisted that all our lovely cut glasses *must* be washed up in the upstairs kitchen, Phyllis had tripped over her long skirt going upstairs and dropped a whole tray of them. I hit the roof and threatened to stop the value out of her wages (how naïve can you get?). I got a severe reprimand from chef Peter for not making sure that our guests arrived in small batches and several other vital lessons were learned. 'See, Peter', I said to myself – 'you don't know it all, and it isn't going to be as easy as you had thought'. I simply hadn't thought things through properly.

Now we came to the real thing and were to quickly discover how cruel life really was. We had probably the most comfortable, elegant restaurant in Bournemouth; we had superb wines and beautiful glasses to drink them from; we had attractive girls, well dressed as our waitresses and we had very good food indeed. We had advertised. All we wanted now were the customers. On our first Saturday night we had a tiny handful daring enough to try us out. The next day, at Sunday lunch, we had nobody and I was even daft enough to stand outside on the pavement greeting everyone who came along with 'Hello, would you like to come inside and see our wonderful new restaurant?' in the hope that they might be tempted to try our food. All that happened was that they crossed over the road to get away from this crank who was accosting them! I was devastated. Where were the thirty covers I had expected for lunch? The other two restaurants down the road were packed as usual. We were empty. Why? I couldn't understand what was going wrong so soon. I decided to put "Plan B" into operation.

I (note: 'I' again) had decided some time earlier that Opus One should be a musical Mecca. With the grand piano in the restaurant, I could play to the customers in the evenings. I could even sponsor young musicians by giving them a platform to play to a real live public audience. I could get singers and instrumentalists and eventually we would have the whole of the Bournemouth Symphony Orchestra flocking to our door. I had planned to hold a musical evening once or twice a month when we would have a set meal of four or five courses, to be followed by a recital of some sort. They were bound to be popular - after all, people liked music and entertainment. I advertised in the Evening Echo for people to apply for audition. I had mums bringing little Johnny to do his party piece and I had semi-professional musicians wanting to earn some extra money and I had everything in between. From the best of these, I organised a series of concert nights and launched them on an unsuspecting world! One of my greatest successes was to discover a guitarist, Paul Hammond, who played music from Spain in the most wonderful Flamenco manner. We advertised him for one of our dinner nights as "playing the music of Paco Peña" and finished up nearly having a standup fight with one obstreperous customer who wanted his money back because he had come to hear Paco Peña himself. We had Paul back again and one of our regular customers, Mr. Black, made a tape recording of him, quite unexpectedly giving it to me as a present. I accompanied an excellent soprano one night, who among her programme sang not only the lovely Elgar "Sea Pictures", but excerpts from "Porgy and Bess" and leider such as Schubert's "The Trout" and Peter Cornelius's "Ein Ton". But somehow or other, she was not a great success with the audience. Rucky Van Mill, my own piano teacher, introduced some of her best piano students to me, together with some of her husband Nick's best string players from Trinity College. I enjoyed the musical evenings and so did those regular customers who looked upon us as having a rather exclusive club. The trouble was that we were still not giving the great Bournemouth public what they wanted. Often the enquiries

would come in over the phone,
'Do you have any music on this evening?'
'What kind of music do you mean?'
'Well, don't you have a string trio sittting in the corner?'
'Good heavens, no.'
'Thank god for that - in which case I'll have a table for two.'

On one occasion, I had finished the cooking for the evening and went out to play a few pieces for the customers. Halfway through Claire de Lune I heard an argument break out at one of the tables. It ended with the husband marching out of the restaurant shouting back over his shoulder to his wife, 'If you want to sit and listen to this rubbish, OK, but I'm going. You can find your own way home.'

We did have our successes though. One evening, Kenneth Montgomery, the conductor of the Bournemouth Sinfonietta, who lived somewhere nearby in Southbourne, came to dinner with some friends of his from the orchestra. After their meals, Ken sat at the piano and played around, eventually giving us part of the Brahms G minor Impromptu. One of his friends, slightly the worse for alcoholic wear attempted the Rachmaninov 2nd. Piano Concerto, but forgot where he was after a page or so. I dug out my score of it for two pianos and we both sat and duetted, playing chunks of it for fun. It was a lovely spontaneous end to an enjoyable evening. On another occasion, Eddie Moors came with a young Japanese girl, Yoko Fujimura, who was a rising star in the Japanese piano firmament. She was on a tour of Europe publicising Yamaha pianos, giving concerts in selected towns. As mine was a Yamaha, Eddie brought her to supper with us in the hope she would play mine, but she steadfastly refused everybody's requests - except mine. She really was quite shy and all she wanted was to have her meal in peace – and I don't blame her.

'Miss Fujimura,' I asked, 'would you kindly play something for us?'

She looked at me with perhaps a weary smile. 'No, I really cannot. I have been drinking with Mr. Eddie and Mrs. Eddie and I really shouldn't.'

'But if I played something first, would you then, please?' I begged - I hoped on behalf of the customers.

'Oh, alright then', she agreed, somewhat reluctantly. Poor

246

girl, she had thought she was coming out for a quiet meal with her host and had got waylaid be me.

I played my first piece, a Chopin Nocturne, which, thank heavens, I managed quite well and got a round of applause from the customers. She played something in return. I said how about one more, and played a piece of Schumann, his Traumerei, or something like that. Finally she gave us the A flat Chopin Polonaise, which Rucky had previously described to me as "The coffee grinder" because of the middle section. This is a continuous and rapid succession of downwards octaves accompanying the melody. It is very, very exhausting. In fact so much so that when Rucky was pregnant at one time, she flatly refused to play it in case it brought on a premature birth!

I have referred to Rucky and Nick and should explain that when I was with SNS and things were going well enough for me to be able to afford it; I bought a small Yamaha grand piano from Eddie Moors' shop in Boscombe. It was a either that or the other grand he had, a huge Russian Concert grand which would have filled a room. Eddie let me have the Yamaha at the special price of about £645 and I had it in what used to be Norman's study in Netheravon. I felt that I had been without a piano long enough - in fact since I left home to join the Army in 1950 and now here we were in 1968, during all of which I had been piano-less. Far too long to be without a piano, I felt. I also thought it would be a good idea to attend evening classes in music study at Poole Technical College. While there, I had asked the tutor, Don Riddell, if he could recommend a good piano teacher. He told me that one of the very best lived right here in Bournemouth. Her name was Rucky Van Mill and she was, or had been, senior piano professor at Trinity College of Music. I rang her and fixed an appointment to go and see her for an audition. I was met at the door by a very commanding lady who spoke English with a somewhat guttural Dutch accent which to me sounded more like German, sprinkling her sentences and answers with "Ja", "Mein Got" and "Neigh's". She took me into her study with its Blüthner grand piano and introduced herself.

'I am the Baroness Rucky Van Mill'. She was also Mrs Roth in private life.

'Vot is your musical background?' She quizzed me about my past training. I told her of my time at Trinity and she knew my old

247

teacher, Professor Audrey Ayliffe very well.

'Vell, play me someting.' I did. The Chopin Waltz in C sharp major I had learned years before. She stopped me halfway through.

'Ken you play someting else?' This time I played the opening of a Schubert Impromptu. Again she stopped me.

'What is dat you play' she asked looking genuinely puzzled?

'The Schubert Impromptu number four in A flat.'

'Oh, this vun.' She leaned over me and played the first page. It was like a waterfall rippling, full of expression, her fingers moving like quicksilver - not at all like my version. Similar, yes. But not the same by any means.

'Ja, ja. Enough. You play OK,' she said, slowly parting her hands, palms upwards, 'but you mek too many misteks. You are careless. You do not read de music. Me, I tek only who I please. I doan tek children. All my students vork hart, very hart end if I tek you, you vill vork hart too, yes?"

'Yes', I agreed.

'Good. Ve start now. We vill do the Schubert.' And so my first lesson with her was begun.

I studied piano with her for several years, becoming friends with her and her husband Nick Roth, who in his day had been a very famous violinist and founder of the Budapest Trio. Rucky herself had been a pupil of Claudio Arrau in Berlin before the second War and perhaps because she was the daughter of a Dutch baron, as a child had not suffered quite as badly as some other Dutch people at the hands of the Germans when they occupied Holland, but that wasn't saying a lot. Of course they suffered – all of them; instant execution if suspected of spying or of acts of resistance against the occupying German forces and much worse. Arrau had predicted a brilliant future for her if she really wanted to devote herself to the piano and nothing else. But - she had wanted to be a wife and mother, raising a family and so had to forgo a glittering career as a concert pianist, contenting herself with being an outstandingly good pianist: making the odd record here or there, particularly for one LP recording of all John Field's Nocturnes (he was Chopin's predecessor who introduced the term Nocturne); a performer of concert standard, sometimes playing in public; sometimes accompanying some of the great fiddle players of the day such as Ruggiero Ricci and making a name for herself in Europe as a

248

harpsichordist rather than concert pianist. She sublimated her career for her husband, Nick Roth. I remember going with Norma and Mark to The Wigmore Hall in London one evening to hear her give her "Retirement" Concert. The hall was packed out and her audience were not disappointed. She gave a wonderful recital to much applause. Some years ago now, I made a copy of Nick's entry in Grove's, the world's foremost Musical Encyclopaedia and for posterity's sake I reproduce it here.

ROTH, Nicholas. Born Budapest 3.5.1909.
English violinist of Hungarian birth. Taken as an infant to London and brought up as a British subject. At age 9 won the Gold medal at the Bristol Eisteddfod and at 11 a scholarship to Trinity College of Music where he became a pupil of Emil Sauret. After a somewhat difficult time during World War I, he was able to go to Budapest where for two years he was a pupil of Jeno Hubay. After this, with his brother George, he started The Budapest Trio and has continued to devote most of his energies to chamber music. An invitation to take part in the musical organisation of the Dutch Broadcasting Company AVRO caused him to settle in Holland and for many years past (except between 1940 and 1945 when he was interned in Germany) he has been Director of Chamber Music for that organisation. In 1935 with Johan Feltcamp (flute), Carel van Leeuwen Boomkamp (viola da gamba) and Hans Brandts Buys (cembalo) he formed the quartet Musica Antiqua for the performance of old music.

BUDAPEST TRIO
A violin, 'cello and piano team formed in 1920 under the leadership of Nicholas Roth, a pupil of Jeno Hubay with his brother George ('cello). The personnel of the trio varied slightly from time to time, consisting now of the brothers Roth and pianist Ilona Kabos. Its headquarters was for many years London, but is now in Amsterdam. The trio has toured almost every country in the world and has been the means of bringing forward a number of original works.

MUSICA ANTIQUA
Formed 1935 in Amsterdam. Music from 17th. and 18th. centuries. Each piece is discussed by the players, but there is no leader as

249

such. Original manuscripts (sometimes unknown for two centuries)
have been revived and followed as closely as possible. Half the
pieces performed were of unpublished works.

Through my studies with Rucky, I managed to pick up the
threads of my earlier studies and get back to playing moderately well
and thanks to her teaching, I improved sufficiently to be able to give
recitals of my own at Opus One, including playing two or three
pieces each evening after I had finished work in the kitchen. But
gradually it dawned on me that having the piano in the restaurant
was an embarrassment - unless I could turn it to a positive
advantage. So I gave it one more try. Through Eddie Moors, I
contacted a jazz pianist by the name of Gordon King who had played
in the Piano Bars of New York and on the Atlantic liners. He was
brilliant. He could play anything and do so in anyone's style, Art
Tatum, Oscar Peterson, etc. I engaged him to play for us three
evenings a week and it was great to hear superb light music and jazz
played live instead of listening to taped music. But then we got
complaints from certain customers that they couldn't hear themselves
talk for the music. That really pissed me off, because Gordon did his
best to play gently and softly, but I suppose our restaurant area was a
bit too small even for that. So I had to cancel my arrangement with
him. Finally, I had had enough of trying to satisfy the Bournemouth
peasantry and called in a firm of removers to take the piano upstairs
to our flat.

One sultry summer's day they arrived; one middle aged chap
and a youngster in his late teens or very early 'twenties. I showed
them the piano, the staircase and the lounge above where it was to
end up.

'Christ, this is going to be a bit tight', said the middle aged
one.

'Yeah, but we can try now we're 'ere.' replied the younger.

So they took the piano apart, wrapped the main body of it in
blankets and belted it onto "the shoe", the specially shaped platform
used for moving grand pianos. Getting it onto the little wheeled
trolley, they moved it as far as the foot of the narrow staircase, while
I was getting on with the cooking, and listening to the grunted
instructions of one to the other.

'No, you push from below while I lift from the front.'

'Can't. 'Aven't got enough of a grip on it yet.'
'OK, try now.'
'No. It won't go. 'Ave a rest for a mo.'
'OK try again.' Pause, then, 'Go on then. Whacher waitin' for?'
'I'm pullin', aint I?'
'Well, pull a bit bloody 'arder'.
'Can't. Got me bloody foot stuck.'
'Oh 'ell. Put it down again, then'.

Pause for another breather. By now, they had managed to get the piano up about the first six stairs.

'OK, let's try again.'
'Quick, put it down. I think the bloody carpet's movin'.
'Bugger me. If that bloody carpet rips off the bloody grippers, the 'ole bloody lot'll slide down the bloody stairs. You an' all!'
'Yeah, I know. That's what worries me. I'll be under the bloody thing.'
'Oh Christ, let's get some more 'elp from the firm'.

By now, I was silently holding my sides, barely able to stop myself from laughing out loud at this pantomime. The middle aged man climbed over the banisters, leaving his young partner, straining to hold the piano from below to stop it sliding back down the stairs. He came to me and asked if he could use the 'phone.

'Mary, can you get Kev or someone to come and give us an 'and 'ere at Opus One. We've got this 'ere piano stuck 'alfway up the stairs and the bleedin' carpet's startin' to tear away under our feet. We daren't move it any more on our own.' Pause for the reply.

'Well 'ow long then?' Pause.

'Well can I come and pick 'im up in the van?' Pause.

'Right I'll be back at the yard in about five or ten minutes. 'Ave 'im standin' by.'

'Sorry, Guv, gotta go back and get someone else to 'elp. Can you let me mate know I'll be back as soon as I can?', and so saying, he fled, no doubt thankful it wasn't him holding the weight of the piano, through the door.

I said I would and went through to the stairs to break the news to the young man who was by now sweating profusely, straining against the quarter ton of piano that threatened to fall and crush him at any moment. 'Could he hold on, or did he want me to help?' This was a bit of a silly question really, because there patently wasn't room for two people side by side on the staircase, it was far too narrow. But at least it was a gesture on my part. After about ten minutes, I went to have another look at Hercules, who really was drenched in sweat by now and taking pity on him, I asked him if he could do with a nice cold lager, which he admitted he could kill for right now. I went and poured one for him and took it through.

'We'll have to change places while you drink it. So if I squeeze in beside you and take over, is that OK?' He agreed it would be.

Somehow I managed to get alongside him and prepared to lay my weight against the keyboard end of the shoe, but in the change-over, there was a moment between one letting go and the other taking the strain and during that crucial moment, the piano was totally unsupported. Miraculously, it didn't move while I was getting my shoulder into place. I gingerly eased off the pressure and found that I could completely let go altogether. The piano was stuck at a crazy angle on the stairs, standing upright and not moving. My young colleague uttered some very un-Christian words and downed his beer, content now to more cheerfully wait for reinforcements to arrive.

We had parted company with Peter and Irene within a matter of a few months. He got fed up with the work and we got fed up with him and Irene. At this time, my mother was living above the restaurant and she was only too pleased to report on Peter and Irene's movements to me.

'Did you know that when he goes out in his car, he always takes some eggs hidden in his chef's cap?'

'Did you know that every other evening, Irene washes her hair and then lays full length of the floor in front of the gas fire drying it? After all, that's your gas she's using!'

'Did you know that he takes tins of food and loads up his car when it's their days off?'

It seemed there was a lot I didn't know, except that I was not happy with either of them after all. The break came at the end of that first November. We planned to put on a fantastic Christmas Day menu and were taking bookings for it already. Towards the end of the month, Peter said that he and Irene were giving us two week's notice. Despite the inconvenience, that was fine for me. When they went, I closed the restaurant for a few days and became Chef/patron instead of just Patron. I spent those three days making stocks and sauces, revising the menus and so on so that we could re-open without any future hiccups. I remained the Chef until the day we sold, helped out along the way by Norma and one or two other ladies doing sweets and starters. Aubrey continued to be our stalwart "plongeur" and one man vegetable preparation department.

One evening we had a tall, casually, but elegantly dressed young man come into the restaurant with an older friend in a slightly crumpled suit. They sat in the window table and ordered some very large drinks while looking at the menus. They eventually chose a variety of dishes and two bottles of very expensive wine. The younger man gave the impression of being widely travelled and his companion was definitely American from somewhere down the south. They both smoked almost incessantly and after they had eaten, I went out to see them, receiving numerous compliments on the quality and presentation of the food. The young man confirmed his travelling by saying that he had eaten all over the world and what he had eaten this evening was excellent and comparable to the best of anywhere else. His friend agreed and I took this as a great personal compliment, saying that they would be welcome to return at any time which they did, frequently, perhaps as frequently as once a week. They eventually became so well known to us that we used their Christian names, the younger one was Christopher and the American was Wayne. They also took to wandering into the kitchen when they arrived to say 'hello' and what did I recommend tonight? One evening, it was like an excerpt from Norman Mailer's "The Naked and the Dead". Wayne came through to the kitchen. He'd been drinking and was already slightly tipsy and holding an enormous Scotch asked

'What the fuck are you cookin' tonight?' I told him. In Mailer's book, that conversation continued...'Owl shit, what d'ya think?' and the reply to that was 'OK, I thought it was somethin' I couldn't eat!' And I feel that had I answered 'Owl shit'in exactly the same manner, Wayne would have given me the self same answer as the book. They both did total justice to their meal for that evening, but from then on, they would be happy to eat whatever I cooked for them, whether it was on the menu or not. Gradually, our friendship blossomed and we and Phyllis received an invitation to their home,

Gurkhas and a Grand Piano

Smuggler's Cottage out on the wealthy fringe of Bournemouth on the way to Wimborne. This was a beautiful thatched cottage about the size of a mini mansion and delightfully furnished. It was obvious that between the two of them, there was some money there somewhere. Phyllis was overcome and fainted, but for what reason, I can't say. According to Christopher it turned out that he and his brother had inherited money from their late grandfather. The brother was of a parsimonious nature and so carefully put his money away. Christopher, on the other hand, spent his travelling the world, living for some time in America and had crossed the Atlantic so many times by Cunard Line that whenever he rang to make another reservation, they automatically gave him the Chairman's suite. Now he was back home in England and here to open a business somewhere in Bournemouth, which he eventually did in Westbourne. His Unicus Galleries specialised in expensive, hand-crafted items of jewellery, ceramics and glassware imported from the finest craftsmen in Europe, but unfortunately, it failed after about one year of trading. Either it was in the wrong place in town, or as with us, Bournemouth just wasn't ready for such high quality goods. According to Wayne, he was from Texas. He had been in the US Navy during the war and had his back broken in an accident and invalided out. He had gone into finance and become a top trouble shooter for Chase Manhattan Bank or some similar organisation. Before leaving the Navy, while recuperating from his back injury, he had got into a game of Poker and won a game in which the last player had gambled a freehold parcel of land down in Mexico somewhere. Wayne won and the land became his. It had been just a dusty parking lot in the desert when he won it. But by the time we knew him it had become a highly valuable strip of land between two competing hotel giants who wanted it for their own development. But before the whole thing could be legally sorted out, Wayne had died and instead of the land going to Christopher, it went to Wayne's sisters in Texas.

Life at Opus One was not without its amusing interludes. As Christopher became a firm friend, he took to calling into the restaurant to see us quite frequently, even during the daytime if he happened to be anywhere in the vicinity - which really meant that he had made a special trip to see us and was finding something else to do to justify it. I was working in the kitchen one morning and was

254

suddenly disturbed by a tremendous crashing sound outside by the lane which ran behind the restaurant. Our end garden fence then fell inwards, followed by the bonnet of a large Volvo estate. Christopher had only just taken delivery of it and was still finding out how (or how not) to use the automatic gearbox and he hadn't yet quite got the hang of parking. On another occasion one evening, one of our waitresses came into the kitchen looking very worried and asked if I could go out into the restaurant as we had a spot of bother. This turned out to be a young man in his mid 'twenties standing halfway up the room with his throat cut and holding a large piece of broken glass. The blood was tricking down his front and he looked pretty fearsome. Where my inspiration came from is still a mystery, but I strode straight towards him, fixing him with my eye, held out my hand and demanded that he hand of the sliver of glass. 'Now!' He meekly did so and I made him sit down while I sent for a towel and at the same time asked that someone ring for the Police and Ambulance. As he had seemed to be calming down now, at least the towel was stopping the blood from going all over the carpet and chair. Not long after, a police car arrived and two constables came in. The young chap jumped up and took up a defensive position in one corner and shouted that they weren't going to take him away. After a lot of strong-arm stuff, the police managed to get him out of the front door and into the ambulance, but not without a hell of a struggle. I felt very sorry for him, as he was obviously suffering from some kind of persecution, perhaps mental, perhaps physical and his throat cutting had been his cry for help. At least, I hope that's what it was. It cost us a free drink all round to our stunned customers who all started talking excitedly about the episode in loud voices as soon as the front door was safely closed once more.

We usually opened in time for 7pm and one evening, the moment we unlocked and opened the front door, an old tramp came in, accompanied by the most appalling smell. He sat down, demanded a menu and chose a table d'hôte dinner. Our evening waitress came out to me and told me what had happened, so I went out to see him. I spoke to him in a conciliatory voice and explained that I didn't think he was really in quite the right sort of place. Could he perhaps try another restaurant farther down the road. He looked most affronted and accused me of insinuating that he couldn't pay for his meal, to which I agreed. I really didn't think he could afford it.

He quickly put me right by opening up his grubby old holdall and throwing a large bundle of ten and twenty pound notes on the table, letting me know in no uncertain terms that he had enough there to eat in our place every night of the week for the next six months if he so chose! I can't remember how, but eventually we managed to get him out of the place and had to spray loads of air freshener around to get rid of the terrible smell he left behind. Later, in the kitchen, Pauline, Norma's friend who came to do starters and sweets said 'Oh, that's old "Smelly". Yeah, he's quite rich really. Got some sort of gangrene in his legs and has to go into hospital every now and then to have them cleaned up and new dressings put on.' Hence the awful smell.

Our landlord rang one day to ask if it was OK for his contractor to come and do some work on the front of the building. He erected some scaffolding, which was a bore, and later that afternoon asked if he could just move one of the two arc lamps which we floodlit the exterior with. Once again, I said OK. As usual, we switched on the floodlights for the evening. About 8pm, Phyllis came to me and said she could smell burning. Could I come out and have a look. Sure enough, the restaurant smelled quite strongly of smoke coming from somewhere near the front bow windows. Quite by luck I saw a wisp of smoke coming up through a tiny gap where the carpeting met the front wall. So whatever it was must be down in the cellar. I had to get two tables to move to get at the large trapdoor and stairs down to where all our precious wines were stored. As soon as I opened the trapdoor, the smoke billowed out and with a torch and a wet cloth round my face, I went down to investigate. There certainly wasn't any fire down there, but I could see new smoke coming in from just below pavement level where the front door was above. I went back upstairs and out onto the pavement and to my astonishment found part of our fascia board alight with the smoke being sucked behind it and downwards with the cold flow of air between the front brickwork and the boarding. What I hadn't known was that the contractor had actually undone the whole fitting and let it hang against the front fascia board of the restaurant so that the hot halogen bulb was touching the wood. We called the Fire Brigade and evacuated the restaurant - fortunately we were not that busy. The Brigade were very enthusiastic and from their mobile tender hosed hundreds of gallons of water all over the front of the shop and down behind the fascia, totally soaking our beautiful brown velvet curtains and a large area of carpeting and giving me quite a pond to clear away from down in the cellar the next day. At about midnight, when it was all over, we made the most of it by offering them all a drink, but all they wanted was tea or coffee. We all went to bed in the early hours of the morning and the next day notified the newspapers for the little bit of publicity.

The summer of 1976 was one of the hottest, if not *the* hottest since records began back in the 1700's and in the late spring of that year, a young Australian came to ask if I could give him a job. He said he was a chef and that his name was Ted Malthouse. He had come over from Alice Springs to see what England was all about. I couldn't pay him a great deal, but thought that he could be useful, so took him on. He turned out to be very useful indeed, particularly as Norma would come across an interesting recipe, I would refine it for our own use and Ted would add a few twiddly bits of his own devising. He became a dab hand at making chicken tajine, which became quite a favourite with the customers, as did our Arabian lamb with prunes and cinnamon. As the summer wore on and it became hotter and hotter with the temperature up into the top 80's and early 90's, it became imperative that we install air-conditioning. I did a deal with a firm and bought one of their units and doing the carpentry myself, installed it over the front door. This spoilt the look of the pediment, but it was unavoidable. Without trunking, there was no other easy place to fit it. Still, it did its job and certainly made the restaurant a much more pleasant temperature to sit in. We sweated our way through the rest of the summer without so much as a one day respite from the intense heat, increased in the kitchen of course by all the blazing hot stoves, grill and bain-marie. When we heard from the weather forecast that this heat-wave was set to last several more weeks, to make conditions a bit more tolerable for us in the kitchen, Ted and I had gone up onto the roof and removed the large sheets of "Georgian" reinforced glass from the big roof-light over the centre of the kitchen and that helped no end. Towards the end of September though, the weather began to break and the forecast now was that we could expect thunderstorms. So after he got back from school, Mark and I got out onto the roof and put back the panels of glass. Unfortunately, we dropped one and it broke, being held together only by the wire reinforcement threads. It would have to do.

257

Later that evening, the thunderstorm struck. It belted down. We had got several people in that evening and Ted and I were extremely busy. The trouble was that a steady stream of water was coming through the broken panel and falling right onto us where we worked at the stove and the only way we could stop the water from splashing into the hot frying pans and all over what we were cooking was by one of us holding up an umbrella. So we cooked three-handed that night and gave everyone who looked through the service door window a good laugh no doubt. Certainly the waitresses thought it was incredibly funny.

From the time we opened, cash flow was a serious problem. The business had not taken off in the way I had hoped and despite all the various petty savings I could make, we limped from one financial crisis to another. Within the first month or two, as John Robins had predicted, my SD shares went up from the nominal 47p I had them transferred to me at, to 56p and then up to about 63p. At that point, I found it necessary to sell some to ease the overdraft situation and so sold a parcel of about 10,000 through a broker in Bournemouth. As 1973 became 1974, I had to sell more to keep "The Listening Bank" quiet. They insisted that now that the shares had eased downwards again, I must let them have more to support the overdraft. And so it went on, me giving them more to support our borrowings *and* having to sell more to reduce those borrowings. I kept telling them that SD was a healthy, vigorous but volatile company and the value would come back up again, but they insisted that I sell more and more of them. By now, in 1975 I was getting only a few pence each for them, even with Norma's uncle Henry handling the sales. In fact, the very last parcel I sold was at 4.5p each - hardly worth the paper they were written on. All my appeals to the bank fell on deaf ears. All they were interested in was having either security, or lower borrowings. The fact that the business was slowly improving meant little or nothing to them. The whole Stock Exchange had crashed in the time of Edward Heath's government, thanks to a combination of a world oil crisis and crippling strikes at home in the UK. The Wilsonian Labour government which followed hadn't helped much either by going to The World Bank to refinance the country following their devaluation of the pound. Great Britain was now in serious economic decline and unfortunately taking us with it. Still, we held on. During 1975 and 1976, even our landlord, Hector Vack was

258

feeling the pinch to such an extent that he asked me if I wanted to buy the freehold of the building for only £12,000 and I simply couldn't raise the finance to do so. Our cash problem was compounded by the wretched Capital Gains tax. As we had started SNS with only £250, the Inland Revenue decided that my SD shares were virtually all gain and at that time, CGT was at 30% and it wasn't until I had sold practically all of them that they pounced, demanding thousands of pounds in taxes. This came as a terrible shock and I made appeal after appeal to them to place a different interpretation on things. Unfortunately, our Accountants, Prince, Croft and Ball were unable to do anything to help either. So I had to run the business as close to the wind as I could, pinching and scraping wherever possible and getting meaner and meaner with it. Eventually, things got so dire that I went to Eddie Moors and asked him if he could give me a loan to keep things going. He handed me £500 in cash which just saw us over the hump. It took me a year or two before I could repay him and he was gracious enough to say that 'he really hadn't expected it back'. Eventually, the Inland Revenue agreed to me paying off my arrears of tax over a one year period, which was something. Otherwise, I was faced with having to pay back several thousands of pounds all in one go. But they charged me interest on the outstanding amount until it was all cleared. It's now a matter of history that the SD shares did rocket back up again to an all-time high of 247p. However within a couple of years of the high point, something went terribly wrong with Sound Diffusion. It crashed completely and became bankrupt, taking all its subsidiaries with it.

After I had left SNS, Rob Jones, the Technical brains behind SNS, Mike Green the deputy accountant and Mike Reynolds the Sales Manager had decided enough was enough with Sound Diffusion. They took a chance and branched out on their own. Very cleverly, as it so happened. By wooing some of SNS's biggest customers, they opened their new business with orders on their book worth £250,000, a staggeringly successful achievement. It meant that from Day One, they never had an overdraft and were in profit from the start. Instead of employing dozens of people making the equipment as SNS had done, they sub-contracted it all out to the network of tried and tested sub-contractors Rob had built up over the past years. Their own direct labour force consisted of a mere handful of the best people from SNS. Within a year, Rob was the proud owner of a large house and a Maserati - and good luck to him. My only regret was that having gone the catering route meant that I had given up the opportunity (which I hadn't known about at the time) to use my SD shares as a financial guarantee for their new company. It would have avoided them having to all re-mortgage their houses to raise the opening funds. As it was, I was able to help them inasmuch as the landlord of their new factory was Leslie Dashwood, one of our regular customers at Opus One and I was able to give him a first-hand report on them and a glowing reference which enabled them to get their factory lease with the minimum of bother. Their new company, Robert Michaels Electronics Ltd did very well indeed.

Struggling to get the economics of business right, and having tried to let the upstairs flat, with only moderate success to the theatre people, we decided that it would make more sense to give up our lovely flat in Netheravon, save whatever rent we were paying to Norman and Maymie and move into the upstairs accommodation ourselves. We gave Mark a bedroom at the top of the house, leaving two rooms up there free. I set up my office on the top landing where I could do all the paperwork and Norma and I had the first floor bedroom looking out over the roof of the kitchen. The front lounge was very large and had swallowed the piano easily. On the first floor, this left us the bathroom and kitchen, the window from which was an ideal exit for the cats, down a plank and into the garden below. Stig and Simba thought it was ok to use the plank, but Jason steadfastly refused, preferring to go through the restaurant kitchen, which meant putting in a cat-flap for him. Timo, the whippet, had no option but to go through the kitchen, but never really made a nuisance of himself except one evening I found him with what looked like an extra silver tongue poking out of his mouth. I pulled, he struggled, I pulled some more and finally drew out a whole side of smoked salmon skin he had found in the bin.

By 1977-8, we had just about ridden out the financial storm and the business was more or less on an even keel. We were taking about £40-50,000 a year, which although not a great fortune was good enough for us to break even *and* live reasonably well. Unfortunately, the Renault on which Mark had learned to drive on our excursions to the New Forest and particularly the old Ibsley airfield, was diagnosed as having rust in the chassis which threatened danger. There was nothing for it but to trade it in against a new car and from Autavia, I bought a red Renault 14TS, a dumpy little car, but one which was to take us many thousands of miles in the search for a new business a few years later. It was also useful for towing our new boat. Bill Benham, a friend of Norman's who had been a Flarepath pilot during the second war had told me about ex-servicemen claiming for hearing disability. By now, I had a constant whistling in my head from all the shooting I had done in my army days. So I went to a specialist, Mr. Bracewell in Westbourne who diagnosed the problem and I submitted my claim to the Army Pensions Board. A couple of months later, they wrote saying that they could not award me a pension, but were prepared to offer a one off gratuity, which considering my rank and service was set at £1,111. With this, I bought a small 16 foot deep-V hulled twin berth boat and equipped it with a Johnson 35hp engine, complete with trailer. The problem was getting it into the garden for parking. I had to take down a lot of the back fencing and create a carport and install a winch to pull it up from the lane to under the carport. It was a squeeze, but with ingenuity, we managed. I named it "Cadenza" and although Mark and I loved it, Norma was not too happy about going out to sea, preferring to potter up and down the Stour. Still, it gave us something to do in the good weather on our days off. I was so pleased with it, that the next time Eddie and Ann Moors came to dinner, I said to Eddie that I had a surprise to show him and took him out into the back garden to admire our boat. He then said that he had a surprise for me and took me out to the front of the restaurant where parked outside was a Rolls Royce Silver Shadow. He was a hard one to out-do! Our next year was even better and I uprated the engine from 35hp to 55hp which gave us greater economy as we could run on the plane at half throttle and nipping across from Christchurch to Sandbanks was only a matter of about half an hour across the bay. Each winter, I had the engine taken off and serviced by Southbourne Marine who stored it and refitted it for me in the spring. Eventually, I fitted Cadenza out with navigation lights, echo-sounder, speedometer, cooker and heaven knows what else. Mark and I slept on her one night, having moored up at Wareham. We hadn't allowed for the tide going out during the night, so awoke to find ourselves lying almost on our side until the water rose enough to refloat us. Mark and I became very slick at launching her and took pride in how quickly we could do it, giving onlookers a superb demonstration of efficiency. Cadenza could take quite heavy weather too, as we proved on one hair-raising trip to Lymington in the teeth of a near gale force wind taking his friend Roderick back to his home town. It was bad enough to scare Mark into refusing to go back the same way, so we had to telephone for Norma to come and get us with the car and trailer, which she did with Christopher's help. Christopher's Unicus Galleries didn't take off at all, despite all his best efforts. In fact, he hit financial trouble and had to leave Smugglers, living for some time with us at Opus One. He tried to help out in the kitchen, but somehow, I just couldn't work with him. I decided we needed the front repainted and gave him the job of doing it, but by then I feared for our friendship.

By 1979, I was mindful of the fact that it wouldn't be long before we were halfway through our lease and began to think about what I really wanted to do. It had to be something in catering - that was all I knew and I concluded that I had now been through my hard apprenticeship and it was time to think about one more, perhaps final, move. Something freehold this time, with its own water or on a river, with some bedrooms we could let and a small restaurant. Having allowed the thought to germinate, I drew up a prospectus of what we were looking for, talked it over with Norma (for a change) as far as I can remember and sent it out to various estate agents. One or two sent me details of properties in and around the Bournemouth area, but none of them was really what we wanted and those that came near, were priced beyond what I thought we could sell Opus One for. It slowly dawned on me that the farther north I looked, the cheaper the properties were. Ireland was also a possibility, although I had never been there. I reckoned that with luck, we might be able to sell Opus for about £35,000 or so as a going concern and so used that as my yardstick as a buying price. In the summer of 1980, Mark and I planned a two week holiday, leaving poor Norma back at the restaurant. We drove through Wales and caught the night ferry from Fishguard to Rosslare in south eastern Ireland and the next morning, drove through County Wexford down towards the south west to stop at the first main tourist mecca, Kinsale, famous for its fishing. Hotel prices for accommodation were quite high and the only place we found to look at was a restaurant with a few rooms over which was on offer at about IR£55,000. As good as it was, we were not unduly impressed, especially when we found that it was only by virtue of the goodwill of the neighbours that the oil tanker deliveryman was allowed access through their property to the tank in the back yard of the restaurant. We stayed only one night in Kinsale, the following morning driving on down to the very south west tip where because of the foul weather couldn't see further than a hundred yards. Probably through my own impatience, we completely missed the friendly, slow-paced hospitality of the Irish and perhaps mistakenly, became demoralised with what we had seen and so drove as quickly as we could cross-country up to Dublin, where we caught the next available ferry for North Wales. A two day excursion through some of the more up-market coastal towns, up into the mountains of Snowdonia by Ffestinniog and we felt we had "done" Wales. What next? Scotland. After a quick detour to look at one or two castles, we headed for Moffat, a central spa town in the heart of The Borders. It was delightful. We had obtained the details of two or three properties in the area and set about giving them the once-over. We were so taken with the beauty of the Borders, the mountains and valleys Yarrow with its St. Mary's Loch and Ettrick that a love affair started which to this day has never really diminished.

We both fell for "Craigieburn" a wonderful, solid old Jacobean house set in its own grounds of about five acres just a mile or so outside Moffat. It had its own waterfall which cascaded noisily all the time and inside, the floorboards were all handmade, some tilting this way and that, giving the house an air of ancient grace and history. The family kitchen, looking out onto the garden and kept warm by the large Aga, was big enough to eat in. Just the kind of room the cats would love, Norma too. The problem was that the owner's wife was none too certain about whether they really wanted to sell or not. In any case, we certainly were not in a position to make any kind of an offer. So we left Craigieburn with its memory firmly fixed in our minds. That was certainly the kind of place that Mark and I would have liked - or so we thought at the time.

* * *

JACOBEAN DREAM

The gently falling floor of polished planks

263

Eased down towards the windows laced with
lead.
Beyond silk curtains, gardens led to banks
that lined the burn, by Annan's water fed.
It thundered down from cliffs above the house
as cascades fall with music full of rhyme.
The water guided now by Nature's course
to give us mortals promises sublime.

From Eastern lands from centuries before,
Bokhara reds of camels' feet I saw.
Above, the gilded cornice, egg and dart . . .
This room, this house, this land transfixed my
heart.

Our home this was to be. Now sell our own.
Too long it took; by then, our dream was gone.

(Sonnet in Shakespearean form)

* * *

Our next property was in the town of Moffat itself. "Ivy
Cottage" sat right on the edge of the pavement and was a delightful
little double-fronted house with downstairs rooms which would have
made either a lovely little tea-shop or very small restaurant to seat no
more than a couple of dozen people in comfort. It had about four or
so bedrooms above and a lounge which looked out onto a steeply
sloping back garden. To get to the garage at the end of the garden
meant walking out of the house and up the adjoining road to a small
lane running behind all the properties. It was nice. Very nice. But
still perhaps not quite what we might eventually be after. There was
still one more property to look at in the town. A big, granite mansion
with stabling behind, a large field in front with some donkeys and
currently being run as some sort of a retirement home. It would have
made a very good private hotel, but once again, we were still only
looking and couldn't commit ourselves. Finally, we saw
"Marchbankwood House" a few miles out of the town towards
Dumfries. Here, the estate agents had described the house well

enough, but got the decimal point in the wrong place when it came to totalling the number of acres that went with the house. It was really ten times what they had stated, giving somewhere in the order of 37 and not the 3.7 they had set out as "the policies". Whether it was on this occasion or not, but one particular property we went to was on the eastern side of Scotland out through Fife to see Solsgirth House, a magnificent mansion set in a lot of ground. It had been the former home of the founders of the Edinburgh Tramway Company and reeked of what money could buy. A huge spiral staircase rose through the centre of the house with a beautiful glazed cupola above. Off the circular landings came the dozen or so bedrooms and on the ground floor were situated the quite magnificent dining and drawing rooms and a superb ballroom. It would have made a splendid hotel and I believe that it is now a corporate luxury hotel, but was rather too expensive for us to buy. The fortnight's holiday was coming to an end and we had seen enough to convince us that Scotland was a good place to go on looking, especially in view of the lower prices being asked there for properties. So it was back to Southbourne and reality and to give Norma an enthusiastic report on what we had found.

Some little while later, we had some more property details arrive, again in Scotland and this time, I took with me Rucky and Christopher. Rucky had latterly expressed the view that she and Nick might consider moving up there, with us. Christopher, on the other hand, was none too sure about Scotland. For one thing, the Law was quite strict at that time regarding homosexuality. We drove up in the little Renault, with Christopher and Rucky changing seats now and again to relieve the cramps. We drove up through the Highlands and saw various properties, including one quite large hotel in Crieff which I did not like, partly because the Gentlemen's' urinals were very smelly and that to me indicated what the rest of the place might be like. We tried to see a property on the Moray Firth, but couldn't find it and there was no estate agent to help. We circumnavigated Loch Ness looking at one or two more, again without seeing just what I wanted at the price I knew we could afford. On the way farther south, we went to Peebles to see two small estates. One on the way to Walkerburn and quite small, although the house was excellent and the other on the opposite bank of The Tweed just outside a tiny village called Cardrona, on the edge of the forest of that name. Cardrona stopped me in my tracks. Apart from the main mansion which was utterly magnificent, there were six surrounding cottages and three self-contained apartments within the stables. The whole place was currently being run as a self-catering holiday complex, with the owners and their family living in the mansion. The asking price for all this, including a wonderful walled garden with peaches and other exotic plants growing in it and the greenhouses, and a mile and a half of fishings on the Tweed was £250,000. Although that was right out of our personal league, it triggered a train of thought in my mind. How about if I could form a consortium to buy it? For the next few weeks when we got back, I worked on putting together a package to offer the cottages and apartments to various people I knew. Rucky was keen, but all the other people I approached were only luke warm, although Mrs. Haining and Mrs. Thompson, two of our regulars at Opus One were quite keen to begin with. Gradually, I realised it was a non-starter, so had to reluctantly put my grandiose ideas to bed. Still, it gave me a further insight into what was available in Scotland and my thoughts that this is where we could eventually find something remained bright. Something would turn up eventually.

Mrs. Haining and Mrs. Thompson were two elderly ladies who lived together in a flat in the centre of Bournemouth. They were quite dissimilar, Mrs. Haining looking and acting more like an elderly ex-nurse or teacher and Mrs. Thompson admitted to having come from a family of quite wealthy hoteliers who at one time had owned or part-owned an hotel in Russell Square, London. They used to come almost every week and have the set dinner and a bottle of wine; nothing desperately expensive, but regular as clockwork. One morning I was busy serving lunches when Mary, one of our waitresses came into the kitchen to say that there was a foreign looking young gentleman sitting on his own who had just ordered curry and a bottle of vintage champagne. Could I please deal with the champagne? Sure, I went out and saw him, showed him the bottle of Veuve Cliquot he had ordered and opened it for him. That was a nice bit of business. We didn't often have anyone come in with that sort of taste, apart from Christopher in his earlier visits when he had money to burn. This chap certainly looked foreign and I put him at Indonesian. He had his lunch and then asked to see me again. He had looked at our Special menu and seen that we offered a "Chinese

Steamboat" as one of our House Specialities. 'Could you do it for ten people?' he asked. Knowing Eddie Moors had had a copy made of our own steamboat cooker, I said I thought I could, so he made a booking for ten people for the following week. Eddie duly loaned me his steamboat and on the day in question we set about preparing all the various ingredients we were going to be serving. That morning, at about 11.30, Mary came into the kitchen with a huge bunch of cut flowers saying that the florists had just delivered them and they were for Mrs. Haining. I couldn't believe it. She hadn't booked for that night. I looked on the greetings card tied to the flowers and saw they were for Muhaini (a Princess, as I later discovered). It looked as though we were going to be having some rather important guests in the party of ten that night. Remembering the champagne and curry order, I got out all the vintage champagne I could find in the cellar and put it to chill. Sure enough, among them was an English couple who had been invited along and they quickly told me that the other eight were all princes and princesses from the ruling families of Malaya who were over here on attachment to Bournemouth College of Technology and out for the night to celebrate Princess Muhaini's birthday. All the vintage champagne got bought, and a lot of other drinks as well that night. The steamboat was a great success, even if Eddie's cooker did burn a hole in the middle of one of the tables! Some weeks later, we had a call from the same prince asking if he could book the restaurant again for another party. This time, his father and mother, the King and Queen would be among the guests. I immediately ordered in a large quantity of more vintage champagne. To my chagrin, though, when they all arrived, the King announced that as strict Muslims, the party would be "dry". Could we please supply them with plenty of mineral waters and juices during the evening. This didn't stop the youngsters coming to the bar and in loud voices asking for Coca Colas and behind their hands asking for double rums or vodkas to be put in them. So drink sales were well down that night. But the whole evening went off very well, with the King handing me his pocket camera and asking me to climb on the table to take a photograph of everyone.

We had another regular, Leslie Sinclair, who used to come in regularly on a Friday night with his lady friend, Shirley Mullinger, with whom he lived at weekends. Leslie was a short, Jewish gentleman whose regular diet was cremated fillet steak. Cooking his steaks well done wasn't enough, they had to be cinderized. He drank generously and tipped so well as to be almost stupid about it. Many times, after he had got to know us well, he would give Mark a £5 note, just for saying hello. If he didn't see Mark, he would make a point of leaving the note for him. He literally "bought" his way into the place. But he did bring us some good business. He was a director of an exclusive Car Hire firm in The West End of London and many great stars and famous people used his cars. When Stefan Grapelli was on tour, Leslie arranged that he should come to us for his meal after the show at the Winter Gardens. Likewise, when Oscar Peterson came over, Leslie arranged not only to give us tickets for the show, but fixed up a special dinner party for ten with Oscar and his manager and agent etc. all coming after the show. Norma and I went to see the show and then dashed back at high speed to open up the restaurant and get everything ready for the meal, the menu for which had been chosen in advance. Oscar was a delightful man and sat talking until the small hours about how he was going to be opening piano bars in Canada and America when the tour was over. Had he asked us to join him in his venture, I would have found it all rather tempting. During the course of his chatting, I asked him how he had managed with the somewhat second rate piano they had provided him with at the Winter Gardens. He said that he always travelled with his own Bösendorfer Imperial, but having got it as far as his opening night in London, when the removal people came to load it for the journey to Bournemouth, they had dropped it and shattered the keyboard. So he was now having to complete his tour of the UK using whatever pianos could be provided. My next question was 'did he go and try them first?' His reply was interesting - 'Hell no, Peter, I jest walk out onto the stage, sit at the piano and play it. If I tried it out first, a bad one would scare the shits out of me for the rest of the day.'

We had lots more stars of the theatre come to eat with us; Roy Castle, Rod Hull (and Emu), Roy Hull, Lulu, Arnold Ridley who wrote "Ghost Train" and appeared in "Dad's Army". Max Bygraves tried to get in one Saturday night without booking in advance and we had to turn him down. 'Do you know who I am?' he demanded. We said we did, but we were still fully booked. Little and Large came and several of the TV and stage actors came and left their photographs, suitably autographed for us. One of our charming visitors was Macdonald Hobley and his wife. "Mac" had been the very epitome of TV announcers in the early days, when all transmissions were still in monochrome. Dressed in his black DJ or white tuxedo, he presented the news and introduced various other programmes in a most gentlemanly manner and was every housewife's heart-throb. Later, when we had eventually moved to Scotland, he and his wife came to stay with us, but he was by then a sick man, having survived one serious illness. He eventually died of cancer after a long illness. Considering Opus One was miles away from the centre of Bournemouth where the stars were appearing, it was quite an achievement to have so many come to eat with us. We had some very knowledgeable taxi drivers who directed their clients in our direction once we became established as a good eating place. We were, after all, in almost every Food Guide going, with Egon Ronay giving us some very complimentary write-ups.

One evening, a dentist from Wareham came to eat with his girlfriend. He appeared very knowledgeable about his wines and came to eat with us several times, even inviting Norma and me to go to dinner with him one night at his home. One time he booked asking if he may bring his own wine with him. When he arrived, he sent a glass of something through to the kitchen for me to blind taste, saying that if I could identify it, I could also have a glass of his special claret to try. In those days, Mark used to help out in the kitchen and was already showing that he had a wonderful palate for wines. We sampled Tony's mystery drink and Mark said he thought it was a very old Madeira and I agreed. He was right and from then on, he quickly developed his knowledge of wines, particularly as we did not stint ourselves when it came to drinking the stock!

On another evening, sometime in 1980, a very tall, commanding looking single gentleman came into the restaurant and asked for a corner table. Due to the layout, we didn't have too many corner tables, but nonetheless, gave him what he wanted. He ordered a simple steak meal and a half bottle of wine. When he had finished, he complimented us and left. Not long after, he came again and the same sequence of events was repeated. By his third visit, we began to treat him on a more friendly basis and he began to open up, introducing himself as John Cottell. I had noticed that he could not shake hands in the normal manner, but offered his left hand upside down to my right hand. His right hand was a bit deformed, although he could manage to hold his walking stick with it. I also noticed that he had a large scar on the back of his right hand, which might have been something to do with his deformity. He told us that he had been commissioned "for convenience" into the RASC, but during the war had been with the SOE, Special Operations Executive, created at Winston Churchill's (our wartime Prime Minister) behest and had been dropped into occupied France to run "The Comet Line" escape route for pilots who had baled out over France. He had fought with the French Resistance and been decorated with the Military Cross and Croix de Guerre for his exploits which included ambushing and shooting up a German general on his way to a high level conference, derailing German supply trains and generally causing mayhem. It was during a fight that he was stabbed through the hand by a German sentry which caused his deformity. During the war, he fell in love with and married a French girl who was a resistance leader, but they had had to part from one another when John was sent undercover to Arnhem where he was betrayed and captured by the Gestapo. His wife was also eventually betrayed and captured, being imprisoned with Odette Churchill and Violette Szabo, two famous female SOE agents. She was executed only days before the end of the war and although John had been sentenced to be shot on the direct orders of Himmler, had been rescued when the Americans overran the prison camp he was in. After the war, John set about finding as many ex-SS and Gestapo officers as he could, even tracking some of them down to South America where he single-handedly executed them in retribution. In the Cold War days, he said he was "the real Spy Who Came in from the Cold", being sent to America as "Condor" when he was too hot to handle in Europe. He was also given the rank of Brigadier and made Chief of Security for Northern Ireland where he had been identified by the IRA and shot in the spine one day. He had to be helicoptered out of his hospital ward as it wouldn't have been safe to try and get him out by any normal means. On his return to England, the IRA had sent a couple of gunmen after him, but he surprised them in his garden one night and shot both of them. Wow, all exciting stuff for a provincial restaurateur. When I visited his home, not far from the restaurant, he explained that he also came from a very famous lineage. Way back, his grandfather's line had been from The Marquis of Granby, another forebear being one of Nelson's aides and John proudly showed me

270

his family seals and warrants to prove his seemingly extravagant claims. Also on the wall of his drawing room was the sword which had belonged to his naval antecedent. Alongside it were Citations for gallantry and a photograph of a very gallant-looking French lady, decorated with the George Cross. She had been his main help at the southern end of the Comet Line, situated down at St. Jean de Luz near the Spanish border. It all seemed genuine enough. As I got to know him more and more, he told me a fantastic story which was so outlandish that it was almost beyond belief, but still just about credible. His daughter was a secretary at King's School of English in Bournemouth and one day, a South American student had been introduced to her there. They had fallen in love and decided to get married. John and his second wife were not sure about such a liaison. They knew next to nothing about this young chap. But it seemed like true love, so they eventually agreed. As John told the story, he said they went off to Brazil where the boy came from and in time, had a baby. John and his wife were invited to fly over for the christening and were met at the airport by a big black chauffeured car, complete with an armed escort. "Home" was a penthouse at the top of a huge block of flats. When John met his counterpart, he was asked whether he had brought a christening present with him from England and said he had, it was a silver christening mug, a traditional English gift. The boy's father said he had also given a gift to the little baby. "He will never need to work - for the rest of his life". His gift turned out to be some millions of dollars. Grandfather was alleged to own the Banco da Brasilia. This all makes fascinating reading and talking about. John had all his facts so straight. I was entranced.

More property details arrived and I organised a tour of south western Scotland, all round Newton Stewart looking at them. Just before I had left, the details of one other place in The Ettrick Valley had arrived which also looked very interesting. I left it till last and it turned out to be just what I had been looking for. Set in its own ten acres, a Victorian mansion house with eleven bedrooms on two floors, a private bridge across the river Ettrick led to the quarter mile drive up to the house and grounds. It all came with the best part of half a mile of salmon and trout fishing rights on the river. Ettrickbridge was about a mile away, Selkirk seven miles and Galashiels fifteen. Edinburgh was about forty miles due north. It looked ideal and I was excited when I went to see it. I arranged to

271

get the keys from the local post office and let myself in. It had been left empty a year or more before and someone had had a hell of a time ripping up the floorboards throughout the house. It looked, and was, neglected. But it held out a great promise of what could be a wonderful place, given tender loving care. There was no water or electricity. That had been turned off long ago. But the rooms looked right. I wandered around sizing things up and quickly realised that it would take ages to put everything in order before we could open it as a business. Still, I wanted it and drove back to the post office, handed over the keys to Mary Wilson, the Postmistress and used the public telephone outside to telephone Norma with the news. I would be home within six hours. I had found it! Now all that had to be done was find that one person who wanted to buy Opus One. I chivvied and chased the estate agents with whom I had placed the sale and eventually, more by luck than judgement, came across Bob Boote who was then the manager of one of the restaurants attached to a New Forest hotel - it might have even been Burley Manor for all I remember. He showed interest, we haggled and we struck the deal. I rang the estate agents and told them that as I had virtually made the sale without any help from them, I was not prepared to pay their full commission, and they agreed. We set the closing date and started the rundown. We decided to hold a farewell drinks party in the restaurant and invited all our best old customers and friends. It was quite remarkable how John Cottell, Nick Roth and Bill Kears, all of whom had at one time or another been apparently involved in some kind of espionage activities found themselves together as a small, elite group with a single common background. A week or so later, John Cottell came to see me offering me his overcoat, complete with grey suede gloves. He said he was selling his house and "going away" and had no further need for it. Although it was a beautiful Crombie coat, it swamped me, so reluctantly handed it back. We never saw him or heard from him again and can't help wondering just where it was he "went away" to. Well, as it turned out, John was a known confidence trickster. Everything he had said was fantasy. I found this out by accidentally reading an article somewhere about three or four of these characters, he being among them. Apparently he had taken the USA in as well, being invited to give tours talking about his exploits to various groups of ladies clubs and associations. I felt a fool to have been a clueless victim, but perhaps being an unwitting romantic at heart had willingly believed it all – as had thousands of others.

The saddest story to relate concerns the three rugs which Norma and I had had sent back home from Singapore. We decided to hang them on the walls of the restaurant where they were not only safer than on the floor, but gave another talking point to anyone interested in Oriental rugs. One lunchtime, a young foreign gentleman came in for lunch and showed interest in one of the rugs in particular. Before leaving, he asked if he may bring his father for lunch one day to have a look at it, which a week or so later, he did. The old chap studied it very carefully.

'Would you be prepared to sell this rug to me?' he asked.

'I hadn't really ever thought about selling any of them' I explained.

'I would make sure you were in no way out of pocket. It is just that it is an unusual rug of Meshed weave from a small nomadic tribe from northern Persia. You see,' he went on, 'I am a conservationist who specialises in contributing to the Persian National Museum such rugs as we consider an important part of our national heritage. I shall have it expertly repaired and taken to the museum in Teheran by my son, who is an officer in the Shah's army.'

We agreed to let him have it for what we had paid for it - about £250. Some months later, he came in for another meal and I asked how "Project Rug" was going on. With tears in his eyes, the old man said that when his son had returned to Persia, it had coincided with the Shah's overthrow and his son, along with many other loyal officers in the Shah's army had been executed by the Ayatollah and his Revolutionary Council.

CHAPTER FOURTEEN

ETTRICKSHAWS

On my first visit, I could hardly believe my eyes. The property details had described the house pretty well, but there was so much else to find out about the place. For instance, it was supposed to have its own private water supply. All I found was an enormous puddle, about four inches deep which stretched over almost the entire front car park. A small burn ran down from the hill above and due to some blockage somewhere, this was contributing to the flood. The front lawns, such as they were, were not much more than bog, having been waterlogged for a year or more since the house had last been occupied. Great rhododendrons sprawled all over the boggy area. There was water everywhere, but not a drop in the taps anywhere inside the house. The great lengths of ripped up floorboards were a bit daunting, but I was confident that I could put everything back, given time. Generally, the interior wasn't in too bad condition, but outside, things were not so good. The boilerhouse had one diminutive rusty boiler sitting in about two feet of water, several window sills were rotting away, but still nothing that couldn't be put right - again given time and money. There was no carpeting anywhere except on the back staircase and what shutters there were were reluctant to open and close. The lawn was two or three feet high in grass and the garden, such as it was on the west side of the house was totally overgrown with weeds. The greenhouse at the far end of the lawn was rotted through and falling down and generally, the whole place had a very sad and sorry air about it. But it had great promise, I kept on thinking.

Having rung Norma from the local callbox by the post office and got home as promised, I spent some time drawing up what I thought was a reasonable Business Plan and it must be said that I didn't take too much advice from Norma about the way things should be done. So from the very beginning, she must have felt somewhat excluded. I suppose I had got the bit between my teeth and was galloping away on my own private crusade. As the weeks went by, I felt another visit was necessary and arranged to take Mark during his

Easter holidays. When we called at the post office to collect the keys, Mary Wilson, the postmistress asked if I was the gentleman who had made a call from the box some weeks earlier? When I said I was, she handed over my little red bag I kept my telephone change in. In my excitement I had left it in the phone box and it had been found the next morning when they went to give the box its daily clean. I was deeply impressed by the honesty and felt it was a good omen. Mark fell in love with "The Shaws" from the moment he saw it. The air was crisp and clear, the daffodils and narcissi were coming into bloom and the sunshine transformed the whole place quite magically into our "Garden of Eden". It *had* to become ours. We went back to Bournemouth full of anticipation about our forthcoming change of life. The sale of Opus One was progressing and we received notice from our Solicitors in Edinburgh that final offers were to be made for "The Shaws" by a certain date. The problem with Scottish Law is that an offer is deemed binding if accepted. No backing out, so if the sale of Opus fell through, we would be stuck with having to find the £52,000 or so we were offering. The asking price was "offers in excess of £45,000" and we felt that it was such a snip that there must be several other people who would be in the market for it. Clearly we had to top them all if we were to stand any chance of getting it. The survey I had made revealed only that the building itself was considered good, but nothing could be investigated in depth because the surveyor had been unable to gain entry to the building. The Midland Bank. in the shape of Richard Vaughan Thomas, the manager, had promised an overdraft against the security of the bricks and mortar, provided I banked with their subsidiary, The Clydesdale Bank, whose nearest branch to us would be Galashiels.

Our deadline grew closer and we could only work on the assumption that Fate would smile upon us and so we proceeded with packing up our home in preparation for the move. Quite by coincidence, Steuart Howie, our Solicitor in Edinburgh who had been recommended by our Surveyors had been to eat with us the previous summer when he was on holiday visiting his parents who lived in Bournemouth. When he had discovered it was we who were wanting to buy "The Shaws", which he knew of, he offered his services willingly and he was now having to really get his skates on. He rang to say that the closing time was twelve noon that day. Did we want to make a firm offer? We took the final gamble and said "Yes. Offer £52,000." Steuart had to have our bid taken round by special runner, who arrived a minute or two before the deadline. The next day he rang back to confirm that ours had been the highest offer, but as the sale was being conducted on behalf of a bank who had taken title to the property due to the bankruptcy of the previous owner, nothing was going to be straightforward. We left Bournemouth, heading for The Borders in the Renault, together with a dog and three cats and a huge bunch of mint which Norman had uprooted from his garden. Somewhere, also on the road were two pantechnicons loaded with all our furniture and even at this late stage, we still didn't know for sure whether we had got proper title to the hotel.

We left Norman and Maymie's in the late evening, planning to drive steadily through the night up the M4, M5 and M6 over The Pennines into the Borders. Mark and I thought it would be a wonderful surprise if we took Norma, who even now had never set eyes on The Borders, let alone Ettrickshaws, via Moffat. That route would take us up the Yarrow Valley, past The Grey Mare's Tail Waterfalls, St. Mary's Loch, over the lower swire into the Ettrick Valley by Tushielaw and northeast past all the wonderful mountains to The Shaws, before reaching the village. The plan nearly backfired when for mile after mile, we passed no other buildings, apart from one or two isolated shepherd's cottages, flocks of sheep high up on the hillsides and saw absolutely no-one. Norma was at that time becoming afflicted by agoraphobia and all this deserted open space was doing nothing to help. We pointed out Ettrickshaws from the road and went on the extra mile to the post office to pick up the keys, only to find that they had been mislaid by someone. A phone call to Steuart confirmed that he was working hard on unscrambling the Title and he *thought* we had scraped home by the skin of our teeth and that subject to the paperwork the Title would be proven and Ettrickshaws Lodge ours. With a sigh of relief, we turned back to see about gaining entry to our new home.

Without keys, this could have been a problem and we had no idea how we were going to manage to get in. Fortunately, Mark spotted a window which looked as though it could be encouraged to open and we lifted him up to it. With a bit of a struggle, he managed to wriggle through and a few minutes later, opened the front doors.

Norma was dumbfounded at the apparent, or perhaps rather real, chaos. Having shut the animals in one room, we wandered around the place letting the full force of what we (in the shape of I) had taken on wash over us. There wasn't one room which didn't need something done to it, although at least the main lounge wallpaper didn't look all that bad. Here we were, mid-morning, sitting in an empty, somewhat smashed up house that looked the worse for wear, carefully having to negotiate ripped up floorboards for fear of putting our feet between the joists. No water, No electricity, no telephone, no nothing - except a case or two of very expensive wines we had brought with us in the car. From the windows overlooking the meadow, we could see Pine Lodge, the original stable house which had belonged to the mansion in its heyday. Fortunately, the people who lived there could help. Colin and Joyce were very hospitable, helpful people. They provided us with containers of water, gave us the use of their telephone and made us some sandwiches and flasks of tea to keep us going until we could sort something out for ourselves.

    While we were wandering around, one of us asked whether anyone had actually given the removal men the address of the hotel? Mark said that while he had been having a cup of tea with them he had told them that it was a Victorian mansion alongside the River Ettrick. That was all. They had nothing else to go on so far as we knew. We didn't even know whether their office had given them any reasonable instructions on how to find the place. We sat on the window seat of the front hall, gazing out onto "our" meadow which ran down to the river, and couldn't help wondering whether our furniture and belongings would ever catch up with us after all. There was a knock on the front door and in walked a couple. They were Americans and were enquiring whether we had a room for the night. We would have thought that the scene of devastation which confronted them would have been enough to have deterred such a question. They explained that they were over from The States searching for "Daddie's grave" which was supposed to be somewhere up the valley in the Ettrick church graveyard. We hadn't a clue where they were talking about and said so.

    All the searching in the world didn't unearth the source of the so-called spring water supply, although my telephone calls to the Scottish Electricity Board had produced a satisfactory result, when

277

they replaced the main 60 amp fuse which had been withdrawn well over a year before. At least we now had electricity. No light bulbs, but electricity! Once again, Colin and Joyce came to the rescue. By telephoning the Telephone Services, and telling them we had taken over to re-open the place as an hotel, they reacted quite quickly and we were promised a reconnection of the telephone within the following day or two. But still no water. I spent some time going through the Yellow Pages at Pine Lodge finding the various numbers of SEB etc. Thinking about the water supply, I wondered whether any local plumbers might be able to help. Colin confirmed that there was a spring on the hillside, because some of his water supply came from it, although he did have a secondary supply of his own. But he had never found out exactly where it was. There was nothing for it but to work my way through them alphabetically. Quite by chance, one of the early names was Brown and Muir, a firm of plumbers based in Selkirk. I rang them and asked if they knew Ettrickshaws.

'Aye, we ken The Shaws. We've kenned it for forty years or more...'

'Aye, there's a wee spring oot on the hill. Not very grand, mind, but nae bad when it rains.'

'Aye, we can come and look at it f'r ye, but not till the morrow.'

Colin and Joyce provided us with more water and some kind of camping contraption which unfolded to make a portable washbasin. We were grateful to have them as neighbours.

It was late that afternoon when Mark spotted the two pantechnicons venturing across the bridge which had the appearance of being an old, unwanted Bailey Bridge of the type used in the Second World War and long since obsolete. This had an 8 ton weight limit sign on it and we had noticed when we crossed it in the car, the planking rattled and sprang as the tyres passed over it. That bridge looked as though it might prove to be a bit of bother, especially as it looked a bit more than average rusty too. Eventually, the vans pulled up outside and before long, the men started to unload. We had to guess which rooms we wanted things in, knowing that inevitably we would be faced with making loads of changes anyway. We celebrated their arrival by opening a bottle of vintage champagne. By the time it was dark they had succeeded in barely unloading the first of the two vans and left us promising to be back the following morning. After a strange night that was like camping out indoors we were up and doing quite early and so were ready for them when they returned. By that afternoon, they had finished and wished us "good luck", rather as though they genuinely felt we needed it.

True to their word, Messrs. Brown and Muir arrived in the morning in the guise of two men called Jock and Dennis, the latter being the son of either Mr. Brown or Mr. Muir, if indeed either of the originators of the firm were still alive. They checked the taps inside and confirmed that indeed there was not a drip of water to be had from them. Next we all went up into the loft and took the lids off the huge storage tanks. These were two eight foot square lead-lined wooden boxes, totally dry inside. Dennis said that it would be wise to reseal them with bitumen before refilling them, so that job was put down as number one. We all trooped downstairs and went outside. Both Dennis and Jock said that they were sure the main tank was up there, pointing to somewhere among the huge Douglas firs and beeches which blanketed the hillside. We climbed and searched and retraced our steps over and over again until with a shout of satisfaction, Jock said he had found "the wee liddy" which is what we were looking for. Whatever it was was beautifully camouflaged by all the grasses which grew in profusion. But there, among the humps and bumps was one bump that was bigger than all the rest. Dennis kicked away at the grass with the heel of his boot and eventually revealed a metal lid. Scraping the dirt away with his screwdriver, he lifted it and shone his torch into the cavern below. As he spoke, his voice echoed eerily within the space.

'Aye, there's some water coming in, but it's running away again doon the
drain. Someone's taken oot the plug. It'll be a day or so before there's enough to
pump up into the roof.'

Borrowing his torch I looked for myself and by hanging head and shoulders into the cavern, I could see the steady trickle of water coming in from a supply pipe high in the far end of the reservoir about twenty feet away. From the size of the tank, I reckoned it must hold about 25,000 gallons when filled. At the rate the water was coming in, that might be sometime next year! The next search was for the actual spring itself and this was made a bit easier when we found the robber hosepipe which acted as the supply pipe. By tracking it back through the swampy undergrowth, it led to a small concrete tank which acted as a primary filter tank and from there on to a sump of some sort where it ended. Flowing into the sump through a metal grille to hold back any leaves and twigs was a thin trickle of water which came from a crack in the ground beneath the roots of a large tree. This was the so-called spring! My heart sank at the prospect of having to rely upon such a meagre source for our water. Borrowing one of my ladders, Dennis climbed down into the tank and replaced the plug, a large metal disc on a length of chain which was fixed to the side of the tank just below the trapdoor.

'As there's nae water in the pipes, ye'll have airlocks in y'r system', he explained. 'Before we can fill the main tanks, ye'll have to have a good supply of water in the main reservoir, otherwise, ye'll just get airlocks again.'

I asked how long he thought this would take.

'Well, we've got to paint the inside of the storage tanks in the roof with twae coats of mastic and let them dry before we can fill them, so I reckon it might be aboot
twae days from noo before ye'll have y'r water.'

So there was nothing for it but to ask Colin and Joyce for more help, which they willingly gave. On the third day, Jock returned with a large foot pump which looked for all the world as though he had just uprooted the village pump. He connected it into the main supply and having confirmed that there was sufficient water in the reservoir started pumping. After what seemed an age, the water began to spurt into the two storage tanks in the roof. Once it was flowing, he checked that the ballcocks were working properly to cut off the supply once the wooden storage tanks were filled and declared the job done. We went round the house turning on the taps and letting them sluice out all the dirt and debris which had accumulated in them for the past year or two. At last we had our own water. Once it cleared, it tasted heavenly and although it was now high summer, was icily cold.

Norma was busy sorting out all the furnishings and belongings and slowly introducing the animals to the layout of the house, doing her best to keep the cats away from any open floorboards, in case they were tempted to go searching beneath them for mice. Outside, everything was growing wildly and it was obvious

280

that we were going to need a mower, a chainsaw and a strimmer to enable us to start to get it all under control. It was also necessary for me to get on with the floorboarding, as until this was all back in place, the house wasn't safe for the cats and we couldn't start to decorate the rooms. The greenhouse was in a state of collapse and Mark invited his school chum, Roderick to come and stay for a week or two and between them, they stripped out all the old glass, so that repairs could be made. I found a firm of joiners to carry out all the timber repairs round the house, and another firm of heating engineers to quote us for upgrading the central heating who also recommended the services of a specialist maintenance man who could revamp the boiler. The painting and decorating I was prepared to undertake myself so as to save money. I also decided to replace all the floorboarding wherever necessary. The trouble was that the original planks had been made to a special width and with metrication, there was now no modern equivalent, so this meant buying another tool for cutting and trimming whole lengths of floorboards to make them fit. In all, I bought just over a quarter of a mile of floorboarding. For good measure, I planned to have the whole house fully wired for a Flexicall radio and TV distribution system, so this meant that before I could even start on relaying the boards, had to lay the maze of wires which would run round the building carrying the necessary programmes to the various rooms. By the time we had spent money on revamping the boiler and installing a new hot water and central heating system, having all the woodwork repaired, having the water reinstated, bought all the floorboarding and cabling and piping for everything, money was beginning to become a problem once again. It was costing much more than ever I had allowed and we had barely scratched the surface yet.

Neighbours began to make themselves known. Thom McCarthy, our nearest neighbour from a bungalow situated halfway down our drive came to say hello. He was an American who had seen service in Viet Nam and was now suffering from agorophobia himself. His temper could be very short-fused, as some of the villagers had found out. Thom had the local pottery and his daily uniform was a check shirt and dungarees suitable splattered with clay splashes. He asked,

'How you doing, man?'

We explained that we were sort of camping out and living off tined food plus what Mary Wilson's local Post Office cum General stores could provide such as eggs, bacon, sausages and bread.

'Frigs man, let's see if we can rustle up somethin' a bit more interesting' for you than that. Come with me.'

I followed him outdoors and down the drive to the bridge where he climbed over the iron fencing onto the bank.

'Since we put these concrete blocks and boulders in to deflect the flow, we've created a couple of hidey-holes for the fish,' he explained and so saying rolled up his sleeve and laying down on the bank felt around beneath the swirling surface.

'Yeah, man, how about that?' he drawled with a broad grin breaking out through his long beard while holding up a writhing, gleaming silver salmon of about five or six pounds in weight.

'We can share this one,' and set off back to his bungalow to cut the fish in half. Needless to say, we dined well that evening.

Our most notable neighbours to call out of courtesy one evening were David and Judy Steel, when David was leader of the Liberal Party. They lived in Cherrydeane, one of the houses in the village and over the years, we got to know them quite well. Gradually we found our way around, getting to know what could be bought in Selkirk and Gala.

Progress was slow at times, as we had to wait for the local Fire Authority to certificate the house, I had to apply to the Ettrick and Lauderdale DC for a liquor license and this necessitated a deputation from the Town Hall to see for themselves what we were doing, plus a subsequent visit by me to the local Sherrif's Court as the prime licence holder. Rob Jones came up from Robert Michaels to supply me with the end equipment for our radio and TV distribution system, together with a Helios fire detection system which was of their own manufacture. Due to the peculiar translation of the regulations by the local Fire Authority, Rob had to make one or two modifications to the fire alarm system before they were satisfied, but with his usual genius, this was accomplished in quite a short time. By now, his personal car was the latest Jaguar XJS with modified this and that. He still had the Maserati, but because it was a left-hand drive didn't drive it that much now he had the Jaguar. The improvements inside continued daily and quite fortuitously we had a van draw up one day with a couple of unshaven looking characters who came knocking at the door. They wanted to know whether I could use "any offcuts of contract carpeting they happened to have on board". As it so happened, we needed quite a lot of it and so without asking too many questions, we bought enough for them to carpet the majority of the house for us. They came back day after day, laying it all and we were satisfied, especially as the whole operation had cost us no more than the equivalent of doing two rooms through a furnishing stores in Hawick. We had a slight spot of bother with the central heating though. Having got all the pipework in and most of the radiators fitted, the engineer had got as far as the main lounge and having fitted the radiators there, it was necessary to bleed the air out of the piping. He opened the valve at one end of the radiator and forgot all about it while he was having his lunch break. I went into the lounge and found the wall, carpeting and our brand new video recorder swimming in water, with a fountain erupting from one end of the radiator. We bought a new video through the insurance and went for the Betamax system, which a few years later was unfortunately phased out in favour of VHS. It wasn't until we had started the alterations that I approached the Scottish Tourist Board to see whether they would be prepared to give us a grant towards the cost of restoration, but it was too late. If I had applied *before* we had started, they might have given us one. But it would have taken three or four months for their decision, the amount would not have been very large and in any case, if we had sold the place before ten years had elapsed, we would have had to refund a proportion of the grant. In any case, we couldn't spare the four months wait if we were going to be open in time for the 1982 season.

What had been the kitchen in the old days was now a scene looking more like a bomb site. The previous owners had smashed out the Aga and left gaping holes in the walls. There was no water or heating of any kind in there, so I decided that we would have to use the old Butler's Pantry as our hotel kitchen. It was tiny, so there wouldn't be much room for anything other than what was absolutely essential and sounds would be easily heard in the dining room just through the adjoining door. This was a distinct disadvantage when I got frustrated and started swearing, which I did fairly often, particularly on a Saturday night when we were busy in the dining room *and* had people in the bar demanding bar snacks instantly. We gave the dining room a lot of thought and decided to go rather extreme on the decor. It had a lovely old wooden fire surround with Delft tiles inset on either side of the grate. To avoid having to keep re-stoking the fire during mealtimes, we had a coal effect gas fire fitted, which although it didn't give out that much heat, looked great. From a hardware shop in Peebles, we bought some wonderful metallic wallpaper which glowed dramatically in the candlelight at night. The chandeliers had six or eight lamps on each and rather than commit ourselves to any one colour shade, we bought four or five different colours and mixed them up. On the walls, we placed black ebonised shelves and mirrors with extra candles. From the limited choice available in Hawick we chose dining chairs in an American Colonial style with high woven backs, warm orangey-red dralon curtains for the bay window and I got some gilt varnish paint to pick out the egg and dart cornice for that extra touch of luxury. After two seasons, we also bought some Wedgewood crockery called "Waterside" which had octagonal sided plates and saucers with a pale green tracery design, the shade of which matched the delicate green paintwork of the doors and windows. We thought it all very elegant, as did just about everyone who ate in it. Egon Ronay's guide gave us the ultimate accolade by describing it as "eccentric". We were making good progress in the downstairs rooms and I arbitrarily took the decision that we would open the bar first so as to get some money coming in for a change. This meant getting Thom McCarthy's shopfitting friends to design and build a bar for us, complete with tiny washhand basin beneath as well as the normal glasswashing sinks. Health regulations were a pain in the neck. . . Looking back on what that bar cost us against the comparatively small amount of revenue it generated, I later doubted it was worth having. With autumn giving way to winter snows and thanks to Norma's imaginative furnishings, our refurbishments were just about finished, so we planned our grand opening for Christmas. One evening, a few days before the 25th. Norma called me.

'I can't get the staff loo to flush properly.'

We checked inside the lavatory cistern and found what looked like a bit of soggy gelatine stuck in the inlet valve. I poked around with the bent end of a coat hanger and dislodged it, but still only a trickle of water. Without thinking of the possible consequences, I got my tools and very unimaginatively, undid the joint completely. Water and bits of frogs exploded everywhere from the disconnected pipe, drenching me and the room - and ironically the cistern now needed flushing every five to ten seconds. I tried to rejoin the two ends but the force of the 150ft. head of water was too great. It seemed enough to power a Selkirk cotton mill.

'Norma,' I shouted, 'fetch some towels – lots of 'em.' I heard the panic in my voice. My hands, swathed in towels and clamped around the gushing pipe were rapidly becoming numb in this ice-water torture. 'Call Brown and Muir and see if they can help,' I pleaded as a steady flow of water was about to surge through the door into the corridor. Following their advice, Norma ran to the boiler house to search for the key to the outside stopcock, but without success. With me verging on hypothermia and standing in inches of nearly zero degree water, they promised to be with us within the hour.

Early next morning I climbed the hill to the reservoir and in my torchlight saw what would have gladdened the heart of a French frog farmer – as a result of now having water in the tank, plus the warm summer weather there were hundreds of the little buggers breast-stroking around, enjoying their own private swimming pool. The trouble was that several would disappear down the outlet pipe each time a tap was opened 150ft. below. Fortunately, I spotted the missing filters and using a long pole from somewhere nudged them back into place. Rather than empty the tank and start all over again, I gave my aquanauts a gangplank to freedom – but was haunted by the thought of them using it as a high diving board for generations to come.

As November had given way to December, the bar was finished. I had been granted my Licence and it was time to start stocking the bar. Our Brewers did a deal with us, making us an interest free loan of about £1,000 in exchange for their exclusivity on supplies and this helped quite a bit, although their range was limited and they certainly couldn't supply some of the fine wines I wanted. This meant doing some further deal with them to enable me to go to other suppliers for what was not in their range. It was all a bit of a pain in the neck, but money was short and I had to play the game their way. Also during November, with Thom McCarthys' help, we had drawn up a list of about 150-180 people who lived in the Ettrick and Yarrow valleys and Selkirk town itself who he thought might become good customers, or be useful to us. By the end of the month, all the invitations had gone out and we had started getting some responses, but not that many. Thom said philosophically,

'Don't worry man, these people will come for anythin' that's friggin' free. They'll come, you'll see'

The weather was quite cold by now and we were glad of the new central heating and the large stockpile of logs we had gathered in one of the outhouses. The coalman had recommended we use Shilbottle, a particular type of coal to burn on our open fires, which was more expensive than the run of the mill stuff, but burned with a clear, bright flame and not much soot and ash. So as to be with us for our first Christmas and my birthday, my mother had come up by coach from Bournemouth to stay with us for about four weeks. I had collected her by car from the nearest coach station in Carlisle, nearly forty miles away. Earlier in the summer she had been very useful, helping Norma with sewing and now in getting those bedrooms ready which I had finished painting and decorating. We had set the last Saturday before Christmas as our grand opening night and the intention was that from 6.30 to 8pm, drinks were "on the house", but from 8pm onward, they would have to pay. On about the preceding Wednesday, the temperature fell like a stone and it froze hard outside. By the Thursday, even the river showed an ice margin along the banks and everywhere twinkled in the frosty atmosphere and sunlight. On Friday, we had a slight fall of snow as the temperature eased a little, but by evening, it had stopped and in the clear skies, the temperature dropped lower than ever. Going round the hotel, I tested every tap to see that we hadn't got any pipes frozen, having lagged all the exposed piping I could find, but sure enough, one or two of our bedrooms were beginning to freeze up. I kept the central heating going, but that still didn't stop the interior of the house becoming like one huge freezer. On the Saturday, conditions got worse and by mid- afternoon, it was snowing once more. Thom predicted that even that wouldn't stop people from coming out to us and sure enough, dead on the dot of 6.30, the cars started arriving, crunching up the drive through the snow, which by now was about six or eight inches deep. Still the temperature fell and as it did so, more sinks and toilets began to freeze up. We kept the central heating on and fires blazing and in those rooms, at least, it was comfortable, but elsewhere throughout the house, despite the central heating it was becoming Arctic. The free drink flowed in great quantities as by now, we had about sixty or so people in the place and boy oh boy, could these people drink? As it was free, they certainly weren't holding back. Mum was busy washing up glasses as fast as she could go, Norma and Mark were serving out drinks to people and I was drinking my fair share too. More pipes froze and soon people were having to be shepherded all over the house as we searched for a loo which was still working. I was glad when 8pm arrived when we could start charging for drinks. It was amazing how quickly everyone changed over to shandies and half pints of beer, or decided it was now time to go home. During that evening about a hundred or more people had come to see the new "Shaws" and miraculously they had all managed to drive away, despite the snow, which had kept falling. We had hadn't even covered our costs. We tidied up as best we could and went to bed, shivering. I had never been so cold. Even our breath was making clouds of steam in the bedroom. The next morning, the snow had at least stopped falling and we now had about two feet of it and although the sun was shining on the other side of the valley, it was not falling on the house, which was locked in the shadow of "Shaws Hill". As a consequence, the temperature indoors was still polar.

On the Monday, I found that Thom had got Davy White, our next door farmer to come up with his tractor and clear the drive. At least this meant I could get the car out - if it would start. I had planned to put on a cold buffet for Christmas lunch in the hope of getting a bit more trade and had ordered my meats and fruit and vegetables for collection that day. Fortunately, the snow ploughs had been along the road to Selkirk and I was able to get there and back - with the utmost care. I unloaded the vegetables into the old kitchen for storage until needed and put the meat into the fridge until I could get around to butchering it. A survey of the house revealed that we were now down to about two bathrooms and two sinks which still worked. The rest was solid. A call to Brown and Muir elicited the fact that there was nothing they could do. As fast as they could unfreeze any pipes, they were bound to refreeze again, so unless I had any bursts causing problems, it was best to wait until it thawed. As I worked on butchering the meat, touching the icy flesh, my fingers developed chilblains, which I hadn't had since childhood. I roasted the ribs of beef, legs of lamb and pork ready for the Christmas Day buffet and although we had advertised ourselves as being open, not a soul turned up. So I thought "bugger it" and decided to batten down the hatches and live as frugally as possible until about February or March, by which time perhaps we might be lucky enough to start getting some people to actually come and stay for a few days. New Year came and went, as did my birthday and we continued to freeze. Unbelievably, the temperature went down lower than ever and because I had set the central heating to run on the economy programme, overnight, when it had been off, the hot water pipes to all the rooms had frozen up beneath the floorboards. So we had no central heating whatsoever with the temperature now having dropped to about twenty seven degrees below! As I opened the vertical freezer doors to get food out, even at minus 18, their correct running temperature, the *warm* air fell out round my feet.

Christmas had been a great disappointment. Although the opening of the bar had been well attended, I don't suppose we took more than forty or fifty pounds during the remainder of that evening, hardly covering our costs. I had got horribly drunk and with the incredible freeze-up, was now sleeping (if you could call it that) almost fully dressed in bed and nursing outlandish thoughts of suicide. I was also continuing to drink too much and the stress of that and the problems we were encountering brought on my stomach ulcers once more, this time causing me to vomit blood from time to time. We had spent so much money getting the place restored and refurbished that I didn't know how on earth we were going to last out until the spring. It was a case of living literally from hand to mouth. By early January, the river was totally frozen over and we were running out of fuel, relying on burning whatever logs we could cut. Norma did a first class job on making up a new brochure from the one or two old ones we had found lying around and we got Walter Thompson, the local printer in Selkirk to print off a small batch of them inexpensively in monochrome. We couldn't afford a colour brochure - that was for sure. The finished article had a sort of warm, homely feel to it - almost deliberately amateur, with a charm that was difficult to pin down. Steuart Howie, our solicitor, came to the rescue by arranging a short term loan of about £3000 through a client of his. The problem was that the interest rate was crippling – 18%. But at least it was a lifeline and I took it. It enabled us to finish equipping the hotel and committing some of the money to advertising.

Before the cold weather had set in, we thought it would be a good idea to get a bit of money coming in by leasing out the front paddocks for grazing and a young couple signed up for a one year lease, putting two horses on the fields. During the big freeze, the horses had been unable to get down to the grasses frozen beneath the snow and had suffered badly. Their owners said they were unable to get through with fodder for them, although Joyce, from Pine Lodge furiously accused them of not caring about the animals. I do believe that the younger horse had died of hunger. They finished up taking the remaining one to another field nearer to where they lived, leaving us with half their lease unexpired and no hope of claiming any rent from them. What we had got didn't even cover the solicitor's charges for setting up the lease in the first place, so letting out the fields on a formal basis was a waste of time. I wouldn't do that trick again.

There was still a little while to go before Mark had to go back to college at Homefield, which, bless him, he did at his own expense from a small legacy Dee had left him. We were out cutting logs one day. It was deathly quiet in the valley, with just the sound of birds and the very occasional, lonely car going up or down the road. We both became aware of a faint sound. It seemed to be hanging in the air somewhere up the valley. It was difficult to pin down what it was. We kept stopping our work to listen and as time went by, the sound coalesced into a far distant rumbling, like continuous thunder miles away. But the sky was clear. The temperature had risen to a tolerable level now and the remaining icicles had begun to drip. Slowly the rumbling seemed closer. It was certainly louder and it was certainly coming from up the valley. We stopped work again and listened. The noise was now getting quite distinct. Slowly it dawned on us. The river was thawing and the ice was on the move. We downed tools and went down to the bridge in time to see the ice breaking up into chunks of all shapes and sizes some as large as tabletops and all about a foot thick. Coming down on the flow of water was an avalanche of mini icebergs, tumbling down to our bridge which was having to withstand the continuous battering as they jostled to crash through between the spans. It was a fascinating sight and quite awesome in its display of strength. Anyone falling into the river now would be crushed to death. The tranquil little Ettrick could be quite brutal after all, as we found later when following a thaw and heavy rain the river burst its banks. The floodwater came right over our front fields and we were grateful that the house itself stood on a promontory of high ground which saved us from further damage. The only way the river was detectable was by the extra swirling and disturbance beneath the surface of the water down by the bridge. This little Ettrick obviously had surprises in store. It turned out to be a typical spate river made worse because of its steep fall to the Tweed seven miles away at Selkirk. In times of heavy rain, it was reckoned to be the second fastest rising and falling river in the whole of Scotland, making the salmon season unpredictable, but interesting for those who could afford to be on the river at just the right time.

Our first season passed off tolerably well. In fact, we were quite pleased with the response to our advertising, when all things were considered. We had taken the house from minus nothing to a reasonable level of business in one year. The bar was quite busy most evenings now with bar meals selling quite well, particularly my curried chicken. The problem was, however, when late in the evening, one or two young shepherds might come in for a pint of beer and make it last for ages. There were occasions when I had still got the bar open at one or two in the morning, just for two or three youngsters who were drinking in ultra slow-motion. As the hotel got busier, I needed my sleep and so became stricter about closing nearer the proper time. I was now busy cooking for hours and hours on end and fitting in the office work alongside it and it was a seven-day-a-week routine, only interspersed with visits to the butchers and greengrocers in Selkirk and McNab's Cash and Carry in Galashiels once or so each week. In between times, I also had to make time to saw down trees and cut up the hundredweights of logs needed to keep the home fires burning. The main lawn needed constant mowing, the flower beds round the house tended and perhaps the most improbable task of all was always trying to improve the flow of water from the spring. This meant hours of backbreaking digging and cutting away at the cleft in the ground which the spring grudgingly seemed to trickle through in the almost forlorn hope that I would suddenly hit upon a second, more major source. I spent ages up in the woods searching for wet areas which might denote another spring, and connecting up what I could through a maze of hosepipes into the main sediment tank.

As each season was busier than the last, we constantly

searched for additional help and found that we had literally drained the valley dry of whatever help was to be had. Two sisters, Babs and Molly were our regular chambermaids-cum-kitchen helpers to do the washing up and potato peeling etc. Glenys from Selkirk was a diminutive Glaswegian firebrand who came in to be a waitress. She turned out to be quite a girl; eventually, after we left, taking herself off to university and getting her degree in History, English or Sociology - something quite unexpected including Teaching English as a Foreign Language in China and Korea. Robin, a handyman who lived the life more of a latterday Robin Hood came to do minor building work for us and the odd running repairs and we found an ex-Borstal boy as a gardener and tree cutter. Our entries in the various food guides were re-instated and it wasn't long before we were getting good write-ups again in Egon Ronay's guides. Mark finished his education at Homefield and came to join us, looking after the wines and the waiting, both of which he did exceptionally well. Norma and I began to drift apart. As I got busier downstairs, she seemed to spend more and more time being upstairs or on her own. We should have been happy with the way the business was gathering momentum and the fact that we were now living in our own place in a most wonderful part of the world, away from the hurly-burly, one hour's drive from Edinburgh. But things were not working out between us. I was slaving away and drinking too much and beginning *not* to enjoy what I was doing.

Each season was an improvement on the last and by the end of 1985 turnover was up to over £80,000 and we had turned away a large number of chance callers. I bemoaned that fact, as with them we could have easily topped the £130,000 mark and made a really substantial profit on the year. But it was not to be. We really wanted another six bedrooms for letting, but this would have involved borrowing a huge amount from the bank, with all the strings attached. We would have needed a better water supply and bigger dining room. We thought over the problem from all angles, even thinking in terms of moving out of our own accommodation and renting a cottage in the valley somewhere. Another alternative was to have bought Pine Lodge when Colin and Joyce sold it. That would have given us a home of our own, rooms for staff *and* spare bedrooms for even more guests. We could have had eleven bedrooms in the main hotel and about three guest bedrooms in Pine

Lodge, giving us a total capacity of about twenty or more guests. The only trouble was that it would have cost us about £90,000 to buy Pine Lodge and furnish it and where on earth were we likely to get that sort of money? To have a mains water supply laid in from the village would have cost a fortune and even if we did have more rooms, the chances are that we would also need more staff. As we had found to our cost, we had creamed off all that was available anyway, so it would have meant getting seasonal living-in staff and that would have meant more bedrooms still, or paying to have them boarded out somewhere in the village. So we were stuck at a limit on expansion, imposed by both geography and architectural constraints. It was like being in the middle of a Hieronimous Bosch picture - a seemingly endless staircase which went nowhere.

Having living-in staff proved not to be a very congenial affair, unless it was one or two young girls whose company Mark might enjoy. During one year we employed a couple as chef and general assistant. They were the only couple who were good enough, yet within the salary range we were offering. I disliked having them but due to having them, at least it allowed Norma and me to take time off, which we badly needed. By then, Mark had left us to go and work elsewhere. He started off becoming assistant manager to The Clifton Hotel in Nairn, owned by a rather eccentric hotelier and found the experience enlightening. But after only six months, he had an offer to join Charles Joseph in his father's wine business, working in Alison's Wine Shop in Edinburgh and living in a flat in Newtown area of Edinburgh. This was a new experience for him and he seemed to enjoy it. We missed him greatly in the hotel, but knew getting away from us was at the time a necessity, like a case of mutual distance lending enchantment. It was enjoyable for us to drive up to the city once we had seen The Shaws settled for the day and have lunch with Mark, sometimes in The Pompadour Room at The Caledonian Hotel, which I found technically quite inspiring.

During 1985, we had achieved a considerable success, being awarded the British Relais Routiers' "Casserole" award for Excellence, making us Scotland's first hotel to be so honoured. This led to us getting a slot on Scottish TV's "Scotland Today" and a radio interview with Jimmy Mack, Scotland's equivalent of Jimmy Young at that time. Although I had been given a list of the questions Jimmy might ask, he slipped in several unplanned, tendentious ones which I answered honestly, causing a bit of a stir as I impugned some Scottish peoples' eating habits. I was not without support though, as we received some telephone calls later in the day at the hotel agreeing with what I had said. When Routiers wanted to come and make the award, we couldn't let the opportunity pass without getting as much publicity from it as possible. So with help from the Scottish Tourist Board, we did Press Releases and we organised a cocktail party to which we invited as many influential people as we could think of, including the Duke of Buccleuch and of course David and Judy Steel. Cynthia Lester, the UK Marketing manager for Routiers came up from London and stayed the night with her boyfriend and during the party, the award was made. This made very good additional blurb to put into our letters and brochure when we advertised.

I forecast that 1986 was going to be a "make or break" year. Our new colour brochure had done us well in 1985 and we were hoping to consolidate the gains we had made the following season. I had been very intermittently keeping a diary during 1983 and '84 and re-started it somewhere towards the end of '85. The entries for '86 didn't make good reading. 1986 became a crunch year. Mark chose to come back to us, lured by my offer of more money and a share of the company. We shed three staff but Mark somehow did all their work single-handed, helping me cook, helping out front and pouring his energy into the place. I though was becoming a nervous wreck and this spilled over once more into the family orbit. I was constantly nit-picking at Norma, belittling her efforts and reducing her self-esteem and confidence. I was rowing with Mark and feeling the sharp edge of his tongue when he got irritable over how things were or were not being done. We had management meetings of sorts to try and agree upon a policy and work routines, but these achieved very little except to stir up anger between us. How we managed to keep the business running at all was a miracle. I retreated into a pattern of more and more work, isolating myself from reality and justifying my hard work by telling myself that it was me - and only me who was keeping the business afloat. My drinking continued to be excessive and my mood became very introspective. Money was a constant worry, as ever, with people like the Scottish Borders Tourist Board sending us final demands for arrears of payments for the advertising space we had taken in their Guide. By now, my health was becoming suspect, although I was loathe to admit it. Over the recent years of Opus One and now The Shaws, I had spent so much time on my feet that I had somehow damaged the nerves in them. I could no longer go through the days standing without changing my shoes about three times. By the time I got to bed each night, my feet were throbbing intensely and each new morning was hell when I came to stand up. I felt as though someone had wired me up to the mains electricity overnight and as I stood, they threw the switch sending the current surging through my feet, creating a numbing, buzzing sensation that was very painful indeed. It was as though I had been in an eastern prison and had the soles of my feet beaten. My remedy was even more alcohol to numb the pain.

Mother had had a stroke which had affected her down one side of her face and body. Being the kind of gutsy person she was, she certainly wasn't going to let such a trivial thing as a stroke worry her though - at least on the outside, the part that the world saw. When she was feeling better and had to a very large extent recovered, she sold her caravan and moved in with Fred Tyson who became her third husband. She came to spend a week or two with us and very generously gave me £1000 from the proceeds of the sale, which needless to say, went straight into the business. She thought I was working too hard and that Norma was nothing more than a lazy bitch. What I found difficult, if not impossible to tell her was that it was more my fault for driving her to it. Looking back on our money problems, it's quite amazing how between us Norma and I poured something like £50,000 of our own money into Opus One and The Shaws. At the time our accountant managed to give us some sort of convincing argument as to where it was in the accounts, but from knowledge I gained later with Allied Dunbar, I'm now damned certain that we lost it through his incompetence. I'm sure he could have safeguarded it better, or made some sort of provision for us to be able to extract it without having to pay tax on it as we did when we finally paid ourselves out dividends and when every last stick had been sold.

Money and marital problems apart, Ettrickshaws did have its lighter, more memorable moments. Lord Rose, a one-time UK Ambassador to the United Nations stayed for a holiday. He was charming and so was his wife, who excused him wearing his carpet slippers in the lounge one evening, saying he always wore them at home when he was in a relaxed mood. Lord and Lady Napier also stayed several times. His full title was Major The Lord Napier and Ettrick who was really the absentee Laird of the valley. He was absentee because of his Royal duties, being Private Secretary to Princess Margaret. He had something of a problem too. Having inherited the old family pile up the valley, he found it rotten with woodworm and in need of extensive repairs which he claimed he couldn't afford to have done. Anyway, he lived in a Grace and Favour Apartment near Clarence House and all he needed was a little "pied a terre" when he came to Scotland. He decided he would demolish the old family home with the help of some of his friends in the Army, so made it available for some demolition training and it was blown up during an exercise. When he applied to Ettrick and Lauderdale DC for planning permission to build a small house on the site, they asked him where his Grade II house was and when told it no longer existed, instructed him to replace it - as was - or so the story went.

In 1984 we had a couple by the name of Featherstone come to stay for about four days. Mr. Featherstone wore a neck brace and on the first morning he came to us in a rather irritable mood.

'I've had a dreadful night's sleep – if you can call it that and we feel we should book out and go somewhere else.'

I recall Norma saying something like, 'Please don't, we will do everything we can to make your bed more comfortable for you. At least let us see whether we can make you so comfortable you won't want to leave.'

'Alright, we'll give it one more night, then.'

We couldn't afford to lose a four day booking just like that and on the second morning he was in a much better mood. That day, we had another couple who were also coming to stay for a short two or three day break. The two couples met at dinner that night and the men spent some little time eyeing one another and finally, in the bar after dinner, Featherstone asked the other man

'I'm sure we have met before somewhere. Were you in the army during the war?'

'Yes, I was a Commando.'

They compared notes and found that one of them had saved the other's life in one of the battles they fought in. On another occasion a single gentleman came to stay and had done so purely on

295

account of our piano being available for guests to play. After he had settled in, during the morning when there were no other guests in the hotel, he began to play and I could hear him as I moved around in the kitchen and dining room. I was riveted when he started to play the Rachmaninov G minor Rhapsody. I stole out into the hall and stood outside the drawing room door listening until he had finished. It seemed as though at that point, he was satisfied with what he had done and finished playing for the time being. I simply had to go in and see him.

'That was fantastic' I said, 'I've tried playing that piece and it's so difficult, but you made it sound so marvellous I wondered whether it was a recording you had dug out from somewhere in my collection.'

As I was talking to him, I was astonished to see that he had got the top two joints of his right index finger missing. I wondered how on earth he could play so well without such an important finger and, perhaps rudely, remarked on it.

'Yes, it is an impediment to my playing, but I manage. It's my own fault. I had this prosthetic finger made for me.' He held out his hand to show me a plastic plug-on finger joint which he fitted whenever he wanted to play the piano.

'I was studying to be a concert pianist when war broke out and was enlisted into the RAF as a despatch rider. My motorcycle had broken down one day when the chain had jumped off the rear wheel cog. I was stupid enough to put it back with the engine running and lost my finger between the cog and chain.'

'Well, I must say, I wish I could play as well as you. You seem to have such an affinity with Rachmaninov – from the little I heard; you really get to the heart of his music.'

'I was lucky, I was referred to (a piano tutor whose name I can't recall) and my teacher's teacher was none other than Rachmaninov himself. I suppose it has come on down the line directly from the Master.'

No wonder he played that piece so well.

You may recall that I mentioned a time in Borneo when I changed helicopters, which as it so happened was my lifesaver, without me having known it at the time. As time went by, as with other odd recollections, I began to doubt the veracity of my memory, such as the wing-tipping of our fighters and the doodlebugs. To my relief, the helicopter occasion was confirmed by a guest I got talking to in the bar one evening. He had been in Brunei at the same time as me, although I didn't recall ever meeting him then. As we exchanged memories of that time, I asked,

'Did you ever hear about the Whirlwind helicopter that came down in the jungle somewhere outward bound from Brunei Town airport early in sixty-three?'

'Oh yes, engine failure. Had a section of Ghurkas on board. It was never found. Poor buggers.'

'I was on it that morning,' I explained and told him what had happened as far as I was concerned.

'God, you were a very lucky chap then, weren't you?' was his rueful reply.

I made a cryptic diary entry for Sunday the 29th. of May 1983 which was the day that David Steel rang up to ask if we could do dinner for about twelve that night. That weekend, he had held his famous "Ettrickbridge Summit" and his dinner party consisted of himself and Judy, Shirley Williams, Roy Jenkins, David Owen, David Penhaligon, Bill Rogers and Lord Chitnis who was a sponsor of the newly formed Liberal Democratic Party. Shirley Williams, David Owen and Roy Jenkins had all defected from the Labour Party and joined a small group of Liberals to create this new break-away party. They all had a good meal and a few bottles of wine, with Lord Chitnis footing the bill for £155. Roy Jenkins must have indulged a little more than the others, because as they were all leaving I asked him how he was enjoying his new constituency (Hillhead North) which he had just won in a bye-election. He mumbled something about it was good but was obviously having difficulty in remembering which constituency it was he now represented in Parliament, until David nudged his toe and whispered "Hillhead" in his ear. For the Summit meeting itself, we were inundated with calls from The Press for accommodation and explained that we had only six rooms, of which three were already taken. 'Never mind', said the secretary who rang from the BBC, 'We'll take everything you've got.' In the end, no-one from the BBC came, so we charged them for the rooms anyway and made a nice little profit in the process. When others phoned and we explained we were booked, they asked for the name of any other hotel in Ettrickbridge, obviously not understanding that it was a fifty-three person village in the middle of nowhere.

During 1983, which was a drought year for us, the spring was a constant cause for concern and we had to place a notice board in the front hall reminding guests that we were short of water, would they please economise. Our message to them all was "Shower or share" and on the whole, most people obliged when they knew why. Not, however, some Americans we had staying. One night at about 11pm I heard baths being run. These unthinking colonial cousins of ours just had no concerns about water shortages - it wasn't something they had to worry about in the good old US of A. The drought conditions not only gave us problems, but the salmon as well. That spring had been an excellent one for the salmon run. The water had been good and we had had plenty of rain so they had no problems with getting up the river to spawn. But when the drought came, it was a different story. Our Bridge Pool was stuffed full of fish swimming round and round waiting for the water level to rise so they could wriggle and swim up to the spawning grounds at the head of the valley. Each day, the poachers came to spy out the land and I kept ringing the bailiffs to warn them. It became a war of nerves. Thom had warned them off and all he got was a load of abuse and threats for is trouble, and between us we got handfuls of tintacks all over the bridge planking to give us plenty of punctures if we had tried to drive across. The poachers were notorious for their criminality. "Nock" Linton was one who had just come out of prison and was in a very threatening mood. The poachers used two methods of bulk fishing - if you can call it that. One was to use "Rake Hooks" which were big and multi-barbed hooks on a line weighted with a lump of lead and simply by throwing them among the swimming fish, they could foul hook them and haul them out. The other way was by throwing a small tin of "Cymag" industrial poison into the water which in an instant de-oxygenated the water, killing off everything including all the plant life. The asphyxiated salmon just floated to the surface where they could be easily netted. We had something like twenty or more fish in the pool and passers by were stopping their cars to come onto the bridge to look at them - and so were the poachers! The bailiffs were so overstretched that they just couldn't watch the hundreds of miles of river-ways in their territory all day, every day and as the poachers were all in touch with one another by short wave radio, they really called the shots. We even had a huge brown trout among our salmon and I went down to the pool one day with my rod. I hooked four fish, but each of them managed to shed the hook, so I caught nothing. I bounced the worms right on their noses as they swam around, but they weren't at all interested in feeding - procreation was uppermost in their minds. At the time, we had a Mr. Graham staying with us just for the trout fishing and he kept reporting back to us each day on the goings on down at the bridge. On the morning of the 14th.of July (1983), he came back to the hotel straight after breakfast saying that all the salmon had gone and there was blood all over the stones on the bank. I went and looked for myself and it was true. I 'phoned the bailiffs who came up and said that the blood was typical of the poachers having rake-hooked them out. It wouldn't have taken them all that long either, especially with the pool being so small and the fish packed in as they were. A week later, Mr. Graham came back with a salmon weighing just under five pounds. He had been fishing for trout in The Loup Pool (part of the water we swapped with Andrew Grieve for our hay) using normal trout tackle with a 3lb breaking strain line and a tiny no. 12 hook. It had taken him almost a quarter of an hour playing it before it tired enough for him to be able to land it and when he did, the hook literally fell out of the fish's mouth. A week later, I bought myself some new trout tackle so I could have a go too. On my first outing I caught three very small trout on a wet gnat fly. I put them all back, poor little things. We had no rain for over eight weeks and the temperatures were in the eighties every day. Everything was bone dry and we couldn't spare the water to water the garden, so all the summer flowers died. Norma was having a lot of trouble with her sciatica and hobbling around the place. I took her to see a specialist in Edinburgh who confirmed her trouble, but was unable to do much about it for her, saying "it was just one of those things."

The 1986 season was not shaping up the way I had hoped. Our bookings were down on the previous year and I began to get very gloomy about the future. Norma and I were fighting like cat and dog far too frequently and Mark was getting involved as well. As my forecasts began to come true and turnover showed itself to be down, we had a family conference. Mark made our situation quite clear to us. We were not pulling together and seemed unable to do so, which made the current situation untenable. He was not going to be a party to seeing us possibly damage our marriage so things inevitably came to the point where we discussed selling the hotel. So by the end of the summer we had placed the hotel in the hands of Christies, the Business transfer specialists in Edinburgh. They came and surveyed the hotel and astonished us by saying that they thought they could sell it for £200,000. I had thought that we might get £120,000 for it at best. This selling price gave me something to do some projections on for our accountant and these formed the basis of the particulars of sale regarding turnover and profitability etc. Even at £200,000 we had some people come and look over the place, but they didn't make us an offer, which was a bitter disappointment. Towards the end of the year, we brought the price down to £180,000 in the hope of attracting a buyer. There was no way we now wanted to continue into another fresh season with all the financing problems that it would entail with the bank overdraft and so on. Eventually, in January of 1987, a couple came to see it. They lived in Surrey and had never run a hotel before, but they had a big house which they were selling and thought that having their own hotel in Scotland would be just up their street. They were totally inexperienced, thinking that a hotel like Ettrickshaws just simply ran itself. After we had left, they eventually found they were mistaken. They said their surveyor had said the hotel needed a completely new roof and offered us £140,000. We argued, saying that we had just brought the price down from £200,000 to £180,000 and that was the price. Eventually, we settled on £160,000 and the deal was done. Solicitors were instructed and a completion date set.

CHAPTER FIFTEEN

AND AFTER ALL OF THAT

I worked on until 1996 finding work that seemed to suit reasonably well and we felt pretty settled where we had ended up, down in the south-west of England. We hadn't ended up with any money but we'd kept our health. Mark visited us often and he was busy carving himself a career in top-end restaurants and hotels. In the year 2000, I discovered that because we were in receipt of State Benefits, we were both entitled to study, free of charge, with The Open University. I also registered with British Executive Service Overseas (BESO). This was an organisation of industry professionals who were prepared to give their time to help overseas businesses in need of managerial expertise. Travel costs were paid by the host organisation and pocket money provided. It sounded interesting. My first offer came for helping an hotel in Ghana, but I felt the project was too large for my range of skills, so I declined. The next, however, I did accept and I'm so glad I took the opportunity as it provided me with a lifetime experience I shall never forget. A small, newly built, 30 bedroomed hotel in Nablus 35 miles (50Km) north of Jerusalem, Palestine (some would argue Israel) was in need of expert help to get it up to International standard and although it would challenge me to the extreme, I felt I could do it. I spent a long time visiting Plymouth library, exploring Catering Industry books by leading experts of the day and condensed their pearls of wisdom into my own Manual of Management, complete with graphs and systems. I learned a lot in the process. Following my briefing at BESO HQ in London, I flew out from Gatwick for my two month stay in a completely unknown (to me) part of the world – the Middle East, land of heat, deserts, ancient and modern cities, Arabs and Jews. I shall not spend time here telling of my adventure, as my Palestine Diary makes a supplement to this autobiography all of its own, complete with a photograph album. Regrettably, I was away for Norma's 67th. birthday, arriving home a few days after, but laden with a strange assortment of presents, ranging from a pair of lidded, clay fukharas (raw, unglazed earthenware cooking pots), to a bejewelled necklace for Norma from Nasser, the hotel owner. I also had some fresh dates and figs in my bag, together with some extra special sweetmeats, made only in Nablus. My departure from Nablus was highly emotional and I sat in the taxi for the first five or ten minutes crying at leaving behind my new-found 'family' of genuinely lovely people; from Ibrahim, the father of Nasser, Salem the hotel's principal manager, Raed his assistant manager, to Mohammed, the ever-cheerful sweeper-upper.

* * *

Mark, after working in many fine restaurants and hotels dotted around England, elected to move back to the Scottish Borders. He had always tended to manage at least one holiday a year up in Scotland so it really didn't surprise us when he chose to move back there to live. The Scottish Borders is a beautiful place, un-crowded and still largely un-spoilt. It did though mean that he was five hundred miles away from us. But then one day he rang us up and suggested that Norma and I moved from the south of England back to Scotland so that we could be closer. What a good idea.

It's funny how things turn out. Now in my mid-eighties, I find myself living with Norma back in the Scottish Borders, not much more than a stone's throw from Ettrickshaws, our hotel back in the early 1980's. Ettrickshaws is now a private home but that apart and a few more houses here and there, the Scottish Borders has hardly changed from thirty years ago. I have less energy these days but can still happily work a corkscrew and whilst I parted company from my grand piano some years ago, there is a piano in the house and when the mood takes me I will play it.

* * *

37492562R00179

Printed in Poland
by Amazon Fulfillment
Poland Sp. z o.o., Wrocław